"Danger, desire,
walks the razor

"[A] must-buy series for paranormal romance lovers."
—*Fiction Vixen*

"Stellar worldbuilding."   —*Publishers Weekly*

"Ashley's Shiftertown books are the closest thing to a sure
bet in paranormal romance." —*RT Book Reviews* (4½ stars)

"With her usual gift for creating imaginative plots fueled
by scorchingly sensual chemistry, RITA Award–winning
Ashley begins a new sexy paranormal series that neatly
combines high-adrenaline suspense with humor."
—*Booklist*

"Engaging paranormal romance."   —*Smexy Books*

"One of my top paranormal romance series with its complex
political and social issues and some intense, hot romances."
—*All Things Urban Fantasy*

"[A] first-rate hero, exceptional storytelling, and a seductive
and sweet romance to satisfy any fan."   —*Fresh Fiction*

"This novel [seemed] as though it was superglued to my
hands because I couldn't pry it from my fingers."
—*Rabid Reads*

"Wickedly sexy . . . Are you new to the Shifters Unbound
series? Already a fan? Either way, I think you'll enjoy your
time with these rambunctious, charismatic, loyal Shifters."
—*Harlequin Junkie*

MIDNIGHT WOLF

JENNIFER ASHLEY

JOVE
New York

A JOVE BOOK
Published by Berkley
An imprint of Penguin Random House LLC
375 Hudson Street, New York, New York 10014

Copyright © 2018 by Jennifer Ashley
Excerpt from *Scandal Above Stairs* copyright © 2018 by Jennifer Ashley
Penguin Random House supports copyright. Copyright fuels creativity, encourages
diverse voices, promotes free speech, and creates a vibrant culture. Thank you for buying
an authorized edition of this book and for complying with copyright laws by not
reproducing, scanning, or distributing any part of it in any form without permission.
You are supporting writers and allowing Penguin Random House to continue to
publish books for every reader.

A JOVE BOOK and BERKLEY are registered trademarks and the B colophon
is a trademark of Penguin Random House LLC.

ISBN: 9780425281390

First Edition: May 2018

Printed in the United States of America
1 3 5 7 9 10 8 6 4 2

Cover design by Katie Anderson

To all the Shifters Unbound readers—you are amazing.
Thank you.

CHAPTER ONE

"You Angus?"

Angus Murray, black wolf of the New Orleans Shiftertown and bouncer in this New Orleans bar, made a show of looking around. Music thumped, the darkness broken by swirling colored strobes and the small white light above the front door. Angus stood in that light's shadow.

"I don't know," he answered. "Am I?"

The man addressing him was a suit—too clean-cut, every hair in place—but he had the craggy face of a man who used to be a soldier. He'd traded military for civilian in a big way, and was polished and slick, way out of place in this Shifter-groupie bar.

"I'm recruiting you for a job," the suit said.

Angus looked down on him from his six-foot-five height and rubbed away a bead of sweat before it could trickle into his close-cropped beard.

"Already have a job." Angus gestured to the packed, five-story bar with a staircase running up the center. Cou-

ples snaked around each other on the dance floors or made
out in dark corners. Shifters and humans mixed—Shifters
because they were bored, humans because they were excited to be around Shifters. "I make sure partying humans
and Shifters don't hurt one another, and themselves."

Case in point—a human male getting in a female Shifter's face. He was drunk, waving his beer bottle at her, and
the next second, he hit her with it.

Female Shifters could take care of themselves, so Angus
didn't move until the female rose in a snarl of rage and tried
to tie the human into a knot. Her Collar went off in an attempt
to dampen her violence, but it didn't stop her from hanging
the man upside down by his heels.

Angus waded to her. "Put him down, love."

The woman, a Feline Shifter, had a bruise on her cheek
and fire in her eyes. "The dickhead *hit* me. Because I didn't
want to go do dirty things in the alley with him."

"I know. I saw. But you have to let him go."

Angus spoke sternly. He was supposed to keep Shifters
from hurting humans, no matter what the idiot humans did,
so Shifters wouldn't be arrested and executed. No violence
against humans. That was the rule. The Feline was from his
Shiftertown, but Angus couldn't cut her any slack.

The Feline gave Angus a sudden smile, her long wildcat
teeth showing. "Sure thing," she said, and dropped the man
on his head.

The man howled and scrambled around, trying to get to
his feet. The Feline dusted off her hands and disappeared
back into the crowd, to the cheers of her friends.

Angus helped the human to stand. "You should go."

The man jerked from Angus's grasp. "Don't touch me,
freak. I want that bitch arrested. And I'm suing this place."

Angus gripped his shoulder. "Not a suggestion. *Go.*"

He put just enough growl into it. Angus was large and
strong, and usually scowling, which helped. His cub, Ciaran,
said it made him look like a wolf with a toothache.

The man opened his mouth to argue, got a good look at Angus's eyes, gulped, and spun away. He slouched unhurriedly out of the bar, muttering that he was tired of this place anyway.

The suit materialized from the shadow where he'd retreated. "I'm right. You're exactly who we're looking for."

That didn't sound good. "To do what?"

The man beckoned Angus to follow him and turned away.

Angus didn't like beckoners. The raised, curling finger was annoying, the gesture saying the beckoner believed himself to be in charge. This guy was clearly Shifter Bureau, because only one of them would walk into a Shifter bar and order people around.

Angus followed the suit for two reasons. One, his shift was almost over and another bouncer had arrived to take his place. Two, Angus feared in the back of his mind that if he didn't make a show of respecting Shifter Bureau agents, they'd use his son as leverage. Ciaran was all Angus had. Ciaran's mum had gone to the Summerland, dead and dust, but she'd been dead to Angus years before that. The one love in Angus's life was the little wolf cub with the smart-ass mouth.

The suit led him to the manager's office. It was empty; the manager rarely came in here.

As the man shut the door, Angus leaned against the desk, folded his arms, and crossed one booted foot over the other. *Closing yourself off, Dad,* Ciaran would say. *You have to let other people in.*

Other Shifters, sure. Not assholes who worked for Shifter Bureau.

"What's the favor?" Angus snarled the words. "You don't mean a job with pay."

The suit shook his head, unworried about being alone back here with an irritated Lupine Shifter. His dark hair shone in the office's light, his eyes sharp and blue. One edge of his suit coat drifted back to show Angus the butt of a pistol in a holster. The pistol looked odd—probably a tranquilizer or Taser. Whatever.

"No pay," the man confirmed. "But you'll do it. We need you."

"I'm touched." Angus stood up, wanting his full height advantage when he told this dickwad what to do with himself. "I'm also busy."

"It's not a suggestion." The man echoed Angus's earlier words, another mannerism that annoyed him.

"Okay, look," Angus said. "I know you Bureau shits think you can come and tell Shifters what to do, but you have rules too. I'm working a job to keep my cub fed and clothed. I'm allowed to do that, without interference. I don't have to drop everything to do favors for Shifter Bureau whenever they want extra muscle."

The suit reached into his coat pocket and withdrew a card and a small manila envelope. He held out the card to Angus, and when Angus made no move to take it, he dropped it on the desk.

"I'm Jayson Haider, special operations. We're recruiting you because you're a tracker, a good one, and we need you to track a particularly evasive target."

Haider pulled a couple of grainy photos out of the envelope and slapped them on the desk.

The first photo showed, from a distance, a woman with long hair, her face half turned from the viewer as though she had no idea she had a telephoto lens on her. There was just enough resolution to make out that she had a pointed face, a lot of hair, and a scowl that could match Angus's for fierceness.

The second and third photos were from even farther away, and showed an animal—no clue what it was from that distance—running away.

"The subject is Tamsin Calloway. She's Collarless, on the run, and needs to be brought in."

Angus touched the photos, willing their blurriness to clarify, but they remained fuzzy and hard to discern.

"By me," Angus stated.

"By you."

"Why?" Angus shoved the photos away. "If you want to round up a Collarless Shifter, I'm sure you have plenty of Shifters at your beck and call to do that dirty work. I don't know this woman."

"No?" Haider actually looked surprised. Did he think all Shifters were best friends with one another? What a dickbrain. "She knew your brother."

All the air rushed out of Angus's lungs. By the time he inhaled again, rage seared every inch of his body. "You shut the fuck up about my brother."

Gavan, Angus's older brother, was dead, killed years ago when he'd tried to break Shifters out of captivity. He'd been the leader of a covert group who'd tried first to negotiate with Shifter Bureau and the governments of various countries to free Shifters, and then had turned to violence.

Gavan had led marches and attacks against Shifter Bureau offices, wanting to show the threat Shifters could be if they chose. At least that's what Shifter Bureau claimed they'd wanted. Angus hadn't seen Gavan since the night he and Gavan had argued and then fought with teeth and claws about Angus joining him.

Angus had thought the group was pointless and stupid and would only get Shifters killed. Gavan had called him a coward and an ass-licker. They'd parted in fury. The kicker was that Angus's mate, April, had taken Ciaran and joined Gavan.

The next time Angus had seen Gavan was when he'd been dead, shot and laid out next to the rest of his followers—including April—waiting for the Guardian to send them to the Goddess. Angus and his Shiftertown leader had insisted that Shifter Bureau let their funeral be in the Shifter way—their souls released and their bodies rendered to dust when the Guardian thrust his magical sword through their hearts—rather than having them buried in a mass grave. Shifters had a horror of burial. If Shifters' bodies weren't reduced to dust, their souls could float free, easy pickings for anyone magical, like the Fae, to enslave.

The New Orleans Shiftertown's Guardian had dispatched first Gavan, then April and the others, while Angus had shielded Ciaran from the sight.

If this woman in the photo had been one of Gavan's, why was she still alive and roaming around when those who'd followed Gavan were dead and gone? And how close to Gavan had she been?

Or was this all bullshit on the part of Shifter Bureau? Angus wouldn't put it past them to rile him up over his brother to get him to find this woman for them for whatever reason. Maybe Angus's name had come up when they'd drawn the *who-should-we-be-a-pain-in-the-ass-to-today?* lottery.

"I'm asking again," Angus said. "Why me? Don't you have other bloodhounds to round up Shifters for you?"

"She's been seen in the area," Haider said without changing expression. "If she was close to your brother, she might trust you."

"Doubt it. Why do you want her so bad? What can one fairly young female Shifter do to chafe the hide of Shifter Bureau?"

At last Haider showed some emotion—weariness, frustration, and anger. "She stirs up other Shifters, sabotages Shifter Bureau vehicles, breaks into offices and destroys records, and harasses agents. It's a possibility that she killed two agents in Shreveport a month ago. We need to bring her in."

"A possibility?" Angus could sympathize with a Shifter who riled up the Bureau, but Shifters weren't killers. Fighters, yes, but not murderers.

"Two agents were found cut to pieces," Haider answered in clipped tones. "A Shifter did it, all right."

"Let me get this straight. You want me to chase after a woman who *might* have killed two humans, but you don't know, and all I have to go on are these blurry photos? And she once upon a time knew my brother?" Angus held up his hands. "Forget it. I'm not in love with the Bureau enough to help you fix your screwups."

Haider's eyes narrowed. "You will do it, or we can revisit just how much you had to do with your brother's revolt."

Angus only gave him a tired look. "I was cleared of that years ago. I'll be cleared of it again. I had nothing to do with it and everyone knows it."

"All right." The man straightened up, his mouth tightening in a grim line. "I didn't want to do this. I hoped you'd cooperate, but you're forcing my hand."

"No offense, Haider, but piss off. I'm clocking out and going home." Angus moved to the computer on the desk to tap out his code to finish his hours, but Haider spoke again.

"Your son. Ciaran."

Angus stilled, his fingers hovering above the touch screen. "What about him?"

"He isn't home. My agents have orders to look after him until you bring in Tamsin Calloway."

Angus didn't hear anything after the first few words. He launched himself over the desk and into Haider, slamming the man against the nearest wall.

"First rule," he snarled, his face changing to the beast between his human form and his black wolf's. "Don't touch the cubs."

"He won't be hurt," Haider said, calm for a man with a wolf's claws around his throat. "If you cooperate."

"Fuck you, dickhead—" Angus's words cut off in a crackle of electricity and searing pain as his Collar and the Taser in Haider's hand went off at the same time.

Two hours later, Angus walked into an illegal gaming den down in the bayous, acting on a tip Haider's agents had received. For the last week or so, Tamsin Calloway had been seen hanging out in the area of Houma and smaller towns, coming and going, up to something—who knew what?

She'd been visiting this old plantation house that held card games in one of its back rooms—the games were known to local police but deliberately ignored. Someone along the line was probably getting a kickback.

Angus drove from New Orleans in the car Haider had lent him, a pathetic old station wagon from the last century. Angus had taken one look at it and objected in disbelief, but Haider said, "She won't notice you're Shifter in this. We need a quick capture. Do everything right, and you and your cub will be going home together tonight."

Angus only kept himself from strangling Haider by reminding himself that Ciaran's life hung in the balance. Shifter Bureau might not go so far as to kill a cub—such an act would have repercussions, even for Shifter Bureau—but they could take Ciaran away from him, foster him with a Shifter family far away, forbid Angus to see him again.

Might as well send him to dust, Angus thought bitterly. He didn't have much in his life anymore besides Ciaran. His son was his whole world.

Angus parked the car in a closed-down gas station a little way from the plantation house and proceeded on foot. He reasoned he didn't want to come out dragging his quarry to find himself hemmed in by other vehicles. Or maybe he just didn't want to be laughed at, a big bad Shifter emerging from a faded, wood-paneled station wagon.

Cars and motorcycles were parked haphazardly in the dirt around the house, showing he'd been right about the possibility of getting blocked in. Popular place.

Old plantation houses in this area either became tourist attractions, if there was money to fix them up, or slowly fell apart in the hands of private owners. This one looked to be in better repair, its columns ghostly white in the fog, lights flickering in its windows.

Angus moved stiffly, his nervous system recovering from the multiple shocks from his Collar and the Taser.

Haider hadn't needed to tase him, but the man was a bastard. Angus had known as soon as Haider mentioned Ciaran that he'd be chasing down the Shifter woman. He'd attacked Haider to make him understand what would happen to him if Ciaran was harmed in any way. There was no need to subdue Angus to get him to obey.

A guard stood inside the door of the plantation house, a human who was almost as large as a Shifter. He gazed at Angus with narrow eyes until Angus gave the password. Haider had known that too.

Again Angus wondered why the hell Haider hadn't simply sent in a bunch of Bureau commandos with black fatigues and tranq rifles to grab her. The man wasn't telling Angus everything.

As Angus stepped inside the dimly lit interior, he saw that this place was more than a backwoods casino. To the right of the main hall was a large living room, lit with darkly shaded lamps. People lounged on sofas together— very close together. From the scents Angus caught, they were human and Shifter.

Humans and Shifters were upstairs as well, from the scent of things. Interesting. Was someone running a brothel or was this a house where humans and Shifters could mingle without anyone getting in a twist about it?

A black-skinned Shifter came down the stairs, the man almost as tall as Angus but not as big, his muscles more ropy. Angus placed himself in front of him.

"What are you doing here?" Angus asked in a quiet voice. He didn't say the Shifter's name, though he'd known it for years—Reginald McKee, currently second in command in his Shiftertown. Names and ranks might not be a good thing to throw around here.

Reg halted on the bottom step, looking, if anything, embarrassed. "Just hanging out. You?"

"Looking for someone." Angus kept his voice soft as a

breath. Reg, being Shifter, could hear him, but anything louder and every other Shifter here would too. "Shifter female."

Reg huffed a laugh. "Can you be more specific?"

Angus leaned forward and whispered the name into Reg's ear. Reg looked thoughtful, then shook his head. "No idea, my friend. Sorry."

"Help me look?"

Reg's amusement died. "Why? Her mate pissed off at her or something?"

Angus rubbed his hand over his uncombed hair. "It's complicated."

Reg's wildcat was mostly serval, a small creature, but wickedly fierce. His lack of bulk made him quick, canny, and cautious.

He knew Angus was being evasive, but Angus couldn't explain. Not when Ciaran's safety depended on it.

"I'll scout around," Reg said. "What does she look like?"

"Red hair, young—" Angus broke off in frustration. That was all he knew, and Haider hadn't even told him what kind of Shifter she was. Maybe Haider didn't know.

Reg raised his brows. "Right. If I see her, I'll tell you. I won't grab her myself."

"Probably for the best," Angus agreed. "Where's the card room?"

"Back there." Reg gave Angus another skeptical eye. "We'll have to talk, my friend."

"Yep, we will."

Reg had taken over being second in command to the Shiftertown leader when Angus had been forced to step down from the position because of Gavan. Reg had felt bad about it, but Angus had never blamed him . . .

"Good luck." Reg nodded and skimmed back up the stairs to start searching, the litheness of his wildcat evident.

Angus took his plodding wolf self down the hall where Reg had pointed, finding the card room after peeking into two other chambers. No guards stood at the door—it seemed that anyone could walk in and throw his money away on a poker game if he wanted.

This room, like the others, was dim except for lights directly over the card tables. Smoky too—no one had decided to ban cigarettes and cigars here. Ashtrays on and next to the tables overflowed, the stench of used cigarettes cloying.

Through the haze, Angus saw her.

Tamsin Calloway looked younger than in her photo. She had a wave of bright red hair flowing back from a broad forehead, her face narrowing to a somewhat pointed chin. He couldn't tell the color of her eyes from this distance, but her skin was the pale hue of a true redhead, one from the northern climes of Scotland. Angus had seen Fae inside Faerie with hair that color.

She sat at a table that held seven other men, all human. Her cards hung negligently in her hands while she leaned forward with a little smile, as though eager for the next bet. They were playing Texas Hold 'em. The cards showing on the table were two queens, a jack, and a ten. Plenty of money sat in a pile in the middle. No chips, just cash.

As Angus paused, trying to decide on his approach, one of the men at the table glared at Tamsin. "I'll raise you a hundred." He shoved in a stack of twenties.

"I'll see that," Tamsin said without losing her smile.

Four of the other men groaned and tossed down their cards. "Fold," they each said, with one saying, "I'm toast."

Three men and Tamsin left. Two put in their money, leaving it to the man who'd raised the last time. He plucked up two more twenties and a ten and let them drop into the pile. "Another fifty."

Tamsin shrugged and added her money. Another man threw his cards down in disgust. "I'm out."

Now it was Tamsin and the other two. One man looked at his cards, the ones on the table, and the pot. He sighed and pushed his chair back. "Damn it."

The remaining man watched Tamsin. He hunched forward, anger in every line of his body. If he didn't win, things might go badly for Tamsin.

"Call," the man snarled.

Tamsin laid down her cards. "Two little ladies make four of a kind."

A string of foul words came out of the man's mouth. His cards fell from his hand, nowhere near anything to win.

"You cheating bitch!"

Tamsin raked the money to her and rose. Ignoring the raging man and his friends, who were telling him to suck it up, she looked across the room and straight at Angus.

Angus froze in place, doing his best to be just another Shifter looking to relieve boredom in this backwoods casino.

Tamsin wasn't fooled. The eyes that met Angus's told him she'd already seen him, recognized him for Shifter, and knew why he was here. Her eyes were a hazel shade, the light over the table showed him, almost golden, the color of whisky. Her faint scent came to him over the stench of humans and smoke—warm, like nutmeg.

Tamsin stuffed double handfuls of cash into her pockets, at the same time moving back from the table on quick feet.

"Gotta go, boys. Thanks for the game."

Two more strides, a flash of a grin over her shoulder, and she faded into the shadows.

Angus charged across the room after her. A heavy curtain hid the wall she'd run toward, and Angus jerked it back to find a window, wide-open and letting in the fog.

Angus scrambled through the window, jerking his bulk through the tight fit, and landed on the veranda that surrounded the house.

Mists flowed between him and the trees beyond, and there was no sound. Tamsin, her flame hair and nutmeg scent, had vanished.

CHAPTER TWO

Cut that close—way too close, Tamsin admonished herself as she ran through the trees, the wet ground sucking at her feet.

What the hell kind of hunter had they sent after her this time? She'd smelled him all the way across the room. Shifter, Lupine, and highly pissed off.

Damn it. Wolves were fantastic trackers—she'd have a hard time getting away from him.

Tamsin moved as fast as she dared. Any faster and she'd make plenty of noise to alert the wolf to her presence. Shifting would be the best way to escape, but then she'd have to leave her clothes and money behind, which wolf-man would find. *Asshole.* What self-respecting Shifter worked for Shifter Bureau?

He might have nothing to do with Shifter Bureau, a voice inside her reasoned. He might be working for Shifters who wanted to catch her for their own purposes. It happened.

No matter what, Tamsin needed to get the hell out of here. She ran, heading for deeper darkness. The problem was, she hadn't had time to scout this place as much as she'd have liked. She'd thought she'd have plenty of time to walk to her motorcycle and ride back to the B and B, no need for running through the bayous. She wouldn't have come here tonight for another game at all if she hadn't needed the money.

The road was in that direction. Right? Tamsin sniffed, but her human nose wasn't as sensitive as her Shifter's. She couldn't see as well in the dark as her Shifter either.

So now she was running through unknown woods, her sense of direction screwed up, trying to get away from a *wolf.* The Goddess was not smiling on Tamsin Calloway tonight.

Mists gathered under the trees; this part of the bayous was liable to become treacherous swamp at every step. Tamsin preferred hills and woods that were drier, with clear, crisp air, but fugitives couldn't be choosers.

She ran along, slipping in mud that clung to her boots and spattered its way up her jeans. She was hot in this muggy air, her jacket and jeans not made for the warmth of early September in southern Louisiana.

Hot damn, there's the road. Tamsin spied the damp strip of asphalt in a patch of light from a streetlamp between the trees, and made for it. She would let the road guide her out of here, back to the intersection where she'd hidden her motorcycle.

Wolf-boy would find it more difficult to track her on pavement, but not impossible. Tamsin gave a look and a sniff behind her, but she saw and smelled nothing. Heard nothing either, and her human hearing was pretty good.

Maybe wolf-man hadn't bothered to come into the woods after her. There were some nice-looking human females in the plantation house who were eager for Shifter guys—maybe the Lupine had stayed and let himself be distracted by them.

Long enough for Tamsin to get away? She hoped wolf-boy was horny.

She moved quietly from the darkness under the trees to the road, hurrying down the damp pavement.

"Now, where are *you* running off to?"

Damn it. Tamsin pulled up, finding herself facing not the wolf-man but one of the guys from the poker table. No—three of them. They'd parked their truck along this stretch, and now they were standing next to it, arms folded, watching Tamsin. Had they gotten lucky and found her? Or did they know where the only dry path behind the plantation house came out?

"Not running anywhere," Tamsin said lightly. "Just heading home."

"With our money," the man who had lost the most consistently said.

"Which I won, fair and square. Good night, gentlemen."

She tried to walk around them, but the loser stepped in front of her. "You're a cheating bitch and you know it."

He'd been singing this refrain all night. "I don't cheat." Tamsin glared at him, offended and wondering why she was letting herself have time to be. "I'm a good player."

"Let it go, dude," his friend said.

Yes, let it go. Tamsin again started past them, needing to be on her bike before wolf-toes finished getting his rocks off and came after her.

"But she's got our money," the loser said. "And she's all alone out here. Poor little lady."

Tamsin smothered a sigh. She could probably fight off one of them—all three at the same time, maybe not. Plus, if she fought, they'd figure out she was Shifter. She'd have too much physical strength for a human, a small-looking female one at that. If she shifted and scared them shitless, she'd drop her keys and her money, and maybe not have time to dress again before the Lupine caught up to her.

The man who'd told his friend to let it go brightened. He might be a reasonable guy in daylight in the middle of a town with people watching him, but at the moment, he was on a back road, in the dark, with his asshole friends, facing a young woman who was alone and carrying a wad of cash.

This was not turning out to be her night.

Decision time. Fight. Shift as a last resort. Tamsin shucked her jacket, but they didn't wait to see what she was doing. As soon as the jacket hit the ground, they were on her.

Tamsin's advantage was that two of her assailants were drunk. The third guy, the one who might have been reasonable in other circumstances, was more or less sober, and he attacked her the most viciously.

Loser staggered back when Tamsin's boot landed in his middle. She spun, landing a punch on the second guy's face, and struck out at guy number three, the sober one.

Sober Guy sidestepped her, then caught Tamsin in an armlock, lifting her from her feet against his chest. The second guy recovered quickly and grabbed Tamsin's legs as she flailed and fought.

"I get her first!" Loser yelled. The yell was more of a choke—he was still recovering from her kick.

Tamsin twisted her leg out of the second man's grasp and swung her foot at him. He managed to dodge, but at least Tamsin had her leg free.

She twisted again, but the man still holding her clamped down, shoving his arm across her throat to cut off her breath.

Loser unfolded himself, an angry sparkle in his watery eyes. "Hold her steady. I don't want to bruise my dick on her."

Tamsin had a foot free—she'd kick his dick straight off if he bared it. If only she could breathe, damn it. Stars swam before her eyes, and she worried she'd pass out before she could shift and squirm away.

A rumbling growl that vibrated the ground flowed from

the trees and onto the road, and the mists swirled in a sudden waft of air.

The second man darted a scared look to the woods. "What the hell was that?"

Sober Guy tightened his grip. "Probably a stupid dog. Don't worry about it."

"Didn't sound like no dog to me. You know these woods are haunted, right?"

"Don't be an idiot," the man holding Tamsin scoffed. "Let's get her into the truck. We'll take her someplace and teach her not to mess with us."

These guys were getting annoying. Tamsin struggled and they laughed. She started to feel kind of sorry for them.

The growl came again. He was warning them—what a nice Lupine. The growl basically said, *Run now, and the worst that will happen is you'll have bad dreams.*

Trouble was, humans didn't speak Shifter. The second man gave a little scream and headed for the truck, but Loser and the guy holding Tamsin paid no attention.

Loser grabbed Tamsin by the face. "We're going to make you real sorry you messed with us, woman."

"Now, don't be like that," the man holding her said. "We'll treat her nice. She'll like it. All she has to do is—"

Whatever she had to do, Tamsin wasn't to know. A black shadow streaked from the trees and bowled over Loser and then the guy running for the pickup. The shadow came up snarling, in the form of a huge black wolf.

The hold on Tamsin's throat loosened. She gave a backward thrust with her elbow, hard into Sober Guy's gut. He folded over, and she shook off his grip, snatched up her jacket, and ran.

The wolf jumped at the man who'd held Tamsin. Sparks flew into the night as the Lupine's Collar went off.

Good grief, why had they sent a *Collared* Shifter after her? Collars inflicted pain deep into the Shifter's nerves, which was why Tamsin had refused to put one on twenty years ago. That refusal had made her a fugitive from that day to this.

She knew Shifter Bureau occasionally got their hands on un-Collared Shifters and forced them to do their bidding, but they'd dragged *this* guy out of a Shiftertown, the bullies.

Great, now she was feeling sorry for him too.

Wolf-boy had his hands full with the humans, who were slowing him down. They weren't fighting him but flailing around in panic, one yelling to grab their gun, the other two smacking into each other trying to figure out how.

Tamsin grinned as the wolf's snarl turned into one of frustration.

She put on a burst of speed straight up the road, no more dodging through unfamiliar swampy woods. She'd stick to the pavement and find her motorcycle—then wolf-dog wouldn't be able to catch her.

She heard the pickup start, its engine roaring. A few moments later, the truck's lights struck her, the pickup heading straight for her.

Tamsin jumped into the ditch, swearing when she landed in muddy water up to her knees. The guys in the truck didn't look her way, probably hadn't even seen her in their panic.

Tamsin struggled out of the ditch and ran after them, sprinting for all she was worth. She could leap into the truck bed and get away from the wolf, then drop out again near her bike. The least these guys could do for trying to capture and rape her.

The truck sped up, its tailgate skimming out of her reach. "Assholes!" Tamsin yelled at them. "You'd leave a helpless woman out here with a big bad wolf?"

Apparently they would. The truck kept accelerating, throwing mud from its tires, screeching away until it turned and was lost in the darkness.

"Total scum-bucket gobshites!" Tamsin declared to the night. At least she'd relieved them of their money during the game. Fair and square—she didn't cheat. They were just bad players.

Tamsin slid on her jacket as she ran, keeping to the side of the road, her breath coming fast. She heard nothing behind her but the faint creak of wind in the trees and the whisper of whatever critters inhabited these woods. No sound of the wolf.

Tamsin knew better than to turn around and check whether he was following. He would be. Lupine trackers didn't give up. She needed to keep running, make it to her motorcycle, and put as much distance between the two of them as she could.

Her only warning was a huff of hot breath on her back. Since she'd more or less expected it, Tamsin didn't stumble or let surprise slow her. Her Shifter senses of smell and sight might not be as good in her human form, but her cunning wasn't blunted. There was a reason her kind hadn't been rounded up when Shifters were outed long ago.

Tamsin dodged left, then as the wolf leapt at her, ready to take her down to the sludgy ditch, she dodged right, back to the road's pavement. The black wolf, intent on the take-down, couldn't stop his momentum. He plowed into the ditch with a giant splash.

His savage growl of rage would make a sane person's blood run cold. Tamsin laughed out loud.

"That's what you get for working for Shifter Bureau!" she yelled.

Meanwhile, she was hauling ass out of there. Extracting himself from the mud wouldn't stop the Lupine, but it would slow him down and give Tamsin her chance.

She put her head down and pumped her arms and legs, faster, faster. She'd rest when she was safe.

She'd parked her motorcycle around the next bend, close enough to the plantation house to reach quickly in case she needed to get away, far enough for it to not be found and associated with her. Tamsin's breath hitched in her side, but she kept going.

There was her bike, tucked into the shadows near a gas station, closed now for the night. Two vehicles sat in the parking lot, a rusting SUV that had been there when she'd arrived, and a station wagon from years gone by.

Tamsin gave both cars a passing glance, saw that no one sat in or near them, and raced past them to her motorcycle.

With a rush of wind and hot fur, the wolf landed on Tamsin and sent her sprawling.

She struggled to regain her feet, but the Lupine rolled her onto her back and pinned her with one great paw. Tamsin fought and kicked, desperation giving her strength.

The wolf was strong. His fur was completely black, a cloud of darkness under the one light by the gas station. His eyes were gray and filled with as much fury as determination. The look told her he wouldn't give up until she was completely under his control.

Tamsin continued to struggle, though she was tired from all the running and the fight with the human men. Her advantage though was that Wolfie was Collared. The more violent he became, the more his Collar would hurt him.

There—the Collar burst into sparks, a blue arc racing around the wolf-man's neck. He snarled and shook, but he didn't let Tamsin go. Gritted his teeth, took the pain.

Shit, the Bureau must truly have him under their thumb. They'd known the only way to catch Tamsin was to send out someone more afraid of them than she was. Goddess, she hated those people.

The wolf was on top of her, his weight pressing her into the damp ground, rocks beneath her jabbing into her back. His claws, very large, held her shoulders, though he didn't dig in. What a sweetie.

His face came close to hers, his eyes red-tinted with anger, his very white teeth big and too near. Sparks from his Collar rained onto Tamsin's skin, stinging and biting.

"Nice wolfie." She squirmed, but he held her fast. "Let's talk about this."

The wolf shuddered, then shivered, and with a growl and a groan, morphed into a large, hard-muscled, very naked, black-haired man.

The eyes remained the same—wolf gray, focused intently on her,

"Nothing to talk about." His voice was guttural, the wolf still strong in him. "I'm bringing you in."

"The hell you are!" Tamsin jabbed her knee straight at his bare groin.

Wolf-man deflected the blow with the ease of a professional and grabbed Tamsin's wrists in a hard grip. "Quit or I'll tranq you."

Tamsin ceased struggling, but not because she surrendered. "Shifter Bureau scum."

"I do *not* work for fucking Shifter Bureau." Pure rage flashed in the man's eyes, making her believe him.

"Then why are you hunting me?"

He didn't answer. The man was strong, athletic, and would be good-looking if he wasn't covered with mud and glaring like a fiend.

Next tactic. Tamsin let her eyes go wide and her lower lip tremble. "Please. You can't take me to them. You can't."

She saw the plea reach him, saw the anger deepen. Not at her—at Shifter Bureau for making him do this.

Whatever they'd threatened him with must be worse than whatever he thought they'd do to her, because his eyes went hard again. "Sorry, sweetheart. Be nice, and I won't have to chain you up."

He was much bigger than she was, and seriously strong. He had himself and Tamsin up before she realized it, his grip like manacles on her wrists. He turned her around, his muscular body pressing into her back, and started to march her toward the vehicles in the gas station's lot.

Only one thing to do. Tamsin held her breath . . . and shifted.

The process was smooth and quick. Not all Shifters changed with ease, but Tamsin always could. Must have something to do with small bones.

She dropped, feeling her clothes flow away from her. No ripping—she shrank down to her animal instead of grew, which gave her a slight advantage. While other Shifters waited for her to rise into some sort of giant beast, she was zipping off between their legs.

As she did now. Tamsin resisted reaching up to give the wolf-man's bare thigh a chomp as she hurtled out from under him and raced for the woods. Her clothes fluttered in the breeze she left as she dashed under the trees, becoming one with the night.

CHAPTER THREE

Son of a *bitch*.

Angus swung around to see *something* streak into
the woods, churning wet leaves in its wake.

Whatever the hell kind of animal Tamsin was, she was
tricky, and fast. Some kind of cat, maybe—perhaps a serval, like his friend Reg.

Hadn't smelled like Feline, though. Angus had no clue
what she was. Fucking fantastic.

She'd left her clothes. Angus went down on one knee to
look through them—tank top with spaghetti straps, bra,
jeans, underwear, boots and socks, a jacket. The jeans held
a wad of cash in the pockets, winnings from tonight's
game. A key with a Harley key fob, which probably went to
the motorcycle parked out of sight, but not out of scent
range. Another key looked like it went to a room in a small
motel—it was a real, metal key, not a key card. No label to
say which motel though.

That was it. No wallet, no ID, no cell phone, just cash

and keys. Nothing to say who Tamsin Calloway was, or *what* she was.

A killer? Her actions screamed of guilt. Fleeing out the window, ready to risk the men who'd been beating on her to get herself away from Angus.

Angus gathered up her things, unfolded to his feet, and carried them to the car. He had a change of clothing for himself in the station wagon, but he didn't bother to dress. The clothes he'd arrived in were back at the plantation house, where he'd shucked them to chase Tamsin. He knew Reg would take care of them for him.

One useful thing Tamsin had left behind was her scent. Angus held her shirt to his nose and took a good whiff, letting the tendrils of smells seep into his wolf brain. Nutmeg came to him again, along with her fear and the need to flee.

Angus laid the shirt on top of the pile of her clothes, closed the station wagon door, morphed into his wolf, and started off on her trail.

The Shifter woman led Angus on a merry chase. Through the woods, across streams, down into swampy ground. She kept heading south, deeper into the bayous, the land of alligators and too much water. Wolves liked drier land—at least this wolf did.

Angus's rage kept him going. He would grab this woman, drag her back to his joke of a car, tranq her, dump her at Haider's feet, take Ciaran, and go home. Any twinge of remorse about giving her to Shifter Bureau had died when she'd tried to kick him in the crotch and called him Shifter Bureau scum. Which he was.

But damn it, if they touched Ciaran . . .

All of him wanted to be with Ciaran, the small black wolf who gamboled around in his cub form and made fun of his dad. Angus needed to hold his son, feel his warm body next to his heart, make sure Ciaran was all right. He felt bad for Tamsin—she'd looked truly afraid—but his son would win this battle.

Her scent led him onward. Angus had smelled nothing like her before, and he'd had to put up with the stench of a lot of Shifters. In the club, the sweaty smell of a hundred Shifters dancing and prowling mingled with the pheromones they let loose as they chose partners for the night—enough to make Angus wish for a bad cold.

He'd smelled every sort of Feline, Lupine, and Bear, but never anything like Tamsin. What was she? Though Reg was a rare type of Shifter cat, he smelled like Feline no matter what form he took.

Angus would finish this, tell Haider to stuff himself, and go home. That is, if he didn't split Haider and his minions in half for touching his son.

His agitation made his Collar start sparking. Angus forced his emotions down, making himself focus on the mission. He was a good tracker, one of the best, or used to be considered so. Gavan's ill-fated rebellion had taken Angus from being trusted second to ordinary guy looking for a job in ten seconds flat.

The scent grew stronger, which meant Angus was catching up. He allowed himself a wolf grin. The swamp was slowing Tamsin down as much as it was Angus, which meant she wasn't an egret Shifter. Or a duck Shifter.

The trail crossed and recrossed itself. Tamsin had doubled back several times, had run straight down the middle of a stream and come out farther down the bank, had even retaken her own trail. A wolf with a lesser nose would have lost her. She was good.

Was that why Shifter Bureau wanted her? To teach them her evasive maneuvers?

And why did Angus care? If she'd been part of his brother's group and fled while Gavan got himself and the other Shifters killed, he'd happily hand her over and go out for pizza. With Ciaran.

Angus put on a burst of speed. He heard a splash, almost turned to track it, then kept on his original course. He wouldn't put it past her to toss something into the water to distract him. Angus calculated the trajectory of the splash in relation to the path he'd already been following, and focused on the point where she must be.

Then he heard a scream. Not a woman's scream, but the cry of an animal in terror.

Angus sprinted toward the noise. The animal had not been a bird or one of the many small creatures that lived out here. Something not from this swamp had gotten herself into trouble and was shrieking in pain and fear.

Angus plowed through standing water, his wolf's vision assisted by moonlight glowing on the mist.

Gator. Angus halted several yards from an alligator that had to be seven feet long. The end of its mouth was clamped over a struggling ball of fur.

As a wolf Shifter on the large side, Angus wasn't afraid of much in the animal world, but he'd developed a healthy respect for gators. They didn't care if an animal was Shifter or wild or someone's pet—they just ate it. Driven by hunger and a small reptilian brain, they acted on instinct alone, and it was best to stay the hell out of their way.

Angus took in the situation with lightning speed and leapt toward the gator. As he barreled past it, he grabbed the red ball of fur by the scruff and yanked it from the gator's mouth.

Tamsin's animal shrieked in pain and fear, blood spraying everywhere, but Angus didn't stop. Alligators could move fast, and this one would home in on their trail of blood. Angus had to get her out of here and into a moving vehicle as fast as he could.

He kept running, his mouth full of fur, but that didn't slow him down. He'd carried Ciaran to safety often enough—a male wolf cub could get himself into so much trouble.

Tamsin wasn't much heavier than Ciaran. Angus hadn't

gotten a good look at her animal, but it was small with wiry fur. Cublike in size, but Tamsin was no cub. She was a fully grown female Shifter past her Transition, and dangerous. No doubt about that.

Angus sprinted through puddles and streams, making his way northward to drier land and his borrowed car. He went as fast as he dared, hearing the gator crash along behind him, and prayed to the Goddess he didn't stumble into *another* gator along their path. The thing Angus hated about living in the New Orleans area Shiftertown, besides the humidity and hurricanes, was the wildlife that could best a Shifter.

After a time, Angus no longer heard the creature behind them. He could no longer smell it either, which he hoped meant it had grown bored and given up, slinking off to find slower prey.

Angus, sides heaving, slowed and then stopped, dropping Tamsin to the ground.

She unrolled from the ball she'd been in, her right foreleg soaked in blood, pain in her light-colored eyes. Her left foreleg, unhurt, was soot black. Angus looked down into a terrified face covered with fur as red as her human hair. The lower part of her nose and throat, by contrast, was white.

Two furry ears stuck up from her head, which was a little lighter than the rest of her coat. That coat was rust-colored all over, except for the darker patches of red around her eyes and the pure white of her underside. All this red and white culminated in a multicolored tail that was almost as long as she was.

Angus gazed down at her in disbelief. Shifters like this didn't exist. The Fae had made wolves, cats, and bears, and that was it.

Angus shifted to human, painfully in his exhaustion, and continued to stare at Tamsin as he crouched on hands and knees. She was hurt, bleeding, not running anywhere soon on that leg.

He drew a strangled breath. "You're a fox!"

Tamsin morphed to human woman so fast Angus scrambled a few inches backward. He'd never seen anyone shift so easily in his life.

"Thanks. You're a sweetie," the red-haired woman said. She held up her mangled and bloody hand, and regarded it sadly. "Got anything for a gator bite?"

"You are damned lucky," Angus reminded her for the hundredth time.

"Yes, yes, yes." Tamsin gritted her teeth on pain as she hobbled alongside the wolf-man, who supported her with a very strong grip. That grip wasn't letting her get away, but right now, she was too shaky and sick to run anywhere. "I know. The big bad wolf saved my life."

"I mean that the alligator didn't bite down like he could have. Prying their mouths open can be impossible. He'd grabbed what was moving past and hadn't made up his mind whether to eat it or not."

"Thank you, yeah, I got it." Her hand and arm were a mess—Tamsin needed a healer, but where the hell were they going to find one out here?

She'd never been attacked like that before, by a silent predator in the dark. One moment she'd been running gleefully along, the next, trapped by teeth and strength, watery panic rushing through her.

She wouldn't tell Wolfie how relieved she'd been to see him.

Any minute now, she'd lose her Shifter indifference to nakedness and realize she was walking in the embrace of a very well-made man. He was tall like most Shifters, solid with muscle that didn't take away his grace. His hair was black, like that of his wolf, and his gray eyes remained the same color in both forms. His arms bore tattoos, flowing vines on one arm and geometric squares that looked 3-D on the other. He had plenty of stamina, marching Tamsin along without breaking a sweat, and this after chasing her for half an hour and then rescuing her from a gator.

Tamsin was a fugitive, but she was also a Shifter female in her mating prime. Her instinct was checking him out even as her reason told her to flee him as soon as she was able.

Hormones were hell. They triggered a picture of herself under him, his arms tight as he braced himself, his gray eyes full of fire as he looked down at her. She'd trace the muscles of his back while she arched up to him, begging for him with her body, while he opened her to hot joy . . .

Tamsin swallowed and forced the vision from her head. She had no business thinking about him like that. She was hurt, which was making her groggy, and he was the enemy.

The Lupine walked her back to the gas station parking lot and the ugly station wagon with the wooden sides. What did humans call it? Oh yeah, a woody. Great name for a car.

The wolf-man opened one of the back doors without unlocking it—but really, who was going to steal this thing?

Tamsin's clothes and boots lay inside, along with her money. She smothered her sigh of relief.

The Lupine stood Tamsin against the cold side of the car and tossed her shirt, underwear, and jeans to her. "Get dressed. Then we'll see to your hand."

He rummaged inside again, showing her his tight backside, and brought out a T-shirt and jeans for himself.

Once they were both clothed, the wolf-man examined her arm, his touch surprisingly gentle. "Lucky, like I said. We can probably save it." He towed her to the passenger side of the car and opened the door. "Sit there and don't move."

Tamsin plopped down into the seat, in too much pain to argue. Her blood had ceased gushing, but it still flowed, and she held her arm away from her body to keep from dripping on her clothes.

Wolf-man shut the door for her. Tamsin noticed immediately that the handle on the inside of the passenger door had been broken off. Must violate all kinds of safety regulations these days.

The wolf-man slid himself over the long hood of the car to get to the other side quickly, probably fearing Tamsin would lock the doors, hot-wire the station wagon, and take off. Which she would if (a) her hand worked, and (b) she knew how to hot-wire a car.

He slammed himself into the driver's seat, gave Tamsin a warning look, took the key from under the visor above him, and cranked the car to life. He then reached into the back seat and brought out a clean towel, handing it to her in silence.

"Where are we going?" Tamsin asked in an eager tone, as though he'd asked her out on a date. She wrapped the towel around her arm. "Someplace nice?"

"To get you fixed up," the man growled. "All you need to know." He put the car in gear.

"Wait!" Tamsin thrust her good hand out in panic. "My motorcycle. I can't leave it. You know someone will steal it. It's over there, in the trees."

Wolf-man shot her an angry look. "What do you expect me to do about it?"

"I don't know. Put it in the back. This car's a gunboat. There's room."

Another scowl. He was sure cranky. "I'm not bringing along a getaway ride for you. Tell you what." He retrieved a cell phone from a compartment in the dash. "I'll call a friend and have him look after it."

His cell was an old flip phone—no latest tech stuff for Collared Shifters.

"Reg," he said abruptly into it after he'd punched a few buttons. "Look for a motorcycle hidden near the gas station at the crossroads. Get it to my house for me, would you? Oh, and grab my clothes. I had to shift in the woods, and didn't have time to go back for them."

Tamsin heard the Shifter on the other end clearly—no mistaking the gruff tone for anything but Shifter. "Sure. Everything all right?"

"Fine. Mission accomplished. Thanks, man."

"Great. Catch up with you later," the other Shifter said.

"Yep. Tomorrow."

They both hung up without saying good-bye. Typical male Shifters.

"Who was that?" Tamsin asked. "Boyfriend? Bromance?"

Wolf-man briefly rolled his eyes, then backed out the station wagon and pulled onto the road. He drove carefully, as though unused to handling giant metal cars manufactured before Tamsin had been born.

"Where do you even gas this thing up?" she asked curiously.

He grunted. "Engine's been converted. Runs on unleaded. So they tell me."

"Not your car, I take it."

"No," he snapped. He seemed more worried she'd think this car belonged to him than that she'd believe he worked for Shifter Bureau.

He said nothing more, only headed along the dark road. Going north, Tamsin noted.

She tamped down the fluttery fear in her stomach. She tried to reassure herself that she'd squirmed out of tighter situations in her life, and she could squirm out of this one. Wolfie wasn't wrong that she needed her arm seen to, and once she felt better, she'd get herself away from him. She'd been unlucky in the woods, in spite of him declaring the opposite. If the stupid gator hadn't lunged at her, she'd be free now, heading out of state on her motorcycle at a rapid pace.

Tamsin cradled her arm against her chest, leaned back, and propped her booted feet on the dashboard.

"Something to be said for giant cars. Roomy. I'm Tamsin, by the way. Tamsin Calloway. But you knew that already. And you are . . . ?"

Another growl. "Angus."

She waited but he said nothing more. "That's it? Just Angus? I thought only bears didn't have last names."

A sideways look. "You don't need to know it."

"Hmm. Sounds like someone has *issues*." Tamsin crossed her ankles. "Want to talk about it?"

"No."

"Angus. That's Scots, isn't it? A lot of Shifters spilled into Scotland from Faerie, didn't they? Back in the day?"

"I don't know." Angus hunched over the steering wheel, the tattoos playing as his muscled arms moved. "I'm not that old."

Tamsin let out a laugh. "What, you don't remember the Shifter-Fae war? That was what, thirteen hundred something? Or twelve hundred? I'm not good at history. I'm exactly forty-seven Shifter years old. What about you?"

"None of your business."

"Oh, come on. I'm only trying to get to know you. It's a bit of a drive back to the New Orleans Shiftertown."

"We're not going there."

Ah. Interesting. "Or Shifter Bureau's office in the city."

"Stop fishing. Not going there either."

Tamsin looked at him in true surprise. "No? Where, then? Aren't you capturing me for the Bureau?"

"Maybe. But first, like I said, we're getting your arm fixed. All you need to know."

Tamsin fell silent but she couldn't let him think he had her cowed, no matter how terrified she truly was. Shifter Bureau wanted to know what was in her head, and they weren't going to be nice to get it. Their interrogation methods for rogue Shifters weren't exactly full of sugar and sweetness.

She began to hum, then sing. Singing always helped keep down fear. When words ran out, Tamsin scatted guitar parts, drumming her good hand in time to the beat in her head, as though she didn't have a care in the world.

Angus said nothing, though he shot her frowns from

time to time. She could *feel* the growls from him even though he kept them stuffed inside.

He drove to the river and turned onto a highway that ran alongside it. They weren't far from New Orleans now, which meant not far from Shifter Bureau. Tamsin would have to act soon.

The alligator's teeth had gone right into her wrist, tearing flesh, muscle, and tendons down to the bone. Tamsin couldn't move anything from the elbow down, so who knew what had been shattered. The blood continued to seep out, turning the towel bright red.

She knew she needed more help than a bandage and a Shifter's natural ability to heal quickly, but she hid the pain and kept singing, tapping her foot to a rocking beat.

Angus remained quiet. Every line of him was tight with rage, but Tamsin sensed the fear behind it. Shifter Bureau must have some kind of mighty hold on him. She could work with that.

She started screeching lead guitar, but got no response from Angus other than more irritated looks. He left the main highway and drove down a winding road past warehouses and river dockyards. After about five miles—Tamsin kept careful track of where they were—he turned through an open gate of rusting wrought iron and went slowly along a lane under an arch of ancient-looking giant oaks.

Tamsin peered around in surprise, her singing trailing off. The darkness parted as they reached the end of the drive, and moonlight illuminated a house towering above them. Big. Old, with trees around it, vines fluttering over pale brick.

Angus drove all the way to the porch steps and shut off the engine and the lights.

"This isn't Shifter Bureau," Tamsin said. They favored square, anonymous, sterile office buildings.

"No kidding."

Angus took the keys out of the ignition and closed them

in his big hand, as though again fearing Tamsin would grab them, shove him out the driver's side, and take off. If Tamsin wasn't hurting so bad, she just might.

Because her door had no inside handle, she had to wait for Angus to come around and let her out. The window was an old-fashioned crank-down kind—no electronics in this old tank—but she couldn't get her good hand around to roll it down.

Angus yanked open the door, reached in, and hauled her out, careful not to touch her injured arm. What a guy.

He took her up the porch steps to a wide veranda filled with rocking chairs and a porch swing—a lovely place to sit on a summer day with a mint julep and watch the world go by. Tamsin wanted to find out how to make a mint julep just to sit on this beautiful porch with one.

On the other hand, her fox did *not* want her to go into that house, which Angus unlocked with a key he took from under a flowerpot. The vibes were making her fur itch.

"Don't tell me you live here." Tamsin peered at the glossy painted door with stained-glass sidelights and then up at the hanging porch lamp that looked new. The lamp swung a bit, though there was no wind. "Collared Shifters are allowed to live in giant plantation houses now, are they? Dark, creepy ones?"

"Belongs to a friend," Angus said, his words clipped. "I look in on it for her."

"*Her.* Oh, very interesting." She shot him a knowing glance, which only earned her another scowl.

Tamsin didn't know why she was bothering with nonchalance. Angus was Shifter—he must have already scented she was a terrified pile of mush under her bravado.

So, why wasn't he browbeating her or laughing maniacally, maybe evilly rolling his hands and saying things like "You're in for it now, my pretty"?

Instead, Angus looked angry as hell that he was doing this. He'd brought her to a place that didn't belong to Shifter

Bureau, but it must belong to a human—Collared Shifters weren't allowed to own property. Tamsin wasn't wrong when she said the situation was interesting.

Angus rattled the key in the lock, cursing under his breath. The door remained closed.

"Having trouble?" Tamsin asked brightly. "Maybe your girlfriend changed the locks. She's sending you a signal."

"Fucking hell." Angus stood back and glared at the door. "Just let me in."

The lock clicked. Tamsin's cheeky words ran out as the door slowly opened, a cold draft of wind pouring at them from inside.

No one was behind the door. Angus grabbed Tamsin by her good arm and hauled her into the house. A flick of switches flooded the downstairs hall with light.

The old house was in excellent repair, with varnished wooden panels, solid doors, and modern lights made to look vintage. Carved and polished chairs and inlaid tables stood along the hall, the tables filled with trinkets and vases of colorful silk flowers.

Someone with wealth and taste lived in this house—so what was a tamed Shifter from a Shiftertown doing freely entering it?

Angus led Tamsin into a bathroom that was tucked under the stairs and shoved her down onto the closed toilet lid. He rummaged in a tall, narrow cabinet next to the sink and brought out bandages, gauze, and antiseptic.

Tamsin flinched at the sight of them, knowing what was coming would hurt.

Angus snapped on the water in the sink, lifted Tamsin to her feet, peeled away the now bloody towel, and eased her hurt arm under the stream.

She was right—it hurt like hell. Tamsin sucked in a breath, and Angus, concern in his eyes, gently sloshed water over the wound. He touched her so carefully his fingers barely brushed her torn skin.

Once the blood was washed away, Angus ripped open a packet of gauze, soaked it in the antiseptic, and gingerly touched the gauze to her torn skin.

"Holy . . ." Tamsin whispered.

"Hurts, but it will help against infection," Angus said without softening. "Shifters are only so invulnerable."

"No kidding." The worst of the blood and dirt were gone, but Tamsin's arm was torn all to hell. Shifters healed quickly, but very bad injuries could kill a Shifter as hard as they could a human.

Angus finished the torture with the antiseptic and then wrapped gauze around her arm and secured it with a long bandage.

"Should help," he said.

Before Tamsin could thank him—or say anything—he had her out of the bathroom and back into the hall. The gentleness with which he'd tended the wound didn't mean he was going to let her go. Not at all.

Angus opened a drawer in a hall table and extracted a pair of handcuffs. He growled when Tamsin's eyes widened, and he said, "Don't ask."

Tamsin grinned. "Kinky."

Her bright word died as Angus clicked one of the cuffs around her left wrist and locked the other around a thick newel-post of the staircase.

"Stay there," he rumbled. "I need to make some phone calls."

CHAPTER FOUR

Tamsin waited for Angus to move down the hall before she partly shifted to her fox to slide her slim paw out of the handcuff.

It hurt like hell to do it, because she couldn't change only one paw—both had to go, and her legs and face started to shift as well. Her injured arm protested, and she spent a moment biting back tears as she resumed her human shape. The fox could move faster, yes, but Tamsin would need her clothes and her money, so human she had to stay for a while.

She followed the sound of Angus's voice to a room in the front of the house, next to the front door.

He'd hear her or see her if she slipped past the room—a human might not, but Angus was obviously a tracker and it was in his best interests to bring her in. He wouldn't be careless.

Back door it was.

Angus's words rang down the hall. "I don't care if he's

hibernating for the winter. He said *anytime*. Was that just bullshit?"

Whoever Angus spoke to had him furious. Tamsin couldn't hear the other voice on the phone at this distance, but no matter—it was clear Angus was calling for backup.

One wolf she could handle. A pack of Shifters cruel enough to give one of their own to Shifter Bureau she could not.

Tamsin crept down the hall to the back door.

That door slammed open, and a man stepped in, talking hard into a cell phone. He was on the short side—at least shorter than a Shifter—with black hair and very black eyes, tatts on his arms and neck, and his scent was . . .

Tamsin stepped back, snarling.

He eyed her in irritation, but his attention was on whomever he spoke to on the phone. "I told you I'd ask. He can be tetchy. His mate can be too—she hates for him to be called out for every bump and scrape, and I don't blame her."

"Well, tell him it's an emergency," Angus's voice came from down the hall. "I wouldn't ask if it wasn't important. Jaycee will vouch for me." His tone lost confidence. "Maybe."

Tamsin swung to look down the hall, then back at the smaller man, who eyed Tamsin up and down. "Yeah, it does look pretty bad. I'll do what I can."

A growl came from the far room, and Angus stepped out and glared down the hall. He lowered the phone and bellowed at the smaller man, "What the hell? Why didn't you say you were right outside?"

A shrug. "I wasn't. Until just now." The man nodded in Tamsin's direction. "What is she?"

"What are *you*?" Tamsin countered. She did not at all like the whiff of otherworld she caught from his scent.

"Not Fae," the man said with emphasis. He clicked off his cell phone. "The name's Ben. Or Gil. Take your pick. *Not Fae*. Got it?"

He pushed himself around Tamsin—very carefully not

touching her hurt arm—and strode down the hall toward
Angus.

He left the way to the back door clear, and Tamsin
headed swiftly for it.

Ben hadn't bothered to close the door all the way, and it
remained tantalizingly ajar. She heard Ben on the phone
again, speaking jovially to whomever they were summon-
ing to keep her here.

Two more steps, and she'd be gone. She could outrun
wolf-man and not-Fae dude easily, but if Angus brought in
more backup, she'd be in deep shit.

"She's safer if she stays here," Angus said behind her.
"Seriously."

Tamsin swung around. Angus wasn't talking to Ben,
who was in the room at the front, still on his phone. Angus's line of sight was the stairs, but as Tamsin looked
wildly at them, she saw no one.

Screw it. Tamsin bolted for the door.

Just before she reached it, the door swung closed and
quietly clicked shut. Tamsin grabbed the knob, but the door
wouldn't open. She frantically searched for a bolt or lock
that held the door in place, but the deadbolt was undone, the
knob turned easily, and no chains were in sight.

She beat on the door with her fist before she told herself
not to waste energy. Better to find a window, slide through
it—hell, change to fox and climb out through a chimney if
she had to.

Tamsin turned to find Angus right behind her, holding
the handcuffs.

"Just sit here and wait for the healer," he said. "Unless
you want your arm to fall off."

Tamsin shook her head with emphasis. "I'm not staying
while you call in Shifter after Shifter to keep me prisoner.
I'm outta here, wolf-boy."

Angus snapped the cuff around her good arm, the steel
cold. "No. You're sticking with me, sweetheart."

The other cuff didn't go around the staircase this time but around Angus's broad wrist.

Tamsin glared at him. She focused her energy, partly shifted to fox again, and slid her hand from the cuff. Angus blinked at having a fox face so close to his, and then Tamsin was human again, darting into the nearest room and to its long window.

Angus followed Tamsin, unlocking the manacle from his wrist as he went. He'd pretty much figured she'd be able to get out of the cuffs, but he'd had to try. Cuffs were psychologically subduing, he'd learned in his bouncer work. Even the drunkest, most obnoxious human could fall down in a blubbering mess once he was cuffed.

Tamsin moved on light feet across the house's drawing room, dragged back the draperies, and tried to open a window.

It wouldn't budge. Tamsin screamed between her teeth. Instead of beating on the window as she had the door, she glanced around, grabbed the nearest chair she could lift with one hand, and drew it back, ready to throw it at the window.

Angus wrenched the chair out of her grasp and set it back down. He didn't think the window would break if the house didn't want it to, but she could wreck the chair trying.

"Be careful," he said. "I told you, the house belongs to a friend of mine. She won't be happy if you destroy the furniture."

Strictly speaking, Angus had met Jasmine, the young human woman who owned the house, exactly once, when she and her Shifter mate had come out to spend some time in it together last month. Ben was more or less the house's caretaker in Jazz's absence, but she'd made it clear it was open to Shifters who needed to use it as a getaway as long as they didn't damage anything.

Tamsin glared at Angus with wide amber eyes. He saw bald fear in those eyes, her defiant spark fading.

Did Haider know she was a fox Shifter? Was that why he wanted her? Besides the fact that she was a rogue, un-Collared, and had caused a lot of trouble?

Angus would love to shake out of her exactly what was going on, and why Haider was so interested in her. Shifter Bureau kept an eye out for those Shifters they'd missed catching and Collaring, but they didn't usually single one out to go after with such zeal. And why choose Angus for the job?

Conclusion—Tamsin Calloway knew more than she was telling.

Angus took hold of her uninjured hand in a firm grip, but he tossed the cuffs to a table and left them there.

"You hungry?" he asked. "There's always plenty to eat in this house. Might be a while before Zander can get here."

Tamsin tried to hide her flicker of interest. "Zander? Who's that?"

"A healer." Interesting that she'd never heard of him, because Zander was Collarless as well. But then, he was a healer, and healers were elusive, reclusive, and sometimes downright crabby. Zander had a mate now, and being asked to leave her side made him even more irritable. "Come on—let's see what's in the fridge."

Tamsin didn't fight as Angus led her out of the drawing room and down the hall. Only when he started up the stairs did she hang back.

"Why are we going up there?"

"That's where the kitchen is. Ground floor is for tourists."

Tamsin drew in a breath as though she'd argue, then she gave Angus a nod and started with him up the stairs.

He didn't turn her loose until they walked into the big room that was a modern, airy kitchen with retro-looking appliances, a large kitchen table, and a giant walk-in pantry.

"Sweet!" Tamsin exclaimed. She went to the refrigerator

and opened it, bending to stick her head in. "Oh, nice. Who lives here? They know how to keep the place stocked."

She backed out with packaged meat and cheese. She dropped that to the counter, then went back for a bag of lettuce and a large tomato. "All we need is bread . . . Ah, here we go."

She opened a bin on the counter and pulled out a loaf, set it on a wooden cutting board, and started rummaging in the drawers. Angus put his hand on her wrist before she could pull out a hefty knife. He twisted the knife away from her while she stared at him in surprise.

"How am I supposed to cut up my tomato?"

"I'll do it." He pointed at a chair with the tip of the knife. "You sit."

"Let a hot guy make dinner for me? Sure thing." Tamsin sauntered to the table and sat down, leaning back in the wooden chair to cross her ankles.

Angus had to turn away from her to start laying out the bread for sandwiches, but Ben had followed them in and now seated himself at the table with her.

Angus had felt Tamsin shaking when he'd taken the knife from her. He suspected that was not only from the pain of her injury, but exhaustion and probably hunger. She had the pinched look of a person who hadn't had a full meal in a while.

"Don't let her get up and run around," Angus told Ben. "She's hurt more than she lets on. Zander on his way?"

"Yep," Ben said. "He's not happy about it, but he contacted Marlo, and Zander will be here soon." Marlo was a private cargo pilot who covertly flew Shifters around the country. "I told Zander it was your fault—I was just the messenger. Why are you talking about Tamsin like she's not in the room?"

Angus only growled.

"I'm a rogue Shifter," Tamsin said to Ben. "We aren't real people to the Collareds."

Angus stifled a grunt of impatience. Why couldn't she be the sullen, crazed, evil woman he'd pictured? He could have dealt with that—he'd have had her tranqued and trussed up in the back of the station wagon and already on his way to the bizarre location where Haider wanted to make the exchange. Haider had told Angus where to meet him with a smirk on his face—glad the man was so amused.

Instead, Tamsin was funny, brave, resourceful, and in serious trouble. Why else would she be running around alone, playing poker for cash when she hadn't eaten in a while? Now that Angus had her trapped, with her hurt, she acted as if she'd only hit a temporary setback.

Angus had to admire her guts, but he didn't have a choice other than to turn her in. If Ciaran weren't involved, he'd be more than tempted to help her get away—hell, he'd have done it by now.

But Ciaran was the stakes, and Angus would wrestle down the Goddess herself to win him back.

Tamsin continued to chatter to Ben, asking him about himself, while Angus made sandwiches with the meat, cheese, lettuce, tomato, onions, and condiments Jazz always made sure were on hand.

This house had become a refuge for Shifters needing to get away from the confines of Shiftertowns for a while. Shifters like Angus weren't supposed to leave the state they lived in without permission, which they had to apply for well in advance. Couldn't have Shifters running around where they pleased, in case they all turned violent and ate the entire population of humans, could they? Why Shifters would want to do such a thing, Angus didn't know, but old fears died hard.

Humans didn't come to this house, except on planned tours through a tour company, because the house was haunted. Or at least it was very good at giving that impression.

Angus wasn't sure how much he believed in the house's

powers, but he'd seen a lot of weird things happen inside it.
Doors leading to other worlds, things moving around on
their own, the doors locking and unlocking at the house's
whim. Downstairs, he'd asked the house to keep Tamsin
inside, and the house had complied. Because it wanted to,
Angus knew. When it decided to let Tamsin out, there was
nothing he'd be able to do about it.

"A gnome," Tamsin was saying behind him. "How cool
is that. Hey, Angus, did you know Ben was a gnome?"

"Or a goblin," Ben said. "But those are human terms.
We don't call ourselves either one."

"Yeah?" Tamsin asked in curiosity. "What do you call
yourselves?"

"Well, there's only one of me that I know of now, but the
name for our people is *Ghallareknoiksnlealous*."

"Oh." Tamsin went silent as Angus sliced the sandwiches
and put them on plates. "How about we stick with *goblin*?"

Ben chuckled. "Probably for the best."

"Why is there only one of you?"

Angus carried plates to the table, setting one each in
front of Tamsin and Ben before going back to fetch his.
Tamsin didn't look at the sandwich Angus brought her—
she kept her gaze on Ben, waiting for his answer.

"Fae killed them all." Ben picked up his thick sandwich
filled with roast beef, ham, and cheese, dripping with mayo.
"Or as good as."

Tamsin stared at him, openmouthed. Ben didn't notice,
focusing on his sandwich.

Tamsin glanced at Angus as he sat down, and he gave
his head the slightest shake. Ben might pretend to be blasé
about the Fae slaughtering his people and then exiling the
few that remained to the human world—Ben had told him
the story one day—but he lived in boiling fury about it.
Had for about a thousand years now.

Tamsin shot Ben a look of sympathy that he didn't see
and took up her sandwich with her unhurt hand. Her other

hand lay curled on her chest, the bandage stark against her cotton shirt.

Tamsin closed her eyes as she chewed the first bite of her sandwich, letting out a tiny sigh of relief. Angus had been right—she was hungry, terribly so, which wasn't going to help her injury.

What the hell was she doing running around half-starved and evading Shifter Bureau? What had she done that they wanted her so much? Haider said he thought she killed the Shifter Bureau agents, but Tamsin's small paws couldn't have made the large claw marks on the men in the gruesome photos Haider had insisted on showing Angus.

Angus's resolve to simply hand Tamsin over and not get involved was crumbling. That was his problem—he had the habit of getting involved. He wanted to help people and keep them safe, and he couldn't seem to stop himself.

Meanwhile, Tamsin was enjoying the hell out of her sandwich. She took another bite, eyes closed again as she savored the meat and bread, lettuce and tomato. She chewed slowly, sitting back in her chair, a look of rapture on her face as though the simple meal were ambrosia.

"Mmm." She made the sound long and sensual. Tamsin swallowed, opened her eyes, and bathed Angus in a warm smile. "Been a while since I was able to sit down and eat. You have talent. Ever thought about being a cook?"

Her eyes were so full of mischief Angus wanted to grin back at her.

He resisted. She was playing him, trying to get him to trust her. The minute he did that, she'd be gone, leaving Angus wondering what the hell happened, and Ciaran at Haider's mercy.

"No," he snapped.

Tamsin ate slowly, bite by bite, as though determined to enjoy every ounce of her food. When she finished, she tilted her head back and sucked the last drops of mayo from the tips of her fingers.

"Wow," she said softly. "That was *good*."

Ben snorted a laugh. "Save it, sweetheart. I'm too old, and Angus is unseducible. He's a bouncer in a New Orleans club. Scantily clad women try to get on his good side every night, the poor guy."

"A bouncer?" Tamsin opened her eyes and looked at Angus in surprise. "I thought you were with Shifter Bureau."

"No," Angus said in a hard voice. "I don't work for those dickheads."

"Except tonight." Tamsin leaned toward him, her red hair falling forward. "Why are you working for them tonight?"

"Because an annoying woman is causing trouble," Angus returned. He stood up, gathering the empty plates, and stamped with them to the sink.

"Touchy, touchy. Struck a nerve, didn't I, Ben?"

"Yeah, Angus, I think we need to know what this is all about," Ben said. "She doesn't *look* like a dangerous criminal. And you hate Shifter Bureau. So why are you at odds instead of working together? Talk, both of you."

Angus clattered the dishes into the sink. "No offense, Ben, but this is none of your business."

"*Everything* is my business. I'm everyone's friend, me. Plus I have some useful abilities. Why are you running from Shifter Bureau, Tamsin?"

"Well," Tamsin said, "I was born in the shack of a rogue Shifter and have been stealing and conning my way across the country since I was three. I'm wanted in twenty-seven states for so many offenses I forget them all. I stay one step ahead of the law with my cunning, and all the cops let me go because I'm a sweet-talker."

"And all of that is a big fat lie," Ben said. "I'm as good at detecting them as Shifters."

"I'll bet it isn't *all* a lie," Angus said, watching Tamsin. "But I don't care. We'll get you healed up, and then I'm done with you."

Tamsin's face paled, though she tried to hide her nervousness. "Aw, and I was starting to have a big crush on you."

"You need to rest." Angus returned to the table. "There are plenty of bedrooms to lock you in."

He wrapped his hand around Tamsin's shoulder and hauled her to her feet.

She stood up readily. "Oh, sweetie, and we only just met."

"You know, you are really starting to grate on me," Angus said with a growl. "If you want to save your ass so much, you'll shut up."

The look Tamsin shot him was full of fear but also calculation. Her chatter and silliness hid the fact that behind her eyes, she was gauging the situation and running through many plans to get out of it.

Angus needed to hand her over to Shifter Bureau as soon as possible, before he started to help her do just that.

Tamsin woke hours later, stiff and sore in spite of the soft bed. Her chewed-up arm hurt like hell, but she had to admit the sleep had done her good. Her edge of exhaustion had gone, and the sandwich, first solid meal she'd had in a while, had restored some of her energy.

The faint gray of false dawn touched the window. Tamsin sat up, dragging her hair back from her face. She hadn't meant to sleep so hard, or even fall asleep at all.

After Angus had shoved her into this bedroom and slammed the door, locking it, she'd searched for any possible exit. The closed window would not budge. Any attempt to break the glass had failed—it was damned good glass. She picked open the door's lock with a hairpin she'd found in the dresser drawer, but the door refused to open. No fireplace in this room, so no chimney, and she couldn't find a secret passage anywhere. What self-respecting old house didn't have a secret passage?

Tired, Tamsin had lain down on the bed to rest before she tried again. The wind outside had been soothing, whispering through the wind chimes, and she'd fallen asleep before she could stop herself.

A key scraped in the lock, and Angus opened the door.

He did so cautiously, as though expecting Tamsin to be waiting behind the door with a cosh, and looked surprised to find her blinking at him from the bed.

"The healer is here," Angus said abruptly. "Come on."

CHAPTER FIVE

Tamsin rolled to sit on the side of the bed and groaned. Her hand was on fire, her arm too stiff to bend. The gauze and bandage grated on her torn-up skin.

"What kind of healer won't come to a patient's bed?" She struggled to stand, and stumbled, a moan dragging from her throat.

Angus was next to her in an instant, his arm around her waist, his warm strength keeping her from falling.

Tamsin considered collapsing against him, letting him hold her up, giving in to her need to forget all this and be normal. Have friends, a mate . . . cubs. The wanting for that suddenly rose up and nearly choked her.

But *normal* meant living in a Shiftertown with a Collar around her throat, her cubs captives, her movements restricted. Her own mother lived in a Shiftertown near the Canadian border, and Tamsin was rarely able to communicate with her, hadn't seen her now for five years. Their last encounter had been covert and heartbreakingly brief, and they hadn't been able to meet since. Tamsin's sister was long dead, killed by a Shifter hunter twenty years ago when un-Collared Shifters had been fair game for hunters. There had been no penalty then for killing an un-Collared Shifter; in fact, it had been encouraged.

Angus, on the other hand, had chosen to live in captivity and round up Shifters like Tamsin.

He'd showered sometime while she'd been asleep, and his skin smelled of soap, his black hair damp. He'd trimmed his beard, which brushed his jaw and chin without hiding it. This close she could see the tiny lines around his eyes, and the glittering gray of those eyes, clear and now full of concern.

A bouncer, Ben had said. Angus had the strength and the bulk for that job, but also the caring. Bouncers were protectors—they kept out the troublemakers and expelled those endangering others.

Tamsin felt hard muscles through his T-shirt, and she'd seen plenty of them when they'd run around the woods. He was clean, solid, and steady—attractive. Tamsin, on the other hand, was hurt, smelly, and disheveled, and she wouldn't say no to a bath. Foxes weren't quite as fastidious as cats, but they came close.

"You all right?" Angus asked her, his voice vibrating through her.

Damn it, don't let him make me believe he cares. He's healing me, so I don't croak before he gets me to Shifter Bureau.

"Hmm." Tamsin pretended to consider. "I'm being held prisoner in a weird house with a wolf and a goblin, an alligator tried to eat me, and you're going to drag me to Shifter Bureau. I'd say the answer is no, I'm not all right."

She held herself rigid to keep tears from coming. That was all she needed—to break down into a blubbering fool in front of her captor. She wouldn't give him the satisfaction.

"Zander can take away the pain at least," Angus said. "He's asking you to come down because he says he needs space."

"Space for what?"

Angus's shrug moved his body against her. "Hell if I know. I don't know him that well, but he's a good healer. Come on."

He guided her toward the door. Tamsin hissed as her arm moved, and Angus stopped her, gently peeling the bandages away.

The wound did not look good. Her skin was lacerated to the bone, and blood had seeped out again, as had yellow pus. Tamsin shivered, which didn't help the pain.

Angus replaced the towel, concern in his eyes. He steered her to the door, his arm still around her, and they went out into the hall, where he guided her to the stairs. Ben was waiting at the bottom, looking up at them anxiously.

Damn it, why were they both being so *nice*? Ben and Angus weren't her friends. It would be a big mistake to like them and start to trust them. She'd been down that road before.

Tamsin knew that without Angus supporting her every step of the way down the stairs, she would have fallen. Her right arm wouldn't move at all, she was weak, and she wanted to barf.

A breeze sprang up outside as they reached the ground floor. Wind chimes on the back porch fluttered and rang, the sound soothing and somehow easing her nausea.

Angus led her down the hall and through a set of double doors into a huge room hung with crystal chandeliers, which were fully lit. The drapes had been pulled back on the room's three long windows, letting in the dawn light.

This was a dining room, Tamsin saw, but they'd moved the table and chairs against the far wall. The room was big enough to be a ballroom, and maybe once upon a time it had been.

A man and a woman, both Shifters, waited in the middle of the room. The man was enormous. He was taller than any Shifter Tamsin had ever seen, and had a dark, close-cut beard like Angus's and snow-white hair. Not because he

was old—his hair was a pure white-blond, like a Viking's.
Most of his hair was short, but two braids full of beads
hung down on either side of his face. He wore a long black
duster coat and motorcycle boots over jeans and a black
T-shirt. The most striking thing about this Shifter, however,
was that he had no Collar.

The woman next to him *did* have one. Her dark hair hung
in one long braid, and she wore a duster coat to match the
man's. The most striking thing about *her* was the broadsword on her back, its hilt sticking up over her left shoulder.

A Guardian.

"Shit," Tamsin whispered.

Guardians didn't guard Shifters' bodies—they guarded
their souls. When a Shifter died or was on the brink of death
without hope, the Guardian came and drove his broadsword
loaded with Fae magic into said Shifter's heart, which dissolved the body to dust, and released the Shifter's soul to the
afterlife. Tamsin had heard the story of the Choosing for a
new Guardian in Montana, and for the first time in Shifter
recorded history, the Goddess had chosen . . . a woman.

"You're *her*," Tamsin said in astonishment.

The woman's dark brows went up. "I'm Rae Moncrieff.
Is that what you mean?"

"You all think I need a Guardian?" Watery fear swamped
her. Tamsin usually didn't lose it in front of people, but she
started to shake. She was going to the Summerland *now*?
She wanted to say good-bye to her mother, kick some
Shifter Bureau ass, free all Shifters . . . she had way too
much to do to die today.

"Have a little more faith in my skill," the big man next
to Rae rumbled. "You look bad, sweetie, but I can fix it.
Rae only came with me because she's my mate. And last
time I was here, I went on an adventure, and she got worried, and well, you know . . ." He made a vague motion with
his huge hand.

"I told him he wasn't going on another one without me."

Rae's gray eyes twinkled. "I can't let him have all the fun. But don't worry. Zander's the best. Let her sit down at least, Angus. The poor thing is about to fall over."

Tamsin wouldn't fall with Angus holding on to her so solidly. He led her, step by step, to a chair set under one of the chandeliers, where she sat, both nervous and grateful to Angus for his support.

Zander slid off his duster and dropped onto the carpet. Rae rolled her eyes, picked up the coat, smoothed it out, and draped it over a chair.

Anything amusing about Zander faded as he came to Tamsin and went down on one knee beside her. He removed the rest of the gauze and examined her arm, which looked not so much like an arm now as a chewed-up piece of meat. *Which was exactly what it had been*, Tamsin thought with giddy hilarity, *to the gator*. She must be delirious if she found that funny.

Zander's touch on her shoulder above the wound was so light she barely registered it.

"What did you put on it?" he asked.

"Water and antiseptic," Angus answered. "All I could find at short notice."

The chandelier overhead creaked the faintest bit. Tamsin looked up quickly, but the light hung silent and still.

"Okay," Zander said. "I can't promise this won't hurt, Tamsin, but it will get better."

He placed his hand over her hurt arm, barely touching, then bowed his head and closed his eyes.

Angus took up a place on the other side of Tamsin, right against her chair. She'd suspect him of making sure she didn't leap up and run away if he weren't watching Zander so hard.

Zander's touch stung on Tamsin's peeled skin, and she clenched her teeth against the additional pain. It was nothing to the bone-deep agony of the bites, but every bit added up.

Zander began to drone a low chant, strange words flowing from his mouth. Tamsin recognized a prayer to the Goddess—she didn't know the exact phrases, but her mother had whispered a similar prayer over Tamsin when she'd been a cub.

Tamsin's eyes grew moist as she remembered the happy times with her family, long before her dad had died, when she and her sister, Glynis, had thought their cozy life would last forever. They'd been hungry sometimes—it wasn't always easy to find food, living in the remote parts of Canada as they had. Most Shifters had hidden themselves from human eyes before Shifters had been outed, but fox Shifters *truly* hid.

Her dad had been the fox—her mom was a small Feline who was mostly bobcat. Shifter cubs of mixed parentage took the form of one parent, not both, and Tamsin had definitely been fox. Glynis had been bobcat, like their mom, but she hadn't been able to run fast enough from a Shifter hunter's bullet.

Tamsin heard whispered words that followed Zander's and realized Rae chanted along under her breath. Rae was watching her mate in love and concern, her lips moving in the prayer. Zander swayed, his braids swinging, his eyes closed, face drawn. Outside, the wind chimes shimmered music, keeping time with Zander's chanting.

Tamsin's pain lessened. Not much, but she was able to draw a breath, her injury no longer the focus of her entire world.

Zander lifted his hand from Tamsin's arm to skim his T-shirt off his torso. His skin beneath gleamed with sweat, and his breathing was labored. When he grasped Tamsin's arm again, his fingers gripped tighter, but now it didn't hurt as much.

The chandelier jangled overhead—no mistaking it this time. The shadows under the chandelier moved, but there was no breeze, no breath of wind in the room.

Zander continued his droning. Angus pressed closer to

Tamsin's side, which made the already warm temperature of the room hotter. Tamsin began to perspire, drops of sweat trickling from her temples to trail down her spine.

Tamsin sucked in a sharp breath as sudden pain seized her. The agony grew, filling all the spaces of her body. Tamsin couldn't breathe, couldn't think. She would have screamed if she could only form a sound.

Zander's chanting became hoarse, the words barely emerging from his throat. His outline blurred as Tamsin's eyes flooded with tears that spilled down her cheeks, though she couldn't so much as sob.

"What the hell are you doing?" she heard Angus growl.

"Leave him be," Ben said firmly at the same time Rae said in worry, "No, don't touch him."

Angus closed his mouth, though he didn't leave Tamsin's side. He was the one thing she could feel through the pain, a solid rock of Shifter against her.

Another lightning flash of agony seared her, and then, in one swift movement, Tamsin's wounds closed. Her bones fused in a brief moment of torture, her muscles knit, and her skin closed. The red streaks vanished, blood dried, and Tamsin's skin became whole, pink with scar tissue. Even the scars faded in the next moment, leaving only a few white streaks to show she'd been hurt at all.

Tamsin gaped down at her arm, which was smooth and strong. *Holy shit.*

She looked up to pour forth thanks to Zander, and then froze. Zander had climbed to his feet, his face twisting in pain, and he was struggling to rip open his belt and jeans. *What the—*

"Get back!" Rae yelled.

Tamsin hesitated in perplexity, but Angus was already dragging her chair away from Zander, Tamsin with it.

Zander kicked off his underwear right before he vanished and a couple of tons of polar bear filled the space where he'd been.

Tamsin leapt from her chair and ran to the far side of the room, Angus a step behind her. She understood now why they'd moved the furniture and why Zander claimed he needed "space." Not to meditate, but so he could shift into a gigantic, no-one-should-be-that-big polar bear.

A polar bear roaring in pain. Zander's black eyes shut tight, disappearing into his mass of white fur. He held his right paw across his chest, and rose and rose until he was on his hind legs, his great head barely missing the chandeliers. He opened his mouth and bellowed, cradling his right front leg in the exact way Tamsin had her hurt arm.

"What's wrong with him?" Tamsin yelled over the noise.

A whiff of fresh scent brushed her as Rae moved to her side. "He takes on the pain of those he heals. Not the injury itself, but the psychic part of it." She cast a worried glance at her mate. "Yours wasn't that bad, so he won't have to fight it long."

It had been bad enough, but also terrifying. Tamsin's small fox had been up against a huge alligator that had ruthlessly attacked her. The shock and fear of that had been almost as devastating as the pain.

Zander's face twisted, showing all Tamsin's horror and panic as well as the anguish of her injury. He threw his head back, narrowly missing the polished ceiling, and roared again.

Rae rushed to him. Tamsin started to follow, worried that the flailing, bellowing bear would hurt the young woman, but Angus held her back.

When Zander ceased weaving around, Rae darted in and wrapped her arms around him as far as she could, sinking into his soft fur.

Angus's hand rested firmly on Tamsin's shoulder. "We should leave them to it."

Ben waited for them at the double doors. Tamsin looked back before she exited to see that Zander had calmed a little, his left paw resting on Rae's back as she rubbed her cheek on the fur of his chest.

The touch of a mate healed, Tamsin's mother and father had taught her. Rae murmured to Zander, and he quieted, lowering himself to all fours, though keeping his weight from his right front leg. Rae leaned across his back, stroking his head, kissing it.

The sight of them taking care of each other brought a lump to Tamsin's throat. How wonderful to have a person to trust and lean on. Her peripatetic life had not let her grow close to anyone, to let down her guard. The few times she had, she'd paid the price. But watching Zander and Rae showed her what she'd missed.

Zander brought his head around to nuzzle Rae, and Angus shoved Tamsin out the door and closed it.

"I guess we're off to Shifter Bureau now?" Tamsin kept her tone light, but her heart bumped as she waited for his answer.

Angus turned her in the direction of the stairs. "Shower first. We'll have some breakfast and then we'll go."

Tamsin stared at him, trying to hide her confusion. "Well, aren't you the polite host? Why did you even bring me here, Angus? You could have dragged me straight to Shifter Bureau and let them deal with doctoring me."

Angus gave her a frown. "You were hurt. Human doctors can't fix up Shifters very well, and I knew a healer."

So very logical. Tamsin shook her head, ducked away from him, headed straight to the back door, and tried to open it.

It wouldn't budge. It was unlocked—the handle moved fine—but as before, the door remained solidly closed.

Tamsin sighed and turned to find Angus pinning her with his fierce glare. She shrugged. "Had to try." She laughed at his expression and tripped lightly up the stairs, out of pain, strong, and optimistic once more.

* * *

Angus walked outside with Zander and Rae. The house let them exit without hindrance, the front door opening readily. Angus worried that the house would arbitrarily let Tamsin leave as well and asked Ben to station himself upstairs in the kitchen to keep an eye on her while she ate.

Tamsin had showered in the large upstairs bathroom, singing at the top of her lungs, then came out toweling her bright red hair and went straight to the kitchen. Ben had cooked breakfast, and Tamsin sat down and began to shovel it in, but Zander and Rae declined the invitation to stay.

Outside, a motorcycle waited under a wide-boled tree. Marlo had flown them in, Zander had said, then they'd rented the bike to bring them to the house. Zander, Collarless, could easily rent vehicles where a Collared Shifter might be turned away—Angus suspected Zander's large size and slightly crazed forcefulness had humans doing whatever he wanted, in any case.

As Rae moved to the motorcycle, Zander gestured Angus aside, crowding him against the bottom step of the porch.

"You really taking her to Shifter Bureau?" The anger in Zander's black eyes sparkled in the early light. "I see that she's a handful, but . . . All right, don't let me mince words. What the fuck?"

"They have my cub," Angus said quietly. "I don't have a choice."

"Oh." Zander took a step back, his anger redirecting itself. "Oh, man. I'm sorry. Tell you what. How about you, me, Rae, and Ben go break out your cub and blow town. I'm guessing we can recruit plenty of Shifters to help."

Angus thought of Haider and the strange, cold gleam in the man's eyes. "Too risky. He might hurt Ciaran."

"We'll go in under the radar. No one will know we're coming—"

Zander broke off as Angus locked his fingers around the

lapel of his coat. "*No*. The guy who has Ciaran is careful enough to keep him well hidden and mean enough to kill him in front of me. Don't even think about trying to rescue him on your own. If you get Ciaran hurt, I'll kill you."

Zander gazed down at Angus from his height, not even angry that Angus had grabbed him. "I get it. But, my friend . . ." He put his hand on Angus's and gently but forcefully removed it from his coat. "If you need us to help, you call. I'll stick around the area—maybe go visit Austin or Kendrick. I'm more than happy to kick some Shifter Bureau ass."

Angus nodded once. "I'll keep it in mind. Thanks."

Zander's face split with a sudden grin. "They say you're a man of few words but deep thoughts. I'm guessing they're right. Goddess go with you."

"And you," Angus said. "And your mate."

Zander glanced at Rae, who'd climbed onto the motorcycle and had it started, then he bent close to Angus. "She hasn't said anything yet, but I think she might be expecting." Happiness radiated from the big man. "So I know how you feel. If anything endangered Rae and the cub . . ." Zander shuddered and shook his head. "But remember—you *call*."

He took a few steps back, pointing at Angus, then he swung around, duster flying, and strode to the motorcycle. "No, no, I'm driving," his voice boomed, and Rae's softer tones answered him—firmly. Angus guessed who would lose that argument.

Angus was right—he looked back from the top of the porch steps when he heard the motorcycle rev, and watched them pull out, Rae in front, Zander behind her. Zander lifted a long arm and waved, and then they were gone.

The front door jerked open, and Ben looked out, wild-eyed. "I don't know how she did it," he said. "But she's gone."

CHAPTER SIX

Angus raced back into the house, cursing Tamsin, Ben, the house, and himself.

He hadn't mistaken that Tamsin had been in pain, vulnerable, and scared, but he'd let himself grow too protective of her. Angus had understood how much Zander's healing process would hurt Tamsin, and he'd stuck by her, ready to catch her if she fell.

She'd bravely held herself together—no screaming or weeping, only a few silent tears. She'd been grateful to Zander and showed compassion toward him. Angus had seen that Tamsin was a real and caring woman, not the crazed, murdering insurrectionist Haider had made her out to be, and he'd let his guard down.

And look what happened. Tamsin had been waiting for her moment, and she'd taken it.

"Where is she?" he bellowed at the house as he ran into the front hall. Maybe she'd beguiled the place to her side, and it had let her depart while he'd been conversing with Zander and feeling sorry for Tamsin.

"I looked everywhere," Ben said breathlessly. "I started clearing the breakfast dishes, I turned around, and she was gone. I thought she'd stepped into another room, but no. I'm sorry, Angus."

"Not your fault. She's tricky." Angus strode into the middle of the paneled hall. "Show me where she is, damn you."

A rush of wind blew through the house, bringing with it the fresh smell of morning. Five panels along the wall slammed open, revealing niches from tiny to wide enough for a large man to walk through.

Angus peered into the niches, but most were shallow and empty. The largest one opened to a narrow hall that bent out of sight.

Angus stepped into the passage and followed it around a corner to find that it ended in another blank panel. He felt around for hidden catches, and finally depressed a piece of molding that let the panel swing open.

Behind it was a very small room, about seven by four feet, which held an old but well-preserved desk and chair under a tiny, high window, the only source of light.

Tamsin sat on the chair behind the desk, her red head bent as she went through a wallet and its contents on the desk before her. When Angus entered, she began reading from a small, laminated card.

"Angus Murray. Shifter type: Lupine. Born 1918. Mate: None. Cubs: One, Ciaran Murray, Lupine. Shiftertown: New Orleans West. Employment: Security, the Dark Moon Club, New Orleans. Approved. Residence: 1442 St. Charles Place. Nice picture."

She held his Shifter ID, the one that all Shifters were required to carry at all times. On the desk was a slim stack of cash, a few printed photos, and bits and pieces Angus had stashed in his wallet for no reason. He didn't know when, but sometime this morning, she'd obviously picked his pocket.

Tamsin looked up at him over the ID, her face holding an anger he couldn't interpret. "Murray," she repeated. "As in *Gavan Murray*?"

Angus saw no reason to lie. "My brother. He was, anyway, before his assholery got him killed. You should know—you were one of his followers."

Fury smoldered in her eyes as well as a stark pity. "I wouldn't say I followed him. More like I was in the same place at the same time." She dropped the card and rubbed her fingers over her temples. "I have to process this."

"You have to get up and come with me. It's time to go."

Tamsin lowered her hands, her tawny eyes still, her anger and bravado gone. "Damn it, you should have told me you were Gavan's brother. I had no idea . . . Goddess, I'm so sorry."

"Sorry about what? That you fell for his garbage?" Angus snarled, his bitter rage rising. "And what about those dead Shifter Bureau agents in Shreveport? Did you do that?"

"Angus." Tamsin rose from behind the desk, her hands flat on its surface. "I did not kill those agents. I promise. Do you believe me?"

She held his gaze, something in her eyes speaking of desperation, as though his answer was very, very important to her.

"I haven't decided yet, and you not killing them doesn't mean you weren't there."

Tamsin looked stricken. "I *was* there. But I promise you I didn't kill those men, or tell anyone else to kill them. It was awful, and I took off."

"Tell me what happened," Angus commanded.

For a moment, he thought she'd refuse, then Tamsin sank to the desk chair and covered her face with her hands. "I was with this Shifter—Dion. I thought he had the same goals I did, which is to get Shifters free of Shiftertowns and Collars. He seemed reasonable when I first met him."

She sighed. "But after a while it was clear he was just crazy. I planned to get away from him, but I was still with him when two men from Shifter Bureau found us. They tried to arrest us, but they didn't call for backup. I guess they thought Shifters would be scared and contrite if we were threatened with tranqs, Tasers, and Collars. But Dion was out of his mind. He went into his half-beast form and attacked. I tried to stop him, tried to fight him away from them. But he killed them—I couldn't do anything. I knew if I were found anywhere nearby, I'd be executed. So I ran."

Her words grew more shaky as she spoke, and when she finished, her shoulders moved in silent sobs.

Damn it, now Angus wanted to hold her, hug her, soothe her. Tell her he felt sorry for her for taking up with a murdering Feline.

"What happened to this Dion?" he asked abruptly. "Did they catch him?"

"I don't know. Probably not if you were sent to bring me in. They obviously knew I was at the scene."

Tamsin remained hunkered over, her damp hair spreading across her shoulders in an orange-red wave.

Angus hid a growl, moved across the small room, and rested his hand on her back. She was warm through her shirt, her shaking coming to him.

He firmed his touch, his natural instinct to comfort taking over. Shifters helped one another with direct contact, which was why embracing perfect strangers and those of the same gender—for long, soul-healing hugs—wasn't odd to them.

Tamsin's horror was unfeigned. Angus imagined she'd have been happy taunting and evading the agents, as she had Angus, but she would not have wanted them dead. Whoever this Dion was, if he was still alive, Angus would catch up to him and explain a few things.

"I'll help you tell them what happened," Angus said. "If you weren't responsible for the killings, I won't let Shifter Bureau pin that on you."

Tamsin raised her head. She sniffled, then dug into the pocket of her jeans for a tissue. "Wake up to reality. They won't care if I didn't actually commit the murders. I'm a Collarless Shifter. That's enough to get me caged and terminated."

She wasn't wrong. When Collarless Shifters were found, many were simply forced into Collars and put into Shifter-towns, but if one was considered violent and dangerous, termination was the usual result.

"I know people," Angus tried. "Powerful Shifters from Texas—both with Collars and without. They can help you. But I have to take you in first."

Tamsin turned to look at him, but she didn't try to dislodge his hand. He could tell his touch was helping, because her shaking had lessened and her voice no longer quavered. "I can't make you understand, can I?"

Her face was slightly pointed, like her fox's, her nose a little longer than most humans would find pretty. Angus thought it fit her perfectly. He also noted that the tips of her ears were very slightly pointed—her fox again. "I can't let you go, Tamsin. I'm sorry." He drew a breath. "They have my cub."

Tamsin's eyes widened. "What?" Her lips remained parted, moisture behind them.

"They're making me choose between you and my cub, and I have to pick my cub. So I don't have the option of letting you go. I've already taken too long, but you were hurt . . ."

Tamsin swallowed. Her breath touched his skin. "You should have told me."

"Would it have made a difference?"

She nodded, her warm hair brushing his hand. "I would

have tried harder to get away from you. Not your fault if you couldn't catch me."

Angus frowned. "You mean you *weren't* trying hard to get away from me?"

"Not as hard as I could have. The house is starting to like me. It showed me this room—I *knew* there would be secret passages. It will let me go eventually if I can convince it that it's in our best interests."

"You don't sound very worried that you're inside a haunted house."

"A sentient house," Tamsin said. "There's a difference. I've heard of them, though I've never seen one. Very, very rare. Have to be on a ley line, built by a person of certain magic, and then it needs to be given time."

"And you know all this because . . ."

"I read books." Tamsin's impish look returned. "You know, they have covers with paper in between. Or they're words that magically appear on your phone. At least *my* phone, since I have one made in this century. Or I did. Too risky to carry something around that always wants to know your location."

Angus didn't bother answering. He couldn't seem to stand up either, to rise and walk away from her.

He'd pretty much shut down all interest in female Shifters since April had told him she'd always preferred Gavan and had only accepted Angus's mate-claim to get close to his brother. He and April had never formed the mate bond, and he'd understood why the day she'd taken off with Gavan, leaving a note in case he worried about Ciaran. Angus had tracked her down—he was one of the best trackers in his Shiftertown, far better than Gavan had ever been—took Ciaran, and let her go.

He'd been completely absorbed in raising his son and keeping Shifter Bureau off his back from that day to this.

But maybe he should have sated himself with a few females, perhaps one of the human women groupies who tried to entice him at the club. Then he wouldn't be inhaling Tamsin Calloway's nutmeg scent and wanting to close the space between them.

He did close it, and she didn't pull away. Her gaze flicked to his lips. Angus's blood fired, his heart banging hard.

The moment hovered, with their faces close, breaths mingling. Tamsin's lashes moved as she met his gaze, her whisky-colored eyes flecked with green.

Angus waited for his natural cynicism to return, for his common sense to clamp down over his impulses. But he felt need building deep inside him, the frenzy that all Shifters could fall into when they wanted to mate.

He knew Tamsin was not unwilling. A Shifter female made it very clear when she didn't want a male, in the harshest words possible if necessary, with a follow-up of claws and teeth. Males, unless they were total dickheads, got the message and backed off. The total dickheads usually ended up bloody, or dropped on their heads, as the Shifter female had done at the club.

Tamsin only looked at Angus, as though waiting for him to make the first move. If Angus kissed her, it would lead to more, and more, and this situation would deteriorate from captor and captive very fast. Which was probably what she wanted.

So Angus should back away. Get up, walk out, demand that she follow him, and lock her in a room until they left. Any minute now . . .

As he debated with himself, Tamsin leaned forward and brushed his lips with hers.

Something electric flashed through Angus's body, and for a second, he thought she'd tased him. But her hands were empty, her eyes closed, and only her mouth touched his.

Her lips were smooth, soft, perfect. The half kiss broke open something inside him, and heat came flooding out.

Angus attempted to pull back, but the ache that would

have caused wouldn't let him. His hand moved before he could stop it and cupped her cheek, pulling her closer so he could strengthen the kiss.

Tamsin stilled, then her hesitancy left her. She leaned into him and met his kiss with a sudden hunger.

Soft, sweet woman under his hands, yet she was strong. Tamsin's lips moved on his, seeking, giving at the same time. She might have started off trying to distract him, but now she simply wanted to kiss him.

Angus responded in kind. He pulled her closer, slanting his mouth over hers, a groan leaving his lips. She was a fugitive he needed to bring in, but right now, she was a woman, Tamsin, beautiful and fragrant. Her hair was like living fire against his palm, heating, not burning.

If he could send the world away, he'd lift her against him and onto the desk, tearing away clothes to find her.

He parted her lips with his tongue, tasting the mint bite of toothpaste barely covering her own spice. She welcomed him, her small fists digging into his back as she pulled him down to her.

The kiss went on, their mouths connecting, erasing all urgency but this joining. The world spun away, the years of heartache and loneliness, of Angus blaming himself for losing his mate, dissolving to mist. Nothing mattered but this woman and her fiery kiss, her arms around him, their bodies fusing as though nothing else existed in time and space.

A breath of wind touched Angus, but he couldn't be bothered to wonder where it had come from. Tamsin was real and warm in his arms, her kiss deepening. She made a faint noise in her throat, a sound of surrender.

They were spinning, falling, floating, but no, they hadn't moved. The floor was still beneath Angus's feet, his knee hard against the desk. But he felt nothing, no sensation except where he connected with Tamsin.

A voice boomed in the echoing main hall. "Did you find her?"

Tamsin gasped, the touch of it on his tongue. She pulled away, breaking the kiss, her face scarlet.

Reality returned with a slap. Angus was supposed to be her jailor, taking her in in exchange for his cub. He had no business kissing her, touching her, tasting her, and wanting to do it again. No business savoring her, drinking in every second of it.

"Yes!" he roared back. "We're leaving."

Tamsin couldn't catch her breath. She struggled for it as Angus pulled her up, grabbed his wallet and money, and dragged her out through the secret passage to the main hall where Ben waited, a worried look on his face.

She still couldn't breathe as he towed her to the front door, plucking a hooded jacket from a coat hook along the way, the keys to the awful station wagon in his hand. Tamsin hoped the house would imprison him as well, but no, the door flung itself open as soon as Angus touched it.

He wasn't really going to take her to Shifter Bureau, was he? They'd had a moment. A kiss.

One hell of a kiss. The sensation of that was what kept Tamsin's breath from her, not Angus's rapid pace.

Plenty of men in Tamsin's life had tried to kiss her or more, and she'd evaded most of them. She hadn't wanted to evade Angus. She'd brushed her lips against his because she'd had the sudden urge to discover what it felt like to kiss him.

Now she couldn't pump enough air into her lungs. His kiss had been strong but not brutal. He had Tamsin in his power, and he knew it, in spite of her refusal to cow to him. Yet he hadn't thrown her to the floor and ravished her, taking what he could from his prisoner.

He'd kissed her as though he'd wanted to learn her as much as she wanted to learn him. She still did. Never mind that he was taking her to her execution and he was Gavan Murray's *brother*.

Tamsin's head told her to fight him, get away from him, run like hell. Her libido kept fantasizing about what it would have been like if he had taken her to the floor, covering her with his hard body.

Her heart said . . .

Her heart was all screwed up and always would be. No use asking her heart.

Tamsin dug in her heels as they approached the car. Ben had followed them out, his dark eyes enigmatic. He didn't like what Angus was doing, but he didn't try to stop him either.

She jerked against Angus's hold, but he didn't release her. "You can't." Tamsin continued to yank at him, but she didn't have any more luck extracting herself than her fox had had pulling its paw from the alligator's mouth. "Angus, come on."

Ben reached them, brow puckered with concern. "You know they'll kill her, Angus. Let me take her—she'll go so far away Shifter Bureau will never find her, and you'll be off the hook. They can't expect you to track someone who's thousands and thousands of miles from anywhere."

That solution didn't sound much better. Tamsin didn't know exactly what Ben was, in spite of his glib explanation of being a gnome or a goblin—whatever she wanted to call him. Running thousands and thousands of miles away where no one would ever find her wasn't exactly what she had in mind.

Angus growled, his grip tightening. "She's coming with me. I'm turning her over and taking Ciaran home. If Haider is too incompetent to hold on to her after that, if she gets away from him right after I'm gone, *which I know she can*, and if there's *a Shifter waiting around the block* to help her out, then Haider can suck it."

Tamsin ceased struggling as she listened, her mouth forming an *O*. Angus gave her a long look, gray eyes glittering.

Wait until I have my cub safe and then give this guy Haider the slip, he was trying to tell her. *Run like hell, but backup will be just around the corner.*

Angus wasn't interested in pleasing Haider—he only wanted to rescue his cub. If Tamsin kicked Shifter Bureau in the balls and ran far, far away, he didn't care. As long as he got his cub first, Angus would be happy.

Tamsin gave him a little nod, hoping she hadn't misunderstood.

She turned and flashed Ben a big smile. "See you, Ben. Who knows, sometime I might need to take you up on your offer to get me far from here. Is it someplace exotic?"

Ben considered. "Exotic-ish."

Tamsin hugged him—with one arm, as Angus wasn't about to let her go. "What a sweetie you are. Why don't you have a mate? Or do you? Tucked away in this exotic-ish place?"

"Huh. I wish." Ben returned the embrace, then backed from her, hands out as though showing Angus he hadn't given her anything. "No one wants an old geezer like me."

"Don't sell yourself short. I think you're wicked sexy. All right, all right, don't push." The last was directed at Angus, who had the passenger door open and was trying to angle her into the car.

Tamsin lowered herself onto the seat, her shakes returning. Angus shut the door, and Tamsin cranked down the window and blew Ben a kiss.

"Thanks for breakfast, Ben. I'll send you a postcard."

Angus said nothing at all. The car jostled as he dropped into the driver's seat and cranked the engine to life.

A heavy wind sprang up, bending the trees and making the vines on the house dance. The chimes on the porch rang and jangled.

Tamsin laughed in delight. "It's saying good-bye to me." She waved at the house as Angus pulled the car around the arc of the drive. "I'll be back. Don't you worry."

Ben watched them go from the foot of the porch steps, arms folded. Tamsin waved until Angus rounded a stand of trees and Ben and the house were lost to sight.

Angus drove out through the rusting gate to the narrow road that skirted the river. He hunkered over the wheel, a silent bulk of male Lupine, his gray eyes light in the morning sunshine.

He said nothing, no mention of the kiss, no more advice for what she should do when in Shifter Bureau's clutches. He might have been alone in the car for all the attention he paid her.

Tamsin leaned back in the seat and rested her feet on the dash. "So, where exactly are we going?"

CHAPTER SEVEN

"New Orleans." Angus's words came out a grunt.

"Oh, that sounds nice," Tamsin said, pretending her fears weren't rising. "I can go shopping. And grab some great food. Food's the best part of Nawlins, isn't it? While I love walking in Jackson Square and doing the music scene, it's the food that brings me back."

Angus glanced at her. "You go there often?"

"If you call twice in my life often, then yes. Last time was with my sister . . ."

The words died as Tamsin's throat closed. She couldn't keep up her false chirpiness when she thought about her sister.

Angus glanced at her again. Goddess, he wasn't going to ask about Glynis, was he?

"What happened to your sister?"

He was. "She died," Tamsin said in clipped tones. "Shifter hunter. We were trying to avoid being rounded up. Happy now?"

"Why the hell would I be happy hearing that your sister was killed by a fucking Shifter hunter?" he asked with a Lupine snarl. "We all had shit like that happen. No one was spared a tragedy when Shifters were outed."

"Which is why we need to fight them," Tamsin said, sitting up straight. "Get ourselves the hell away from Shiftertowns, Collars, rules, Shifter Bureau. You know it."

Angus sent her a glare. "If you start the freedom-fighting Shifter shit in this car, I'm throwing you out. While it's still moving."

"So you *don't* want Shifters to be free?" Tamsin asked, eyes wide.

"I didn't say that. This is where Gavan and I disagreed. His stupid rhetoric and raging only got Shifters killed. Including cubs. Is that what *you* want?"

"No," Tamsin had to admit. "But . . ."

Angus swerved toward the side of the road, gunning the car as he did so. "I mean it. I'll tell Haider you fell out trying to escape. Nothing I could do. Got it?"

Tamsin took one look at the fury in his eyes and realized she'd touched a nerve. A terrible, raw nerve that brought up a lot of pain. She glanced at the side of the road rushing past her and made her decision. She shut up.

New Orleans, even in the morning, was a busy place, with tourists flocking to Bourbon Street and Jackson Square, hoping to get a glimpse of the stereotype of life in the Big Easy. Were there really voodoo priestesses and scantily clad ladies, Dixieland jazz bands going full blast?

For the tourists there were. Tamsin remembered coming here with Glynis, walking arm in arm through the hot nights, eating fabulous shrimp and crawdad concoctions in every restaurant they entered, dancing to the bands set up in the middle of the street.

That had been a long, long time ago, before Shifters

were outed. Tamsin and Glynis had pretended to be human tourists, no shifting, no teeth and claws.

"Except this one time." Tamsin had started telling Angus the tale as soon as they hit the main streets of the city, as though the stories had taken over her tongue. "A guy and his friends tried to pick us up. Four of them, and two of us. They wouldn't take no for an answer. So we let them chase us into a dark alley—seriously dark, no lights back there at all. Glynis changed to her bobcat form and just stood there, snarling. One guy had a flashlight, and he shone it over this tough-looking wildcat with yellow eyes and bared teeth. While he and his friends stood there gibbering, I ran behind them and started biting their asses. They were screaming bloody murder. We'd never seen anyone run so fast . . ."

Tamsin trailed off, laughing, but tears gathered in her eyes and threatened to spill out.

After a period of silence, Angus cleared his throat. "I'm sorry about what happened to her."

Tamsin wiped her eyes. "Hey, it wasn't your fault. It was Shifter Bureau who gave the authorization for un-Collared Shifters to be hunted down."

"They killed my brother too," Angus said quietly.

Tamsin knew that. Gavan Murray had been caught, arrested, interrogated, and executed. His secrets were supposed to have died with him.

She flipped her hand. "There you go."

Angus growled. "Sweetheart, I'd love it if the whole pack of Bureau agents disappeared, Shiftertowns vanished, and these stupid Collars were off our necks. But we have to be careful. Not long ago, a group of Shifters got so desperate to be free they made a deal with the Fae. You hear me? *The Fae.* They went from one slavery to another. I tried to help bring these Shifters back home, but most of them didn't want to come. They wanted to stay in Faerie and be the Fae's Battle Beasts. How fucked-up is that?"

Tamsin frowned. "Your brother never had anything to do with the Fae."

"I know." Angus's voice rose to a shout. "It's an *example*. It's what can happen."

"Sure, what can happen if you're stupid and gullible."

"Exactly," Angus snapped. "And who is being taken to Shifter Bureau now instead of puttering at home in her Shiftertown?"

"Under a curfew, wearing a Collar," Tamsin pointed out.

"Taking care of her family!" Angus said, voice hard. "That's what we do. We take care of the people we love so when shit happens, if another Shifter-Fae war comes, if Shifter Bureau moves against us, we can be there to defend them."

Tamsin thought of her mother and flinched. She could be with her now, if she'd meekly taken the Collar and moved with her to her Shiftertown. But then, some clans and families had been split up. There was nothing to say she'd have been housed with her own mother.

"I couldn't have prevented Glynis's death," Tamsin said, "if that's what you're accusing me of. Glynis made a run for it when Shifters were being rounded up by Shifter Bureau, interviewed, and 'processed.' I wasn't with her. I couldn't do a thing."

"Did I say that?" Another glare. "Quit putting words in my mouth. I meant in general. We stick together. We help each other."

Tamsin flushed. "You know what? You're a shit. I'm sorry I kissed you."

"I'm not."

Tamsin opened her mouth for more hot words, but they died on her lips. "What?"

"I'm not sorry you kissed me." Angus stretched, pushing his hands against the steering wheel. "It was a good kiss."

Tamsin tried to think of a snide retort—she had one for

every occasion—but nothing came to her. She could only say faintly, "It was?"

Damn it, she sounded like a Shifter girl just past her Transition, thrilled a hot guy had noticed her.

"Yes." Angus's frown returned. "It was."

Tamsin cleared her throat. "You rate your kisses? It was awesome, pretty good, or meh?" There, that was more like her.

"No." He resumed his harsh tone. "Take the compliment. Don't ruin it."

He had a point. Tamsin clamped her lips shut and looked out the window.

Streets went by, bringing back memories. This town had seen a lot of damage since she'd been here with Glynis, but its spirit hadn't been broken. They drove slowly through an area where wrought-iron balconies on stucco buildings hung over brick sidewalks.

Clouds had gathered, and it started to rain, a gentle autumn rain. Farther along, they passed parks and gardens open to walkers, the pavement damp and the greens lined with brilliant flowers.

Angus thought Tamsin was a good kisser, did he? A warm shiver went through her.

What is wrong with me? He's taking me to this Haider guy, who I'm going to kick in the balls and run away from, after Angus's cub is safe. I'll never see Angus again. Safer for him if I don't.

The regret that thought brought unnerved her. With the life Tamsin had chosen, any connections she made could only be temporary ones. She knew that. She should be used to it by now.

But she wasn't. She was lonely and disheartened, tired of the people she met who shared her outrage turning out to be completely crazy. Tamsin wanted Shifters free but safe, able to live life on their own terms. She didn't want to overthrow human governments or join up with Fae or slaughter every man in Shifter Bureau. Rough them up a little maybe, because they'd done some horrible things, but that was all.

Mostly she wanted Shifters to have true freedom—to live where they liked, with whom they liked, go where they liked and when.

Many Collared Shifters she'd met had thought her a dreamer. *Look,* they said, *we're not starving anymore, women don't die bringing in cubs, those cubs have a better chance of growing up, and we'll live longer than the humans around us anyway. One day, we'll have what you want.*

Maybe, but she hated seeing cubs given their Collars when they hit their teens, hated that Shiftertown rules kept her mother from seeing her own daughter. Tamsin was convinced that waiting would only give the Bureau time to come up with some new way of keeping Shifters under their thumbs forever.

She pushed the thoughts out of her head. Now was the time to come up with a plan of escape. She'd save idealism for later.

"Where are we meeting the dirtbag Haider?" she asked.

"He wants me to go to the cemetery in the Garden District." Angus kept his eyes on traffic and turned the giant car through small streets. Tourists were everywhere in spite of the rain, rambling on foot, riding in horse-drawn carriages, even sitting at sidewalk cafés.

"Sounds ominous," Tamsin said.

"I'm not meeting him there. He told me to go there and call in."

"Still sounds ominous."

"I know that," Angus said sharply.

Tamsin fell silent as Angus navigated the streets. The walkers through the old district stared at their incongruous car as much as they did the lovely, well-preserved houses around them.

How Angus would find a place to park, Tamsin didn't know, but somehow he managed to squeeze between the front and rear of two cars against the curb.

Beside them was the wall that separated the road from the historic cemetery. Across the tree-lined street were houses, stately and large, with trimmed lawns and gardens.

"Have to wonder how spooky it is to live across from a cemetery," Tamsin said as Angus turned off the engine. The lack of the engine's roar didn't mean silence—plenty of cars rushed past, and people walked up and down the street, while cyclists pedaled by serenely. "Must be creepy at night."

Angus didn't answer. He climbed from the car when the traffic was clear and came around to help Tamsin out.

She could run now. She could make a dash for it before Angus took her into the cemetery, blend in with the people strolling through the neighborhood, leap onto a bus, and lose herself in the throng of downtown New Orleans.

From there she could figure out a way to get the hell out of town, out of the state, out of the country if necessary. She could go to Mexico and regroup—Mexico had enough problems with drug cartels and border violence that they didn't have time to pay attention to stray Shifters. She'd have to dodge the drug runners and human traffickers, true, but one thing at a time.

But if she made a run for it, Shifter Bureau might keep Angus's cub to coerce him into going after her, or maybe they'd hurt the little guy to punish Angus. Tamsin had seen the terrible fear in Angus's eyes—he hadn't been lying about Shifter Bureau holding Ciaran hostage. Why was Haider torturing Angus like this? Retribution for the trouble his brother had caused?

Tamsin made her decision. She'd let Angus take her into the cemetery and call Haider so he could have his cub back. She'd at least wait for that. Once the cub and Angus were gone, then she'd get away and hope the backup Angus promised appeared. Maybe he'd talked Zander into helping her—the thought made her spirits rise.

As they walked through a gate that stood half open, the noise of the street traffic died behind them.

The main path was lined with small stone buildings, their facades decorated with pediments, some curved, some triangular. Plaques adorned the walls with faded names and dates, or words about death and finality. Some of the tombs were in disrepair, some deliberately damaged. She shuddered. Who would be weird enough to vandalize a tomb?

Tamsin shared the Shifter wariness of burying the dead, and sensed the ghosts that lingered here, the chill of souls left too close to their bones.

"Give me a Guardian anytime," she said in a low voice to Angus, and he nodded.

Tourists moved in a clump down one of the walks as though huddling together for comfort. Cemeteries could be spooky, or they could be peaceful. This one was a little of both.

Angus led Tamsin down an empty lane, tombs closing in on them. Some of the monuments were simple flat graves with markers, which looked even more exposed and lonely than the enclosed tombs. At least people had left flowers to brighten up some of the graves, even though the dates listed on them were nearly two hundred years in the past.

Angus looked as uncomfortable as Tamsin felt. "I hear you," he said.

"They have to bury people aboveground in New Orleans," Tamsin said, chattering to break the humid silence. "The water table's too high for them to dig graves. So they brick up their families in these buildings instead." She shivered.

"I know." Angus's answer was subdued. "I've lived in southern Louisiana for twenty years. I know all about the water table."

"Can't wait to get back north," Tamsin rattled on. "I bet you'd be happier in dry woods too. All this humidity must play hell with your fur."

Angus's dark hair was damp with perspiration and misty rain. "You get used to it. If you like northern woods so much, what were you doing running around the bayous?"

Tamsin shrugged, but her heart beat faster. "If I don't tell you, they won't be able to beat it out of you later."

"Mmph." Angus grunted. "Whatever."

Tamsin had no intention of confiding the real reason she'd been in Shreveport with Dion—she wasn't wrong that it would be dangerous knowledge, dangerous to Angus and his cub. Besides which, Angus was Gavan's brother. Angus struck her as an entirely different person from Gavan, who'd been a total asshole, but maybe that side of Angus's personality just hadn't manifested yet.

Dion had claimed he'd known about Gavan's plans, and she'd been trying to *prevent* him from finding out if he was right, not assist him. And then he'd gone insane and attacked the Bureau agents who must have been following him, instead of simply evading them and disappearing. She'd had to run before checking out whether the information she had was still good. And now she'd have no chance, with Shifter Bureau all over her ass.

The quiet grew more intense. Angus halted under a tree, which rained droplets upon them. The tomb next to the tree held seven people, Tamsin read, a whole family buried there from 1878 to 1934. Their names were fading, forgotten. Sad.

"Like I said, I want the Guardian's sword when it's my time to go," Tamsin whispered.

Angus opened his flip phone. The beeping as he pressed the numbers sounded irreverent in this place.

"I'm here," Angus said into the phone, his tones clipped. "Where's my cub?"

His eyes narrowed as he listened. Tamsin couldn't hear

the person on the other end, which was strange. Was there such a thing as a Shifter hearing baffling app?

"Fine." Angus's word was sharp. "Just hurry up. I'm getting wet."

He closed the flip phone without a good-bye and bent a gaze on Tamsin.

"Well?" she asked.

"He wants us to stand here. He's coming."

"He's bringing your cub *here*?" Tamsin folded her arms, pretending she wasn't shaking. "That's kind of mean."

"I don't care. As long as he brings him."

Angus closed his mouth and looked away.

Another opportunity to run. She could shift into a fox and stream around these tombs and over the wall into the city before Angus could turn around and see her go. Humans weren't quite as amazed when they saw a fox, even one larger than most wild ones, as they were when they caught sight of a wolf or a leopard or a lumbering grizzly bear. How many grizzlies ran through the swamps of Louisiana?

Foxes were far more common in the wild. The downside was that, instead of fearing foxes, people tried to shoot them. Foxes ate chickens and generally made nuisances of themselves. It was a popular sport in England to dress up in fancy riding clothes, gather about fifty hounds, and ride twenty horses over the countryside in pursuit of one itty-bitty fox. Obviously that fox was a terrible monster that must be subdued at all costs.

Tamsin had always wondered if the Fae had created a few fox Shifters as a big joke. They'd think it funny to let loose fox Shifters in front of an English hunt.

Her mind was babbling these things to keep herself from thinking about what was to come. Her instincts were coming alert, looking for her chance to get away. She'd wait until Angus's cub was safe, and then—gone.

But who knew what Haider would do? Would he try to

tranq her right away or wrap her in spelled cuffs so she couldn't shift? Were his guys carrying Collars? Or would they not bother with a Collar and take her straight to a firing squad?

Four men materialized out of the trees, one in a suit, three in black fatigues. A suit? Really? In this weather?

But yes, the lead man wore a suit with a coat and tie, and shoes that looked like they'd cost a wage worker a month's salary. His own stupid fault if they were ruined by rain and mud. The man in the suit had dark hair and blue eyes, and a pistol in a holster just under his coat.

The three guys in fatigues had tranq pistols in hip holsters, and probably more weaponry hidden on them somewhere. They all carried radios that for the moment were silent.

The leader stopped about two yards from Angus and Tamsin. The men in fatigues circled around behind them.

Angus fixed the leader with a hard stare. "Where's my cub, Haider?"

He didn't mess around, Angus. Haider met his stare, then gave a brief nod to one of the guys in fatigues. The man turned away, his radio crackling to life. "Bring him," he said.

Behind them, down the row a little, a door in one of the larger tombs opened. A man in black fatigues emerged, another following. Between them, the second man's hand on his shoulder, came a boy of about eleven years old, dark haired and gray eyed, with the squared features of his father. He'd be a heartbreaker when he got older, Tamsin thought. He even had a scowl that matched Angus's in intensity.

Angus's scowl was vividly present as he glared at Haider. "You kept my son in a *tomb*? What the hell is wrong with you?"

"Relax, it's empty. We put a bed in there, and Ciaran got to play video games and watch movies."

"Lame ones," Ciaran muttered. Tamsin wanted to burst into nervous laughter. He sounded just like his dad.

"Let him go." Angus's eyes were turning lighter gray, his wolf wanting to come out and play. If he turned himself into his between-beast and struck out hard and fast, he could take out all six guys very fast.

His Collar would go off and burn him with pain if he did. Then the guys with the tranqs would land him on the ground, and he'd be chained and hauled away. What they'd do with Ciaran, Tamsin didn't like to speculate.

She lifted her hand in a friendly wave at Ciaran. "Hi there. I'm Tamsin, the big scary Shifter all these guys are after."

Ciaran looked her up and down, his dark brows rising, then turned to his father. "You mean I was stuck all night in a crypt with Shifter Bureau, and you were with *her*? Not fair."

"I didn't have a choice, son." Angus's voice held a gentleness Tamsin hadn't heard in it before.

Ciaran gave Tamsin a once-over again. "Good taste, Dad. She's hot."

"Hey." Tamsin gave him a mock frown. "I'm old enough to be your . . . aunt."

"Yeah. My *hot* aunt."

Tamsin winked at him. "I was right. You'll be a heartbreaker. I bet you already are."

Ciaran looked puzzled by this, then turned back to Angus. "I'm all right, Dad. Just bored."

And scared. Tamsin scented that on him, but he wasn't about to let on in front of the Shifter Bureau goons how afraid he was.

"Let him walk over here," Angus said. "Then we're leaving. Right? I did what you wanted. Now my son and I are going home."

"You took your time." Haider motioned for the men with Ciaran to walk him forward. "Where did you disappear to?"

"Running after *her*." Angus jerked his thumb at Tamsin. "Where do you think?"

"Hm." Haider looked skeptical but didn't pursue it.

Ciaran reached Angus. The goons stepped back, and Angus crouched down and pulled his son into a smothering hug. "You all right, little guy?"

Tamsin's throat went tight as she saw the relief and love on Angus's face. Ciaran, who clung to Angus a long moment, clearly loved and trusted his father. She remembered her own cubhood with her mom and dad, the family hugs that could make every trouble melt away, and her heart ached.

Angus unwound himself from Ciaran and straightened up, keeping hold of his cub's hand. "I'm taking your car back to the club," he told Haider. "My motorcycle is there, and I'm not walking with my cub across the city. Pick it up yourself."

Haider nodded, as though he didn't care one way or the other what happened to the car. "Leave the keys on the front seat. I doubt anyone will steal it." His lips twitched.

Angus showed no amusement. He tightened his hold on Ciaran and walked him past Haider, past the men in fatigues, and down the walkway between the tombs.

Ciaran glanced back at Tamsin, worry on his face, but Angus never turned around.

Because he feared any look would give away what he'd told Tamsin to do? Or because he was absorbed in Ciaran and ready to put this situation well behind him?

Either way, they turned a corner, father and son gripping hands tightly, and disappeared.

Tamsin did not like how watching them go made her feel. Empty. Lonely. Mournful that she'd never see Angus again.

She stopped herself from analyzing these feelings and concentrated on the fact that she was alone with six guys from Shifter Bureau.

Her chest tightened, and her fight-or-flight instincts rose. She'd be fighting or fleeing very soon. Probably both.

"Ms. Calloway," Haider said. "Shall we go inside?" He motioned to the tomb in which they'd kept Ciaran.

"Nah, I like the weather." Tamsin stuck her hands into her jacket pockets. No way was she entering a confined space with Haider. She'd be able to get away much more easily if they remained in the open air.

When Haider didn't move, she continued, "So why did you send a master tracker like Angus after little ole me? What have *I* done? This time, I mean."

The quirk of Haider's lips hadn't left him. Tamsin hated people with the I-know-something-you-don't look.

"You interest me," Haider said. "I could reel off the list of your crimes and your associations with known agitators, but I'll do that later. You'll tell me where they all are in time. You also know a few things about Gavan Murray I will make you tell me. But I'm also very curious about *this*."

He dipped his hand into his pocket, and Tamsin tensed, but what he pulled out was an ordinary smartphone. He tapped an icon, gave it a few swipes, tapped again, and held it up facing her.

The screen of the phone was dark for a moment, then a greenish light spread over it, giving the trees and plants it showed a strange fuzzy outline. In the middle of these trees was Tamsin, her skin glowing in the green light. She was naked.

Before she could voice her disgust that someone had spied on her with a nightscope and *filmed* it, the Tamsin on the screen morphed rapidly and smoothly into her fox.

Shit.

Haider smiled as he turned the phone around and tapped it to make it dark again.

"What are you going to do with that?" Tamsin asked, pretending nonchalance. "Post it on a Canine porn network?"

"I'm going to find out what makes you tick," Haider said. "I want to know why there are fox Shifters when no one knew it, and *how* there are fox Shifters. I'm going to find out everything about you."

"How, by dissecting me?" Tamsin's voice went shriller than she meant it to.

"Not right away," Haider said smoothly. "I'll want to talk to you first. About Gavan and his little group. About everything. We will do quite a lot of talking."

Interrogation, he meant. With torture, drugs, whatever he could think of to make her spill all she knew.

Then he'd cut her apart to find the secret of what made Tamsin herself.

He was crazy enough to do it—Tamsin saw that in his eyes. She noticed that a couple of his goons weren't thrilled by what he was saying, but she figured they'd obey orders no matter what. If they had true scruples, they wouldn't be here at all.

Only one thing to do. She wasn't sure Angus and Ciaran had made it to safety yet, but she couldn't wait.

Tamsin launched herself at Haider.

She knew he'd be expecting something like that, so she turned in midair to hit the guy five feet away from him instead. She rammed into the startled man in fatigues, then jumped away from him, his tranq pistol in her hands.

The problem with tranq guns was that they only had one shot. Tamsin picked her target, and fired the tranq dart into Haider's neck.

He swore at her the second before he crumpled into an unconscious pile, and in that second, she was gone.

Tamsin dodged the goons before they could coordinate to grab her. She heard their tranq guns go off, but none hit her, and then came the pop of pistol bullets.

Tamsin thrust the tranq pistol into her jacket and nimbly leapt from the ground to an ornamented frieze to the top of a tomb, then ran, jumping from one tomb to the next, dropping down at the end of the row to another walkway. The large human men in combat boots would have to run around, but they were trained, and they were fast.

Tamsin bolted down the main walkway toward the open gate, running with all she had in her. She emerged onto the street where Angus had parked. The station wagon was still there, Angus and Ciaran about ten feet from reaching it.

The Shifter agents were right behind her. No time to search for whomever Angus had arranged to pick her up.

"Change of plans!" Tamsin shouted as she barreled toward them and the car.

Angus and Ciaran exchanged a startled look, and then they were running.

All three reached the car at the same time. Tamsin yanked open the back door of the station wagon and dove inside. She hunkered down on the seat as Angus and Ciaran slammed themselves into the front, and Tamsin sent up a fervent prayer to the Goddess.

"Awesome!" Ciaran shouted. "Go, Dad! *Go!*"

CHAPTER EIGHT

Angus swung into traffic, diving in front of a speeding SUV that had to slam on its brakes. The driver leaned on his horn and gave Angus the finger. Angus didn't slow, leaving the narrow street behind as fast as he could.

"What the fuck was that?" he demanded of the lump in the back seat.

"Me blowing your mission." Tamsin's voice was muffled. "I don't care where you throw me out, but don't take me back to Haider."

"You want to tell me where you think I can take you? In this shitbag of a car? With all of Shifter Bureau on our asses?"

"You don't know it's *all* of Shifter Bureau, Dad." Ciaran's tone was reasonable but his eyes were lit with excitement. His face and arms were dirty. If any of those goons had hit him . . .

"It will be once Haider reports in," Angus growled.

"We'll have to ditch the car." There was a rustle as Tamsin righted herself but she remained hunched down in the seat. "It stands out a mile, and I bet he put a tracker on it."

"Why would he have to?" Angus's barked question was cut over by Ciaran.

"You mean you didn't look for a tracking device? Seriously, Dad."

Tamsin nodded. "Remember, he asked where you'd disappeared to? Probably meant he lost your signal at some point. I bet it was when we were at the house. Ley line, sentient house. Makes sense."

Ciaran's eyes widened as he turned around and studied Tamsin. "You took her to the haunted house? Nice one, Dad."

Angus gripped the steering wheel, irritated at himself. His son and Tamsin were no doubt right. He hadn't bothered looking for a tracking device because it hadn't mattered. He'd planned to do what Haider wanted anyway—why try to do it stealthily?

But now they needed to be invisible—hard to do in a wood-paneled station wagon from the 1970s.

Angus drove as fast as he dared through the narrow streets, which were heavy with traffic, heading for the broad expanse of St. Charles Avenue.

Ciaran peered interestedly over the dashboard. "What are you going to do? Carjack someone?"

"*No.*" Angus bent a hard look on his son. "We're not criminals. I had Ben arrange backup for Tamsin if she needed it."

"Isn't he sweet?" Tamsin said from the depths of the back seat. "Is Zander hiding out waiting to carry me off? He's not exactly inconspicuous."

"You met Zander?" Ciaran's eyes widened with admiration. "*And* Ben? Man, I always miss all the fun."

Angus glanced at him, noting that, despite his wide-eyed interest, Ciaran was trembling. Angus put an arm around him and drew him close.

"If they hurt you, Ciaran, tell me, all right? Don't hold back. If they did, I'll kill them." He rested his hand on his son's back, all of him rejoicing that his cub was safe. "I'll probably kill them anyway—I'll just do it a bit harder."

He noted Tamsin watching him in the rearview mirror, surprise in her eyes. What had she thought, that Angus would lie down and roll over for Shifter Bureau? He'd have Haider's balls on a platter for abducting his son.

"They didn't," Ciaran answered, subdued. "Just scared me. Or tried to. But I wasn't scared, Dad. I knew you'd come find me."

Ciaran's shivering told Angus he *had* been scared, terrified. Haider would pay for that.

"You were brave, son. Never let on to those Bureau shits that you're worried."

"I didn't."

"Good lad."

Angus pulled around the corner to St. Charles Avenue, a broad boulevard divided by an island along which streetcars clacked. It was lined with houses large and small, all old and stately.

A beige SUV, unassuming and so like every other SUV on the road as to be almost camouflaged, waited in a side lane that led back toward the cemetery.

Angus pulled the station wagon in behind it and stopped. He quickly got out of the car, scanning the roads in case Haider and company were charging down them. Angus calculated they'd have a minute or so, maybe, to get out of here.

A tall black man with a runner's body climbed of the SUV, tossing Angus a set of keys.

"Thanks, Reg," Angus said. "You haven't seen us, right?"

Reg folded his arms as first Ciaran and then Tamsin darted out of the wagon and hurried to the SUV.

Ciaran threw open one of the rear doors. "I'm in back. You get shotgun," he said to Tamsin.

He didn't call her by name. He was already learning.

"I haven't seen *anything*," Reg said. "In fact, I'm not even here. I'm jogging by the lake."

He started for the station wagon, but Angus shook his head. "It's probably being tracked. Leave it. Can we drop you somewhere?"

"Sure. The lake."

Without another word, Reg climbed into the back with Ciaran and shut the door. Tamsin was already in the front seat as Angus slid behind the wheel. She rummaged in the glove compartment and pulled out a pair of sunglasses.

"Cool shades," she said to Reg. "Mind?"

Reg shrugged. Angus could tell he was dying to know who she was and what the hell was going on, but like a good tracker, he knew when to keep quiet.

Tamsin pulled on the square sunglasses, checked her reflection, smiled at it, and hunkered down into the seat.

Angus started the SUV and made a quiet but swift U-turn. He drove sedately to the end of the block, though his heart was thumping with the need to hurry, and turned back onto St. Charles Avenue. This time, he blended in with the traffic, slowing when it slowed, stopping when it stopped.

Every instinct told him to floor it, screech away, and drive like hell, but Angus fought the compulsion. The best way to evade pursuit was to not call attention to himself. This SUV looked like every other one on the road, its windows tinted enough to keep people from seeing clearly who was inside. Reg had chosen well.

"Where did you get this?" Angus asked Reg as he drove carefully along the street. "It's perfect."

"What do you mean, where did I get it? It's mine."

Angus stepped hard on the brake and glared back at Reg. "Registered with Shifter Bureau?" They'd have a record of the license plate and could easily track them.

Reg frowned at him. "No, no. I'm not an idiot. Bought it under the radar and have been modifying it. You said you needed something inconspicuous."

"That's us," Tamsin said, grinning at him. "Inconspicuous. I'm Tamsin, by the way." She stuck out her hand to him. "Fugitive from Shifter Bureau. It was nice of you to help out."

Reg shook the offered hand, mystified. "I'm Reg McKee," he said as Angus drove on. "Hey, Angus is a friend and fellow tracker. He says come to Lafayette Cemetery and give a ride to a red-haired Shifter woman on the run, I do it. He said I couldn't miss you. I see why." He shot Tamsin a smile that had Angus bristling.

Tamsin returned the smile as she withdrew her hand. "I like him," she said to Angus.

Angus let out a snarl, and then wondered why he was becoming so defensive.

"Is that them?" Ciaran pointed over the back seat out the dark rear window.

A sleek black SUV had pulled from St. Charles Avenue into the lane where they'd left the station wagon.

"Looks like it," Angus said. Only Shifter Bureau would drive something that flashy while trying to be covert. "Are they coming?"

Ciaran watched for a time as Angus drove slowly onward. "No," he said, righting himself in the seat. "I bet Haider's yelling at them all. One of the guys was nice—he let me keep playing games when the others wanted me to sit there and be quiet—but the rest of them . . ." He made the small growling sound of an angry wolf cub. "Shitheads."

Angus relaxed a bit. They hadn't broken him. They might have threatened him, but Ciaran hadn't let himself be bullied.

Angus continued along the street, behaving like any other motorist trying to get somewhere. Not attracting attention.

The question was where to go next. Even if they'd ditched Haider, Angus couldn't go home or back to the club. Haider would have men waiting at the gates of Shiftertown and at the door to the club. Angus had to take them away somewhere—forever, or at least until Haider died of old age.

This was his own fault. When Tamsin had bolted down the street behind them and leapt into the station wagon, Angus could have kept walking. The keys had been in the car's ignition, and he'd retrieved Ciaran. Angus could have walked away with Ciaran, found Reg, and had him drive them back to Shiftertown, leaving Tamsin to get away from them best she could.

But no, Angus had turned aside, gotten himself and Ciaran into the car, and sealed his fate. He'd made the choice to give up his sedate life to help an un-Collared fox Shifter on the run, one who'd been a follower of his crazy brother, and he didn't know why he'd made that choice.

Tamsin watched him from behind the sunglasses, as though discerning his thoughts.

"You can dump me out anywhere," she said. "Tell Haider I coerced you to drive me away, threatened your cub or something. He'll believe it. I stole one of their tranq pistols."

She brought it out from her jacket pocket.

Angus swerved as he eyed it. "That thing loaded?"

"Not anymore. The dart is buried inside Haider." She laughed, a warm sound. "Let me out wherever, tell Haider I jacked you, and you'll be off the hook."

Reg and Ciaran said nothing behind him. Angus felt the weight of their silence, while they waited to see how he'd respond.

Tamsin had a point—Angus could let her off in any of the neighborhoods between here and Shiftertown or take her back out to the bayous, and then drive to the club, fetch his motorcycle, and drive Ciaran home. He could tell Haider and his men she'd forced him to take her to wherever he let her out, and she'd run off again.

Angus would be free of her, of this situation, and he could go home with Ciaran. Make sure he was all right, catch some sleep, and be back at the club for his shift tonight.

Tamsin would be left to run alone from Haider and Shifter Bureau, to fight off whatever tracker Haider coerced to go after her next time.

Fuck that.

Angus stepped on the gas, darting down a side road that led to an on-ramp to the expressway going north. He'd take Tamsin somewhere safe, make sure she was well hidden, and then go home. He'd worry about what to tell Haider and Shifter Bureau later. Angus had Ciaran with him, which gave him a huge advantage—there was nothing else in the world Haider could hold over Angus to force his obedience.

Ciaran knew without being told what Angus had decided. He whooped.

"Yeah, we're badasses now!"

Reg looked relieved. The man had no clue what was going on, but he hated Shifter Bureau as much as any Shifter did, and he didn't mind causing them a little grief.

Only Tamsin looked worried. "Seriously, Angus, don't get into trouble for me. I'll be all right."

"I'm already in trouble." Angus didn't look at her, keeping his eyes on the cars he had to avoid. "So sit back, relax, and accept that I'm helping you out. All right?"

Tamsin sat back, but she didn't relax. Angus drove with fierce determination, his eyes as gray as the rainy skies outside. This morning, he'd been her captor, ready to take her to Shifter Bureau at all costs. Now he was assisting her, risking being labeled a fugitive with her. The only thing that hadn't changed was his grim look.

The last thing Tamsin wanted to do was drag Angus and Ciaran into her troubles. They didn't deserve that.

So why did her heart lighten? Why was she so relieved she wouldn't have to say good-bye to Angus and his cub right away?

She tamped down those thoughts—time enough for regrets and soul-searching later. For now, Angus was helping her, and he was right—shut up and take it.

After about fifteen minutes on the expressway, Angus drove off on an exit that led to the lake. Cute, older houses with well-kept lawns lined the road that wound its way north. Tamsin imagined the sorts of people who'd live in these houses—they'd be retired, mostly, and like to garden, read, cook, and take care of their grandkids. Tamsin envied them as Angus drove calmly past.

Shifters should be able to have this, she thought. Angus had claimed that Shifters already did—in Shiftertowns.

But that was wrong. They had the illusion of a decent life, not true freedom.

Angus turned along a grass-lined drive to a park that skirted the huge Lake Pontchartrain, lying blue-gray and untroubled under the rainy sky. Joggers moved along the path at the water's edge, lovers strolled hand in hand behind them, and kids played in the grass. The other side of the street was lined with tiny, narrow lake houses, quaint and inviting.

"This is me." Reg had the door open. "Unless you want me to go with you." He gave Angus an inquiring look.

"I want you to have nothing to do with it," Angus told him firmly. "I'll be ditching this ride too, but I'll leave it somewhere safe and let you know where it is. You going to be all right getting home?"

Reg descended and came to Angus's window, nodding without worry. "I'll call Casey to pick me up—he needs something to do." He gave Angus a pained look. "Don't scratch it, all right? It might look boring to you, but I have it running fine and it's good for hauling supplies."

Tamsin wondered what supplies. But Reg looked harmless and normal, so it couldn't be for anything sinister.

"One piece, I promise." Angus reached out the window and gripped Reg's shoulder. Shifters, especially friends, usually embraced when they parted, but Angus didn't have time, and two large men in a fond hug in the middle of a park would draw attention. "Tell Spence not to worry about me. That is, if he notices I'm gone." The last came out with dry bitterness.

Reg returned the squeeze, gave Ciaran a thumbs-up, and then turned away, jogging out to the path along the break-water. As Tamsin watched, Reg started to run, his dark legs in running shorts moving faster and faster.

"Holy crap, look at him go," she said, her jaw dropping. "What kind of Shifter is he?"

Ciaran leaned forward between the seats. "Serval. Reg can seriously run."

"I see that." Reg overtook several joggers, passing them with ease. His high-necked shirt hid his Collar, and the joggers simply moved aside for him without worry. "What supplies?" Tamsin asked in curiosity as Angus turned the SUV to head out of the park.

"Woodworking." The answer was short, to the point.

Ciaran filled in the rest. "He's really good at it. He makes furniture—they're like artwork."

Tamsin looked back to try to see Reg, but he was already out of sight. "Serval, huh? That's unusual. But explains a lot. The smaller cats are usually fast." She laced her fingers as she sat forward again, happy that her hand was whole and well. "So are foxes."

Angus scowled at her as he turned the SUV onto the street. Ciaran hung on to both front seats as he stared at Tamsin. "Wait, you're a *fox*? I didn't know there were fox Shifters."

"We're rare." Tamsin winked at him.

"Dad, you really need to do some full disclosure. They didn't tell me *anything* when I was trapped in that crypt."

"Once upon a time," Tamsin began when Angus only

frowned, "a fox was being chased by some mean Shifter Bureau agents. But they couldn't catch her, so they sent a Lupine tracker to find and capture her." She pointed at Angus. "But the fox was sooo cute, and sooo nice, that he couldn't stand to give her to the mean agents. So he busted his son out of prison, and now he's taking the fox Shifter . . . somewhere. And maybe they'll all live happily ever after." She gave Ciaran a big smile. "I guess we get to find out."

CHAPTER NINE

Tamsin wasn't familiar enough with New Orleans to know exactly where they were, but Angus navigated with ease. He had them on a road heading west, and soon the city fell behind, as did the suburbs. Not long after that, they were out into bayou country.

The freeway became a bridge stretching across a watery landscape. Flat, swampy land poked up along stretches of gray water, the occasional boat zipping by beneath. Clouds had rolled in to make the sky bleak, and rain pattered on the windshield, swept away by the SUV's wipers in a steady rhythm.

Tamsin leaned back against the seat, humming a tune in her throat, but tension kept her muscles stiff.

Ciaran was the only one of the three who was excited. He peered eagerly through the windows at the rain and traffic.

"Are we going to the haunted house, Dad? I bet Tamsin's right that it blocked the tracker on the car. We can hide out there."

Angus shook his head. "He'd find the house sooner or later. He'll start from where the tracking device cut out and search in a circle from there."

"Oh," Ciaran said, disappointed. "You're probably right."

"Ben will be there," Tamsin said in concern. "Should we warn him?"

"Ben and the house can take care of themselves," Angus answered. "Ben's not Shifter. Shifter Bureau has no jurisdiction over him, and the house is owned by a human woman. They'll have to leave it alone."

"What is Ben, exactly?" Tamsin asked, trying to distract herself. "He said gnome or goblin, but those are human words, used in place of that unpronounceable name he told me."

"He's a forgotten race from Faerie," Ciaran said with the confidence of one in the know. "They were exiled a thousand years ago. The Fae killed almost all of his people and banished the rest to the human world. Most of them died out, and Ben is left."

Tamsin listened with growing sympathy and horror. "Stupid Fae bastards."

"That's what I said." Ciaran studied Angus. "Then where *are* we going, Dad?"

Angus didn't take his eyes off the road. "Somewhere you'll be safe."

Ciaran's face fell. "Aw, don't dump me. I want to go with you."

"I'm not dumping you. We'll go to Kendrick's compound, and you can spend some time there. You like visiting Dimitri and Jaycee, don't you?"

"Yeah, but I'd rather stay with you." Ciaran's brows came down, jaw tightening in rebellion.

"I'd rather you stayed safe with Shifters who know how to hide you," Angus said. "You've already been captured by Shifter Bureau once. How many times do you want it to happen?"

The scowls of father and son were so identical Tamsin wanted to laugh.

"Tamsin can stay there too," Ciaran announced. "They're un-Collared Shifters, hiding out," he told her. "They have a big ranch—it's so cool."

"Which is supposed to be a *secret*," Angus said with a growl.

"It's all right if Tamsin knows. She's un-Collared too. Besides, you just said we're going there."

"I was keeping the details to myself."

Ciaran heaved a long sigh and slammed himself into his seat. "Fine. Whatever."

Tamsin slid off the sunglasses and gave him a look of understanding. "Where is this supersecret enclave of un-Collared Shifters?" she asked Angus.

The answer came from behind her before Angus could speak. "Middle of Nowhere, Texas."

"Awesome. I've always wanted to go to Texas."

Angus said nothing. He was tense all over, hands tight as he concentrated on the road.

He was a hard man, tough. Tamsin had seen him soften when he'd crouched down to Ciaran in the cemetery, making sure he was all right, and again when he let Ciaran lie against him in the station wagon. He'd softened a little bit also when he'd told Tamsin the kiss they'd shared was good. Started a shiver down inside her, those words had.

She ran her gaze over the well-muscled arms, taut as he clenched the steering wheel, his chest hugged by his T-shirt. His close-cropped beard framed his square face, and his dark hair managed to be wolf shaggy, even cut short.

His eyes were as gray as the sky above them. Clear gray, rain gray.

Her hunter and captor had switched to being her savior. Why, Tamsin wasn't sure. Feeling sorry for her was one thing. Spiriting her away from Shifter Bureau was something else.

Tamsin had been stunned to learn that Angus was Gavan Murray's brother. The two men couldn't be more different. Gavan had been electric, outgoing, courageous, and, in the end, utterly selfish. Angus was closemouthed and growling, but his love for his cub shone like a beacon of pure light.

His mate had left Angus for *Gavan*? She had to have been crazy. Tamsin hadn't known Angus long and not under the best of circumstances, but she already recognized he was the better man.

"So, who's Spence?" she asked him.

"Our Shiftertown leader." Angus closed his mouth immediately, indicating this was another subject he didn't want to get into.

"He fired Dad," came the answer from the back seat. "Dad was his second. Then Uncle Gavan went off the rails and Shifter Bureau came after Dad and Spence. Spence booted Dad out of being second in command to save his own ass."

"He didn't have a choice," Angus said tightly. "They'd have removed him as leader and replaced him with a total dickhead. I understood. I stepped down."

"That was eight years ago. I was just a baby," Ciaran put in. "But Spence hasn't asked Dad back to be his second, or even to be a tracker for the Shiftertown again. Reg is second now—he's a good one, and everyone likes him— but it should be Dad."

"All right," Angus said firmly. "That's enough."

"Dad is in Spence's clan," Ciaran rattled on. "Reg's clan is down in the pecking order, though Reg is pretty dominant. Even Reg thinks Dad should be second, with Reg as third."

"I said *enough*," Angus said in a hard voice. "It's the way it is. Talking about it doesn't change it."

"Oh, I don't know," Tamsin said. "I think talking can change a lot of things. It's helped me out of trouble so many times. Maybe you should tell Spence how you feel."

The look Angus turned on her could have flattened a forest. "I'm not talking to Spence about it. He won't make me second again just because we get all touchy-feely and sing campfire songs. Doesn't work that way in a Shiftertown."

"I wouldn't know." Tamsin made a sweeping gesture. "I stay far away from those."

"Which is why you're on the run, taking help from a Lupine you met last night. Is this what you're going to do the rest of your life?"

"If I have to. You going to take shit from Shifter Bureau the rest of your life?"

"If I have to." Angus scowled at her. "As long as Ciaran is safe, that's what I'll do."

"Gee, thanks," Ciaran muttered. "Blame it on me."

"Ciaran deserves better," Tamsin said. "My mother thought Shiftertown was the safer place for her family. Glynis ran away because Shifters were being taken in to be experimented on. Running was a better option, or so she thought. I ran too, but in a different direction." She tasted sorrow, anger with herself for not being with her sister on that fateful day.

"I'm sorry." Angus's eyes held sympathy, but his voice was harsh. "But if you're questioning how I take care of my son, you can bail out."

Tamsin sat up and looked around for a likely spot to dive and roll. "There," she said, pointing to a wide place on the shoulder. "Dump me there. I'll hitch to Middle of Nowhere, Texas, and tell them you sent me."

Angus didn't slow. "Stay where you are."

"Hey, you told me to bail out." Tamsin clasped the door handle. "If I stay, I'll keep on asking questions, so I might as well go."

Tamsin had no intention of diving out of a vehicle moving at seventy miles an hour, but she couldn't resist seeing how far Angus would take his threat. She pushed the button to unlock the door.

Angus reached out with alarming swiftness, wrapped

one arm around her, and hauled her to him, never slowing or swerving the SUV. Tamsin found her nose buried in his side, where she inhaled warmth and the scent of male.

"Oh, this is nice."

Angus started to unwind himself from her, but Tamsin burrowed in, nuzzling him and closing her eyes. In spite of the console between them, she was able to nestle into his shoulder, enjoying his strength.

She'd had a long night, little sleep, and a long day. The touch of Angus's body against hers, the soothing rocking of the SUV, and the rhythm of Angus's breath under her cheek unwound all the knots inside her. Tamsin fully meant to tease him a little and rise back to a sitting position, but her exhaustion took over, and she dropped almost instantly into sleep.

"I think she likes you." Ciaran's voice was hushed.

Angus kept his arm around Tamsin's shoulders as he drove with his free hand. Her red hair spilled over his lap like a stream of fire, her head resting trustingly against his side.

He couldn't think of a way to answer so he settled for, "Mmph."

As far as Angus could tell, no one had followed them out of New Orleans. Abandoning the station wagon and driving carefully away in Reg's anonymous SUV seemed to have done the trick.

The best place to leave Tamsin was in Kendrick's capable white tiger paws. Kendrick knew how to deal with rogue Shifters, seeing as he was the biggest rogue—or un-Collared Shifter—out there. He'd held together a group of rogue Shifters in freedom for more than twenty years.

Kendrick's band lived in secret and had to be very careful when interacting with humans. They also wore fake Collars when they went to Shiftertowns so no one would report a Shifter without a Collar running around there.

Kendrick wouldn't thank Angus for bringing in a fugitive. This would only work if they didn't pick up a tail.

They'd have to switch from Reg's SUV before they hit the Texas border. Reg had said he hadn't registered it with Shifter Bureau, but other Shifters would know he owned it, and if Shifter Bureau went sniffing around the NOLA Shiftertown, they might mention it, even in innocence. And not all Shifters were loyal to Spence and Reg. Jostling for dominance happened all the time, and if a clan thought being in thick with Shifter Bureau was the way to advance, they might tell the agents what close friends Reg and Angus were, and all about Reg's missing SUV.

Angus slid his cell phone from his pocket and handed it behind him to Ciaran. "Call Dimitri. Ask him if he has a ride we can borrow. Keep the details to a minimum."

Ciaran took the phone with an expression that showed he was proud to take on this responsibility. He flipped open the phone, expertly scrolled through Angus's contacts, and touched a button.

In a moment, Dimitri Kashnikov's voice came through the phone.

"This is Dimitri. What's your pleasure, Angus?"

"It's Ciaran." Ciaran adopted a nonchalant slouch as he spoke. "We need wheels, Dimitri. Can you get us some? There's three of us—me, my dad, and a hot chick he picked up. She's on the run, and he's helping her. Meet up on the Louisiana side of the border?"

Dimitri's carefree tone vanished. *"What?"*

"I said we need—"

"I heard you, kid. I'm just stunned. Let me talk to Angus."

"He's busy driving. We're running for our lives."

Angus growled. "Keep the details to a minimum, I said."

"Dimitri's cool," Ciaran told him. "Can you do it, Dimitri? Where should we meet up?"

"Put me on speaker," Dimitri's voice said.

Ciaran punched a key without having to search for the

right one. Angus always marveled at how adept his cub was with technology.

Dimitri's flowing tones filled the air. "Angus, what the h-hell are you doing?"

Dimitri, a red wolf, used to stammer quite badly, but since he'd mated with Jaycee, a beautiful leopard Shifter, his stammer had all but vanished. He had to be very agitated now for it to return.

"Running from Shifter Bureau," Angus said. "Long story. I need to switch vehicles. We're ahead, but before long, they'll figure out what we're driving and where we are."

"Right." Dimitri's voice faded a moment, but Angus could tell he was talking to someone in the background. His voice came back. "There's a diner in Lake Charles, near the bus station but off the beaten path. Wait for me there. They have great po' boys."

"Awesome." Ciaran bounced on the seat. He'd taken to Cajun food as soon as he'd had the teeth to chew. Any kind of food, in truth. Ciaran could put it away.

Dimitri gave more specific directions to the diner, then said, "See ya, Ciaran. Keep your old man out of trouble."

"Not easy, but I'll try," Ciaran said. "Bye, Dimitri. Give Jaycee a kiss for me."

"Now, there's something I can enjoy." Dimitri laughed and then the laugh cut off as he hung up the phone.

"Mmm," Tamsin stirred under Angus's arm. "Po' boys. I could eat a good sandwich."

"We won't be going into this diner," Angus said abruptly. "We're switching cars in the parking lot and getting the hell out of town."

Tamsin rose from his side, stretched, and yawned. "Sure, whatever. Who was that? He sounded cute."

"Dimitri Kashnikov," Ciaran answered. "He's a red wolf and lives in the secret compound in Texas with his mate, Jaycee. She's gorgeous, and really fast, and a seriously good fighter. If they let her fight in the fight club, she'd beat everybody, I bet."

Tamsin listened with interest. "What's the fight club?"

"Not important—" Angus tried, but Ciaran couldn't be stopped.

"It's where Shifters fight each other for fun and profit. Every Shiftertown has one, or at least one nearby. It isn't allowed, but Shiftertown leaders pretend they don't know. The leaders never attend, so they're not sure where it is, and we change up the location from time to time. That way, if the Shifter leaders are interrogated about it, they really have no idea where it is or how many Shifters go."

Angus broke in. "Ciaran, we really need to have a talk about *discretion*."

"It's all right," Tamsin said. "Ciaran understands all about need-to-know. And I need to know." She leaned around the seat to him. "Why don't they let Jaycee fight if she's so good? Because she'll beat everyone?"

Ciaran looked surprised Tamsin had to ask. "Because she's female. Females don't fight in the fight clubs. They might get hurt."

"You think? So could males."

"Yeah, but males can't have cubs. What happens if a female is hurt so bad she can't have cubs anymore? That would be terrible."

Tamsin looked thoughtful. "I agree, it would be. But males also could be hurt so much they couldn't have kids. What happens if his nuts are torn up? Or hit so hard they stop functioning?"

Angus had to halt this conversation. "For the Goddess' sake—"

"There are some rules," Ciaran went on without blinking. "No killing. No outside interference—no one can run into the ring and help you. And no targeting balls and penises, in human or animal form."

Tamsin grinned. "You mean, no hitting below the belt."

"No one's wearing a belt," Ciaran said, puzzled. "Everyone fights naked so they can shift."

"I so have to go to one of these," Tamsin said in delight. "Is there one close to where we'll be?"

"They're all over," Ciaran said. "You just have to know where to look for them. And they're not held every night. About once a week, or maybe once every two weeks so Shifters can rest in between."

Tamsin turned her gaze to Angus. "Take us to a fight club, please, Angus? Why not? If they're so secret I've never heard of them, I bet Shifter Bureau doesn't know where they are either."

Angus raised his voice to cut through their chatter. "No. I'm not taking a night off running from Haider to go to a fight club. Cubs aren't allowed anyway."

"Cubs might not be *allowed*," Ciaran said. "My dad is one of the best fighters of the New Orleans fight club. I've seen him. He's never been beat."

Angus glared into the rearview mirror. "Are you telling me you go to fight club fights?"

Ciaran contrived to look innocent. "Only to watch you, Dad. Reg takes me."

Angus hadn't known that. Angus went to the fight club to take out his frustration about the losses in his life: his mate, his place in the hierarchy, the trust of other Shifters, his brother. Ciaran was supposed to have been home with his babysitter while Angus let out his aggressions—the babysitter being Angus's trusted best friend, Reg.

"Son of a—" Angus thumped the steering wheel. "I need to have a serious talk with him."

"Why?" Tamsin asked. She lowered her seat back, resettling her sunglasses over her eyes. "Reg seems like a nice guy. Letting you use his car without question, agreeing to pick me up when he didn't know anything about me. He must be a really *good* friend."

"He is." Angus's voice lost its hardest edge. "When I was

accused of being in with Gavan up to my neck, he stuck by me."

"You see?" Ciaran spread his hands. "So it's fine to go to the fight club with Reg. He looks out for me."

"Still going to talk to him about that. And if we weren't heading down a freeway to a covert meeting in a diner parking lot, you'd be grounded."

Ciaran's face puckered in the scowl that was so like Angus's own, then it cleared, his good humor returning. "Good thing we're on the run, then."

Tamsin laughed. "I really like your cub, Angus."

"I like you too." Ciaran sounded slightly surprised but pleased at this revelation.

"Aw." Tamsin twisted to reach around the seat for Ciaran's hand. Ciaran held hers for a moment, relaxing the same way he did when Angus hugged him.

The two smiled at each other. Angus glanced at them and couldn't stop the twinge of foreboding inside him.

Lake Charles was a town hugging the lake of the same name, a spread of houses, stores, and gas stations, no different from most small towns in the states Tamsin had seen in her life. The land was flat and green, landscaped trees soared in yards, and lawns separated neighbor from neighbor.

The diner lay down a side street that contained shops, a church with a square steeple, a few restaurants, a self-storage center, and a lumberyard.

The day was waning as Angus pulled around the block to the parking lot behind the diner. The lot was small, sharing space with other businesses and a large Dumpster.

Angus parked the SUV in the lot's one empty space, turned off the engine, and let out a tired breath.

The guy had to be exhausted. Tamsin had slept at the haunted house and again as they drove, but she didn't know when Angus had. He'd showered at the house, but the red lines around his eyes and the droop of his body told her maybe he hadn't laid his butt down in a long time.

Shifters didn't require as much rest as humans—they could go for days if necessary—but they needed *some*. Tamsin guessed Angus had been awake nonstop since Haider had recruited him.

Tamsin unbuckled her seat belt and opened the door. When Angus didn't move, she said, "You coming?"

Angus's gray eyes fixed on her. "I told you, we're not going in."

"*I* am," Tamsin said. "I'm starving. So is Ciaran. I bet Haider didn't feed him in that crypt."

"Not well," Ciaran said with a shudder.

"Too dangerous," Angus snapped. "We wait."

Tamsin hopped out of the SUV and looked back in at Angus. "There's an old fox saying—*You're not the boss of me*. Now, what am I in the mood for? Barbecue beef? Maybe some shrimp? Or debris?" Roast beef with its gravy made rich with roast-beef shavings—Tamsin had only had a debris po' boy once, but she never forgot it.

"Mmm." Ciaran almost moaned. "Come on, Dad, *please*? I'm hungry, and we gave Haider the slip. It will take Dimitri a while to get here, though maybe less if he lets Jaycee drive. If you put on your jacket and keep it zipped up, no one will see your Collar."

Angus frowned at him for a long time, but Tamsin saw when the tide turned. Ciaran needed to eat, Tamsin was going inside no matter what, and Angus knew he wouldn't win this battle.

The breath he let out had a snarl in it. "All right." He grabbed his jacket from the back seat where he'd tossed it and shrugged it on. "We'll go in. But keep a low profile, and *no talking*." He moved his finger from Ciaran to Tamsin.

"Sweet!" Tamsin slammed her door and opened Ciaran's. "Come on, Ciaran. Let's go eat everything in sight. And then have dessert."

CHAPTER TEN

Tamsin walked into the diner behind Angus, who was leading, as Shifter males liked to. She held Ciaran's hand, absurdly pleased that he let her.

Angus dropped his hood as they went in, but the jacket covered his throat. Other men in this diner wore hoodies, as the rain was pelting down outside.

Ciaran looked like a human kid, even if he had wiry muscles and a gray-eyed stare like his father's. If the people here weren't used to Shifters, they wouldn't jump to the conclusion that Angus and Ciaran weren't strictly human.

Angus received a few startled glances, being as large as he was, and all Shifter males had something of the beast about them. But the fact that he was with Tamsin, who'd never be large, and Ciaran, who was adorable, softened the looks. The big bad male couldn't be so bad if a harmless-looking woman and cute little boy followed him without fear.

It was a seat-yourself place, so Angus led them to the rear of the dining room, sitting down in the chair that let him put his back to the wall. From there, he could observe the entrance as well as the hall that led to the restrooms and rear exit.

Tamsin, living without a Collar and hiding her Shifterness for years, was less wary about those around her. Most people were out for dinner with families and friends, and because this was a local place, many of the diners knew one another. This town was on an interstate, however, which was only a few blocks away, and so the locals saw nothing odd in strangers stopping for a bite on their way through town or to the lake.

Ciaran lifted the menu, which was almost as large as he was. "Can I get anything I want?"

"Sure," Tamsin said at the same time Angus barked, "No."

Angus shot Tamsin an irritated look. "If you eat too much and get sick, you'll slow us down," he said to Ciaran.

"I won't eat too much," Ciaran scoffed. "If I get one steak and shrimp po' boy and one sausage, that will be enough. Barely. Those guys *really* didn't give me much to eat." He made sad wolf-cub eyes over the menu at Angus.

Tamsin hid a laugh. Ciaran knew how to milk a situation, even a bad one. Good. Kept him from being traumatized. Tamsin knew all about trauma.

"Get the steak and shrimp one," Angus said. "If you finish that, *then* we'll order more."

Ciaran let out an aggrieved sigh. "Oh, all right."

The waitress stopped at the table, beaming a wide smile. "How are y'all? What do you want to drink?"

Before Ciaran could speak, Angus ordered glasses of water, which the busboy was already slamming down in front of them, and coffee for himself.

"And a giant sweet tea for me," Tamsin said. "The sweeter, the better. With lots of ice in it."

"Oh, Dad, let me have a sweet tea. It's all right—it's not like sodas. Dad doesn't let me drink those," he confided to Tamsin.

The waitress looked at "Dad" for confirmation. Angus gave a grudging nod. "Not too much."

The waitress bustled away to fetch the drinks. She was back with them soon, the glasses beaded with condensation on this humid evening.

They ordered the po' boys and the cheerful waitress sailed away again.

Tamsin studied Angus while pretending to keep an eye out around the diner. Angus's gray eyes were focused on the door, waiting for whatever trouble might come through it. His body was tight, his fists curled on the table. If a Shifter Bureau agent *did* come through the door, Tamsin sensed Angus would have her and Ciaran down the restroom hall and out the back faster than fast.

An agent *wouldn't* come in, Tamsin was willing to bet. She'd gotten good at knowing when she was being followed and when she was in the clear for a while. They'd given Haider the slip for now.

But he'd be coming for them eventually, she was well aware. Hopefully Angus and Ciaran would be safe from the man before then.

Angus was a good fighter though, as Tamsin had already seen. He was also nice-looking. His face had clean lines, though his nose might be a bit long—but he was a wolf, couldn't help that—and his eyes had a way of pinning you even when he wore a neutral look.

As though Angus felt her watching him, he turned his head and met her gaze. Tamsin's cheeks warmed, and she quickly looked away.

The food came. Long sandwiches on flaky bread piled with meat and dripping with gravy oozed on the plates, and the waitress plopped down a huge basket of potato chips for all of them to share.

"Tamsin," Ciaran said. "This is how I eat mine. Watch." He took off the top bun of his sandwich, swept up a handful of chips, and pressed them on top of his roast beef. Fried shrimp slid from under the meat, but Ciaran patiently re-placed them. He jammed the top piece of bread back on and opened his mouth wide for his first bite.

Sauce and shrimp squirted out of the sandwich along with a few chips. Tamsin burst into laughter. She expected Angus to snarl at his son, but his lips twitched, and he said nothing.

Tamsin lifted her sausage and hot sauce sandwich and bit down. Her eyes watered as soon as the food hit her tongue, but she chewed enthusiastically. Good stuff, and she was hungry. The breakfast Ben had cooked very early this morning was a long time ago.

Angus was watching her. He had ordered a roast beef with debris, but he hadn't eaten any of it yet.

Tamsin realized half her sauce had spilled onto her chin. She reached for the pile of napkins the waitress had left, but Angus had already lifted a napkin, and he touched it to the corner of her mouth.

Tamsin stilled, the spice from the sandwich and the warmth from his unexpected touch burning her. Angus's gentleness manifested as he carefully wiped her lips and then her chin, catching a drip that threatened to trickle down her throat.

Tamsin's heartbeat was off the scale. She wondered if Angus could feel her pulse banging against his fingertips.

I'm just horny, she told herself. Shifters liked to mate—had the instinct ingrained. She rarely trusted anyone enough to let herself be vulnerable to either a Shifter or a human male, so she'd avoided any kind of sexual encounter, or even opportunity, for a long time. Years, she realized.

Angus wasn't offering her sex. Hell, she'd had to convince him to come in here and give her food.

He was simply wiping her mouth, like he would for Ciaran. Except he hadn't reached for a napkin for Ciaran—*he* was busy scrubbing at his face with half the pile. Angus leaned toward Tamsin, his gray eyes flicking down as he concentrated on dabbing sauce from her chin.

He looked up, and their gazes met, as they had in the hidden room in the house. Right before they'd kissed.

Tamsin wanted to kiss him again. More than wanted to. She craved it. She wanted to kiss him, wrap her arms around him, and keep kissing him. She'd let her hands explore his body, the muscles under his shirt, his tight stomach, his firm buttocks. She wanted his weight on her, his mouth parting her lips, his hands learning her, his thumb brushing her breast and bringing her to life.

She struggled for breath. Angus's gaze moved to her lips, but he straightened up in the next moment, dropping the crumpled napkin to the table.

Ciaran had ceased eating to watch them, and his expression held hope.

Tamsin smiled feebly at Ciaran, but when she lifted her sandwich again, her hands shook so hard she had to set it down and eat its innards with a fork.

They'd nearly finished the meal—Ciaran had changed his mind about ordering the second sandwich after he took the last bite of the first one—when Dimitri and Jaycee walked into the diner.

Angus didn't bother waving for their attention. They'd have known where the Shifters were right away, even over the scents of hot sauce, sausage, gravy, and barbecue. The diner would never shake those scents, Angus had the feeling, even when its remains were unearthed in a thousand years.

Dimitri, a tall, red-haired man who walked with an easy stride, was a red wolf, his Shifter beast fast and powerful. Jaycee, who followed him, was on the short side for a Shifter woman, but she had even more grace, though she was restless with it. She wore her dark blond hair pulled into a ponytail and had the tawny eyes of a leopard. She and Dimitri were the best trackers Angus had ever met, including himself.

Discretion wasn't going to rule here. Ciaran was out of his chair, arms outstretched as soon as the pair walked in. "Dimitri!"

Ciaran flew at Dimitri, who caught him and raised him high, spinning around before he hugged the cub.

Jaycee watched with an indulgent smile, then took note of Tamsin and came alert, her smile fading.

Jaycee had known Tamsin was sitting there—she'd chosen her moment to look at her, but not aggressively. Jaycee was a little more careful than that. Her assessment was calm, a tracker sizing up a newcomer to discover whether she was threat or ally.

That Jaycee had come with Dimitri at all surprised Angus. She was pregnant, and Dimitri had become highly protective of her. Of course, Jaycee wasn't one to let a male Shifter tell her what to do, even her mate. Angus imagined she'd announced she was coming along and that was the end of it.

Dimitri dragged a chair over, sat down next to Tamsin and planted his elbows on the table. Dimitri's hair was almost as red as Tamsin's, though a different shade. Red wolf and fox. Both with attitude.

"So, who are you, then?" Dimitri asked her.

Jaycee seated herself next to Ciaran and across from Tamsin. "Don't mind my mate. He's rude as hell. I'm Jaycee." She gave Tamsin a cordial nod.

Tamsin studied Jaycee's neck, commenting without words about Jaycee's lack of Collar. Jaycee studied Tamsin in return, clearly thinking pretty much the same thing.

"I'm Tamsin," she replied. "A stray Angus picked up."

Jaycee gave her a hint of a grin. "Angus does that. He picked up me and Dimitri once."

"And that was the stuff of legend," Dimitri said. "Get

the story out of him sometime. I know he didn't tell you already. He doesn't like to talk much."

Angus didn't. He'd learned the truth of the saying *Least said, soonest mended*. Dimitri, a man who'd had a speech impediment most of his life, rarely stopped talking.

"Oh, I want to hear *this*," Tamsin said.

Angus cut through the happy getting-acquainted party. "Did you bring it?"

Dimitri didn't look offended. "We wouldn't be here if we hadn't." He laid his hand, cupped palm down, on the table in front of Angus. When he lifted away, two keys on a key ring rested next to Angus's plate.

No electronic key fob, so it must be an old car. Fair enough.

"Sorry it took so long," Dimitri said. "It's not the fastest vehicle on the road. But I've fine-tuned the engine so it goes quickly enough. Just not like, say, a Ferrari."

"Anything is slow the way *you* drive." Jaycee rolled her eyes. "I followed him on my bike so I can get him back home. He was going to hitch or take a bus, can you believe it? I almost ran over him about twenty times, the way he crept along. But he insisted I stay behind him."

"It's what Shifters do," Dimitri said, giving his mate a meaningful look. "Males go first, to make sure the way is safe."

"*You* go first to be a pain in my ass."

"Yeah, but you like looking at *my* ass, so there you are."

Jaycee gave him an exasperated glare, but she didn't argue with him.

Angus had known Jaycee and Dimitri were madly in love with each other the moment he'd met them. When Dimitri had gotten himself captured, Angus had gone with Jaycee to help find him, knowing Jaycee would run after him on her own, no matter how many people tried to dissuade her. Angus hadn't wanted to see her die, so he'd gone with her to protect her.

It was his curse, the need to protect people. Would get him killed one day. Nearly had already.

"Have you eaten?" Tamsin asked. "The po' boys are spectacular."

Ciaran nodded in agreement, pinching the last crumbs of chips and loose debris between his fingers. "Bloody terrific."

"Come to think of it, we are hungry." Dimitri sent his warm look to the waitress, who hurried over.

Angus frowned at them all once she'd taken their sandwich order—one crawdad and one beef. "We're trying to be inconspicuous."

"Doesn't mean we can't eat," Dimitri said. "This is a restaurant. It would be more conspicuous if we *didn't* eat."

"Stay relaxed," Jaycee advised. "The more natural you act, the less attention you attract. We're just old friends meeting up, as far as the other diners are concerned."

"She's smart," Tamsin said to Angus, then turned back to Jaycee. "You've done this before."

"All my life," Jaycee said. "You get used to stealth, Angus. After a while, you'll be great at it."

"I'm a tracker," Angus said, pitching his voice low. "I know what I'm doing."

Jaycee reached over and patted his arm, giving Angus the excuse, when she released him, to slide the keys into his pocket. "He's my hero, Tamsin. Stood up to some scary people with me, and helped Dimitri and me get home safe."

"That's my dad," Ciaran said proudly.

The restaurant's business was picking up, as it was the time humans usually had supper, and they had to wait a while for Dimitri's and Jaycee's orders. But there was something to what Jaycee said. As they talked about nonsense things, Tamsin taking easily to Jaycee and Dimitri, the other patrons ignored them. Angus and his group weren't behaving any differently from the other humans crowding around the tables.

Jaycee and Dimitri enjoyed their food, praising it, sharing bits with Ciaran, who declared he could eat more now. Tamsin then ordered a piece of cheesecake, which she split with Ciaran and Dimitri.

Finally, finally, the food was eaten, the bill presented. Angus started to dig for cash, but Dimitri beat him to it, tossing money onto the little tray the bill came on and telling the waitress to keep the change. She thanked him graciously.

They strolled out of the restaurant and around to the parking lot as though they had nothing more to do tonight than go home and watch TV. Angus made sure, however, that Tamsin and Ciaran walked in the middle of the pack.

Jaycee's motorcycle was parked near Reg's SUV, but Dimitri didn't head for it. He led them instead to a vehicle that sat on the street, deep in the shadow, and was too large to fit into the tiny lot.

"There you go." Dimitri waved a hand at it. "Wheels."

"Cool!" Ciaran said in an enthusiastic whisper. Tamsin looked pleased, but Angus halted in dismay.

"Seriously?" He swung on Dimitri. "You want me to get away in *that*?"

CHAPTER ELEVEN

Angus's wolf growls rumbled next to Tamsin, filling the air.

The vehicle Dimitri had brought was a huge black box sitting high on double wheels, its windows tinted and dark. It was the cab of a semitruck, polished and glinting even in the shadows.

"I hitched a ride in one of these once," Tamsin said. "I loved it. Trucker wanted too much to show me the bed in the back though, so I hopped out as soon as he slowed down."

She spoke lightly but he'd scared her, that scumbag. She'd leapt to the ground in the tiny town he'd had to decelerate to drive through, and had run to the nearest gas station, hiding in the women's bathroom until he was gone. But she'd liked the truck—wasn't its fault it had been driven by an asshole.

"We're trying to be under the radar," Angus told Dimitri.

Dimitri shrugged, the streetlight glinting on his bright hair. "No one will be expecting a Shifter in *that*. You'll blend in with all the other truckers. If anyone asks, you own the cab and are between hauling jobs, heading out with your family somewhere or other."

"*His* idea of stealth," Jaycee said, cocking her head.

"Hiding in plain sight," Dimitri corrected her. "A person tiptoeing around, glancing furtively over his shoulder is way more suspicious than a man going about his business. Just like eating in the restaurant."

Angus looked irritated as hell, but Tamsin saw him tamp down his anger. "Thanks, Dimitri. I appreciate the help."

Jaycee laughed. "It hurt you to say that. I argued with him, Angus, but Dimitri said the truck has a legit license in the human way, registered to an independent trucker—he calls himself Rufus Trucking. *Rufus* for *Canis Rufus*, Red Wolf. Hilarious, right?"

"I like that," Ciaran sang out. "Uncle Dimitri is smart."

"Hey, the truck is nothing connected with Shifters," Dimitri said. "I found the cab in a scrap yard and refurbished it myself." He cast a worried glance at the gleaming black chassis. "Don't bang it up, okay?"

Tamsin snatched the keys from Angus's hand. "We'll take great care of it. Come on, Ciaran. Let's see what's inside."

She and Ciaran darted forward before Angus could stop them, and Tamsin unlocked and opened the passenger side door. She boosted Ciaran inside and then followed him.

The cab was tall, with several steps leading up into it. The front bench seat was wide, with padded headrests, a big radio, and a dashboard with plenty of dials and buttons. In the back was another bench seat and a large storage space, which indeed contained a bed. The bed was wide enough for two, and possibly three if that third person was as small as Ciaran.

"Bet I know why Dimitri put in such a big mattress," Tamsin said to Jaycee, who had opened the back door. "Your blush says it all."

Jaycee climbed up inside, settling herself on the back seat. She was a gorgeous woman, all curves and sleek hair, her leather motorcycle pants and dark top hugging her body.

She gave Tamsin a frank look from her golden eyes. "Not to be nosy, but who exactly are you? Angus is going to a lot of trouble for you."

Tamsin let out her breath. "I know he is. And I'm Trouble with a capital *T*. I can't tell you everything you want to know, but I promise you, as soon as I can, I will keep Angus as far from my problems as possible."

"You could leave right now," Jaycee pointed out. "While he's busy chewing the fat with Dimitri, take whatever car you came in and go. If you need to hide out, I'll tell you how to contact Shifters who are good at hiding people—like Zander and Dylan."

Tamsin hadn't heard of Dylan. "I already met Zander."

Jaycee pulled out her phone, which was a modern one, not Angus's ten-year-old model. "Then he'll probably be willing to help. Dylan is even better, but he's iffy. You never know what Dylan will do."

The slightly worried look in Jaycee's eyes when she mentioned Dylan's name was concerning. The thought of Zander and his let's-get-this-done attitude was more reassuring. Zander had a mate though, with a Collar, and Tamsin didn't want to endanger her. The pair had already risked a lot to help her.

But she couldn't throw away the possibility of his assistance. "All right, give me Zander's number," she said with reluctance. "In case. You'll have to write it down the old-fashioned way. I ditched my phone a long time ago."

Jaycee rummaged in her pockets and found a scrap of paper, and Tamsin unearthed a pen from the catchall tray in the dashboard. As Jaycee wrote, Ciaran watched, his mouth open.

"No," he said abruptly. "You're not leaving."

Jaycee looked up, brows rising, and Tamsin settled on

the front seat and gathered Ciaran to her. "I might have to, sweetie. I don't want to bring Shifter Bureau down on you or your dad."

"No, we go *together*." Ciaran's voice held a hint of tears. "No matter what, we stick together, and we'll be all right. That's what my dad says."

Jaycee exchanged a glance with Tamsin, then went back to writing.

Tamsin smoothed Ciaran's hair. "Honey, that might not be practical in my case. Shifter Bureau already nabbed you once, and frightened you a lot. I know you won't admit it, but they did scare you. Scared Angus even more. You want that to happen again?"

Ciaran squirmed away from Tamsin and knelt on the seat. "It won't happen now that I'm with my dad. He'll take care of you. Of *us*. You can't go."

"Ciaran—"

"Dad!" Ciaran did a one-eighty on the seat as Angus opened the driver's-side door. "Tamsin's trying to leave. Tell her she has to stay."

"Tamsin, you have to stay," Angus said. "Jace, are you going with Dimitri or are we giving you a ride back to Kendrick's?"

Jaycee unfolded herself and scrambled down from the truck, but not before palming the slip of paper to Tamsin. "I'm out of here. See you soon."

"Make sure Reg's SUV is left somewhere safe," Angus said before she could disappear. "Tell Dimitri to mail him the keys."

Jaycee landed lightly on the ground, her leopard's grace in evidence. "Stop worrying. Dimitri and I will handle it. We're good at this." She sent Tamsin a look. "Take care of yourself." Then she slammed the door and was gone.

At the same time, Angus started the truck. The engine was surprisingly quiet but powerful enough to send intense vibrations through the cab.

Angus slammed the door. "Ciaran, get in the back seat and buckle up. Tamsin, keep your hand off that door handle. If you try to jump out, I'll haul you into the back and tie you up."

Tamsin glanced at the bed, her heart beating faster. "Promise?"

"Yes. But it won't be any fun." Angus gave her a hard look, but his cheekbones stained red.

A shy wolf. Wasn't that sweet?

He'd be a strong and tender lover. Angus's big hands would caress her as he pinned her with his weight, his kisses gentle yet powerful.

Tamsin swallowed and looked away. She went through the motions of putting on the seat belt but couldn't have sworn afterward how she got it buckled. The thought of being in the bed with Angus, his body bare for her touch, her lips, pushed everything else out of her brain.

Definitely horny. One cold shower, and I'll be fine.

Tamsin knew, as Angus pulled the truck from the curb and Jaycee and Dimitri waved, their arms around each other, that she'd never be fine. Angus had touched something within her, and she wouldn't shake that anytime soon.

Angus drove carefully into the night. Dimitri had been right that no one gave the truck cab a second glance, except to move out of its way. Plenty of truckers drove lone cabs between loads or rode home in them to sleep. Once Angus got onto the interstate, they'd be pretty much invisible.

"You know how to drive one of these things?" Tamsin asked him.

She'd drawn herself up to sit cross-legged on the big seat, and was now busy checking out the compartments and buttons and levers on the dashboard.

"Yes," Angus answered as he geared down for a turn. "I

drove a rig for a while, back before Shifters were outed.
Good way to make a living."

"You did?" Ciaran asked. "You never told me that."

Angus shrugged. "That was a long time ago, son. Can't
do it anymore."

He hadn't wanted to talk about it. But it felt good to sit
high above the road again, the big steering wheel in front
of him. Angus had driven all over the country for several
years, earning enough to support himself and then a mate,
back when Shifters had to hide what they were. Shifters
weren't allowed such jobs anymore, as humans worried that
Shifters, with their stamina and strength, would push them
out of the workplace.

The humans probably weren't wrong. Shifters were
smart, driven, and tireless. At least some Shifters were. Others were complete idiots. Shifters came in all flavors, as did
humans.

Maybe one day humans would understand that. Maybe
they'd realize that Shifters were just trying to live life, and
would never be a threat.

"Are we still going to Kendrick's?" Ciaran interrupted
his thoughts.

Angus took the on-ramp onto the I-10, heading west. If
Dimitri and Jaycee on Jaycee's bike were following, Angus
couldn't see them.

"Best place," Angus said, although he was having
second thoughts.

Tamsin would be safe with Kendrick, without doubt.
She'd be in the middle of a horde of un-Collared Shifters
who'd lived under the radar for twenty years and knew how
to keep hidden. Dimitri and Jaycee would take care of her.

But if Shifter Bureau was after Tamsin as hard as they
could be, Angus might be leading Bureau agents straight to
Kendrick and those in his care. In spite of Dimitri's assur-
ances about the anonymity of the truck cab, in spite of An-

gus's firsthand knowledge of the security of Kendrick's place, it was starting to feel not right to him.

He glanced at Tamsin. She turned a dial, and a radio blared to life. Smiling happily, she began to push buttons, trying station after station until she halted on one belting out country music.

"Hey, I love this song." She leaned back and started to sing at the top of her lungs.

Angus hadn't heard the song, which seemed to be about a man and woman kissing in the moonlight, and then both of them thinking about the kiss, alone, all night long. Tamsin's voice couldn't quite hold the tune, but she sang with enthusiasm, squeezing her eyes shut to warble out the emotional phrases. Ciaran leaned forward, listening in fascination.

Tamsin tasted joy in every second of her life, Angus realized. She was on the run, being hunted by Shifter Bureau, wanted in connection with Angus's brother's activities and more recently a murder, and yet she took time to find delight in a simple love song.

Angus had once had that joy in him. It had surged when Ciaran was born, when he'd held his tiny cub in his hands, marveling that this was his son.

The song wound down. The next had a jumpy, rock beat and was about a man and his lady making love somewhere along a back road.

Tamsin sang this one word for word, and Ciaran joined in, his treble cutting through Tamsin's faulty alto. Angus hadn't known Ciaran liked country music, especially the kind with raunchy lyrics.

The truck filled with song, and with laughter when Tamsin and Ciaran both attempted a sexy "mmm-hmm" in the middle. Tamsin's laugh was as musical as what came through the radio.

Something inside Angus loosened as he drove through

the darkness, the voices of his son and the fiery woman he'd rescued weaving together and nestling in his heart.

Texas was much bigger than Tamsin had imagined. Less than an hour after they left Lake Charles, they were crossing the border, heralded by nothing but a green sign that read "Texas State Line." They came to a turnoff to a travel information center with tall flagpoles poking up beside the freeway. Tamsin wanted to stop, but Angus sailed past.

Another hour and a half and they were in Houston, a giant city that went on endlessly. Two hours after they left the heart of Houston, they were in a dark, flat, empty plain that stretched all around them. Still Texas, Angus said. They'd traversed only one small part of it.

It wasn't simply the distance Tamsin felt. The land opened up around them, the darkness beyond the road unbroken by lights, buildings, trees. The sky arched high above, dark and silent. This was a place of vast spaces and silences.

The radio was off now that Tamsin and Ciaran had sung every song they could, some of them twice. When the stations segued into endless commercials, Tamsin had shut off the noise, and Ciaran slid into sleep.

"You don't look happy," Tamsin said to Angus.

Angus gazed down the road, one hand resting negligently on the large steering wheel. She believed him when he said he'd once done this for a living—he drove in a relaxed way, as though far more used to taking a rig across country than chasing fugitives through swamps.

He glanced briefly at her. "Why am I supposed to look happy? My cub should be home in bed, waiting for me to get back from the club. Instead I'm in a borrowed truck, heading down the freeway in the opposite direction."

"I mean, you don't seem relieved you're taking me to a safe place. What's wrong?"

Angus let out a breath, not looking surprised she'd read him right. "I don't know. Maybe I just feel like it's too easy."

"Mmm." Tamsin studied the road ahead of them, other vehicles few and far between now. "I think it's more than that."

"Probably." Angus shifted in his seat, his left hand coming to join his right on the wheel. "My instincts don't like the idea of going to Kendrick's. What if Shifter Bureau follows us there? That's a huge chunk of innocent Shifters to put in danger."

"But no one is following us," Tamsin pointed out. They'd seen no signs of pursuit since New Orleans.

"I know—that bugs me too. How did we lose Haider so easily? Why didn't they have Shifter Bureau people all over the place at the Texas border? Shifters aren't allowed to cross into other states without permission, so it's a great place to put a checkpoint."

Tamsin had been having the same thoughts, but she'd tried to put them aside. She'd learned to worry about the here and now, not possibilities, to be cautious but not paranoid.

"Maybe they're tracking us, sitting back to see where we go. Is there GPS on this truck? Or was there on Reg's SUV?"

"Dimitri would have taken out any GPS devices before he lugged the cab out of the junkyard. Reg would know if someone had stuck a tracker on his SUV, and he'd have told me. Wouldn't have brought us the SUV at all, if that were the case. You can't surreptitiously track a Shifter vehicle— all Shifters know their cars and trucks and motorcycles inside and out. We have to work on them constantly to keep them running." Angus huffed a short laugh. "Shiftertowns are great places to learn auto mechanics."

"Or Haider already knows about this guy Kendrick and will be waiting for us at his compound."

Angus shook his head. "Kendrick is careful. I've never met anyone so careful. Dimitri and Jaycee had to talk a long time before he let me out there a few months ago when they had their sun and moon ceremonies. Kendrick doesn't trust anyone. I had to swear to keep the location of the compound a deep, dark secret, on pain of death. Which I have."

"Except now you've told *me*. Maybe that's what your instincts are warning you about. I could be a spy, leading Shifter Bureau right to your friends."

"You could be," Angus said without worry. "But I saw how terrified you were when I took you to Haider. You kept your chin up, but I know you were afraid."

Tamsin shivered. She'd been arrested before, interrogated by Bureau agents before, but never had she met one with eyes as cold as Haider's. "I don't know what's up with him, but he has pure hatred in him. More than what should come from him believing I killed those agents in Shreveport."

"Which you said you didn't do." Angus glanced at her, the gray of his eyes glinting. "I believe you."

Tamsin remembered telling him about Dion, right before he'd kissed her. Her lips tingled and she went on hastily. "Yeah? How do you know I wasn't feeding you a line of bull?"

"Instincts again. They're pretty good. I can imagine you spitting on Shifter Bureau agents, telling them off, pulling down your pants and mooning them, but I can't see you going insane and clawing them to death. Anyway, that was done by a larger Shifter, a Feline or Lupine. Your claws aren't big enough to have made those marks I saw in the photos."

Tamsin looked at her hand, her pale fingers that never could hold a tan. "No, they're not."

"So why is Haider so interested in you?" Angus asked.

"He knows what I am." Tamsin folded her arms over her stomach, moving uncomfortably. It hadn't bothered her for Angus to find out her true nature, but it had creeped her out when Haider had showed her the video. "He has footage of me shifting to my fox. He had it on his phone and played it with a big smirk on his face. He wants to dissect me. That's why I ran, why we're here right now."

Angus turned to stare at her, and Tamsin kept her face straight. She suspected that Haider wanted to know not only Tamsin's secrets but Gavan's, which Tamsin wanted to keep tucked firmly into her brain.

Angus jerked his attention back to the road. "I'm glad you ran. I'll dissect *Haider* if I see him again."

"You didn't have to help me. I keep telling you to let me out, and I'll go off on my own."

Angus scowled. "I wasn't going to leave you for Haider to catch again. I'm not that much of a dickhead."

"But it's *my* problem. My whole life is my problem. Nothing to do with you."

"It became my problem when Haider came into the club and ordered me to find you," Angus said angrily. "When he took Ciaran from me. When he said you worked with my brother. I decided to make it my problem."

Tamsin lifted her brows, hiding her nervousness. "I sense a big sibling rivalry here. I mean, more than your mate running off with him, the ungrateful cow. Want to talk about it?"

"No," Angus said, the word abrupt.

"Struck another nerve, did I? You have a lot of those."

"Why are you so interested in counseling me? I could ask you—"

The jangling noise of his cell phone cut into his speech. Angus snarled and grabbed the phone from his belt, flipping it open. The good thing about an old-style cell phone was that it didn't have tracking in it. Tamsin had ditched her smartphone and used burners if she used cell phones at all.

Angus checked the number calling before he said a cautious, "What?"

A voice came through, male, with an Irish accent. "Sean here. My dad wants a word."

"Does he? Then why isn't *Dylan* calling me? Never mind—put him on."

"I don't mean he's here with me. Our dad is never that straightforward. He wants a meet."

"Don't have time. Busy. I'll catch him later."

The easygoing lilt in Sean's voice changed, the man's dominance coming through to Tamsin. "It's not a suggestion. Dylan says it's urgent, and I'm not to let you blow him off. His very words. I know you're driving Dimitri's souped-up rig, and I know you're heading to Kendrick's, so take a turn north and meet in our usual spot. Please don't make me tell him you're not coming."

"I have Ciaran with me. I'm not racing off for one of his meetings with my cub."

"Dylan knows Ciaran's with you," Sean went on. "He says bring him. And the red-haired woman. Do it for me, Angus. If I can't persuade you, I'll never hear the end of it. Don't do that to me, my friend. Take pity on me, please."

Angus's jaw tightened so much Tamsin feared he'd break his teeth. "Fine," he snarled. "I'll be there."

He snapped the phone closed and tossed it down, slamming his hand back to the wheel as though resisting the urge to crush the phone in his bare hand.

CHAPTER TWELVE

"Jaycee mentioned Dylan," Tamsin said, sounding casual. "Who is this guy?"

Angus didn't look at her. He sped up, feeling the need to move faster. "Dylan Morrissey. Full of himself Shifter with way too much power."

Sean's statement that Dylan, former Shiftertown leader of Austin and now a liaison between Shiftertowns in South Texas, knew about Tamsin made Angus's hackles rise. Every misgiving leapt into his brain.

On the other hand, he knew Dylan would track them down more diligently than Haider ever could, and at this moment, Angus wasn't certain which man was more dangerous.

"You agreed to meet with him," Tamsin said. "Why, if you don't like him?"

"Because he's *Dylan*. He'll find me if he wants to."

"Dad works for him." Ciaran's sleepy voice came from

the back. "At least sort of works for him. I don't know what he does for him."

Angus kept his mouth solidly closed. Dylan had approached Angus a few months ago, right after Dimitri and Jaycee's mating ceremony, with a proposition. He was quietly gathering Shifters to train for a fight against the Fae, who were gearing up on their side of the gates for a full-scale war. The Fae were coercing Shifters to fight *for* them, promising them all kinds of shit if they would become the Battle Beasts like in the old days.

Dylan and his sons, and other Shifter leaders like Kendrick, believed the Fae had been instrumental in having the Shifters exposed to humans, Collared, and rounded up into Shiftertowns. The Collars could be triggered by special swords the Fae had made, another method of keeping the Shifters under their power.

Shifters, led by Dylan, were secretly removing the Collars—a slow and laborious process—and replacing them with fake ones. The weaker and less dominant Shifters were being freed first as they would suffer the most if the Fae came.

The Fae had more tricks up their flowing sleeves, however. They were busy recruiting Shifters who were devout Goddess worshippers, filling their heads with the nonsense that the Goddess—who'd created Fae as well as Shifters— wanted the two reunited.

Angus had spent some time in Faerie during his adventure with Jaycee and Dimitri, and he had firsthand knowledge that the Fae were cruel and crazy bastards who would do anything to win.

Angus hadn't talked about what he did for Dylan to anyone, least of all Ciaran. He did not need those he loved to be tortured for his illegal activities. The less they knew, the better.

"This is interesting." Tamsin was studying Angus, the

lights from the dashboard glowing on her face. "Do you trust him?"

"Dylan used to be the Shiftertown leader in Austin. Stepped down so his son could take over. Retired."

Tamsin cocked her head. "Retired? Didn't know Shiftertown leaders could do that. In the wild, when a clan leader got too old, he let his son kill him and the Guardian send him to the Goddess."

"Times have changed."

"Obviously. And I thank the Goddess for it. I'm just surprised. Maybe I *should* meet this Dylan. I like a Shifter who changes the rules."

"He changes the rules to suit himself and his purposes. Don't trust him."

"I didn't say I'd trust him. I said I wanted to meet him. Big difference."

Tamsin leaned sideways against the seat to watch him, her body drooping. It had been a long day and night for her—for all of them. She needed rest and so did he. Another reason a summons from Dylan was not welcome.

Angus took an exit to leave the I-10 and headed north. The highway he turned onto snaked toward Bastrop, east of Austin. The farms around them rendered the night black, few buildings in sight, though city lights were a faint glow against the sky in the west and south.

In a town that was close enough to Austin to see its lights, but far away enough from its Shiftertown and South Texas Shifter Bureau for secrecy, Angus pulled into the parking lot of a small, two-story chain motel.

He turned off the engine and the lights, letting the quiet and stillness fill the cab. "I'll go in and see what he wants. You and Ciaran use the bed, try to get some sleep."

"No way," Ciaran said immediately, his words echoed by Tamsin's, "Nothing doing."

"We stick together," Ciaran finished.

"He's right." Tamsin unbuckled her seat belt. "Whatever this Dylan wants, we face it. Besides, there's nothing to say he won't have some of his guys stationed out here to nab us while you're talking to him. Dylan sounds like the type to have henchmen, am I right? Trackers loyal to him?"

Tamsin was completely correct. Angus was one of those henchmen now, and Dylan would expect Angus to obey him.

"Anyway," Tamsin said, not realizing Angus had already agreed. "This looks like a decent place to get some shut-eye. I'd prefer a bed that isn't on wheels."

"All right. We all go." Angus bent a glare on Ciaran. "But both of you, stay quiet. *No* talking until we find out what Dylan wants. I mean it, Ciaran. He can be tricky, and his motives aren't always clear."

Ciaran looked puzzled. "He's one of the good guys, isn't he? He doesn't like Shifter Bureau either."

"Dylan is his own person." Angus knew this for a fact. "He's on the side of Shifters, yes, but that doesn't mean we can trust him completely."

Dylan had been known to kill Shifters, and even humans, who endangered other Shifters, especially those who endangered his family.

Sean's directions led them to a room on the second floor in the back of the motel, the position Angus would have chosen. The motel was in a U shape around a central pool, with all doors facing inward. From the room in the center back, Dylan could watch all comings and goings.

Angus had Ciaran firmly by one hand, with Tamsin holding Ciaran's other hand. Angus didn't think Dylan would hurt a cub—he was a doting grandfather to his sons' cubs—but Angus had no intention of letting Ciaran be anywhere but plastered to his side.

Angus knocked. The door was opened, cautiously, not by Dylan but by his son Sean, a Shifter with deep black hair and very blue eyes. The hilt of the Sword of the Guardian stuck up over his shoulder.

Sean was a little more easygoing than his older brother, Liam, and far more than his father, Dylan. Guardians tended to be more thoughtful than other Shifters, having seen enough of death to not want to court it.

Sean's presence either meant Dylan was in a negotiating mood, or that he'd need someone to quickly send their dead bodies to dust.

No one spoke until all three visiting Shifters were inside and Sean closed the door.

"Dylan," Angus said in greeting.

Dylan, who waited in the exact center of the room, had hair as dark as Sean's and eyes as blue. The only sign of Dylan's venerable three hundred years of age was a bit of gray hair at his temples.

"Angus," Dylan returned. He gave Ciaran a cordial nod as well—Dylan did not like to pretend cubs weren't in the room.

Sean moved to the cabinet under the television and opened it to reveal a small refrigerator. "Want anything? I have water and . . . water. No minibar in this room, such a sad thing."

"Ciaran will have a water," Angus rumbled.

Sean came out of the refrigerator with two water bottles dripping with condensation. He handed one to Ciaran, who looked pleased at being waited on by Sean, a Shifter he admired.

Sean held out the second bottle to Tamsin, giving her an inquiring look.

"I'll take a large latte with whipped cream and a mountain of chocolate sprinkles," Tamsin said, and shrugged. "Or I could settle for water." She gave Sean one of her giant smiles as she accepted the bottle from him. She opened it and leaned back to drink half of it down. *"Ahh,"* she said as she came up, swiping her hand across her mouth. "I needed that."

Ciaran watched her in fascination, and then mimicked her. *"Ahh.* I needed that too."

Sean's eyes twinkled, but Dylan became suddenly more watchful.

What had he expected—a meek, terrified little Shifter falling at Dylan's feet and begging him to be gentle with her?

Maybe not, but Dylan obviously had expected Tamsin to be cowed and nervous. Tamsin *was* nervous, Angus could tell from the way she clutched the bottle, but she wasn't about to let Dylan and Sean see that.

"What do you want?" Angus asked without preliminary. "We're tired, and Ciaran needs to sleep."

"I want to talk." Dylan gestured to one of the beds. "Ciaran can lie down if he needs to."

"I'm not tired." Ciaran's sagging body contradicted the statement, but he lifted his chin in defiance.

Tamsin walked past Sean and then gave a sudden twisting leap to land on one of the beds, her back to the headboard. "Come and sit with me, Ciaran," she said, patting the covers. "We'll let the big bad Shifters talk."

Ciaran went readily to the bed, setting his bottle on the nightstand, and climbed up to settle in next to Tamsin, his back to the headboard. Tamsin smiled down at him as Ciaran snuggled into her, and slid her arm around him.

Sean took a chair from the desk and straddled it wrong way around, resting his arms on its back. Dylan remained standing, and so did Angus.

"Just a chat, lad." Dylan's voice was deceptively quiet. He could sound like the most reasonable man alive, living only to throw back a pint with his sons and friends. Then he'd look you in the eye and tell you what he really wanted. "I heard through the grapevine that you were helping an un-Collared Shifter woman run from the Bureau."

"That would be me," Tamsin said, lifting her hand.

Sean sent her an amused look. "We figured. By *the grapevine*, he means Ben, who mentioned it to me. Ben's motive wasn't to get you into any trouble," he said quickly to Tamsin. "He was worried about you. So this Bureau shit took Ciaran?"

Ciaran answered. "Yep. Locked me in a crypt. I didn't even know what a crypt was until I was in one. At least it had a TV. But they mostly used the TV for a computer feed. Weird place for a hideout."

"Clever place," Dylan said. "Humans don't mind looking at monuments to the dead, but they don't like going inside the tombs, especially at night. The agents knew they'd be relatively undisturbed."

He switched his stare to Tamsin. Tamsin looked boldly back at him, not dropping her gaze like a good submissive. Tamsin had either learned to suppress the instincts that all Shifters had to not make eye contact with one more dominant, or else she was dominant herself. Or maybe fox Shifters had a different view of the hierarchy.

"So you ran with Gavan?" Dylan asked her.

Angus jumped. He didn't remember talking to anyone but Tamsin and Haider about that.

"Ran a *little bit* with Gavan, a long time ago," Tamsin said. "Why?"

Dylan glanced at Angus. "Gavan was, you could say, a bit extreme. I checked you out, Angus, pretty thoroughly before I talked to you, because of what I heard about your brother. He had good intentions but bad tactics."

"He didn't have any tactics at all," Angus said impatiently. "Except to have his own way or kill everyone else trying to get it. He ended up dead in the end, didn't he?"

Dylan acknowledged this with a nod. Neither of them mentioned the other person who'd ended up dead because of Gavan—Angus's mate, April. Angus didn't like to bring that up in front of Ciaran.

"You didn't know much about Gavan's activities," Dylan said. "You told me that right away, and I believed you. But *she* knows."

He turned his body so he could take in Tamsin without giving Angus any attack advantage. Dylan had spent his entire life making sure he held the best position in the room.

Tamsin gave him a bright look. "You want to know Gavan's favorite color and what movies made him cry? I hate to disappoint you all, but I wasn't as close to Gavan as everyone thinks. I was idealistic and naïve when I joined him, and I left when my idealism faded. I wasn't his bestie, or his lover, or even his dreamy-eyed admirer."

"Doesn't matter," Dylan said, pinning her with his blue gaze. "You, lass, are one of the few left who knew him and what he did. Tell me what you remember."

Tamsin touched her chin. "Let's see. His favorite color was puce, and he really liked *The Sound of Music*. Wept every time the kids stood on the stairs and sang before going up to bed."

"Oh, hey, I saw that movie," Ciaran said. "I liked when the nuns sabotaged the cars so the family could get away from the Nazis."

"Yeah, I liked that too," Tamsin said. "The song is how I learned to say *Auf Wiedersehen*. It's German for *until we see each other again*. Such a nice, succinct phrase."

"Is that what that means?" Ciaran tried it a couple of times, and Tamsin helped with his pronunciation.

Dylan, who must have met and dealt with Shifters from every type of personality in his long life, waited patiently until she and Ciaran finished.

"Anything you can tell me will be a help," he said, his voice calm.

"Goddess, does no one believe me when I say I don't know anything? Gavan never confided in me." Tamsin sat up straight and tapped her chest. "I. Don't. Know. Anything."

Dylan only gave her a quiet look. "I'm an old Shifter, as my sons like to remind me. That means to me, you're little more than a cub, and I have several hundred years of experience on you. I also have a finely developed sense of smell, even in my human form. I can scent a lie at a hundred paces. You know more than you admit, Tamsin Calloway."

She didn't blink. "I lie about tons of things. Which one are you scenting?"

Ciaran gave a gleeful chuckle. Angus could see him storing up the line to use himself one day.

Angus took a deliberate step and put himself between Dylan and the bed. "Enough. She knew my brother but he didn't confide in her. She told me all this—you could have asked me instead of bringing her in for an interrogation. Ciaran's tired, and it's time to go."

Dylan didn't move. "I agree—you should take your son home, or at least somewhere to sleep. The house I share with Sean is open to you, and I'll keep Shifter Bureau off your back so you can take us up on our offer of hospitality."

"Or we could stay here," Angus said. "I can come up with the price of a motel room."

"If you'll take advice from a father who raised three sons from hell, best you get your cub indoors in a real house. He'll be safer in a Shiftertown and have a home-cooked meal. Sean and his mate will see to that."

Angus noted several things about this speech. First, that Dylan mentioned *three* sons—Sean, Liam, and Kenny. Kenny had been killed by feral Shifters years ago, and Dylan rarely spoke of him. Dylan was noticeably conferring trust on Angus by this oblique reference.

Second, that Dylan didn't say *his* mate would see to the home-cooked meal. His mate, Glory, was a powerful Lupine, a clan leader, and didn't do anything so tame as cooking. Sean was the chef at the house he and his mate shared with Dylan, Glory, and now Sean's cub.

The third thing Angus noted was that Dylan made no mention of Tamsin. Dylan clearly wanted Angus to take Ciaran far from this motel, possibly having Sean accompany them, while he and Tamsin remained.

Angus folded his arms. "This seems like a nice place. I

haven't noticed Shifter Bureau running around outside, it's quiet, and it's off the beaten path."

"Dylan means he wants to interrogate me without you breathing down his neck," Tamsin said, not sounding worried. "So—if we stay here, Angus, are we sharing a room? *I* don't mind, but other people might get the wrong idea."

The thought of curling up next to Tamsin in bed, body to body, her warmth against his skin, licked sudden heat through him. Angus felt himself flush.

Tamsin grinned. "Isn't he adorable when he blushes? Excuse me, I need to use the bathroom. Talking about my interrogation is making me have to pee."

Sean rose from the chair and made a gallant gesture to the open door of the dark bathroom. Dylan's eyes narrowed.

Angus scowled at him. "Let her, Dylan. What is she going to do, flush herself?"

"The bathroom has a window," Dylan said.

Sean snorted a laugh. "A little tiny one by the ceiling, for ventilation. Even the smallest Feline cub couldn't get through it, and Tamsin's not Feline." He gave a sniff in her direction. "I've been Feline all my life and recognize one when I smell one. There aren't any giant ducts in the ceiling for her to crawl through either—I checked."

Sean, a good tracker himself, would have located every way into and out of this room before he'd let them in.

Tamsin swung her legs off the bed and landed gracefully on her feet. "I don't think you should prevent me, gentlemen. It's been a long drive, and Angus wouldn't stop at any gas stations."

So speaking, Tamsin sauntered past Sean and into the bathroom, turning on the light and pointedly closing the door.

"Sean," Dylan ordered. "Stand there and make sure."

Tamsin's voice rose from within the bathroom. "Only if he sings!"

Sean folded his arms, leaned on the doorframe, and began to croon. "She was a bonny red-haired lass, from where we do not know . . ."

Tamsin's laughter floated to them. Sean was making up the song, but behind the door, Tamsin began to sing a similar one, a true Irish ballad. Sean switched to that, singing along with her.

Ciaran left the bed now that Tamsin wasn't on it and came to Angus. He stood tightly by Angus's side, though he didn't wrap his arms around Angus's leg as he would have a few years ago.

Tamsin and Sean continued to sing the ballad of a lady who'd lost her love and turned into a ghost. Dylan waited in silence.

The toilet flushed, and the water in the sink began to run, Tamsin continuing the song.

"I'm not leaving her here with you," Angus told Dylan. "Whether we take you up on your hospitality or not, Tamsin stays with me."

"What do you know about her?" Dylan asked, his blue eyes expressionless.

"The same as you do. Her name is Tamsin Calloway, and my brother fooled her into joining his freedom-for-Shifters club. She grew wise to his idiocy and left the group before Gavan was stupid enough to get caught."

"Convenient that she was already gone when that happened."

"You're saying you think she betrayed them?" Angus asked in surprise. "Doubt it. Gavan was careless enough to get caught without outside help. It's out of character for her anyway."

"Even though you met her last night and know as much about her as I do," Dylan stated calmly.

"Yes." Angus hardened his voice. "If you don't—"

"Dad," Sean said in alarm. He rattled the handle of the bathroom door.

The sink water was still running, but Tamsin had stopped singing, and all was quiet.

Dylan strode to Sean. "Get the door open."

Ciaran closed his hand around Angus's, looking up fearfully at him as Sean slammed his shoulder into the flimsy door and quickly broke it open.

The light was off. Sean snapped it on to reveal the faucet pouring water into the sink.

The window above the shower, about four inches high, was wide open, a few moths drifting in, attracted by the light. Tamsin's clothes were on the floor, and Tamsin was gone.

CHAPTER THIRTEEN

Angus smothered a chuckle. The look on Dylan's face was priceless. So few Shifters ever put one over on him.

Ciaran didn't hold back his jubilation. He punched the air. "She got away! Tamsin got away!"

"*How* did she get away?" Sean sounded less angry than amazed. "What's her Shifter? A bird?"

"No such thing as bird Shifters," Dylan snapped. He glared at Angus. "What is she?"

"Good at getting away." Angus moved past Sean and picked up Tamsin's clothes. They held her warmth—she couldn't have been gone long.

"I swore she wasn't Feline," Sean said. "But no way a Lupine and most especially a *bear* slithered out that window. Oh, wait—a snake." His eyes sparkled with mirth. "She's a snake Shifter, isn't she? She'll fit right in, in Texas."

"Her mother is a bobcat, she said." Angus carried Tamsin's jeans, shirt, and silky underwear to the bed she'd been sitting on and began to fold everything neatly. He felt weird touching her underwear, but he sure wasn't going to let Sean or Dylan near it.

"Aha," Sean said. "That might be it. I've never met a bobcat Feline. But still." He shook his head. "Scent is wrong, even for an unusual Feline."

Dylan's eyes had gone hard. "Find her, Angus. Bring her to Shiftertown."

"You're not my leader." Angus smoothed Tamsin's folded jeans. He'd tucked the underwear between the folds, out of sight. "Spence is. I answer to him."

Dylan's growls had Ciaran backing behind Angus, and this time Ciaran did hold on to Angus's legs.

"What she knows could help us," Dylan said, his voice barely controlled. "Gavan was into something big—my intel is full of it. But I don't know what. *We* need to know what it was before Shifter Bureau gets hold of it, do you understand? It could assist what I'm putting together. Make her tell *you*, anyway."

"I'm not interrogating her." Angus met Dylan's stare, even if it wasn't easy. Dylan was far above Angus in any hierarchy, but the fact that Angus wasn't required to answer directly to him helped. "Since I've met her, people have wanted to catch her, trap her, and grill her—including me. Leave the poor woman alone."

"She's not a poor woman. She's trouble. I know that when I scent it. I agree that Gavan had faulty judgment, which is all the more reason we should know what that bad judgment led to."

"You want to put her under your power," Angus said flatly. "You want me out of the way so you can bring her in and set her up as part of the Austin Shiftertown, am I right? That way she answers to you and to Liam. You assure Shifter Bureau you have her under control, and they relinquish the keeping of her to you. I go home and never see her again. Isn't that what you're thinking?"

Dylan was a big man, broad of shoulder. He stood a half

inch taller than Angus and used every micrometer of that height. "Partly. I can smooth the way for you to take your son home and make sure you aren't punished for what she's done. You'll be out of it completely, your cub safe. I can guarantee that. And if you want to see Tamsin again, you're welcome to visit. Though I am not sure why you would. She's sure led you on a merry chase."

Angus's fingers twitched. He believed Dylan when he said he could get Shifter Bureau off Angus's back. The leader of the military attachment of the South Texas Shifter Bureau had mated with a bear Shifter from Austin, and Dylan used him to influence the agents in that Bureau office.

"You might have a lot of power in Texas, but I'm based in Louisiana, and it's a whole different ball game there," Angus said. "This Haider guy—wherever he's from— doesn't look like he'll give up the chase that easily. While we're arguing, she's out there alone, and Haider will be scouring every direction we could have taken from where we left him, probably has alerted Bureau agents every- where to be on the lookout for her."

"All the more reason to find her and bring her to me. I'll protect her from this man. I can, Angus."

But would Dylan be better for her than Haider? Maybe Dylan would stop short of terminating Tamsin, but Angus wouldn't put it past Dylan to use tranqs or heavy intimidation to scare her into telling him what he wanted to know.

Thinking of Tamsin quivering, drugged to the gills, under Dylan's sharp stare made growls vibrate his body.

"I'll find her, but *I'll* protect her," Angus said. "From Haider, and from *you*."

Sean watched, concerned and ready to back up his fa- ther, but also with interest, as though curious to see who would win the debate.

"Would it help if I said *please*?" The dry tone in Dylan's voice meant he wouldn't say *please* if it killed him.

"Nope."

"All right, then." Dylan turned to Sean. "Get on the phone. I need trackers, as many as you can round up. The best. Spike, Ronan . . . Tiger."

Sean's brows rose, but he slid his phone from his pocket and flipped it open.

Angus's blood chilled. Dylan could lay his hands on the best trackers in Shifterdom, especially Tiger, who could locate anyone with uncanny precision. If Tiger was on Tamsin's trail, she'd never get away.

Angus snapped around to Sean. "Sean—don't call. No one is going after Tamsin, because if they do, they'll have to go through me first." He took a deep breath, the conviction of what he was about to do filling him with strength. "I claim Tamsin Calloway as mate."

The words rang through the room. Sean, in surprise, lowered the phone, and then quietly folded it closed. Dylan only gave Angus a level stare.

Ciaran, on the other hand, let go of Angus to turn a cartwheel, his long legs nearly smacking into a chair. "Sweet!" he shouted. "I love Tamsin. She'll make the perfect mom."

"She isn't here." Dylan's clipped words were barely audible over Ciaran's triumphant shouts. "She can't answer."

"But I can still make the claim, in front of witnesses." Angus's heart thumped, but he held himself steady. "So if you want Tamsin, you have to go through me."

"Fine." Dylan struck fast, like the cat he was, his fist catching Angus on the side of the head even as Angus ducked out of the way.

Ciaran shrieked. Angus blocked Dylan's next punch and came up swinging.

Dylan was one of the best in the Austin fight club. Not the top, but not far from it. Except this wasn't the fight club, with its rules, as minimal as they were.

The *no killing* rule wouldn't apply in a motel room in Central Texas. Dylan had a Guardian here to send Angus to dust, and a vacuum cleaner would take care of the rest.

But no way was Angus letting Dylan past him to find Tamsin. She wasn't a flash drive of information to be passed from hand to hand. She was a living, breathing woman, and Angus was now her protector.

He kept punching. Dylan dodged his blows and got in damaging ones himself—to the shoulder, rib cage, jaw. Ciaran's shouts turned to howls as he shifted to his black wolf cub, his distress shrilling through the room.

Sean grabbed his father by the arms and dragged him back. "Dad! Stop! You'll have the cops on us in a trice. Ciaran, lad, shut it!"

Dylan let Sean pull him from Angus. His face was bloody, his breath labored, and Angus tasted blood on his own lips.

Angus caught the squirming Ciaran in his arms. The furry black cub cut off his howls, but he continued to whimper, his gray eyes wide with terror.

Dylan drew ragged breaths. "This is your answer, then."

He stepped away from Sean, wiping blood from his face with the back of his hand. Dylan was a stickler for Shifter law, an ancient code that went back centuries, before humans put forth their restrictions. He wasn't happy with Angus, but he'd abide by his decision.

His laconic words acknowledged the mate-claim. Though Angus and Tamsin weren't officially mated by the claim—and Tamsin, if Angus ever found her, would probably tell him to take his claim and stuff it—Angus now protected her. Every other male on the planet—father, brother, son, uncle, clan leader, Shifertown leader, Dylan—would face Angus's wrath if they went anywhere near her.

Sean looked pained. "Goddess, the pair of ye. Angus, get after her and keep her safe. I can't answer for Dad, but I'll try to keep him hosed down. That lass obviously needs you."

Dylan retreated to the bathroom during this speech and returned with two towels, one of which he handed Angus. "It's important you find her," he said, mopping his face. "I hope you understand how important. I won't hurt her. But please, bring her to me."

Ciaran started howling again. Angus scrubbed the blood from his mouth with the towel and kissed the top of Ciaran's head. "It's all right, son. We'll find her. We'll keep her safe."

Ciaran settled into the crook of Angus's arm. Sean had to help gather up both Tamsin's clothes and Ciaran's, Sean's look sympathetic as he opened the motel room's door.

"Go find her," Sean said quietly to Angus. "Make her your mate in truth. Trust me, lad. It's the best thing."

Tamsin paused at the edge of the farmer's field and gazed back at the motel. Lights glinting between cracks in curtains told of people settling in for the night, watching television, catching some sleep before continuing their journeys tomorrow.

She sat on her haunches, cool wind ruffling her fur. They'd left the rain behind, and the night sky stretched above her, thick with stars.

So why was she loitering in the breeze and the night instead of hightailing it out of there? Angus had known exactly what she'd do as soon as Sean mentioned the window in the bathroom, but he'd done nothing, said nothing. Even his body language, which Shifters were good at reading, had remained neutral, not betraying a thing.

Tamsin had, in fact, become stuck halfway through the window, cursing herself for eating every bite of that po' boy and following it up with cheesecake.

A frantic wriggling and her sleek fur had popped her through, and then she'd had to dig her claws in hard to the concrete wall to keep from falling twenty feet and landing on her face.

A few seconds later, she'd been on the ground, leaping across the asphalt and over the wall to the fields beyond, Sean's shouts fading behind her.

Now she sat thirty yards from the parking lot in the shadow of a stand of trees fed by a trickling creek. Rabbits in the field behind her were cowering, silent, waiting for the predator to go.

Go she should. Tamsin needed to run far and fast before Dylan came out of that motel. He'd turn into whatever bad-ass Feline he was and track her without a problem. His son would be right behind him, and Angus too.

She told herself she was waiting to see whether she could slip inside and retrieve her clothes and money as soon as they bolted out to hunt for her, but she knew that was bullshit.

Tamsin had abandoned clothes and money several times in her past and managed to survive. She'd learned the fine art of resourcefulness and never had to resort to theft. People could be persuaded to part with clothes they didn't want, or they'd pay her to go away if she was enough of a nuisance. She'd do an honest job for wages as well, walking away with a cheerful wave as soon as she got paid. If she could find a nearby poker game, all the better.

Tamsin never cheated at cards. She didn't need to. Humans had subtle changes in scent when they were bluffing. Easy to know when she had the best hand on the table.

Nothing explained why she sat here instead of fleeing. She wasn't certain what had made her turn back, except the pang in her heart when she realized she might never see Angus again.

What did it matter? She could arrange to meet with him—someday, when Shifter Bureau agents and über-dominant Shifters weren't chasing her. They might be twenty years older by then, but hey, what could they do?

Angus would have found another mate by that time. He was fine-looking, kindhearted, and strong, even if he was grumpy. He deserved a mate who loved him.

Tamsin's chest tightened until she couldn't breathe. No wonder she wasn't running—the escape must have exhausted her more than she'd thought.

She tensed when three men emerged from the motel, their height and bulk telling her they were Shifters, one unmistakably Angus. No glimmer of sword hilt marked the one who must be Sean, but he'd probably left the sword locked in the room so he didn't frighten the natives.

They all walked to the black semitruck cab, Angus, carrying a small, squirming wolf cub. Dylan and Sean didn't stop Angus from climbing up into the truck—in fact, Sean opened the passenger door and set a bundle of something on the seat.

Then the two Morrissey men backed off. They didn't wave or say any farewells, only watched as Angus started the truck, turned on its lights, and drove out of the parking lot.

Shit.

Tamsin waited another moment to see which direction Angus headed. Dylan and Sean remained in the lot, watching him go, lights glinting on their dark hair.

In the next second, Tamsin was gone. She dove beneath the trees and leapt the creek, dashing through scrub on the other side. She crouched low and then leapt straight over a barbed-wire fence, scraping her belly along the way, but barely feeling it. Then she was running, running, skimming over the ground on an intercept course to the highway Angus had taken.

Tamsin had never been good at geometry in school, but she could figure the exact angle she had to run to meet the truck, which Angus drove at a steady speed.

Her legs pumped, the furrows of plowed earth dragging at her abdomen, the stubble of cut crops stinging her. She ran straight through a patch of slick mud, slipping sideways before she could regain her footing. The mud slowed her, and the truck was passing.

Damn it. Tamsin changed her angle to compensate, forgetting about breathing as she zoomed across the field, her paws scrabbling to reach the asphalt as the black truck sped past her.

Tamsin hit the highway's shoulder and kept running,

desperately chasing the truck she had no hope of catching. *Like an optimistic dog,* she thought. *I sure hope no one's watching, laughing at me . . .*

Her lungs demanded oxygen. Tamsin's body made her stop before she wanted to, despair exploding through her as air filled her lungs.

The truck's tires squealed on the pavement and the cab skidded sideways. The red glow of brake lights bathed Tamsin, and the truck halted.

The driver's door opened. Angus leapt straight to the ground, the engine purring behind him, and ran for Tamsin.

As Tamsin gasped for breath, Angus reached her, scooped her up as though she weighed nothing, and hugged her against him.

"It's all right. I've got you."

The simple words made Tamsin collapse. She went limp against Angus's chest as he carried her to the truck, lifted her onto the seat, and sprang in swiftly behind her.

Tamsin lay still, panting, legs splayed, her fur matted with mud.

Angus guided the truck back onto the road, speeding up as he went. There was no traffic, no one to slow for as he drove on.

"Ciaran, give her that blanket."

Ciaran leaned from the back seat, a woolen blanket in his small hands. He draped it carefully over Tamsin, his touch steady, his face creased in concern.

Ciaran made sure Tamsin's head poked out—her mud-coated head with its open, drooling mouth. She must look like shit warmed over.

Tamsin lay as a heap of helpless wet fur, shivering and unable to stop. Ciaran petted the top of her head, making soothing noises. His touch, small but caring, started to calm her.

Finally, Tamsin summoned the strength to shift. Ciaran lifted his hand away as Tamsin slid into her human body and drew the blanket close over her naked limbs.

"Hey, sweetie," she said in a hoarse whisper to Angus. "Going my way?"

Angus kept driving, hands on the wheel. He didn't have a clear idea where he was going, which bothered him—he only knew they couldn't stop.

Tamsin crawled into the back and onto the bed, pulling the curtains that hung around the bunk closed. She emerged a few minutes later dressed again.

"Why do you think Dimitri hung up curtains?" Tamsin said to Angus as she slid into the front seat with startling ease. "I think it was so he and Jaycee could sneak inside and close out the world. When the truck is a-rockin', don't go a-knockin'."

Angus ignored this. "You all right?"

"Would love a shower and my hair is a wreck." Her voice was weak. "Running like hell across a mowed field in the middle of the night is harder than it looks. Otherwise, fine. How did you leave things with Dylan? Did he say, *Oh well, I give up. See ya later?*"

"Dad punched him." Ciaran's voice was tired but full of pride. "Fought him off. Sean had to break them up."

Angus felt the weight of Tamsin's gaze. "Then I should be asking if *you're* all right," she said. "I've never met a Shifter like Dylan. He's got a lot of power."

"We came to an understanding," Angus said quietly.

"Huh." Tamsin pulled her feet onto the seat, wrapping her arms around her legs. "Must have been a hell of an understanding."

"Dad claimed you as mate," Ciaran told her. "He made the mate-claim, under the light of the moon, and Sean, Dylan, and me were witnesses. You'll say yes, won't you, Tamsin? You'll be my dad's mate? And stay with us forever?"

CHAPTER FOURTEEN

Angus braced himself for Tamsin's snarl of outrage, for angry questions, even snarky comments, but she remained oddly silent.

He glanced at her. Tamsin was staring straight ahead, watching the road unroll under the glare of the headlights, her face pale behind the dirt streaking her cheeks.

"It was the only way to get Dylan off your back," Angus said quickly. He who didn't like to talk now spilled out words. "You're fair game, by Shifter terms. Unprotected, no mate, no father, no clan leader. If I mate-claim you, then no one messes with you. Not Dylan, not my clan leader, not Shiftertown leaders, *no one*. Even Shifter Bureau has to clear things with me."

Her lips parted as she listened, Tamsin's tawny eyes focusing on him. Those eyes were quiet, the teasing, carefree manner she hid behind gone.

"I wasn't there," she said softly. "How can you mate-claim a female who isn't in the room?"

"It wasn't a completed claim. But it was good enough. I claimed you before witnesses and in sight of the Goddess. It counted in Dylan's eyes, which was why he let me go and didn't give chase."

"So far," Tamsin said. "He hasn't given chase *so far*. But he will."

"I know," Angus said. "But now that I've made a mate-claim, his trackers will back off, because they'll have to fight me to get to you. They know me, and know I won't simply stand aside. Some of them have become friends, and they might refuse to obey Dylan on this."

Ciaran leaned over the seat to her. "All you have to do is say yes, Tamsin."

His voice held hope. April had taken Ciaran away when he was only two, and had died the next year, months after Angus had found her and wrested Ciaran back from her. Ciaran didn't remember much about April, but he felt the loss. He'd never had a proper mum, and he knew it.

Tamsin sent him a glance, then fixed her gaze on Angus again. "I've been mate-claimed before. Twice. I turned both claims down."

"Why?" Angus demanded. "Were the Shifters who made them assholes?"

A ghost of Tamsin's grin touched her mouth. "Well, yes."

"I did it to protect you, to add the layer of my fists between you and the world," Angus went on. "You do so many crazy things, you need someone to fight for you."

Again Angus waited for her derision, her laughter at him for doing something so stupid.

"You don't have to put yourself in danger for me," she said, her voice quiet. "I'm always running from bad people—I must be a bad-people magnet. But some of them turn out to be dangerous, like Haider. Seriously. Don't officially be their enemy too."

"I didn't do it to be a hero." Angus swerved around a slow-moving car. "I did it to save your ass from Dylan. He was going to call down all his trackers on you, including Tiger. Tiger's a big, messed-up Shifter bred in a lab in Area 51. He's not like normal Shifters. If Dylan sets *him* on your trail, you'll never get away, no matter how far you run or where you hide. But Tiger's a good guy at heart—he's got a mate and a cub, and he'll respect that I've made a mate-claim. Doesn't mean he won't find you; but he'll understand that I'm your protector, and he won't simply take you. He's a tracker for Dylan and his son Liam, but Tiger doesn't mindlessly obey anyone. He makes his own decisions."

Tamsin didn't answer for a moment, and when she did, her tone was thoughtful. "You know, I've never had a male try to scare me into a mate-claim by threatening me with a super-tracking Shifter from Area 51." She looked out the front window again. "I'm going to have to think about this."

"Are you not accepting because he has a cub already?" Ciaran asked, worried. "I'm usually good. I even clean my room sometimes before my dad remembers to tell me to do it."

Tamsin turned around and clasped Ciaran's hands, kissing each one. "Oh, sweetie. If I could have you as my cub, I'd love it. It's not you I'm worried about—it's your dad. I'd have to live with *him*."

"No," Angus said abruptly. "You do what you want. But no one touches you if I'm your mate."

Tamsin squeezed Ciaran's hands again and released him. "This is the weirdest mate-claim I've ever heard, I have to say. Are you sure you're not just overly tired, Angus? You need some shut-eye. You'll wake up horrified you ever thought of such a thing, and you'll want us to forget all about it."

"Nope." He shook his head. "Situation will be the same whether it's the middle of the night or the light of day. A mate-claim is binding. All other males will back off. The only way it ends is if you say no."

Angus clamped his mouth shut, willing himself to stop

talking. He expected the next words out of Tamsin's mouth to be *All right, then. No.* But she said nothing.

They went on, Angus cutting south of Austin, skirting San Marcos, and north into darkness again. Ciaran dozed behind them, worn out from the excitement and his worry that they'd lose Tamsin. It had been Ciaran who'd caught sight of her leaping from the field and yelled at Angus to stop.

"We need to pull off somewhere so you can sleep," Tamsin said sometime after Austin's lights had faded behind them. "Ciaran too. I'll keep watch."

Angus gave her a quick look. "You really think I'd do that? First, no way am I letting you decide to run off while I'm asleep. Two, there's nowhere to stop. Kendrick's place is out—Dylan will simply corner us there. Every Shifter in Kendrick's group and the Austin Shiftertown will know by now that Dimitri lent me this truck, so they'll be looking for it. We need to find different transportation and only then a safe place to rest—far, far from here."

"Wherever here is," Tamsin said, peering out into the dark. "Too bad—I like this truck. I hate to give it up. It's cozy."

"It's conspicuous. Shifter Bureau might not know about it, but every Shifter in Texas will soon."

"Out of the frying pan, into the fire. That's the saying, right? Where are we, do you think?"

"River country west of Austin. At least that's what the signs all say. There's a map in the dash."

Tamsin pulled out a thick, folded-up paper map. "Oh, I love maps. The paper ones are much more visceral than ones on a phone screen, right?" The map rustled as she unfolded it, then she flipped on an overhead light to study it, while Ciaran, who'd awakened, looked over her shoulder. "Let's see. Here's Austin. There's the lake. The river goes that way to—Llano?"

"Passed it. We're on the 71." A sign flashed by to confirm that.

"Next town is called Brady." Tamsin's finger touched it. "Not much out here. Very small towns. I like small towns, but I kind of stand out in them."

"No kidding." With Tamsin's brilliant red hair and laughter, bouncing in and out of people's lives, she must make herself memorable. "We'll head for San Angelo," Angus said. "It's a big enough town to let us be somewhat anonymous, and we can find another ride there."

Tamsin traced the line on the map. "Yep, that's where this road goes. How do you know so much about the middle of Texas?"

"I'm a tracker. I know a lot about a lot of places. Plus I used to drive all over the country when I was a trucker. And the biggest clue is we just passed a sign that said San Angelo was eighty-five miles from here."

"Smart-ass," Tamsin said. "Can you stay awake that long? Maybe I should drive." She gave him an eager look.

"Yes, I can, and no, I'm not letting you drive. You and Ciaran try to get some sleep, and I'll wake you when we get there."

"All right," Tamsin said. She shook out the map, folded it perfectly—Angus could never get the things to fold up again—unbuckled her seat belt, and climbed into the back with Ciaran.

"Not on the bed," he said. "Too dangerous if I have to stop suddenly or someone runs into me. You could go flying."

"Sheesh," Tamsin said in mock outrage. "I haven't accepted the mate-claim and already you think you're my lord and master." She buckled herself in next to Ciaran. "Let me tell you, Mr. High-and-Mighty, I don't care if I accept your claim and do the sun and moon ceremony with you. I'm not about to be an obedient, submissive little mate who does everything you say."

"Good." Angus stepped on the gas. "I'd gag if you were."

"Just so we understand each other," Tamsin said.

"Oh, I think we do."

Angus's tension eased a bit as Tamsin stuck out her tongue at him, then drew Ciaran against her, leaned back, and closed her eyes. Ciaran snuggled happily into Tamsin's side, opening one eye to give his dad an admonishing look.

She hadn't instantly rejected the claim. For some reason, this made Angus warm, and a hope he hadn't felt in years rose. A need as well. He looked forward to reaching San Angelo, finding a place to rest, and continuing the conversation.

B right lights flashed in Tamsin's face. She jumped awake, fearing to find police and Shifter Bureau bearing down on them, but what she saw made her sit up straight and point over Angus's shoulder.

"Hey, there's a good place to hide."

There was a carnival, a wide empty lot covered with machines bearing screaming people aloft, lights flashing and blinking, music reaching them through the closed windows of the truck.

Plenty of semitrucks were parked around the periphery, with cabs of all colors. RVs and trailers mixed with them, the carnival workers' traveling homes.

Angus was silent, as though trying to think up an argument. There were plenty—the carnival people would notice them slipping their truck in among theirs, they weren't pulling a trailer, Ciaran might eat too much cotton candy . . .

Angus slowed the truck and turned, rolling across a cattle guard to a dirt road that led to the lot full of semis. He drove carefully, easing the black cab in between a red one and a brown, killing the lights and the engine.

It was quiet back here, the carnival starting to die down

this late, but the lights were still on and stragglers soaked up their evening.

"If they start loading up to leave, they'll notice us," Angus said, his voice a rumble.

"They won't." Tamsin watched people drifting around the rides, daring to rest her chin on Angus's shoulder. "The carnival will be here at least the whole weekend, probably moving out Monday morning. We can befriend them and travel with them."

Angus sent her a skeptical look, and Tamsin flashed him a brief smile.

She hadn't recovered yet from the shock of his mate-claim. It shouldn't count if she hadn't been there, should it? In the old days, it would have. A hundred years and more ago, Shifter males picked out their mates and declared it to the world, whether the female was around to protest or not. The female could say no, but it was in the male's best interests to get the claim in before another male did.

Mated to Angus. To have him in her life, for always.

She barely knew him. She didn't know what movies he liked, or if he even liked movies. Or his favorite foods, or if he liked to sleep in on Sundays or if he woke up at dawn and watched the sunrise while offering prayers to the Goddess.

On the other hand—Tamsin knew all the important things about him. He was a loving father who'd do anything for his son. He stood up for the underdog—or in her case, the under-fox. He was protective of those in his care. He bristled and growled but always did the kind thing. He didn't let other Shifters or the shits in Shifter Bureau intimidate him.

To sum up, Angus was strong, confident, caring, intelligent, and an all-around great guy. And he was hot.

How could she forget hot? He had a well-honed body and was sexy as hell. Tamsin hadn't averted her gaze back in the bayous when they'd shifted from animal to naked humans—she'd looked her fill.

If she accepted the mate-claim, her fantasies about him—Angus making love to her while covering her mouth in heated kisses—could be real.

The mate-claim did mean no one could legally touch her while Angus was alive. She had the feeling, however, that Haider would simply kill Angus to eliminate that obstacle.

The breath left Tamsin's body. The trouble with caring for people was that she now had someone to lose.

Refusing the mate-claim and running off into the Texas desert would do away with that problem. So her choice was this: Flee and eat her heart out missing Angus and Ciaran the rest of her life. Or stay and endanger them.

She wanted to cry.

Angus cupped her cheek with his broad hand. "You and Ciaran get into bed and sleep. I'm going to scout around."

Tamsin kissed his palm, liking its roughness against her lips. "The carnies might tell us to leave. Or toss you in carnival jail. Do they have jails at carnivals?"

"I don't plan to be seen." Angus brushed his thumb over her lips. "Go to sleep. Watch over Ciaran."

Tamsin nodded. If he'd told her not to run away, she wouldn't have listened and made her own decision. Charging her to take care of Ciaran had the strength of a chain. She'd never disappear and leave Ciaran unguarded.

Angus slid his hand behind her head, pulled her close, and kissed her.

Tamsin's body tightened to a point of pleasure. She leaned into Angus as he swept his tongue into her mouth, rising need burning her blood. She opened her mouth for his, suckling his tongue, drinking his warmth into her.

Angus drew back, but not hurriedly. He skimmed his fingertip across her lips, the corners of his mouth curving upward as Tamsin caught his finger lightly between her teeth.

"Get some sleep," Angus whispered.

Tamsin nibbled his finger, then licked it. Angus's cheeks grew redder in the flash of lights from the midway, but he didn't pull away. Tamsin kissed his fingertip and sat back, a ball of heat gathering in her chest.

Angus caressed her cheek with his thumb, turned from her to grab his jacket, and slid out of the truck to the ground. He shook himself when he landed, then pulled on the jacket, quietly closed the door, and faded into the darkness.

Tamsin let out a long breath. She gave herself a shake as Angus had, trying to snap out of the hunger that roiled inside her.

A fox and a Lupine. That was never going to work.

She found Ciaran's eyes open, his look knowing. "You'll be his mate," he said with conviction.

"Maybe." Tamsin pulled him close and kissed the top of his dark head. "Let's hit the sack. Your dad's out there taking care of us."

She believed this without having to reason it out. Angus wouldn't desert her or Ciaran, nor would he let anyone near them.

Ciaran burrowed under the blankets, and Tamsin lay on top of the bed, pulling a loose cover over herself. Ciaran snuggled down trustingly and soon was asleep.

Tamsin lay awake, staring at the ceiling above her, trying not to listen for every noise, and to sort through the jangled thoughts in her head.

Angus walked quietly but purposefully from the shadows of the trailers toward the carnival. He'd learned to blend into the human world by looking innocuous—as innocuous as a large man in a hoodie with a Collar could.

For this moment, he'd be a silhouette, just another human shape in this field, navigating his way around the vehicles.

The carnival was set up in what looked like a fairground,

with rides up and down the length of a very large field, and a grandstand beyond where rodeos must be held. Tents and booths formed aisles, though most were being closed and locked for the night. This carnival was using about half the grounds, probably a small traveling operation that set up where they could get space.

Angus stayed to the deeper darkness, trying to look non-chalant, as though he belonged, worked there. Plenty of other shadowy men were carrying things to trailers and trucks, locking doors, shutting down rides. The last human visitors were being herded out the gates.

A decent place to hide, he'd decided, both from Haider and from Dylan. Dylan expected Angus to pry knowledge about Gavan from Tamsin, but Dylan could suck on it. Angus didn't give a crap about what Tamsin knew about Gavan—which was probably little.

Angus had known Gavan better than anyone—he might have boasted about something, but he'd been all talk and no substance. *All hat and no cattle* was a saying among ranchers. Gavan and his followers had been found and killed because they were stupid, and Angus wanted to forget him. Whatever Tamsin knew—if she knew anything—could stay in her head. Dylan would have to find out the information another way.

Angus heard a step behind him. His first thought was *Tamsin—What the hell?* But it wasn't Tamsin.

He heard a growl, scented the sudden whiff of predator. Angus spun in place, going into a crouch. Red eyes that glowed with rage and possessiveness blazed out at him from the gloom.

The eyes belonged to a solidly muscled bear, its mouth pulled back to reveal teeth gleaming in a savage snarl. No Collar glinted around the bear's neck, but Angus knew bloody well what he faced. *Shifter.*

CHAPTER FIFTEEN

The bear attacked. Angus sidestepped and spun, tossing off his jacket at the same time.

He dodged the bear's swiping claws—*brown bear*, he thought distractedly. *Not grizzly.* He didn't want to shift, but his wolf started to push its way through. Angus tamped down on the urge with effort.

"Enough!" he said in the voice that could make even Ciaran freeze and fall silent.

The bear paused a step but his snarls didn't lessen.

"I'm passing through." Angus held up his hands to show he'd not sprouted claws. "Need a place to rest." He gestured—carefully—at the bear's neck. "You don't have a Collar. That's cool with me. I'm not a tracker for Shifter Bureau. For anyone."

The bear's snarls cut off with a wheezing huff as it began to shift. This bear had to do it slowly, as many Shifters did, his limbs changing and reforming in a painful, lengthy process.

The man at last stood up on human legs. He was lankier than most bear Shifters, who tended to be all bulk, but he had the height. His hair was red-brown and unruly, and his eyes were a rich brown, at the moment tinged with anger. He had a longish face, blunt chin, and large limbs. His chest was furred, as most bears' were, the same color as his bear's coat.

"Who the hell are you, and what do you want?" the man demanded, his voice the bass rumble that characterized bears.

"I told you. Passing through. Looking for a place to sleep." Angus clamped his mouth shut without mentioning Ciaran. A wise Shifter didn't reveal his vulnerable mate and cub to a stranger until he knew the lay of the land.

"How'd you get in here?"

"Drove. Parked over there." Angus nodded to the crowded truck lot. The bear would scent which vehicle belonged to a Shifter sooner or later, so no sense in trying to hide it.

The bear watched him. Sniffed—testing for lies. He put his hands on his hips, a less defensive stance, but his scowl didn't show trust.

"Name?"

"Angus Murray. You passing through too, or do you work here?"

"Angus Murray, from . . . ? What clan?"

He spoke as one who'd never been to a Shiftertown. Shifters these days asked each other what Shiftertown they came from, who the leader there was.

"My clan is scattered," Angus answered. "I was sent to New Orleans."

The bear's eyes narrowed. "New Orleans? I guess if you let yourself be shut in a Shiftertown, one in New Orleans might not be so bad."

"It's not in the city; it's an hour away."

"Huh." The noise was reminiscent of a bear's growl. "What the hell are you doing in the middle of Texas?"

"Told you. Looking for a place to sleep."

"Are people hunting you? They must be. Why else would a Collared Shifter be sneaking around my carnival in the middle of the night? I hear you poor slobs aren't allowed to leave the state where you live without permission and a ton of paperwork."

Angus didn't move. "I'll sleep; I'll go."

"Last thing I need is a shitload of heat. How far behind you are they?"

"Not sure. Haven't seen them since New Orleans." Angus decided not to mention Dylan, who was a better tracker than Haider could ever hope to be.

"I admit, this is a good place to hide," the bear said. "Been hiding here twenty-two years myself."

Though his stance was less hostile, Angus didn't relax. "You said *my carnival*. You run it?"

"I own it." The bear folded his arms, muscles moving in the dark. "Bought it before Shifters were rounded up. Carnival people are tight—no one betrayed me."

"They know you're Shifter, then?"

"Most do. New ones don't always. I keep a low profile."

"Like attacking strangers in the dark, as a bear?"

"First time a Shifter has wandered through my carnival," the bear said. "Name's Dante. Like the poet. Sleep tonight. Might give you breakfast in the morning, but don't be offended if I have my people watching you."

"That's what I'd do. Well met, Dante. The Goddess's blessings upon you."

This was a standard Shifter greeting from one who was invading another's territory, which Angus was. Angus extended his hand. If Dante accepted him completely, he'd gather Angus into a brief hug, showing he trusted Angus not to gouge him with teeth or claws. Or Dante could shift back to bear and rip the hand apart.

Dante kept things impartial, gripping Angus's forearm. Angus gripped his in return, and Dante brought his left hand around to squeeze Angus's shoulder.

Acceptance for now, if not total trust.

"Go to that tent when you wake in the morning." Dante pointed to a white, fairly large tent at the end of one aisle. Not where Dante lived, Angus knew—the tent would be neutral ground. "And I'll see you're fed. Good night. Give my greeting to your mate and cub."

Dante grinned at Angus's discomfiture—but of course Dante would have scented Ciaran and Tamsin. He was being polite and not demanding that Angus tell him about them.

The fact that he'd called Tamsin Angus's mate said that the mate-claim was already becoming ingrained—Shifters could scent when one Shifter claimed another.

They exchanged wary good-nights. Angus walked away first, careful not to turn his back until he was at least twenty feet from Dante. This was Dante's territory—Angus would make himself be deferential.

He noticed several shadows following him, human by scent, likely Dante's backup, keeping an eye on Angus. Angus walked quietly to the truck, not trying to lose them, letting them see where he went.

Angus very much doubted Dante would report him. Dante was un-Collared, and he'd want to stay far from the notice of Shifter Bureau. Obviously the bear had successfully avoided being rounded up, just as Tamsin and Kendrick and his group had. But unlike Kendrick, Dante had chosen to live among humans and not seek out other Shifters.

Angus silently opened the truck's door and climbed into the cab. He heard the quiet but deep breathing of Ciaran, and the quicker but equally sleep-filled breaths of Tamsin.

He parted the curtain around the bed a crack to find Tamsin curled on her side, his son sleeping trustfully against the curve of her body.

Angus's tension started to ebb. Tamsin was here, protecting Ciaran, sleeping the sleep of the just.

And the exhausted. Angus let the curtain fall, then

closed and locked the truck's doors, stretching himself out
on the front bench seat. He didn't intend to sleep, but between one blink and the next, he must have succumbed,
because when he opened his eyes again, the sun was shining hard through the windows.

The bed's curtain was open, and both Tamsin and Ciaran were gone.

Tamsin kept hold of Ciaran's hand as they entered the
white tent, which held about forty people and a buffet.
Sunday brunch, the overly tall man who called himself
Dante told her.

When Tamsin had leapt down from the truck, wanting
the bathroom too much to wait for Angus to wake up, she'd
been surrounded by five human males, who'd greeted her
politely if not warmly. Two had led her and Ciaran, who
had scrambled out after her, to a trailer that held a somewhat decent bathroom. Tamsin had done her best to wash
her face, but she longed for a shower.

She'd emerged, then guarded the door while Ciaran used
the bathroom, and then they followed their guides to the tent.

Dante had been waiting outside the tent's open flap.
"Where's Angus?" he asked without greeting.

Tamsin stared at him, as did Ciaran, not so much because he was a Shifter, un-Collared, but how he was
dressed. His shirt was black silk, and over it he wore a gold,
purple, and silver striped velvet coat that hung past his
waist. Black jeans and gray cowboy boots completed the
outfit, and he held a purple top hat with a stream of black
feathers rippling from under its wide black ribbon.

He watched her take in that he was Shifter, and he gave
her an acknowledging nod that he knew she and Ciaran
were too.

"I met Angus last night," Dante went on. "We do brunch
Saturday and Sunday mornings, but the rest of the time,

you find your own meals." He gestured with his ornate hat. "Come in and meet everyone."

Angus must have won Dante over—Dante would never have made an offer like that if he hadn't decided to trust them.

The people inside the tent regarded Tamsin curiously, but they were welcoming, in a low-key way. They let Tamsin into the line, and before long, she had a full plate, Ciaran an even fuller one. Steaming eggs, crisp bacon, a pile of pancakes, toast, juice, coffee—everything Tamsin and Ciaran could want.

The cook was a large man who looked as though the shower wasn't his favorite place, but he could cook, Tamsin discovered as she ate. She went through her plate and returned for seconds, Ciaran right behind her.

Halfway through her refill, Angus stormed into the tent. His gaze went to Tamsin and Ciaran, and his stark worry turned to glowering anger.

"About time you got up," Tamsin said, licking syrup from her fork. "You were sleeping hard. You snore, you know. Loudly."

Ciaran guffawed around a mouthful of sausage. "He does."

Angus glared, but he said nothing, his relief at finding them apparent.

"Grab a plate," Tamsin told him. "It's good. Then I'm going to make Dante tell me where I can take a shower."

"You met him, then."

"He's right over there." Tamsin poked the air with her fork. "I couldn't miss him."

"I meant—what did you think of him?"

Tamsin studied the bear Shifter, whose coat glimmered as he moved. "Quick assessment? Too sure of himself. But if he's lived off the grid all this time, he's good at it. Do I trust him? The jury's still out."

Angus gave her a nod. "I was thinking about the same."

He eyed the half-empty trays of food on the long table. "Might as well eat."

He strolled off, as though he could take food or leave it. He'd acted the same about sleep. Angus had been heavily asleep though when Tamsin and Ciaran had crept quietly out of the truck. His face had been relaxed, his hair rumpled, lashes curled on his skin. He'd been exhausted, the poor wolf-man. She wondered what he'd say if she told him she'd wanted nothing more than to cuddle up to him, to lie back in the circle of his warm arms. He'd probably rumble and growl, and then blush. She loved it when he did that.

Angus finished loading his plate at the buffet table, but he set his food down quickly as Dante approached him. With him came a woman, one that had Tamsin jumping out of her chair and rushing to Angus's side.

The woman had very blond hair caught in a braid that fell to her waist, and dark eyes under light brows. She was almost as tall as Dante, with a slender build and a pointed chin.

Tamsin, with Ciaran on her heels, arrived in time to hear Dante say, "This is Celene."

A snarl clogged Angus's words. "She's Fae."

The scent of Faerie—sulfur and mint—came to Tamsin, though in a subdued way. The woman wore slim jeans and a tie-dyed shirt, very un-Fae-like garb.

"She's my mate," Dante said. "Don't judge."

Celene turned an interested smile on Tamsin. "I'm half Fae. Does it bother you? I forget about my lineage most of the time—my parents weren't my fault. Everyone thinks I'm human, so that's what I am now."

Tamsin gave her a careful shrug. "Hey, we all have pasts."

Celene peered at her very obvious lack of Collar and then at Angus's black and silver chain glinting from the shadows of his jacket. "I guess we do."

Dante looked down at Ciaran, his very brown eyes assessing, nose twitching as he took in scent. Tamsin saw him understand that Ciaran was Angus's but not Tamsin's. "Hello, cub," Dante said cordially. "Don't worry. I won't eat you."

Ciaran lifted his chin. "My dad wouldn't let you."

Dante laughed, the deep laugh of a bear Shifter. "You're probably right. High five, kid."

"That's lame." Ciaran tried to scoff, but he darted around Tamsin and slapped Dante's offered palm.

"Our cub is about your age," Celene said to Ciaran. "Maybe you two can play while you're here. She's helping the ticket taker get ready. She likes to do that. She can show you around."

"A *girl*?" Ciaran asked, incredulous.

Celene sent him an amused look. "You'll be surprised by her, I'm sure."

"We won't be staying long," Angus began, but Tamsin slid her hands into her back pockets and nodded at Dante.

"We might as well stay for the day, as long as we can keep our truck hidden. But only if you have showers. That's a deal breaker."

Angus had to admit he felt better after bathing and putting on fresh clothes, which Dimitri had thoughtfully supplied in a duffle bag Angus found in the truck. The clothes fit Angus fairly well, but they smelled of Feline, which meant Dimitri had borrowed them, possibly from Kendrick, who was about the same build as Angus.

Tamsin had showered first in the long RV Dante had led them to. The interior held human scent, which meant Dante wasn't yet trusting enough to leave another male Shifter alone in his own home. Smart of him.

The human who used the trailer was absent, working already. When Angus emerged, he saw Dante set his outlandish hat on his head and yell, "Heads up! The good folks of San Angelo are about to stream in. Let's show them a fine time today, people."

The lights of the midway began to flash, music pumping from first one ride, then another.

Tamsin, holding Ciaran by the hand, had been in intense conversation with Celene, the three of them standing in the middle of an aisle of booths. They broke off as Dante hurried Celene away to whatever job she did, and Tamsin shaded her eyes to watch Angus jog to her.

The smell of frying meat drifted from one booth, the burned odor of cotton candy from another. Other stands sold junky souvenirs, and more had games, giant stuffed animals crammed on their shelves as prizes.

"Sun's bright out here," Tamsin said when Angus reached her and Ciaran. "This redhead needs a hat." She peered into the booths around her, and then pointed. "Ah. *That* one."

With Ciaran at her side, Angus a cautious step behind her, she glided to a brightly decorated stand where a human man with long dark hair in a ponytail was straightening merchandise on the shelves.

"How much for that?" Tamsin waved at a tall, crooked top hat with orange and red stripes that rested in the middle of a shelf.

The man gave her a faint smile. "Not for sale, sweetheart. You have to win it." He gestured to the floor, which held a jumble of glass bottles of various shapes and sizes. He dropped three rings on the counter in front of her. "Three rings for five dollars. Fifteen rings for twenty."

Tamsin dug into her pocket and slapped down a twenty-dollar bill. Ciaran stepped up to her excitedly. "What are you going to do?"

"Win my hat. How many do I need to get?" she asked the man.

"Eight."

"Fair enough." Tamsin took up the rings in her left hand and eyed the rows of empty glass bottles—tall ones, short ones, long skinny ones, squat ones with thick necks.

Tamsin's first toss went astray, but her next one ringed a bottle. Ciaran cheered. Tamsin narrowed her eyes, tilting her head. Angus could see the fox in her when she did that, imagined her in animal form, sizing up whatever trouble she planned to get into.

Tamsin tossed the next ring, and the next and the next in rapid succession. Each one found a bottle's neck, caught it, and spun down it with a ringing note. Tamsin missed one or two, but she reached eight with a couple of rings to spare. Ciaran danced around in a circle, chanting, "Go, Tamsin, go!"

The booth tender watched, openmouthed, as she had success after success, then closed his lips, an angry glint in his eyes. Tamsin tossed her last ring and turned to him with a broad smile.

"My hat, please."

The man sighed, plucked it from the display, and handed it to her. Tamsin brushed it off and set it on her head.

The hat was oversized, and the top bent askew, but somehow it looked exactly right on her.

"Sweet," Ciaran cried. "Win me one, Tamsin."

Tamsin eyed the row of ridiculous hats and slapped another twenty on the table.

She ended up winning a Mad Hatter–looking hat for Ciaran and a baseball cap for Angus. Angus tried to refuse it, but Tamsin sidestepped his protesting hands and jammed the hat with a Texas Rangers logo on his head. "There. Now you look normal. Well, mostly."

Angus adjusted the cap with a grunt of irritation, trying not to like how Tamsin had swarmed up him. Her warmth lingered, and her breath tingled his cheek even after she'd turned away again.

Tamsin's wins had drawn a crowd. The booth operator looked less annoyed as more and more people stepped up to buy rings for a chance to win. Tamsin had made it look easy.

The man slipped out from behind the booth when they turned to go. "Hey, come back later and play some more," he said to Tamsin. "You're good for business. I'll even give you a cut."

Tamsin paused, lips pursed. "I'll think about it. I might need a job."

The man nodded, hurrying back into his booth to soothe the impatient kids and adults waiting their turns.

Tamsin held Ciaran's hand as they strolled away, Ciaran reaching up to touch his new hat every once in a while.

The fairgrounds were filling up with people looking for entertainment after church on a Sunday, and Angus glanced around uneasily.

"I think it's about time to go," he said.

"Why?" Tamsin peered up at him from the shadow of her absurd hat. "This is a perfect place to hide out. I don't think Haider or Dylan would expect to find us *here*."

She had a point, but Angus preferred hiding places deep in the woods, in shadows, where his black wolf would be almost invisible.

This field was wide-open, crammed with lights, music, food, people, bright colors, and confusing sounds. Impossible to guard all approaches.

On the other hand, they did more or less blend in with all the other moms and dads taking their kids to the carnival. Even Tamsin's and Ciaran's gaudy headgear didn't look odd, as plenty of people walked around with weird things on their heads—balloon rings, plastic crowns, antennae on springs.

"We can lie low here for a while," Tamsin went on. "Celene says they're always looking for people to help out. Dante and Celene own the carnival together, but they only have a few rides and games of their own—the rest are independent contractors. But everyone needs help loading and unloading, running the rides, or taking tickets, plus they have sideshows. We could be a sideshow act—I could run around as my fox, jumping through rings or something, and you could pretend you'd trained me. Then I'd do whatever I wanted no matter what you said—you know, make it a comedy."

Angus listened in growing irritation. "That wouldn't be a show—it's your real life. In any case, you're not revealing your fox to an audience. Word of the smart-ass fox at the carnival would get around."

Tamsin frowned. "You're right. How disappointing." She brightened. "But don't worry. I'll think of something else."

"I'm going to see if I can trade Dimitri's truck cab for someone else's," Angus said as she stared off into the distance, no doubt coming up with another alarming idea. "One less conspicuous. I'll send Dimitri the money for it."

"No rush." Tamsin moved closer to him as another surge of people pushed past. "I haven't felt this safe in a while. Or had as much fun." She glanced at the midway, as giant arms of rides began to rise into the air, lights flashing as they swung and spun. "Which one do you want to go on, Ciaran?"

"No rides," Angus tried, but he knew he'd already lost that battle.

"We can pick whichever one we want," Tamsin said, completely ignoring him. "Celene gave me some passes. Your choice, Ciaran."

Ciaran gazed around, wide-eyed, his excitement evident. Ciaran had never seen a carnival before. Though he'd lived near New Orleans most of his life, Ciaran stayed in Shiftertown, only venturing out to attend the nearby school. Angus didn't consider New Orleans a safe place for cubs.

"That one."

Ciaran pointed eagerly at a tall machine with enclosed cages that rose up a pillar and went down the other side. Didn't look so bad until the cages started going faster and faster and spinning around themselves. Then the main pillar leaned over sideways and then turned upside down, even as the cages continued zooming around the ride's vertical axis.

"The Zipper," Tamsin said with enthusiasm. "Good choice."

She darted forward, but Angus grabbed Ciaran's hand and yanked him back. "You are not taking my cu—my son on that contraption."

Tamsin sent Angus a pitying look. "I've been on it lots of times. The ride is only like two minutes long. Come with us if you're so worried."

Angus watched the Zipper move upside down, its cages spinning, spinning. "You seriously want *me* to get on that thing?"

"Please, Dad?" Ciaran looked up at him, hope in his eyes. "*Please.* All those dads are taking their kids. I want to be like—"

Ciaran closed his mouth before the rest of the words came out, but Angus knew what they'd be. *Like a real family.*

Ciaran never blamed Angus for his mother leaving him, or for his mother's death. Angus never blamed himself either—any guilt rested squarely on Gavan and April. But Angus had made it clear he hadn't forgiven Ciaran's mother, and he knew that must be hard for Ciaran to live with.

Ciaran had latched on swiftly to Tamsin, giving her more trust than Angus had ever seen him bestow on anyone. It would be very hard for him when Tamsin finally decided to go.

"Death trap," Angus muttered.

"See, look, it's stopping," Tamsin said. "All those riders are fine, and more are getting on." She grabbed Angus's hand and Ciaran's and tugged them forward. "Come on, Angus. It'll be fun. You do know what *fun* means, right?"

"I know I'm going to regret this," Angus said.

Ciaran bounced up and down. "Yay! Come on!"

He started through the crowd, pulling Angus and Tamsin behind him.

Tamsin's body tingled as the ride operator, a brisk young woman with arms covered in tattoos, shut them firmly in the cage and secured it. Ciaran wriggled with excitement between Angus and Tamsin. He'd had a moment of worry—he had to be a certain height to get on the ride—but he'd passed.

Angus clutched the bar beside him, gritting his teeth and looking grim.

But he'd done it. Tamsin had seen the terror in his eyes when he'd watched the Zipper go around. The big bad wolf who'd chased her through the bayous looked like he wanted to put his tail between his legs and run home. But he'd sucked it up and gotten on the ride—for Ciaran.

"This is how I should have gotten away from you," Tamsin told him as she removed her hat and secured it between her knees. Ciaran copied her movements. "I should have run to the nearest fairground and hopped on a ride."

Angus shook his head, every line of him tight. "You'd have to get off eventually."

"That's a fair point. Oh, good. We're starting."

The ride's motor began to grind, the cage rising gently, no more frightening than a slow Ferris wheel. Angus breathed out, relaxing a little.

The Zipper sped up, their cage reaching the top. The cage suddenly flipped end over end, and Angus groaned, clutching the bar.

The ride began to move more quickly, the cage spinning first forward, then backward. Tamsin laughed; Ciaran screamed in delight. The whole structure began to rotate, faster and faster, spinning and jerking, spinning again.

Tamsin was pushed back in the seat, then shoved forward. She might be locked into a cage, something she feared as a Shifter, but in this one with Angus and Ciaran, she felt suddenly free.

Freer than she had ever been in her life. She'd run from Collars, from Shifter Bureau, from Shiftertowns, from Shifters themselves, seeking independence, her own life. Running, running.

Now she was squashed against Angus and his cub, the Shifter Lupine who'd tried to capture her and then had turned around and saved her life.

Angus, the snarly Lupine who trusted no one and loved his son so much, squeezed his eyes shut, his cap falling off to release his unruly short hair.

"I'm going to die now," he roared over Ciaran's happy cries. "You're a shit, Tamsin!"

Tamsin smiled, her heart filling as Angus abruptly opened his eyes, turned his head, and glared at her.

His gray eyes, caught in the sunshine that sparkled through the grid, were the most beautiful things she'd ever seen in her life.

"Yes!" she yelled.

The eyes narrowed. *"What?"*

"I said yes! Angus Murray, in front of witnesses, under the light of the Father God, I accept your mate-claim!"

CHAPTER SIXTEEN

Angus's body turned inside out as the cage spun around and around.

But no, the ride was slowing, the cages flipping right side up and remaining so. Two minutes, Tamsin had promised. Two minutes of perfect terror.

Tamsin held his gaze, her tawny eyes full of sudden excitement but also worry about what impact her words would have on him.

She'd just said she'd be his mate.

A shrill keening cut through the air, obliterating all thought. It was Ciaran, yelling in joy.

"Dad—did you hear what she said? She accepted the mate-claim!"

Tamsin swallowed. She clutched the bar in front of her, though the cage had ceased its rocking. "I'll have to say it again, when Dante's around. Need more than one Shifter witness, right?"

Angus couldn't remember at the moment. Did a cub, and his own, count as a witness?

And who cared? The mate-claim was a personal thing. The witnessing had begun in the days when Shifters were first free of the Fae, and males grabbed any female they could. If a mate-claim was witnessed, then all Shifters would know that female was no longer fair game.

"I heard her." Angus's voice was guttural, sounding wrong. "I heard, son."

"Well?" Tamsin's lips shook once. "Do you accept my acceptance of your mate-claim?"

A big lump lodged in Angus's throat. "Yes," he croaked out.

Ciaran cheered again. The woman operating the ride unlocked the cage, opening it wide so they could step out.

"Sounds like you liked it," she said to Ciaran.

"Sure did. Can we go again?"

"No!" Angus hauled Ciaran down and away. He heard both Tamsin and the woman laugh.

That is, Angus tried to lead Ciaran away. Angus's legs wobbled, and walking was suddenly impossible.

Tamsin staggered into him. "You know the ride was great when you forget which way is up."

"I'm thinking I'm sorry I ate breakfast." What the hell had made Angus want to devour all those pancakes?

Tamsin steadied Angus with one hand, recovering her equilibrium quickly. "Let's find Dante. We have a lot to tell him."

Angus couldn't remember what. He only knew that when he clasped Tamsin's hand, it felt right, that his heart warmed and his stomach ceased roiling.

To hell with Dante. Angus wanted a soft, private place to be alone with Tamsin.

The carnival was in full swing by now. Crowds filled the space, people yelled at one another, laughed, squealed, shouted. More screams came from the Zipper as a new set of victims went aloft. The octopus ride sent its arms careening toward the barricades between it and the crowd, to abruptly pull them back at the last second.

Angus knew only the lightness of Tamsin's hand in his, the connection that came from their touch.

He had a mate. After all the years of loneliness, of Shifter women avoiding him because of the taint of his brother's perfidy, Tamsin had smiled and said she would stay. Hell, he'd mostly avoided the Shifter women, to be honest. Hard to be with women who knew his mate had walked away from him.

Tamsin didn't care. She sympathized but didn't blame him for April's faithlessness. She looked at Angus, and wanted to be with *him*.

Angus knew it was impossible. They faced huge obstacles, such as his Collar, the Bureau wanting to capture Tamsin, Dylan trying to use her, and them having nowhere to live, nowhere to be safe. The carnival was fine for today, maybe even for tomorrow, but what about after that?

The practical thoughts dove to the back of Angus's mind. None of it was important at the moment.

The front of his mind told him Tamsin was his *mate*. A beautiful woman to bury himself inside and maybe risk losing his heart to.

Tamsin halted next to him, stepped against the startled Angus, and kissed him.

The crowd faded. Angus wrapped his arms around Tamsin, pulling her to him, burying his fingers in the warmth of her shirt. Her silly hat, which she'd resumed, fell from her head, but Ciaran caught it before it thumped to the dust.

Angus slid a hand under her hair, burying his fingers in the silken strands. He pulled her up to him, opening her mouth, tasting her laughter, her excitement.

Her lips parted his, her tongue a point of spice, her mouth moving on his. Tamsin curved against him, her breasts in the thin tie-dyed shirt she'd borrowed from Dante's mate squeezing against his chest. He could feel the tight points of her nipples, a sign of how much she wanted him.

Angus resisted lowering his hand to cup her backside, something in him remembering they stood among thousands, including his son. His cock didn't want to listen to caution, however, hardening in desire, the like of which he hadn't felt for a very long time.

Fine with him. The world had stopped, letting him deepen the kiss, no rush. Her skin was smooth, a joy to touch, a contrast to his bristles and roughness.

Their lips and teeth bumped, the kiss a little clumsy, but for the first time in many years, Angus felt strain fall away and lightness take its place. Nothing mattered but Tamsin in his arms and her kiss, the touch of his son's body against his calves telling him Ciaran was still with him, and safe.

A human boy whooped. A woman yelled jovially, "Get a room!"

The real world swirled back with all its colors and sounds, but somehow the harshness had gone, the colors had brightened, and the sounds had become music.

Angus was still kissing Tamsin when Ciaran shouted to the crowd, "She said yes! She said yes!"

More whoops, cheers, advice for Angus to run for it, for Tamsin to as well. Applause and laughter.

Tamsin eased out of the kiss. She remained in Angus's arms, her warmth threatening to break him, and brushed moisture from her lips with her fingertips. When Angus gazed down at her, never wanting to look away, she wrinkled her nose in good humor.

A loudspeaker switched on, and Dante's voice blared out. "We have a lost kid, folks. Look around for Natalie, wearing a red top and a black skirt. She's nine and has brown hair in braids, brown eyes. Last seen over by the Amazing Louis show—he's the guy with the three heads. If you find Natalie, please bring her to the office located on the west side of the park. Natalie, your mom says to come find her—she's worried and she won't be mad."

"Yes, she will," Ciaran said as the loudspeaker switched off and everyone looked around to see if a girl with a red shirt was nearby. "My dad's always seriously mad when he can't find me. He yells as me when I get home."

"It's what worried people do," Tamsin said. "Come on. I can find her. Just need to talk to her mom first."

She picked up her hat and headed for the west side of the park at a run, Ciaran two steps behind her. Angus growled in his throat and took off after them.

The mother wasn't worried—she was panic-stricken.

Tamsin found the office, a small trailer that belonged to the fairgrounds, which Dante had taken over for the carnival's short stay.

A sign proclaiming *Lost and Found* reposed over a table holding a jumble of items—plastic toys, dog leashes, cheap jewelry.

Dante, in his colorful coat, tried to comfort Natalie's mother and father, who were scared and trying not to show it. Natalie's mother blinked back tears to thank a girl of about eleven who carried a cup of coffee to her.

The girl who brought the coffee had honey-blond hair and the dark eyes and fine bones of Celene but the limberness of Dante. *One-quarter Fae and one-half Shifter,* Tamsin mused. *That must make for an interesting combination. Bet she's amazing.*

"What can I do for you?" Dante began as Tamsin strode in, but Tamsin ignored him and went straight to Natalie's mother.

"I'll find her, don't you worry," Tamsin said, crouching down next to her. "Sit here and drink Dante's coffee, and I'll have Natalie back in a jiffy."

While Tamsin kept up her cheery chatter, she inhaled

scents—soap, sweat, warm clothes, and terror. Somewhere in there would be Natalie, and Natalie would have her parents' scents all over her as well.

Tamsin turned away and headed out the door, nearly falling over Angus, who waited with Ciaran on the step outside.

"Low profile," he admonished her as they walked away.

"I'll be so low profile no one will even see me," Tamsin said. "I can find Natalie. I'm good at scents. The less time her parents have to fret, the better. And if some sick bastard took her, I'll know that too. And then *you* can kick his ass." She grinned up at him. "See? We already make a great team. I just need somewhere private to shift."

"I want to go with you," Ciaran announced.

For once, Tamsin was the one who said no. "I'll move too fast, and I won't be able to wait for you. Why don't you stay and get to know Dante's daughter better? She's cute."

Ciaran scowled. "I can keep up. Promise."

"We'll both follow you," Angus said firmly. "Natalie might be less scared if she sees a boy her own age."

"As if *I* can be scary," Tamsin said loftily, but she acquiesced.

The carnival was a different place once Tamsin was a fox and darting around the fringes of it. Scents came to her in layers upon layers—the fatty smell of hot dogs, the bite of mustard and relish, the sharp sweetness of cotton candy. Mud, spilled soda, candy wrappers brushed with melted chocolate, the dank odor from the porta-potties. Sweat, fear, excitement, frustration, anger, happiness, hope, desire.

Every emotion had a scent, a body giving off more or less of it as people wound through the gamut of their feelings.

Somewhere in this swirling wilderness of smells was one small child. Was the girl afraid and alone? Gleefully evading her parents? Or taken by someone and terrified?

If she'd been taken, Tamsin wouldn't stop until she tracked them down, and then she'd rip open whoever had nabbed the girl. She'd said she'd let Angus do that, but

Tamsin knew that if she came across a child abductor, she wouldn't be able to hold back.

Angus walked nearby, though not too close to her, with Ciaran. Angus said he'd keep her in sight, and probably scent-sight too, as wolves were fantastic trackers, even in human form. Tamsin had deduced that about Angus the moment she'd laid eyes on him across the room in the plantation house while she'd won at poker.

Angus had chased and caught her, and now Tamsin would be his mate. She called that expert tracking.

Dante's security was searching the grounds, but they hadn't found anything so far. Tamsin shifted behind the porta-potties, alone, with Angus to stand watch, then slipped through brush, wandering around the edges of the fairgrounds. The brush had plenty of thorns that stuck in her fur. She resisted stopping to bite them out, but they drove her crazy.

Dante seemed like a good guy, but Tamsin had seen his watchfulness. Was he a plant—a Collarless Shifter working for Shifter Bureau or Haider? She wouldn't put it past them to recruit or coerce Shifters to assist them. Look what Haider had done to Angus.

Dante didn't smell duplicitous, but he might become very interested in Tamsin if he found out how unusual she was. He was an opportunist, she sensed, which would explain how he'd escaped detection all these years.

A whiff of fear kicked her out of her contemplation, and Tamsin swerved to follow it.

The trail led her out of the grounds and over a rise covered with dust and weeds. More stickers in her fur.

Tamsin continued to scent fear, isolated from the smells of the fairgrounds, but she couldn't find a source. She sat on her haunches on the rise, gazing back over the mass of tents and spinning rides, and at Angus and Ciaran, both in human form, skulking around in the weeds along the property's boundaries.

Her fur bristled as the scent burst to her, stronger than ever. Fear had turned to panic.

Without a word, Tamsin turned and hurried along the small ridge, following it lengthwise. She'd thought it a raised bit of earth to mark the end of a farmer's land, but she realized as she reached the end that it had another function.

Tamsin nearly dropped off an abrupt ledge, unable to see where the rise ceased. She lowered herself to the ground and carefully peered over.

A culvert opened beneath her, its round shape held in place by rusting corrugated metal. The bottom of the culvert held water, about an inch of it, smelling musty and stagnant. A large snake slid its way along it, heading for a child folded up inside. The child whimpered, too terrified to make another sound.

If there was an animal Tamsin feared, it was snakes. Well, and gators. Larger Shifters could scoff about snakes, but a small animal could be killed by the bite of a rattler. Eaten too. Swallowed whole.

Yuck. Stuff of nightmares.

Tamsin didn't have time to wait for Angus, who could kick the snake aside and barely notice. She darted forward, her heart pounding, praying her swiftness would be her best weapon.

She splashed through water, and the girl's head came up, her gasp echoing through the culvert. The snake didn't care—it slithered on. Whether it thought the girl was food, it was just passing through, or it homed in on a warm heartbeat in the darkness, Tamsin couldn't know.

Didn't matter now. Tamsin leapt, bounced off the sloping metal wall with all four paws, and landed on the snake's back.

CHAPTER SEVENTEEN

The snake whipped around, mouth open, striking, but Tamsin was no longer there. She jumped like a cat, straight up, then five feet backward, and scrambled away when she landed.

The snake now homed in on *her*—maybe she was a tastier target in its little snaky opinion. It sped toward her, and Tamsin turned and ran like hell.

She saw the pair of blue-jeaned legs at the end of the culvert too late to swerve. The owner of the legs roared, "Shit!" and Tamsin went right between them and out into the desert.

She kept running, shivering, needing to flee.

"Tamsin!"

Only Angus's full bellow could have stopped her. Tamsin turned, sides heaving, and looked back.

He had the snake in his hand. The reptile dangled from Angus's grasp, Angus clutching it by the head. The snake was still alive, wrapping its diamond-patterned, sinuous body around his arm.

"There are probably more snakes out there." Angus swept his free hand to indicate the direction she'd been running.

Crap, crap, he was right. Tamsin now saw little holes in the dirt around her, perfect for gophers—or snakes.

She spun on her back legs and charged toward the culvert. Angus, meanwhile, walked a long way out into the brush, where he, the traitor, let the snake go.

Ciaran had crouched down to peer into the culvert. "Are you Natalie?" he asked in a calm voice. "I can take you to your mom and dad. They're looking for you."

Natalie said something Tamsin couldn't hear. Tamsin was too busy running in circles, trying to get over the creeps of her brief battle with the snake.

As Angus walked to her, she shifted to human. "I hate snakes." She kept spinning around, stamping her feet, then jumping when she came down on stickers. "Hate them, hate them. Wait—I hate gators too. Okay, I hate *all* reptiles."

Angus put his hands on her shoulders and stopped her spinning. Tamsin looked up at the widest smile she'd ever seen on him.

She stopped, transfixed. Angus's eyes were dancing, his teeth showing in his grin, and then he laughed.

Tamsin stopped. She'd never heard him laugh before. The laughter came from deep inside him, rich and strong.

Worth it, maybe, to go through that little bit of hell to see this?

No. Nothing was worth snakes. "It isn't funny, damn it."

"You are." Angus dragged Tamsin into his arms, lifting her from the sharp rocks and thorns of the desert floor. "My brave, bold mate. You found her, sweetheart. You found her."

Hanging in Angus's arms, happy with her, was not a bad place to be. The warm friction of his clothes on her bare skin made her want to cling to him, maybe rub against him. Kissing him sounded like a good idea too.

Angus's eyes darkened, his skin flushing. His wanting came to her in waves, engulfing Tamsin and making her shivery with need. She knew in that moment she'd been yearning for Angus since she'd met him. She'd run from him, but she'd been watching him, following the lines of his body, doing anything to look into his eyes, his strong face, to feel his hands on her skin. She'd be lying to herself if she denied it.

The sound of children's voices drifted to them. Angus gave Tamsin a long look, then very carefully set her down.

Tamsin gave him a brief kiss on the mouth and looked over his shoulder as Ciaran emerged from the culvert, leading young Natalie by the hand.

Natalie stood close to Ciaran, giving him a look like she was Princess Buttercup and her Westley had just rescued her.

She then gazed at Angus and Tamsin, who hid herself behind Angus's broad body.

"Ciaran, why is that lady naked?" she asked in a small voice.

"None of us know," Ciaran answered gravely.

Natalie was restored to her family at the office, to everyone's relief. Her parents gushed over the little girl, hugging and asking her what happened, asking Tamsin—dressed again—how they'd found her. Ciaran generously volunteered Tamsin's part in the search, saying how good she was, but he of course didn't mention Shifters or foxes.

Natalie explained she'd been following a rabbit out into the field and then found herself lost. Hot, she'd gone inside the culvert to cool off. A snake had been crawling toward her, but a fox had attacked it, drawing it away, and then the fox had run off, and Ciaran had come to rescue her.

Natalie's mother listened to the explanation without much comprehension in her eyes, then she began to scold Natalie for not sticking close by, and then she began to cry, to Natalie's bewilderment. Natalie's dad ushered them out to take them home, Dante returning the entrance fee they'd paid.

Natalie gave Ciaran a longing look as she left, but he only waved cheerfully as he, Angus, Dante, and Tamsin walked them to the entrance.

"I told you her mom would yell at her," Ciaran said after the family moved toward their car, holding tight to one another. "Just like my dad."

"All's well that ends well." Tamsin gave Natalie one last wave. "That's what my mom used to say."

The last words choked her, and she turned away so Angus wouldn't see the sudden tears that flooded her eyes.

She found Dante giving her a watchful look. Dante had been impressed with Tamsin's and Ciaran's stories, praising Ciaran for his part in the rescue, but he knew they'd held information back.

Tamsin returned his look neutrally. Was Dante curious for curiosity's sake? Or for a more sinister reason? How *had* Dante escaped detection all this time?

"You're right," Dante said, softening his gaze. "It ended well. I don't like when cubs get lost. Thanks, Tamsin. You too, Ciaran."

He said nothing about Angus, but Tamsin sensed Angus didn't mind. He wasn't a Shifter who sought the limelight. He didn't have much of an ego, though he did possess deepseated convictions about his strength and ability, convictions he didn't slop onto everyone around him.

Angus, she decided, was a Nice Guy. A hot, sexy Nice Guy. Maybe that was why she'd said yes to the mate-claim.

Tamsin was still puzzling over the impulse that had made her yell her acceptance. Perhaps the Shifter in her had known it was *right*.

"Why don't you kids knock off for the day?" Dante said to Tamsin. "Celene fixed up a trailer for you to use so you won't have to sleep in your truck. It has a bathroom. With a shower." He gave Tamsin a nod, knowing she couldn't refuse.

"Thanks, Dante," Tamsin said cheerily. "You're a brick. Point us to it."

Celene came out to join Tamsin and lead her and Ciaran to the trailer. Behind her, Tamsin heard Dante speaking in a low voice to Angus.

"Celene and I can look after Ciaran for a while," Dante was saying. "You know, if you and Tamsin want to . . ."

He left the words hanging, but Tamsin knew exactly what he meant. Mating frenzy swirled inside her, making her want to take Angus out into the field beyond the fairgrounds, throw him to the ground, and satisfy her urges on him, never mind about all the stickers and the snakes.

"No," Angus said, to both Tamsin's relief and disappointment. "Ciaran stays with us."

Tamsin knew he didn't trust Dante enough yet to leave his cub in the bear-man's care, which Tamsin agreed with. Worry for cubs trumped mating frenzy.

"If you change your mind . . ." Tamsin glanced back to see Dante clap his feathered hat onto his head. "Don't let mating frenzy kill you, Angus. Give in. Give in."

He shot a grin at Tamsin, knowing she'd heard every word, then walked back to his carnival, calling out to people as he went.

Celene slid her arm through Tamsin's. "You'll have time alone soon enough," she said. "All Dante thinks about is mating frenzy."

"You're an interesting couple, aren't you?" Tamsin said. "A bear Shifter and a half Fae. How did that happen?"

"Long story." Celene smiled, her face one of the most beautiful Tamsin had seen. Tamsin thought her own face was too pointed, too full of nose and eyes, but Celene's had perfect proportions.

"I'm a very curious person, so you'll have to tell me someday," Tamsin said. "What did you mean when you said we'd have time alone soon enough?" She had suspicions in bucketfuls, just like Angus.

"Hmm? Oh, I meant we'll be on the move tomorrow, and if you come with us, you and Angus will probably have time alone sooner or later. *Are* you coming with us? We'd love to have you."

"Yes," Tamsin said without hesitation. "Of course we are." Angus didn't know it yet, but . . .

"Just a warning. If you travel with us, you have to work. Dante will hire you if you want jobs, but at the very least, you'll have to help out in some way. We can't afford too much hospitality."

"Absolutely. We'll earn our keep. I was thinking of an act to do as a sideshow. It will be hilarious."

Celene raised her brows. "Does Angus know about this?"

"Not exactly. Not yet."

Celene laughed, and even that was beautiful. "That's how you deal with Shifters. Keep them guessing, so they don't come over all dominant and growling. Oh, no offense."

"None taken. You're totally right. Are you sure you're part Fae? You're too nice."

"I'm supposed to want to see all Shifters in Collars and cages, and I pull wings off flies too, right?" Wisdom lurked in Celene's eyes. Tamsin wondered how old she was. Fae lived a long time—did half Fae?

"The Goddess's honest truth is I've never met a Fae," Tamsin said. "I've only heard the rumors."

"Some Fae are wonderful, some are terrible. Like Shifters. And humans. My mother was Fae, my dad human. I spent some of my childhood in Faerie, some here. My mom had a hard time in the human world, so finally she stayed in Faerie. My dad lived out his human life span and passed about ten years ago."

"I'm sorry," Tamsin said quickly. "My dad's gone too."

Celene nodded. "It's tough. But I met Dante, and he filled up the empty spaces, you know what I mean?"

Filling up the empty spaces made sense. Angus was rapidly doing that with Tamsin, without her realizing it.

Angus reached them. Celene gave Tamsin a broad smile and, to her surprise, pulled her into a hug, Shifter-style.

Tamsin realized with a start that hugging a Fae, her traditional enemy, wasn't so bad. Celene's slim arms were strong, comforting, her scent now familiar, *hers*. Celene released her, leaned down to kiss Ciaran on the top of his head, and left them.

The "trailer" they'd been lent was in reality a large, sleek RV. Tamsin had expected a pickup with a camper shell or a rickety mobile home, but this was an older but well-cared-for camper trailer, the kind people drove cross-country in, living their vacation.

Benches lined the walls just inside the door. Halfway along was a booth with a table and two wide seats across from a tiny kitchen with a sink, stove, a very small refrigerator, and cupboards. Beyond that was a closet, above which was a curtained bunk bed. The bathroom was tucked across from the bunk bed and closet, and did indeed have a shower. In the very back, taking up the rear five feet of the RV, was the master bedroom, which consisted of a large mattress on a platform.

"Nice!" Ciaran instantly climbed up to the bunk bed and pulled the curtains closed. "This is my room."

That left Angus and Tamsin standing in the middle of the RV, looking at everything but each other.

"Awkward," Tamsin said at last.

A flush rose on Angus's face. "You take the bed. I'll get our things from the truck, then go patrolling. I'll sleep there tonight." He pointed at one of the forward benches.

Tamsin reached up and touched his hot cheek. "You know, I've never met a Shifter who blushes about mating frenzy. I like it."

"Patrolling," Angus said. "I'm blushing about patrolling. But I need to do it. Too many risk factors out here."

Tamsin brushed his cheek again, liking the feel of his whiskers under her fingertips. "I don't know. I've felt safer here than anywhere in a long while. I think Dante is all right. Weird, but okay."

"We don't know anything about him," Angus said. "The less we tell him, the better. I'm grateful for his help, but we can't know what he means to do. We'll be out of here tomorrow anyway."

"Um," Tamsin said, lowering her hand. "About that . . ."

Angus's eyes narrowed. "What?"

"I kind of told Celene we'd be traveling on with them. I have this great idea for a show . . ."

"Tamsin."

"Think about it—we're buried in a crowd here. We'll blend in with all their trucks and trailers when we go. We'll be just more anonymous people with the carny. But Celene says Dante will want us to earn our keep, so I'm working up a show idea."

"No shows." Angus stepped closer, irritation wiping away his embarrassment. "The last thing we need is someone telling their friends that there's a beautiful redheaded Shifter woman doing a carnival sideshow. What were you planning? A fox hunt?"

Tamsin stared at him, lips parting. "Did you say 'beautiful'?"

"Yes." The answer was impatient. "Memorable. No one could forget you, Tamsin."

Words stuck in her throat. *That's the most wonderful thing anyone's ever said to me.*

Why couldn't she say that? Smile at him? Make him blush again?

Because it was too important. Tamsin got through her life waving her emotions aside, teasing to cover up her hurt and fears.

What she felt for Angus was too strong to be pushed aside. Joked about. Shrugged away.

Angus obviously saw nothing extraordinary in what he'd said. The man only made blunt statements, no flirtations, seductions, or floweriness. He would only ever speak the truth as he saw it.

Tamsin's heart beat faster, and her world changed.

Ciaran stuck his head out from between the curtains. "If you need to work out the mating frenzy, it's all right. Brina—Dante and Celene's cub—invited me over tonight to play video games." He slid his legs around, preparing to descend.

Angus's face went brick red. "*No*. You stay here with Tamsin. I'm going patrolling."

Without another word, just a glare at his son, Angus swung around and stomped out the door.

At least he didn't slam it. Tamsin pulled it closed after him and locked it.

Ciaran stared down at her from his bunk. "What did I say?"

Tamsin let out a long breath. "Nothing, sweetie." She went to him, rose on tiptoe, and gave him a tight hug. "You're perfect. Don't worry about your dad. He's a growly thing."

"Yeah." Ciaran clung to Tamsin a long moment, his warm, small body relaxing her worries. "I'm glad you're staying, Tamsin. Can I start calling you 'Mom'?"

Tamsin released Ciaran and grabbed the side of his bunk to hold herself up. "Sure, if you want."

Ciaran grinned, leaned down, and kissed her forehead, then squirmed around with the quickness of a wolf cub and jerked the curtains closed.

"Night, Mom!" he sang out.

Tamsin's eyes flooded with tears. "Night, Ciaran."

* * *

Monday, Dante's workers tore down the carnival, and Angus drove the RV in the long convoy of trucks and trailers moving from San Angelo to the next gig Dante had booked at the end of the week. They'd drive Monday afternoon, spend the night in a motel, and enter the fairgrounds on Tuesday to start setting up.

Dimitri's truck cab was now fully covered with bright red, white, and blue logos for the carnival, and was busy pulling one of the booths. Angus hadn't recognized the cab when he'd emerged after sleeping a few hours in the RV on one of the hard benches. He'd only seen it gone and demanded to know what Dante had done with it.

Dante had grinned and pointed it out. Dimitri would shit a brick when he saw the fiery curlicues and big letters all over it—whether it was painted or the logos and decorations merely stuck on, Angus couldn't tell. But the truck was well camouflaged, and Angus would make it up to Dimitri if he ever got the chance.

At the moment, Angus was with his cub and his mate, and that was fine with him. Ciaran rode buckled onto one of the benches—Angus wouldn't let him lie in his bunk the whole way as he wanted to.

They kept up a sedate pace. Travelers in cars honked and waved as they passed the carnival in their brightly painted trailers, the rides on flatbed trucks. They ignored Angus, their RV being fairly ordinary. Tamsin was right—they were hidden in a crowd.

Angus had lent his muscles helping dismantle the rides and booths, most of which were already on wheels. Each booth's sides folded up, and the whole thing was hitched to a semi, like Dimitri's. Whatever Tamsin had been busy doing, Angus didn't know, but she'd kept Ciaran with her and watched his son with a careful eye.

Ciaran had ceased calling her *Tamsin* and now called

her *Mom*. Angus hadn't yet figured out how he felt about that.

As she had in Dimitri's truck, Tamsin fiddled with the RV's radio until she found a station she liked, and she and Ciaran began singing. Her voice blended with Ciaran's, neither of them knowing crap about staying in tune, and brightened the air. Maybe, Angus thought, just maybe, things would be all right.

Angus held on to that shred of hope through the trip down Texas highways. He saw no sign of Shifter Bureau, or Haider, or Dylan, or of any Shifter but Dante.

No sign of Shifters didn't mean they weren't out there. The best trackers were good at staying hidden while they stalked.

But it was easy to get caught up in the carnival's routine. They pulled into a chain motel with an RV park to spend Monday night. The crew enjoyed a night of beds inside four walls and then Tuesday they pulled up to a field outside Wichita Falls, in north Texas, that would house the carnival this weekend. They rested for the remainder of the day, and on Wednesday morning, they started to set up.

While Angus helped with the rides, Tamsin worked on her "act." She and Angus argued every day that she would be putting herself at risk, but she insisted no one would recognize her. When he tried to forbid her as her mate, Tamsin only looked at him doubtfully and walked away to meet up with Celene.

Angus shook his head and got back to work. He'd let her think she was getting away with it for now. When the night came for her show to start, he could lock her in the RV and let her rage at him.

On Thursday evening, they tested the rides to make sure none needed repair or were unsafe in any way. Dante insisted on several tests—if he wasn't happy, the ride didn't run.

"People have gotten seriously hurt or killed on park

rides," Dante had told Angus. "Not often, but never in *my* carnival."

Ciaran had hit it off with Brina, it seemed, and Dante had even let his cub ride with Angus for a leg of the trip. Ciaran and Brina had played games on Brina's tablet the whole time. Growing up without Shifter Bureau restrictions, Brina had gadgets that Ciaran wasn't allowed.

Now the two were strolling around the grounds. Grass grew in the fields beyond the fence, much more green here than in San Angelo, but the grounds themselves were bare dirt.

Angus kept his eye on the cubs as he went to help the woman who owned the Zipper ride lock down bolts and test cages. This ride had scared the shit out of him, and he wanted to make sure there was no way it could hurt anyone crazy enough to get on it.

He heard an abrupt shout. Angus jerked up from tightening a screw, his hackles rising, scenting danger.

The ride that was essentially a giant swing shaped like a pirate ship teetered. The hydraulic lift that raised it from the truck bed had jammed, the sudden halt slamming and rattling the ride's supports.

The swing jarred loose from its mooring and swung out on its smooth axle, knocking down the barriers too hastily set in place around it and heading straight for Ciaran and Brina.

CHAPTER EIGHTEEN

Angus heard Tamsin scream. He sprinted hard across the dusty earth, his focus on Ciaran and the hard end of the swing heading right for him.

If the ride had been at its requisite height as it was when fully set up, the swing would glide right over the two cubs. But now, it would slam into them, and it was heavy, and fast.

Angus was too far away. He saw a streak of red . . . Tamsin. But she was also too far to make it in time.

Dante came out of nowhere. He sprinted at the cubs, catching one in each arm and rolling hard across the ground. The swing sliced over the grass, spurting up dirt, before the frantic operators got the big ship braked.

Dante effortlessly gained his feet, still holding the cubs. He set Ciaran down and rested a hand on his shoulder, making sure he was steady. Then he hugged Brina hard against him.

"We're okay, Daddy," Angus heard her say as he reached Ciaran and grabbed his son into his arms. "You can let me go now."

Dante hugged Brina again and kissed her cheek. "I know, sweetie. Daddy's just worried."

He set her on her feet, and Brina brushed herself off, unconcerned that she'd narrowly escaped being mowed down, possibly fatally hurt.

Angus saw Dante's face as Brina calmly patted dirt from her shorts. It was a look Angus had felt often on his own face, one of complete love and also terrible fear. If anything happened to Brina, Dante would break apart, just as Angus would do over Ciaran. The time he'd lived through when April had taken Ciaran from him had been the hardest of his life.

Ciaran, sharing Brina's equanimity, squirmed to get down. Angus released him, taking a step back as Ciaran rushed to rejoin Brina.

"Thank you," Angus said to Dante, his heart in his words.

"Yeah." Dante, today wearing a more ordinary-looking outfit of jeans and a T-shirt, blew out his breath. "That was close. I need a beer. But first . . ."

He turned around and started for the ride operators, yelling invectives at them.

The red ball of fur that was Tamsin peeked out from behind the office trailer. She waited until all eyes were on Dante cussing out the ride operators and then she darted through the half-open door. She emerged a few moments later, fully dressed, but her face, when she and Angus locked gazes across the open space, held both worry and relief.

The pirate ship was taken away and stowed, and Dante ordered it not to be used until the lift mechanism was fixed.

Angus kept a sharper eye on Ciaran all day, but no more incidents occurred. His respect for Dante rose, as did his gratitude. Dante could have saved his own cub and let Ciaran look after himself. That happened sometimes in the wild, and Dante had never known the touch of a Collar.

Later that evening, Angus bought Dante a beer and they drank quietly together, sitting out under the stars.

As the park darkened on Friday, and the citizens of Wichita Falls, a larger town than San Angelo, came to find entertainment, Tamsin vanished, and Ciaran with her. Angus prowled about looking for them, growling under his breath, until he came to a large tent with a long queue outside it. The sign in front proclaimed "Madame Butterfly and Her Dancing Wolf."

Angus tamped down his fury as he pushed through the crowd and bullied the ticket taker into letting him by. The rest of the audience flowed in around him, taking their seats. Angus didn't bother with a seat, reaching the backstage area just as a woman came dashing onstage from the other side.

Her red hair was nowhere in evidence. She had tucked her real hair under a short blue-black wig, her face hidden by a large mask in the shape of a butterfly. The tip of her nose and her lips were the only things visible.

The rest of the costume was a skintight bodysuit, shining pink and glittering with silver sequins in the form of butterflies. The light bouncing from the silver disguised her height and even her build somewhat—difficult to fix on her with all the blinding sparkles.

Madame Butterfly ran around the small area, arms spread to welcome the guests, who cheered. On her second circuit, she grabbed two large rings from someone on the other side of the stage. The rings were about three feet in diameter, and as sparkly as her costume. She held them out in front of her, spacing them about four feet apart.

From the wings shot a small black animal with pointed ears, black nose, and large feet that covered ground fast. Angus's heart skipped a beat—he'd know that little furry body anywhere.

The crowd made a collective *Aw* sound. Ciaran ran once around Madame Butterfly, then soared through the rings and landed without a stumble.

The audience applauded. Madame Butterfly and the

wolf moved around the stage area, with her holding the rings at varying heights or closer to or farther from each other. When she started throwing and catching the rings with perfect juggler's ease, Angus's breath caught. Caught again when Ciaran leapt through the rings, timing himself exactly right to go through without a hitch.

Angus exhaled when Ciaran landed, a smug look on his wolf face. The crowd loved him, cheering, clapping, and whistling.

Madame Butterfly brought out other obstacles from the wings—hollow tubes Ciaran could run through or jump on, balls she and Ciaran bounced to each other. The audience couldn't get enough of the cute and clever little dog.

Two lanky men ran out from the wings and quickly set up a sort of balance beam consisting of a very, very thin round bar that hung about three feet off the ground.

Angus nearly stormed out and grabbed Ciaran before he could jump up on the contraption, but Ciaran merely ran under it while Madame Butterfly jumped lightly to the bar and started to walk across it. She moved with amazing agility, as though she barely noted how narrow the bar was.

Angus's lips parted as he watched. He knew Tamsin was as light-footed as her fox, but he never dreamed she could balance like that—

"Enjoying the show?"

"Shit!" Angus's bellow was drowned out by the crowd's enthusiasm as Ciaran began leaping through hoops the balancing Madame Butterfly held up.

Angus swung around to find Tamsin next to him, in dark jeans and black shirt, her hair in a braid, a dark baseball cap on her head. He stared at her, jerked his attention to the act onstage, and swiveled back to her.

"Tamsin, what the fuck? I thought that was *you*." He pointed accusingly at Madame Butterfly.

Tamsin gazed at the glittering woman, feigning surprise. "Me? No, that's Celene. She's far more graceful than

I could ever be. She's done this kind of thing before, and thought it was a great idea. That's how she and Dante met. She used to be a tightrope walker."

"Son of a bitch, Tamsin."

Celene danced lightly along the bar, juggling hoops, which Ciaran leapt through, back and forth.

Tamsin laced her arm through his. "You didn't think I would actually perform, did you? Someone might recognize me, even dressed up. Everyone knows Celene. And they think Ciaran's a dog."

Angus's heart thumped. His rage surged, though he didn't know why he should be angry. Tamsin had done the smart thing and not exposed herself.

No, he did know. She was a shit. She'd deliberately let him worry that she was doing something stupid when she'd planned all along to work behind the scenes.

Tamsin's grin told him she knew exactly what thoughts spun in his head.

"How is this earning your keep?" he demanded. "Or are you hiring out Ciaran, like he really is an animal?"

She looked indignant. "I'd never do that. No, I'm their trainer."

"Shit, Tamsin."

Tamsin's musical laughter filled him with warmth. Her heat as she pulled herself closer threatened to burn him up.

The audience loved Ciaran. They oohed and aahed as Ciaran leapt and spun, laughed when he ran in circles, his tail wagging. At last, Celene jumped down from the balance bar, held out her arms, and caught Ciaran as he leapt into them.

Everyone cheered and applauded as Celene let Ciaran spring down. They did a lap together and then ran off into the shadows.

The lights on the stage lowered, and loud music came on, encouraging the audience to leave their seats. They went, talking excitedly about the show.

Angus strode behind the curtain to the other side of the wings. Ciaran was already in boy form, pulling on a pair of sweatpants. He was out of breath, flushed, and starry-eyed.

He leapt to his feet as Angus approached. "Did you see me, Dad? Did you like it?"

Celene had removed her butterfly mask. Close up, Angus saw that while she had the same height as Tamsin, her build was much slenderer, since she had the long, thin bones of the Fae.

"He's a natural." Celene beamed at Ciaran. "Don't be angry, Angus. I did say we should ask you first, but Tamsin assured me it would be all right."

"Oh, I know exactly who to blame." Angus drew a breath, ready to send Ciaran home and forbid him to perform again. Ciaran caught his look, and all the joy went out of him. His head drooped, and he looked away quickly so Angus wouldn't see the tears in his eyes.

This was special to him, Angus realized. Ciaran really had done well—he was agile and strong, and grew more so every day.

Angus let out the breath in a conceding sigh. "All right, Ciaran, as long as you don't do too many shows and are in bed before ten. And it's not forever. Just for now—all right?"

Ciaran brightened, then looked downcast, then brightened again. "Only two shows a night, Dad. And they're short. But it's easy for me. All I have to do is jump around like I always do. Celene holds the rings so I make it every time. She's really good at it."

"Nothing too difficult or too risky," Angus said, trying to sound like a stern parent.

"Don't worry—we rehearsed this," Tamsin said. "Celene knows what she's doing. Ciaran's safety is the most important thing."

"It had better be." Angus scowled. "I'll be right here every show to make sure."

"Good." Tamsin took his arm again. "I'll be right beside you."

Ciaran and Celene performed one more time, to another admiring audience. As Angus and Tamsin left the tent with Ciaran, who'd shifted and dressed, Ciaran asked, "Can I spend the night with Brina? *Please?* She wants to show me more of her games. Dante and Celene will be right there."

Angus gave him a frown, but he didn't dismiss the request out of hand. He knew the cubs really were interested in nothing but games at their age—Shifters had no yearnings for the opposite sex until their Transition, which wouldn't happen for either cub for another eighteen or so years. Dante was proving he could look out for Ciaran, but Angus still had a hard time letting himself trust.

"You can go for a while," Angus said. "But then I'm coming over to take you home. You'll sleep with us."

Ciaran's eyes lit up. "Sweet! Good enough."

He wanted to run off then and there, but he waited for Celene, in her regular clothes now, to join them, take his hand, and lead him away.

Tamsin walked back to the RV with Angus. The carnival was going strong—it was still a few hours until closing. The midway flashed, screams from the rides ebbing and flowing in the breeze. People strolled through the aisles, buying food and souvenirs, kids laughing as they darted toward their favorite rides, adults just as noisy as they enjoyed being kid-like again.

Tamsin gave an exaggerated yawn and sagged against Angus. "I'm beat. All this training and worrying about the performances has worn me out. Being a stage mom is exhausting."

"Go to bed, then." Angus untwined her arm from his but kept hold of her hand. "I'm going to prowl around a little, check the perimeter."

Tamsin's brows drew together, but then she smoothed

her expression, slid her hand from his, said good night, and jogged away, her braid bouncing on her back.

Angus waited until he watched Tamsin go inside the trailer, then he moved to the darkness of the field beyond, undressed, and shifted to wolf. He made a round or two of the entire fairgrounds, keeping eyes, ears, and nose out for enemies.

He saw, heard, and smelled nothing but humans thronging the night. No other Shifters except Dante. No furtive Shifter Bureau agents trying to blend in. Humans who didn't belong gave off a nervous scent, and Angus smelled nothing like that.

He returned to his clothes, shifted, dressed, and made his way to the RV.

Tamsin, instead of being in bed asleep, despite her claims of tiredness, was washing out the few dishes they'd used at lunch. She glanced over her shoulder at Angus as he came in and locked the door behind him, before drying the plates and stacking them in the cupboard above her.

"All quiet?" she asked.

"All noisy as hell," Angus said. "But no one's after us for now."

"Good."

Angus took the last dried plate from her and slid it into the cupboard.

He looked down at Tamsin, who stood inches from him. If he lowered his arm, he could enclose her with it.

His mating frenzy, and Tamsin's, realized at that moment that the two of them were, for the first time in a long time, completely alone.

Angus reached behind him and snapped off the light and then bunched the front of Tamsin's T-shirt in his big hand and yanked her against him for a kiss.

CHAPTER NINETEEN

Tamsin crashed against Angus's chest as he curved down to her. She rose to meet his kiss, which was hard and hot and tasted of hunger.

She opened her mouth for his, his tongue brushing heat inside her.

This kiss was different, demanding, wanting. Before, Angus had kissed with warmth and longing, but at this moment, he was a Shifter, with all veneer of human stripped away, a Shifter giving in to a primal need for his mate.

Angus dragged Tamsin's shirt upward, his fingers strong. Tamsin helped him, wriggling her arms out of the sleeves, her mouth holding his until she had to lift the shirt off over her head.

Cool air touched her skin, her bra a black slash against her paleness. She clutched Angus's T-shirt with the same frantic impatience he had hers, wanting him bare.

Angus backed a step so Tamsin could yank his shirt off him. His torso was hard with muscle, brushed with wiry black hair. She'd seen his full body when they'd shifted back and forth in the bayous, and when she peeked at him while he'd dressed or undressed in the trailer, and she'd enjoyed every second. Now she let her hands cup his waist, feeling his strength. She traced the muscles of his chest, running her thumbs across his flat nipples.

Angus growled low in his throat. The next thing Tamsin knew, she was being lifted against the side of the cabinet, his body holding her in place while his mouth came down on hers once more.

She clung to him, fingers skimming his back, bringing one foot up to encircle his legs.

Angus lifted his head, his breath coming fast. His face was flushed, gray eyes glittering. "I'll give you a chance to run."

Tamsin's heartbeat sped, her pulse throbbing in every fingertip. "Will you chase me?" she whispered in hope.

Heat flared in his eyes, his predator's need focusing on her. "No."

"Well, then, I'll stay here." Tamsin tightened her arms around him, pulling him down for more kissing.

Angus resisted, tension in every muscle. "I don't know if I can be careful, Tamsin. I've been going insane staying away from you."

The words only fueled her excitement. "It hasn't been much good for my sanity either."

"You can say no." His voice held the guttural rasp of his wolf, the words barely coming out. "You can go. Refuse me. We're not mates yet."

Tamsin gently drew him back to her. "Yes, we are."

His eyes went incandescent. The kiss he covered her mouth with was incandescent too, fire burning all the way down Tamsin's body.

She heard a rip, and then her bra was gone, flown who knew where. No cloth now existed between her chest and his, and her nipples grew tight as his body warmed them.

Angus kissed her, bending her head back until it rested against the cabinet, his hard hand sliding into her jeans, cupping her backside.

Two could play at that game. Tamsin thrust her fingers between them and loosened his belt, and then slithered her hands under his waistband, finding his underwear and the sleek, hot skin beneath it. No going commando for Angus. She imagined he'd stare at her if she suggested it, telling her he'd only get chafed if he left off his underwear.

His smooth buttocks were worth the effort to get to. Angus closed himself off to most people—the fact that he'd let her into his intimate world made Tamsin feel glorious.

He brushed his hand over her hip inside her jeans, the button that held them closed straining. It popped as Angus brought his fingers around to her front, and the zipper opened swiftly.

Tamsin didn't go commando either. Her black satin underwear let Angus's fingers slide easily over her, until he touched her heat through the silky fabric.

Tamsin sucked in a breath, breaking the kiss, her eyes widening. No man had touched her intimately in a very long time, and then it had been a fumbling experience with a human who hadn't really known what he was doing.

Angus knew exactly how to touch her. He watched her as he stroked, his gaze focusing as though wanting to see her reaction.

Tamsin stepped her feet apart, tilting her head back and closing her eyes. Angus kissed her, more gently this time, as he cupped her between her legs, sending her need spiraling high.

Tamsin managed to squeeze her hand to the front of his jeans, making short work of *his* button and zipper. She closed her fingers around his hot cock, the smooth skin stretched hard. She slid her hand up and down the shaft, cupping the warm weight of his balls, skimming her fingers along him, as nature and instinct drove them closer to mating.

Nature and instinct weren't going to let them make it to the bed. Angus withdrew his hand to shove her jeans and underwear down, and at the same time Tamsin pushed at his, both of them struggling to get the inconvenience of shoes and boots out of the way.

Angus lifted her, her jeans sliding off so she could open to him. Tamsin was up against the cabinet, her legs coming around him, the laminate creaking behind her.

His blunt hardness touched her opening, which was slick with wanting and from his playing. Tamsin let out a groan, pulling her mate close, encouraging him to come to her.

Angus's growl filled the trailer as he thrust upward, driving straight into her.

He could die now. Die and be sent to dust, and he'd go out with a smile.

Tamsin's little moan of pleasure kicked Angus's need high. She was his *mate*, this beautiful, funny, joyful woman, all his.

She'd put her arms around him when he'd pointed out they weren't officially mated yet—the sun and moon ceremony in front of witnesses would do that—and she'd smiled up at him and said, *Yes, we are.*

The truth of that rocketed through Angus's body. *Mates. Together. One.*

Warmth burned in his chest, a tether that encircled his heart and pulled tight. Mate. *Mine.*

Mate. *Hers.*

Angus thrust again, needing to climb inside her, the urge to be one with her overwhelming. He kissed her, seeking her, her fingers pressing the corners of his mouth to open him wider to her.

Tamsin's hair, still in its braid, fell over his arm like a silken rope. Her fingers now pressed into his back, tugging him closer as she arched up to him.

Her body was liquid heat, drowning him. Angus gladly succumbed. His jeans dragged at his ankles and cool air from the ventilation fan touched him, but where he joined with Tamsin was fire itself.

He thrust again, the joy of it sending all other thoughts, all other sensations, to the wind. Angus knew nothing but Tamsin closing around him, her hands on his back, her mouth open under his, the rise of her breath that slid her breasts against his chest.

She broke the kiss to let out a noise between a growl and a groan, her head falling back.

She'd never been shy with him, and she didn't inhibit herself now. Tamsin's reaction was natural, unfeigned. She moved in his arms, seeking more, curving her body to drive him deeper into her.

Tamsin cried his name, her head banging once into the cabinet as absolute pleasure hit her. Angus shouted at the same time, unable to stifle it. His own release was building, tightening inside him, ready to rob him of this ongoing joy of being inside his mate.

Angus lifted her, sliding her from his now-slick cock. Tamsin gasped as they came apart, her eyes flying open.

He held her against him, kicking off his ensnaring jeans, and staggered with her down the trailer to the bed at the end.

Tamsin fell onto the mattress, laughing up at him as she reached for him, arms welcoming. Angus came down over her, finding it easy to slide back inside where he'd been happy. He was so hard he ached, but she soothed the ache with her astonishing warmth.

The glare of the carnival flashed and glowed against the thin curtains, light chasing shadow over Tamsin's face. Angus kissed her and gave in to the frenzy.

He drove into her, she came up to him, the two matching in need and strength. Shifters could make love for a long time—hours, days—but Angus's desperation for her was too strong for that.

His need built high, a hot wave that swept him up and erased all existence but Tamsin, her softness, her body squeezing him until he was lost. He shouted her name as he came and came, kissing her face. "Tamsin. My mate. My heart."

The words ended in another groan as he gave up to her everything he was.

Tamsin moved against him, her climax as intense, her face beautiful as she released herself into it. She pulled him close, the two hard against each other, seeking, needing.

Tamsin kissed Angus frantically as he collapsed onto her. He surrendered into the soft strength of his mate, who caught him and held him, secure against the world.

Tamsin had never been anywhere she liked better than lying under Angus's warm weight. He pressed hot, openmouthed kisses to her neck and breasts, his fingers gentle as he moved his hand up her arm.

Beyond the trailer's walls, music thumped and bells rang as rides shot screaming humans through the air.

"Better than the Zipper," Tamsin whispered.

Angus let out a soft grunt. "Goddess, I hope so. Never getting on that thing again."

Tamsin threaded her fingers through his mussed hair. "Big bad wolf, afraid of a carnival ride, *and* he blushes about the mating frenzy."

Angus raised his head. He wasn't blushing now, and his eyes held confidence and warmth. "Mating frenzy isn't so bad."

"You're right, it's not." She traced his cheek. "Not with the right Shifter."

Angus kissed her breast, then licked his way down to her nipple. He brought it to life with his tongue, then drew it into his mouth.

He suckled her slowly, then raised his head, finishing

with a little nip. "You're the right Shifter for me." His brows came down. "Am I for you?"

"I think we already had this discussion. On the ride that had you screaming like a cub."

"That was heat of the moment," Angus said. "You were being tossed around until you were dizzy. Maybe it shook up your brain."

"Yeah, that was it." Tamsin gave him a sage nod. "That's why I said I'd be your mate."

Angus darted his tongue over her throat. "I'm finished arguing. We need a clan leader to do the ceremonies. My clan is scattered to the four winds, so it will have to be a Shiftertown leader."

"I'd like my mom to be there," Tamsin said softly, her heart squeezing with a familiar ache. "But it's impossible."

"Maybe not. If we can convince Shifters you don't have anything they want, they'll help us. We can retreat to Kendrick's and have Dylan keep Shifter Bureau off our backs."

He made it sound so easy. "There are one or two things I need to tell you about your brother," she said.

Angus's sudden snarl shook the bed. "I do *not* want to talk about my fucking brother while I'm in bed with you." He let out a heavy sigh. "Oh, go ahead—get it over with. You were his lover?"

"No!" The word burst out indignantly. Tamsin struggled to sit up, but Angus held her down. She'd never once touched Gavan, nor he her. "Not my type. I prefer males with sanity, thank you. And it's not about your former mate. Well, mostly not."

Angus's scowl was fierce. "I don't want to talk about her either."

"Neither do I, really." Tamsin couldn't imagine a woman preferring Gavan to *Angus*. She must have flushed her sanity as well. Gavan had been charming and charismatic, but so were most megalomaniacs.

"They're gone. They were my family, but they're gone." Angus's voice went hard, the walls he surrounded himself with rising once more. "I want *now*. Here. With you."

"So do I." On this mattress in an old trailer in the middle of a carnival packed with humans, Tamsin was more content than she'd been in a very, very long time.

"Good," Angus said. "So no more talking."

He growled again, the sound low and unceasing. He continued to growl as he kissed her, only easing off as he slid inside her again, nowhere near sated.

His hardness opened her, filled her, chasing away all troubling thoughts. Tamsin happily pulled him to her and lost herself in him once more.

At breakfast in the morning, Dante's grin was knowing. "Feel better?" he asked Angus.

Angus's face heated—what he did with his mate was none of the bear's damned business. Angus had made himself leave Tamsin later last night to walk over and fetch Ciaran home. She'd been asleep when he'd returned, and he'd put Ciaran to bed, gone outside into the dark park, shifted to wolf, and exploded into a run.

Sprinting over fields and up and down low hills hadn't calmed him. He'd seen a fox, and he'd pulled up to a dust-raising halt, but it had been a wild creature, as surprised to see him as he was to see it. The way it had vanished reminded him of Tamsin and how fast she could move.

That made him remember how she'd smiled sleepily at him after their third round of lovemaking, softly touching his face before he'd risen and left her.

He could make love to her all night and all day for weeks and still not have enough.

This was why Shifters took mates. So they could lose themselves in frenzy and not come out until the female was heavy with a cub. Not that Shifter females held back when they were pregnant. No, he and Tamsin were fated to have wild sex together constantly, for the rest of their lives.

The thought made Angus spread his mouth in a wolf grin, as did the idea of having a cute little girl cub who looked like Tamsin. Would she be fox or wolf? Mixed breed Shifters were born human and first shifted to the animal form of one of their parents when they were about three. It would be fun to find out which way their daughter or son would go.

Now to convince Shifter Bureau, Dylan, and everyone else tracking them to back off and let them live their lives.

Angus had let out a sigh as he'd trotted back to the carnival. He was now as much of a fugitive as Tamsin, having missed curfew by a week or so, left his state without permission, and harbored a rogue Shifter. The Bureau wouldn't let all that go anytime soon.

At the moment, Tamsin was serenely chatting with Celene on the other side of the tent, her cleaned breakfast plate in front of her. Ciaran had sought Brina immediately when he'd entered the tent, and now the two were bent over another gaming device, the remains of their breakfast around them.

Dante laughed. "You have it bad, my friend. But congratulations. Nothing like finding the right one." He sent Celene a glance that left no doubt that the two had formed the mate bond.

"How did you know she was for you?" Angus asked him curiously. "When she's a half Fae? Shifters rarely jump to that conclusion."

Dante shrugged. "You didn't see her in skintight leather dancing all over a tightrope. She was amazing. I couldn't keep my eyes off her. I stalked her for a while and asked her out. You know, as one does."

Angus huffed. "If one is a nutjob. She was happy with a Shifter bear drooling after her?"

"No." Dante chuckled. "She ran like hell. I had to convince her I wasn't going to kill her, or even hold the fact that she was part Fae against her. Took her a while to not hold the fact I was Shifter against *me*."

"I'm glad it worked out for you," Angus answered with sincerity.

"So am I. Match made in paradise. You never know, do you? When the mate bond will strike."

"Sun and moon?" Angus couldn't imagine Dante coming out of hiding to find his clan leader to preside over the rites, or a Fae readily agreeing to it.

Dante shook his head. "Didn't need one. The sun and moon ceremony is just words to show the rest of Shifter-kind what you already know."

He spoke with conviction, but Angus heard a tinge of regret. Dante wanted to be part of the Shifter world as much as Angus did, but without the captivity, Collars, and the like. Maybe someday it would happen.

Dante turned away, clapping on his feathered hat, his striped velvet coat swirling. "Okay, ladies and gentlemen, let's give the good people of Wichita Falls a memorable day."

Tamsin left her table and made her way to Angus. "Celene will be watching Ciaran and Brina this morning, and then we'll do some training. Have time to talk?"

"I'm helping fix the swing ride this morning." Angus had volunteered to make sure another accident with it didn't happen. "What's up?"

He made his inquiry nonchalant, but his heartbeat quickened. Tamsin had a look in her eye that meant what she wanted to talk about wouldn't make him happy.

He wasn't sure he could take revelations about her life with his brother this morning. Angus had believed her when she'd denied she'd been Gavan's lover—the surprise and disgust in her voice hadn't been feigned, and Angus hadn't scented a lie. Even so, he didn't want Gavan to ruin his happiness again.

Tamsin glanced around. "Someplace private."

"Things I need to do," Angus said, scowling.

"The carnival got along fine without you for a long time—they can give you another hour."

Angus heaved an irritated sigh. "Is it that important?"

Tamsin widened her eyes and nodded. "Oh, I'd say so."

Shit. Angus slid his arm around her waist and started to guide her out of the tent.

As soon as he touched her, he longed to sweep her up and run off with her to bury himself inside her once more. He'd kept himself under control while Ciaran had been in the trailer with them, but he wasn't sure he could keep himself from Tamsin if he retreated someplace private with her.

He stopped her, scooped her to him, and gave her a full kiss.

Tamsin readily melted into it. Angus tasted the sweetness of syrup and behind that, her need, the edge of frenzy that neither of them had sated.

Angus heard hoots and comments from the humans going back to work, but he didn't care. Tamsin was worth their mocking.

"Sure you want to be alone with me?" he asked in a warning tone as Tamsin hung in his arms.

"Have to risk it. *Really* important."

Angus didn't like the sound of that. He took her hand and walked with her, not to the trailer, but out to the fields beyond the edge of the fairgrounds.

Tamsin didn't question his choice. Trailers could be bugged—if Dante or one of his employees had been listening last night, they would have heard an earful. Their own fault for being nosy.

Angus had begun to trust Dante and Celene—no way would he leave Ciaran anywhere near them if he didn't—but the trailer could have been bugged by others for other reasons. Any of the tents might also conceal a listener, and the grounds were now flowing with families as kids dragged their parents in for a day of sticky fun.

The middle of a field was the most likely place not to be overheard. They'd be surrounded by nothing but dirt, grass, mud, water, and furry animals that weren't Shifters.

Angus and Tamsin walked about fifty yards into the wet grass before Angus turned her to him. Anyone watching would decide they wanted to be alone to canoodle.

"All right, what's so important? Am I going to regret the mate-claim?" He spoke lightly, but everything inside him was uneasy.

Please say no. I've already lost part of myself in you. I don't want to live with the hole your absence would make.

"Maybe." Tamsin's smiles and banter fell away, and her eyes took on a sadness and a worry that sent dread into Angus's heart. "I need to tell you about Gavan, and what he was up to. I wasn't his lover—I didn't lie—but he wanted me to be. So he showed me things. What he showed me is why I ran away from him, why Shifter Bureau is chasing me, and why Dylan wants to catch me and squeeze every drop of knowledge from my brain. And why I can't let any of them do it."

CHAPTER TWENTY

"Stop." Angus put his hands on her shoulders, gripping hard. "Stop—I don't want to know this."

Dylan had wanted Angus—expected him—to pry secrets from Tamsin's head, but Angus had deliberately put the command out of his mind. He wasn't about to do Dylan's dirty work for him.

Angus didn't want to hear secrets that would change things between him and Tamsin. What they had—what they'd begun—was good. Better than good. Since Tamsin had come into his life, Angus had woken from the half awareness in which he'd existed, and he'd do anything to never lose that.

"Yes, you do." The sadness in Tamsin's voice pierced his heart. "You need to know what you're getting into with me, so that when Shifter Bureau is filling the syringe to tranq you to death, you know why. Or maybe you can trade the knowledge for your life." She let out a breath. "I also want to tell you to ask you what to do. I thought this was all over and done with, but I guess it's not."

She trailed off, the lingering pain in her eyes enough to make the wolf in Angus want to kill whoever had hurt her.

"Son of a bitch, Tamsin, what the hell did my brother do to you?"

"To me?" Tamsin blinked. "Nothing. What he planned to do to the *world* was pretty horrible."

"What?" Angus allowed himself a minuscule amount of relief. "Gavan wasn't overly gifted with brains. What was he going to do—shed until humanity begged him to stop?"

"I wish it could be funny." Tamsin swallowed, then she looked at him fully, as though knowing her next words could unmake all they'd found together. "He was building up an arsenal."

The relief ebbed. "What kind of arsenal?"

Tamsin spread her hands. "How many kinds are there? Gavan was collecting and storing weapons. All kinds of weapons, from small handguns to grenades. Machine guns. Serious shit."

Gavan had collected this? The man who couldn't find his own pants without a map? "You're sure? Did you see this arsenal?"

"Very sure. He showed it to me to brag about it. Gavan wanted to be a super-dominant Shifter, making all humans and Shifters submit to him. I guess he thought my seeing his guns would make me fall in love with him, want to be his mate. But it only told me he was crazy enough to kill— to kill a lot of people."

"Shifters don't use weapons." Angus's hands balled as he spoke. Shifters disdained them, because the Shifter him- or herself was a weapon. Why use a knife when your claws are sharper? Or a gun when you can launch yourself like a ballistic missile?

"I know that," Tamsin said impatiently. "I couldn't believe what I was seeing. So when we got back to the hide-out, I thanked Gavan sweetly, and then took off the first chance I could."

Emotions churned through Angus's brain, rising and falling like ocean waves. "What about April? I can't imagine her stepping aside so Gavan could mate-claim you."

"She didn't. Gavan wanted to take more than one mate, as Shifters did in the old days. He had other females in his sights as well. April was fine with it. Younger women, she said, could give him more cubs. There was enough of Gavan to go around, in her opinion." Tamsin rolled her eyes. "I was *so* out of there."

The emotion that burst to the top of Angus's brain, surfacing through the others, was rage. He'd damped down that rage to a simmer after Gavan's death, in order to forget what his brother had done and get on with his life. Anger at the dead didn't accomplish anything.

But Gavan had been a first-class dickhead. In spite of his proclamations that he would free the Shifters, all he did was rain down trouble on them. Angus had barely escaped being executed as his accessory. What had saved Angus was Gavan's vehement denials that Angus had anything to do with his plots—not in compassion for Angus but because Gavan didn't want to share the limelight. Gavan had considered Angus a rival from the moment of Angus's birth.

Now Angus was learning that Gavan had wanted to build a harem, one that included not only April, but Tamsin. Gavan had always liked the idea that Shifter males should be leaders of their own packs, that producing offspring through several Shifter females would strengthen them. Apparently he'd been putting theory into practice.

But then, if Gavan wanted to spread around his own sperm, why had he insisted that April bring Ciaran with her? Scared he couldn't produce his own offspring? He'd fought against Angus taking Ciaran back, and only stopped when Angus threatened to sic Shifter Bureau on him.

Angus dropped to the ground and dug his hands into his hair, strangled noises coming from his throat. He stretched out flat on his back and yelled to the sky.

"Goddess, I *hate* that asshole!"

Tamsin sat down beside him, hugging her knees. "Yeah, I wasn't thrilled with him either. That's why I was so surprised to learn you were his brother. You're nothing like him."

Angus scrubbed his face. "Damn it, Tamsin, I think that's the nicest thing you've ever said to me."

"Really?" She grinned at him. "How about *You're hot, you're wonderful, and I want to be mated to you*?"

"You haven't said those things," Angus pointed out. He rubbed his face one more time. "Son of a bitch. An arsenal." He lowered his hands to study Tamsin's face above him. "This is what Dylan wanted to know? Haider too? Why were you afraid to tell me?"

Tamsin drew herself into a tighter ball. "I had to make up my mind about you first. When I realized you were Gavan's brother, that scared me. I didn't know whether you'd be like him. I didn't want to see your eyes get that predatory gleam like his did. And as far as I knew, you were dumping me on Haider and I'd never see you again—even if you so nicely arranged a pickup for when I escaped. I didn't know that was why Haider was after me, until he started threatening to dissect me. I didn't tell you before Dylan questioned us because I still wasn't sure what Dylan knew until we got to the motel room, plus I didn't want you to have to lie to him. He'd scent your nervousness and get it out of you. Or me, to keep him from hurting you. And after that . . . I had to decide how you would react."

"I would react like this," Angus rumbled. "My brother is a fucking shithead."

Tamsin flashed him a faint smile then shook her head. "The real truth is that I didn't want to think about it anymore. I didn't want it to matter. I just want to be with you, and Ciaran, and have this." She stretched out her arms, then lowered them. "And anyway, the arsenal might be long gone by now. That was about eight years ago." She sighed. "But I can't run away all my life. If I'm going to run away with you, you should at least know what you're running *from*."

"Hell," Angus said softly. He sat up, leaning back on his hands, opening himself to the sunshine.

"I'm sorry," Tamsin said. "You can take back that mate-claim. I'll understand."

She spoke glibly, but Angus heard the sorrow in her voice.

Out of nothing, they'd found each other. Angus's brother had done one thing right in his life—he'd brought Tamsin and Angus together. In a roundabout way, years later, after Gavan was dead, and not on purpose. But in a weird twist of fate, he'd been responsible.

"I'm not taking it back," Angus said. "We belong together. I knew it when I saw you, kicking ass at poker and being all smug about it. When you got hurt because I chased you, I knew I'd move heaven and earth to get you well again. I mate-claimed you to save you from Dylan, but I'd have done it anyway, sooner or later. Dylan just gave me the excuse."

"Well, damn," Tamsin whispered. "You're going to make me cry."

"Why? It's the truth. I'm glad you've told me about the arsenal—I mean, *before* you got yourself killed for it. But I'm not sending you away for something my dickwad brother did. You said it might not be there anymore. Do you know for sure?"

"No. I haven't had a chance to check on it."

"Because you're right," Angus said. "It could have been found and reported by now, although I'm thinking a story like that would have made news headlines. I don't pay much attention to the human world, but I probably would have heard *that*. Or it might have been plundered by others, like gangs or militant groups. Which I seriously hope not."

"Like I said, I haven't had the chance to look, and once Gavan was caught, I had no intention of returning to a place he'd been associated with. I didn't have a death wish."

Angus frowned. "Why didn't you report him right away, or at least this arsenal? To a Shifter, I mean. I understand why you didn't rush to the human police, though you could have made an anonymous tip."

"And have a stock of weapons be traced back to Shifters?" Tamsin shook her head decidedly. "Gavan probably left his fingerprints and DNA all over it. What do you think Shifter Bureau would do to all Shifters everywhere if it was discovered one of them had stockpiled weapons? Machine guns and grenades? I'll tell you what they'd do—they'd round up all the Shifters and put them to death, terrified we were more dangerous than previously thought. At the very least—and only if Shifters had good lawyers—Collared Shifters would be locked into even more restricted Shifter-towns, and the few liberties they have now taken away."

She had a point, Angus thought glumly. No one could ever know about this, least of all the fanatic Haider and Shifter Bureau.

"Obviously Shifter Bureau heard some rumor of it," Angus said. "Or Haider wouldn't have wanted to interrogate you."

"Who knows?" Tamsin's shoulders slumped. "Maybe Gavan hinted at it when he was taken in. Maybe he thought it would save his butt or, more likely, he wanted to prove what a badass Shifter he was. I don't know where Haider heard about *me*—maybe one of Gavan's followers mentioned me, and Haider kept an eye out in case I drifted into his territory." She groaned. "I don't know. I didn't tell any other Shifters about the stash, because I was as afraid of them as Shifter Bureau. What if the Shifter I told shared

Gavan's beliefs and wanted to use weapons against humans? Or even other Shifters? There's always a dominance struggle somewhere, and living in Shiftertowns must make you all crazy. You really think Dylan wouldn't want this arsenal for the army *he's* putting together?"

Angus lay down again, suddenly tired. "I wish I could say no."

Tamsin stretched out next to him, turning on her side to put her face close to his. "What do I do, Angus? Keep running and hope they give up? Tell Dylan and trust that he won't blow up the nearest Shifter Bureau compound? Tell Haider and try to convince him it was a one-off, and no other Shifter would dream of doing such a thing? And hope *he* doesn't use it for *his* personal vendetta?"

Angus let out a low growl. "Don't know. Need to think about it."

"See what I mean?" Tamsin brushed a piece of dried grass from his shirt. "If you want to kick me down the road and have no part of this, I understand."

"No," Angus snarled. "I just told you, you're my mate. *Mine.* For always. This is a problem, and we'll find a solution. Then we'll figure out how to be together and live our lives. Even if we have to follow a human carnival run by a bear Shifter with weird fashion sense."

Tamsin's smile lit her face. Angus's heart turned over every time she did that. "I like Dante. He's amazing."

Angus frowned. "We're not telling him about this."

"Of course not. We barely know him." Tamsin exhaled, her breath touching his skin. "You know, I've held that secret in me so long it feels weird to have it out. I never told another living soul. Only you."

"Mmph. I'm not sure how to take that."

Tamsin tapped his nose, then leaned to brush a light kiss to it, her warmth comforting in the cool breeze. "You're the only one I've been able to trust. Since . . . well, ever."

"You didn't take long to decide that," Angus observed.

"With you, I just knew. Or maybe it was seeing how you are with Ciaran. You'd never hurt him—you were willing to throw me to the wolves, so to speak, to keep him safe."

"Which started to kill me." Angus gentled his voice. "I want you both safe. We have to fix this, not only for us, but for Ciaran. He doesn't need to be hurt by it."

"It's another reason I told you." Tamsin traced his cheek. "To help me figure out what to do." Her eyes were on his, golden and thoughtful, waiting for his answer.

"Well, if you figured I was a genius who would instantly solve your problem, you were wrong."

"Of course I didn't think that," Tamsin said with conviction.

"Huh. That could be insulting if I let it be."

"Don't be ridiculous. You're plenty smart, Angus, and I'm smarter. I figured two heads were better than one."

Angus raised himself on one elbow. "If you're smarter than me, why did I catch you so fast?"

"Because I stayed human so I wouldn't lose all my money. And anyway, you didn't catch me, the gator did."

Tamsin shivered, losing her lighthearted look. She'd be haunted by the trauma of that attack for a long time.

Angus slid his hand behind her and drew her down to him. "I'd have done anything to save you. I still will." He brushed back a loose strand of her hair and kissed her soft lips. "We'll get through this, Tamsin. I promise you. Then you and I will say to hell with the world, and spend a long, long time by ourselves."

"With Ciaran." Tamsin settled down into the crook of his arm, while the September sun warmed them. "Sounds good to me."

Tamsin returned with Angus to the carnival, reluctantly releasing his hand when they reached the fairgrounds so they could take up their various activities.

She could get used to this life, she thought, even as she watched Angus's fine ass as he walked away. Working hard, being friends with Celene and Dante, moving on when each weekend was over, heading out to another town, another state. Living with Ciaran and Angus and falling more and more in love with them every day was something she didn't want to let go. She'd been terrified that revealing Gavan's secret would force her to do just that.

Angus hadn't walked away from her or shouted at her that he hated her, nothing like what Gavan had done when she'd turned down his offer to be part of his ménage. Angus was furious—but his anger was directed at his brother, not at Tamsin.

Relief rolled over her in waves. Wasn't there a saying—*A burden shared is a burden halved*?

But did that other person want half of your burden? When he hadn't had to worry about it before?

Tamsin watched Angus stride to the men fixing the hydraulics system on the pirate ship ride and bend to take up a tool. The guys nodded at him, accepting his help without hesitation.

How many of the humans here realized they were Shifters? Dante had won their trust, apparently. Would that trust extend to Angus? Or should he and Tamsin leave, before this haven grew too dangerous?

Life was simpler when Tamsin only had to fend for herself, trusting to her swift feet and fox ability to get her out of any situation.

No, not simpler. Just lonely.

Angus looked up and around, focusing on Tamsin as she moved to the tent where she'd help Celene and Ciaran rehearse. She felt his gaze on her, watching, protecting, warming.

Simple was overrated. She'd take complicated and crazy, as long as she could have the big growly Shifter with the cloud-gray eyes looking out for her every day.

* * *

Saturday and Sunday went off without a hitch. No broken rides, no lost kids. There was an angry father of four unruly children, who decided that the ticket prices were way too high for what was offered and demanded to see the manager. Dante soothed him down with enviable swiftness. He could sweet-talk anyone, Tamsin observed. His colorful coats and hat were distracting, his large build with a hint of predator intimidating. The irate father ended up apologizing and even returning the next day, bolstered by the free coupons to a few of the booths that Dante had given him.

Dante had winked at Tamsin as he'd gone back to work, full of himself.

They tore down on Monday and moved on, heading west for Amarillo. Once there, they couldn't set up because there was a tornado watch, and it was best not to get caught with tents and rides in a high wind. If storms hit, they'd have to hunker down and move on, eating the rent Dante had already paid to the fairgrounds.

"It's why I don't linger in Texas this time of year," Dante told Angus and Tamsin as they sat in his trailer drinking coffee and waiting for weather reports. "I'm heading into New Mexico for the rest of fall, where the weather is better. We'll hit the low deserts by November, in time for snow to start falling in the high country. More people will be in desert cities by that time anyway. Snowbirds are my friends."

Tamsin couldn't fault his logic. She'd never been farther west than Louisiana before she'd met Angus, and to her, every weekend brought a new adventure.

The storms didn't brew up, so the carnival opened on time. Still, Dante watched the sky with a suspicious eye.

That weekend, around training Celene and Ciaran—neither of whom needed much coaching—Tamsin started helping out in the ringtoss booth for a small cut of the profits. She paraded around in the booth's goofy hats and encouraged patrons to try their luck. *It was easier than it looked—see?*

She'd demonstrate, then everyone would want a try. The guy who owned the booth didn't cheat. If people won, they got a prize. If a little kid did really poorly, he or she might be allowed an extra toss for free and something tiny and cheap as consolation.

After hours, Tamsin, Angus, and Ciaran retired to their RV to eat and sleep. Angus didn't sleep on the bench anymore or spend half the night prowling. He curled up around Tamsin, and deep in the night, when Ciaran was well asleep, he made hard, silent love to her.

In their rare moments alone, Tamsin and Angus would contemplate what to do about Gavan's arsenal.

"Where is it, exactly?" Angus and Tamsin strolled on the edge of a farmer's field on Saturday, blue sky arching over flat land stretching for miles.

"In Louisiana. Around Shreveport."

Angus halted, hands on hips. "Where a rogue Shifter killed Bureau agents. Was that rogue Shifter trying to get you to take him to the arsenal?"

"Sort of. He'd heard rumor of it, and he was trying to pry out of me whether it was true. He insisted on going to Shreveport, and I couldn't risk letting him go there and poke around on his own. I was busy playing the stupid innocent when Shifter Bureau interrupted. There was a fight. Two agents died." Tamsin closed her eyes, not wanting to think about the screams, the sharp scent of blood, the fanatic fury in Dion's eyes. "I don't know if they ever caught Dion. The agents were able to report in before Dion attacked them, so they described me. I tried to go to ground, and was doing fine." She swallowed and tried to make her tone light. "But then a Lupine tracker hunted me down."

Angus's scowl clouded the day. "Not my choice."

"I know. I hated you at that moment, but you've grown

on me." Tamsin playfully bumped into his side. "Anyway, I'm pretty sure I can find Gavan's hiding place again. If Gavan didn't move everything before he was caught, or others didn't find it and steal it."

"If it's gone, then we might be off the hook. You can't give up information you don't have."

Tamsin shrugged. "Or Haider might convince himself I'm lying about the location and torture me. I don't want Shifter Bureau finding out about the arsenal at all, because it will blow back on other Shifters. I don't want everyone punished because of Gavan."

"Neither do I."

Angus turned away, studying the sky, his rage making his back quiver. He must feel grief too—while Gavan wasn't exactly a prize, he'd been Angus's brother, his kin, his pack, his family.

Tamsin slid her hand into his, and Angus squeezed it.

"We should check," he said after a time. "See if it's still there. If not, we go on and hope Shifter Bureau forgets about it. They will, in time, if nothing is ever found."

"And if all the stuff is still there?" Tamsin asked.

Angus looked grim. "We destroy it."

Tamsin raised her brows. "How? Blow it up? Because, sure, no one will notice that."

"I don't know how." Angus gave her an impatient look. "Break down the pieces, hide them, bury them. I don't know. How do humans get rid of excess weapons?"

"I haven't the faintest idea. I'd say melt them, but same problem. How do you melt explosives? I don't know anything about stuff like that. I'd kill myself trying."

"*You're* going nowhere near it," Angus said firmly. "You point the way, and I do the rest."

Tamsin jerked her hand from his. "Nothing doing. I'm not going to lead you to a bunker and let you go try to disarm grenades. I'd like my mate to be in one piece, thank you very much. I think Ciaran would agree."

Angus didn't argue. He only stood still, looking unhappy. "We'll have to have help."

Tamsin shook her head until her hair danced. "That means telling people. Who are you going to trust? Dylan?"

"No. Not Dylan. Or his sons—they'd feel obligated to report to their father, or he'd pry it out of them somehow. But I know a lot of Shifters. Let me think about who we can bring in."

"What about Reg? Your friend who gave you his SUV without question?"

"Mmm. I'd say yes, if he wasn't second to Spence. Spence might get such a secret out of him, and I don't trust Spence. He likes his power. But there are others. Ben."

"He's not Shifter."

"Exactly. He's ancient, smart, and as far as I know doesn't crave power. He's a place to start."

Tamsin relaxed. She'd sensed good things about Ben, but ambiguous things as well. "How are you going to get hold of him?"

"I was thinking of using my phone."

"Which might be tapped. Or traced."

Angus shook his head. "It's old, and I went through it when I got it and made sure there were no trackers, bugs, or any kind of doodad on it."

"But phone records are searchable. Shifter Bureau is probably monitoring yours by now."

Tamsin hadn't seen Angus use his phone since they'd fled the motel and Dylan. Now he pulled it from his pocket, looked at it, and then tucked it away again. "I'll think of something."

Tamsin twined her fingers through his once more and grew alarmed at how much heat that simple act sped through her body. "Sorry to dump my baggage on you."

Angus shrugged. "Everyone has baggage. It's just a matter of what kind and how heavy it is."

Tamsin leaned into him. "How did I get so lucky to be hunted and captured by a guy like you?"

"Because of your baggage." Angus slid his arm around her. "Haider sent me after you for it."

"Haider was stupid. He should have known you were kind and sweet and mushy inside."

Angus made a face, very much like Ciaran did when an adult tried to make him eat vegetables. "Yuck. What happened to big bad wolf?"

"Oh, he's in there." Tamsin rubbed Angus's chest, then leaned forward and kissed it. "Very much so."

A growl confirmed it. Angus pulled her close and tilted her face to his for a long, commanding kiss.

Tamsin had learned how to kiss him by now, the way their mouths fit together, how the burn of his whiskers felt on her skin, how he liked to lick across her tongue.

The field around them rolled away to meet the sky, green and blue to the line of the horizon. The fairgrounds were behind them, the dusty earth Angus took her down to warmed by the sun.

It was a long time before they returned to the carnival, their clothes wrinkled and dirt-streaked from being turned into makeshift blankets on the ground. Tamsin's hair was studded with dried bits of grass, and Angus's hands were scraped raw.

When Dante spied them, he laughed uproariously, as though he had never seen anything so funny. Smart-ass bear.

That night Tamsin drowsed with Angus, the lights of the carnival glowing on the curtains above the bed. She wished they could stay in this bubble of calm forever, ignoring the outside world and its problems. The arsenal probably didn't exist anymore. They'd go to Shreveport, look, find nothing, and move on with their lives.

Angus had already contacted Ben, he'd told her as they wound down from making love, and things were in motion.

Tamsin asked him how, if he didn't use his cell phone—had he found a ley line to connect to the sentient house outside New Orleans? She'd toyed with the idea of using Psychic Lorraine's crystal ball, but Tamsin wouldn't know how to tap a ley line, and she'd have to trust Lorraine, a plump, middle-aged woman who was a pretty good psychic, with the private message.

Angus had said, "I went into town and found a phone booth with a working phone still in it," and then dropped off to sleep.

She'd have to wait for him to wake up to tell her what he and Ben decided, which could be a while. Angus's snores filled the trailer, sonorous and slow.

A shadow cut the light from outside. Tamsin looked up, and then screamed as the back window filled with the silhouette of a giant tiger.

CHAPTER TWENTY-ONE

Tamsin's screams jerked Angus awake. "Tamsin, what the hell?"

"I saw it. I didn't dream it. I swear."

Angus dug sleep from his eyes and looked to where she pointed. The curtained window looked normal, flashes of yellow and red from the rides rippling across it.

"Saw what?" he demanded.

"A tiger. I swear to the Goddess it was a—"

Angus was out of the bed, dragging on his jeans, and out the door before she could complete the sentence.

The corner where their RV was parked was relatively quiet. The trailers around them belonged to ride and booth operators who were still working, so their windows were dark, and all was silent.

Angus inhaled, taking in the scents of dust, food, humanity, waste, exhaust, excitement. Somewhere among that he scented Shifter, though that could be Dante. His scent lingered on everything, this being his territory.

Dante himself appeared around the corner of a trailer, his feathered hat a smudge in the darkness. "My bounds were breached," he said with a low growl. "I feel it."

Angus nodded. A Shifter always knew when his territory was invaded by another Shifter, which was how Dante had found Angus the first night.

Angus faced the darkest patch at the end of the trailers, where a fence separated the lot from the open fields beyond. "Let's get this over with," he said softly to the air. "Tell me who sent you."

"Who the hell are you talking to?" Dante asked, but Angus held up his hand for silence.

The darkness seemed to part, and a large man walked out of it. He'd dressed in jeans and a T-shirt, but the clothes pulled at him as though he'd rather be out of them and in his animal form. He carried running shoes in one hand, walking barefoot on dirt, pebbles, and thorns without flinching. He had mottled black and orange hair and yellow eyes that glowed in the lights from the midway.

"Sweet Goddess, what is *he*?" Dante breathed.

The Shifter ignored him, fixing his golden gaze on Angus. "Ben sent me."

Angus let out a long breath, his tightness easing. He smelled no duplicity on the man; he never did. "Not Dylan?" he asked, just to make sure.

"No."

A simple statement, and Angus believed him. Tiger didn't lie—he saw no point in it.

"Thank the Goddess for that. Dante, this is Tiger. He's a friend. At least I'd like to think so. He probably could use a beer."

Tamsin led Ciaran by the hand across the parking area to Dante's trailer. It was lit, and she banged on the door with her fist.

Celene opened it. She took in Tamsin's face, nodded her understanding, and let her in.

"Males make me crazy," Tamsin announced as she stepped into the living area. "Could you bother telling me what's going on?"

She found herself pinned by the yellow stare of a Shifter she didn't know. He sat on a kitchen chair while Dante and Angus shared a padded bench, and he was holding a set of spangled bracelets that Brina had made and was apparently showing him.

The Shifter held the bracelets carefully, as though worried he'd break them. He took in Tamsin and Ciaran standing next to him, and then he turned his attention back to Brina.

"They are very well done," he said, handing them back to her.

"I'm going to sell them," Brina said. "Ciaran's going to help me."

Ciaran, not shy, went to Brina's side. He showed no fear of the giant Shifter in their midst, and in fact held out his hands so the man could gently slap them, Ciaran doing the same in return. Ciaran's tiny hands were lost under the big man's, but Tamsin sensed the Shifter holding back his strength to keep from hurting him.

"This is Tiger," Angus said. "Tiger—Tamsin Calloway."

"Your mate." Tiger lifted his gaze from the two cubs, and his eyes narrowed. "You are a fox."

"Steady." Dante, who'd removed his hat and coat and looked almost normal in his T-shirt, started to laugh. "She's mate-claimed. Keep your thoughts to yourself."

Tiger frowned, while Tamsin's heart thumped. She gave her head the slightest shake, but Tiger spoke again. "I mean, her animal is a fox."

Dante didn't lose his amusement. "No such thing. We have Lupines, Felines, and Bears. Best for last . . ." He trailed off under Tiger's serious expression. Tamsin clenched her fists and tried to glare Tiger into silence.

"Seriously?" Dante swung his gaze to Tamsin, an interested glint in his eyes. "Okay, I'm starting to believe it. That would explain a lot. Like why I couldn't decide whether you were Lupine or Feline."

"How did *you* know?" Tamsin demanded of Tiger.

"I have met one before. His name is Miles, and he is a boat pilot." Tiger clamped his mouth shut as though that was all the information he was willing to part with.

"Well, shit," Dante said. "Who knew?"

"Keep it to yourselves." Angus sent a frown to Dante, Tiger, and Celene.

"I'm cool." Dante took a sip from his can of beer. "I'm trying to convey that you can trust me, Angus. Have been trying for a while now."

Tamsin answered him. "We're naturally a little reticent. Angus more than me. He doesn't have a trusting nature, but I can't blame him. He's had issues."

"Thank you, Tamsin." Angus gave her a weary look, and Tamsin playfully stuck out her tongue. "Tiger and I need to talk."

Dante waved his beer as if to say, *Go ahead,* then realized Angus meant Dante wasn't to be included.

"Use my trailer if you want," he said, rising. "As long as what he's come here for isn't going to hurt my people, mess up my carnival, or bring shit down on me from police or Shifter Bureau, by all means, have your private chat."

"It shouldn't," Angus said. "But no need to give up your space. Tiger and I will take a walk. Tamsin, will you put Ciaran back to bed?"

"No, I will not," Tamsin said. "I'm not letting you out of my sight with a strange Shifter who's bigger than any I've ever seen. Besides, I want to know all the details right away, instead of having to pry them from you later one question at a time."

"You're not going without me," Ciaran said.

"Yes, we are," Angus countered.

Ciaran took on his stubborn look. It was time for Dante or Celene to step in and offer to look after him, but both simply watched, interested to see how this would play out.

Tiger rose. "I will put Ciaran to bed. And then we will talk."

The man had to bend his neck so his head didn't bang the ceiling. Ciaran, instead of arguing, nodded. "Do you tell stories?"

Tiger considered. "I can."

"Then cool. Come on." Ciaran took Tiger's hand and pulled him out the door.

Tiger had some kind of mojo, Angus reflected, that he wished he could learn. Tiger had Ciaran in his bunk, telling him a disjointed story of fighting a contingent of Fae, humans, and traitor Shifters in a battle on the Olympic Peninsula, with Zander and Rae by his side.

Ciaran listened with avid interest, asking plenty of questions, then when Tiger told him it was time to sleep, Ciaran nodded, snuggled down, and dropped off. No trying to stay awake, no insisting he be part of the forthcoming conversation.

"Does your own son obey you like that?" Angus asked. Tiger had a cub, a small boy called Seth.

Tiger thought for a moment. "No. He has much of his mother in him." He sounded proud.

Tamsin sat cross-legged on the bed, where she'd gone after kissing Ciaran good night. "Should we talk here? Or have Celene stay with Ciaran while we retreat to a cold, muddy field?"

Tiger glanced about. "We will talk here. There are no listeners."

"How do you know?" Tamsin asked, tilting her head as she did when she was skeptical, a very fox-like move.

Tiger gave the trailer another once-over. "No listening

devices. They make a sound I can hear. I have very good hearing."

Angus believed him. Tiger had been bred in a lab, and the researchers who'd made him had apparently done some weird shit to him.

"So, Ben told you where we were?" Tamsin went on.

Tiger sent her a nod. "He said Angus had contacted him. He and Angus are to rendezvous at your next destination, which is Albuquerque. Ben asked me to help. I had already been hunting for you, and once Ben told me you were in Amarillo, I was able to narrow down your coordinates."

Tamsin's eyes widened in alarm. "Why were you looking for us? For Dylan? Is he on his way?"

Tiger shook his head. "Ben was worried about you when you left the house. He asked me to keep an eye out. I do not work for Dylan."

"Don't you?" Angus asked in surprise. "You're helping him recruit his army for when we face the Fae. And you're one of Liam's trackers."

Tiger bent his head in another nod. "I work *with* Dylan. He is right to plan for the Fae. But I do not work *for* him. Likewise, I help Liam in return for his hospitality—Carly and Seth and I live in his house," he explained to Tamsin. "I work for no one now. I am free of that."

His emphasis made Angus believe him.

Tamsin pointed at Tiger's bare neck. "You don't wear a Collar. How do you live in a Shiftertown without Shifter Bureau noticing that?"

Tiger reached into his pocket. "I have one." He drew out a black and silver chain with a Celtic cross pendant dangling from it. "It is fake. I take it off when I am in the human world and put it on when I am with Shifters."

"Oh, nice." Tamsin pressed her hands together. "What a great idea. So you can blend in wherever you go. Well, as much as someone like you *can* blend in."

Tiger tucked the Collar into his pocket. "The Morrisseys made it for me. I will have them make one for you."

Tamsin looked alarmed. "I think they'd prefer to kill me. I ran out on Dylan, and he's extremely pissed off about that."

Tiger studied her. "I won't let them kill you. Fox Shifters are too rare, you are Angus's mate, and besides . . ." He squared his shoulders. "No more killing."

Tamsin shot Angus a grin. "I really like him."

Angus did too, but he wasn't sure how far to trust him yet. "What did Ben tell you? All I said was we had a unique problem and that I'd like to talk to him. I picked Ben because he's not Shifter and he knows how to be discreet."

"Ben thought I could help," Tiger answered. "What he said was that you would not have called him if the problem had been ordinary and easy. He has alerted Zander as well. The three of us are strong, we have special abilities, and we can protect you."

"You'll be protecting us from other Shifters, not just Shifter Bureau," Angus said. "Can you do that? Even against Dylan?"

"Especially against Dylan," Tiger said without changing expression. "I will guard you to your rendezvous, and stay until you decide what to do."

"Why would you?" Tamsin asked. "We're asking you to act against Shifters from your own Shiftertown, ones who help you. Why would you do this for us? Not saying I'm not grateful. I seriously am. But why are you choosing our side?"

Tiger gave her one of his assessing looks that said he'd understood everything about her after only one glance. "Ben and Zander told me about you, Tamsin Calloway. They are concerned for you and want you to be well. And Angus has become my friend."

He spoke as though there was no doubt. "Thank you," Angus said warmly.

Tamsin slid off the bed and went to Tiger. "I'd like you

to be my friend too," she said. She carefully put her arms
around him and pulled him into a Shifter embrace. "Sorry
I screamed when I first saw you."

"I am frightening." Tiger rested his hand on Tamsin's
shoulder, the strength of it unnerving. "That is what my
mate tells me. Then she laughs." His face softened. "Carly
has a wonderful laugh."

Tamsin released him and straightened up, giving him a
grin. "Sounds like someone has it bad. Don't worry, Tiger.
We'll get this wrapped up, and you can go home to your
mate."

"And my cub."

"And your cub. Give them both a kiss for me."

Tiger sent her a solemn look. "I will."

Tiger asked no more questions. He refused the offer of a
bed in the RV for the night and departed, saying he
would guard them.

In the morning, he joined Angus and Tamsin as they
made their way to the tent for breakfast. Dante welcomed
him and accepted Tiger's offer to be a security guard for
the day.

Tiger started this job after breakfast and proved to be
very good at it. He stopped six shoplifters and prevented a
preteen girl from being lured from her parents, nearly killing
the predator in the process. Tiger dragged the man off by the
neck to lock him into a porta-potty until the police arrived.

Tiger stayed out of sight when the police came to fetch
the man, and then resumed his duties, finding two lost dogs
and catching a little boy who started to fall from the carou-
sel, restoring him to his panicked parents.

At the end of the day, Dante tried to offer Tiger a perma-
nent job, but he declined. Tiger helped break down the
carnival on Monday, and rode in Angus's RV on Tuesday
down the straight ribbon of the I-40 toward Albuquerque.

In that city in New Mexico, they finally found autumn. In southern Louisiana and across Texas, the weather had been hot, but once they reached Albuquerque's altitude, in the shadow of its big mountain range, the air was crisp, the mornings cool.

Ben met them in a restaurant in the old town, a street thronged with tourists among low adobe buildings. The restaurant served Mexican food with Hatch chiles—the famous chiles of New Mexico that spawned a yearly festival—and handmade tortillas, and it was packed. Ben already had a table and was chatting and being friendly with the waitress. A pitcher of beer and two bowls of salsa waited on the table to go with the mountain of fresh tortilla chips.

"These are awesome," Ben said, waving at the bowls of salsa. He lifted a chip coated in green sauce. "This one is like eating fire. The red one is slightly milder but still very tasty. Hi, Tamsin, sweetheart. I see you haven't ditched him yet."

Ben stood up and gave Tamsin a hug, then a careful one to Ciaran.

"Tiger." Ben gave him a cordial nod. "Don't ask him how his cub is, anyone. We don't have enough time for the answer." He grinned at Tiger, who looked nonplussed. "Now, then, this place is so noisy no one will be able to hear what we say. What can I do for you?"

CHAPTER TWENTY-TWO

They sat down, Tamsin and Ciaran reaching eagerly for the chips.

"Not sure." Angus didn't want to talk about specifics in the middle of a restaurant with other customers three feet away.

"I get you," Ben said. "Let's enjoy the food and then adjourn someplace more private."

Tamsin sat close to Ben, their shoulders and elbows touching as they munched chips. "How's the house?" she asked him.

"Great. I watched Shifter Bureau goons trying to find it—cars creeping slowly back and forth on the nearby roads, but the house kept itself hidden. And me inside it."

Haider must have sent people to search from the point they'd gone off the GPS the night Angus had captured Tamsin. If the house didn't want to be found, then the searchers wouldn't be able to pinpoint it.

"How did you get out?" Tamsin asked. "I assume they left someone in the area to watch. Did they follow you?" She didn't sound unduly worried, only curious.

Ben shook his head. "I'm very good at sneaking around. No one sees me if I don't want them to. Anyway, they don't know to look for me. I'm just a random dude."

"No, no." Tamsin patted his arm. "You're not random. You're very special."

Ben looked pleased. "Aw, you're just saying that."

"A very special goblin. Are there any lady goblins?"

The flash of pain in Ben's eyes was hard to miss, though he hid it the next second. "No. Not anymore."

Tamsin lost her smile. "I'm sorry." She rested her head on Ben's shoulder in true sympathy.

Ben shrugged, but Tamsin didn't move. "Them's the breaks when the Fae hate you," he said. "By the way, you smell a little bit like one. You been hanging around a Fae?"

No rancor, but the hint of anger was there.

"Yes. Celene," Tamsin said. "She's half Fae. A tightrope walker, or former one anyway. She says her days balancing thirty feet above the ground are over. She's mated to a Shifter now."

"Okaayy," Ben said dubiously.

"I like her," Ciaran said. "And her daughter is cute. Brina's teaching me how to sell jewelry. I'm good at it."

Ben switched his gaze to Ciaran, his dark brows rising. Angus knew his hatred of the Fae ran deep, but he'd been known to make exceptions for individuals, once they'd proven themselves. Ben said nothing to Ciaran, only went back to munching chips, loading them with both kinds of salsa.

The waitress returned to take their order. Tamsin went through the long menu and chose several dishes, as did Ben. Ciaran picked out what he wanted, and Angus ordered two plain soft beef tacos with salsa. Tiger asked for a large steak.

Ben, Tamsin, and Ciaran ate food off one another's plates, enjoying tamales, several different kinds of enchiladas that oozed cheese, carne adobada—which was meat in a rich red sauce—burritos stuffed with so much filling it burst out both ends, and carnitas—pork that had been slow cooked all day, rubbed with spices. Green chiles were everywhere, in the sauces, on the sides of the plates, chopped over Tiger's steak. He ate them without a qualm.

"Seriously, that's all you're going to eat?" Tamsin asked Angus, eyeing his two modest tacos, which were slathered with cheese and chiles.

He nodded. "I think better when I'm not stuffed."

"I don't." Tamsin patted her stomach. "I think better when I'm full and warm and a little bit sleepy."

"Don't we all," Ben agreed.

Ciaran watched them both in fascination, then patted his belly in imitation of Tamsin. "Me too."

"Great." Angus pretended to scowl. "My kid is being raised by gluttons."

"Goblins and gluttons." Tamsin grinned. "We know what it's like to be hungry, that's all. We know *not* being hungry is the better state. When you have food—enjoy it."

Angus remembered how shaky she'd been when he'd brought her to the house in Louisiana, how she'd admitted she hadn't eaten in a while.

Never again, Angus vowed. Tamsin would never have to be on the road alone, wondering when she'd find her next meal. No matter what Angus had to do to put things right with Shifter Bureau or convince the Morrisseys to work her into the system as they'd done for Tiger, he'd make sure Tamsin always had a home, food, family. Even if he had to fight the world to do it.

Not content with ordering half the menu, Ben had the waitress bring a platter of sopapillas for dessert. Angus partook, liking the light, puffy pastries covered with cinnamon and honey. He licked his fingers, glancing at Tamsin and thinking what a fun dish it would be to eat with her—alone. He could accidentally drip honey on her neck and lick it clean. Drip it on other places as well, and she could do the same to him.

Tamsin caught his eye, and a slow smile spread across her face as she licked a drop of honey from the corner of her mouth. Angus's cheeks burned, but he refused to look away.

Tamsin gave him a look filled with promise, then returned to her conversation with Ben.

The meal finally ended, the waitress happy with the generous tip Ben bestowed upon her. He might be good at slipping in and out of places unnoticed, but this restaurant would remember him.

Angus had borrowed a pickup from one of Dante's employees to drive downtown, and they piled back in to follow Ben, who led the way on his motorcycle. He knew a place, he said, where they could talk.

The place proved to be a house halfway up the mountain, tucked at the end of an empty lane. The house was fairly new—built in the last decade, it looked like, with an ultramodern kitchen that took up half the living space.

"Belongs to a friend," Ben said as he unlocked it with a key and tapped in an alarm code.

"I see," Tamsin said as she looked around the spacious interior. "A lady friend?"

"Sadly, no. Guy and his wife I used to work for. When you live a thousand years, you get to know a lot of people."

He spoke in a matter-of-fact way, but Angus saw another flicker of pain. When you lived a long time, you lost a lot of people too. Shifters didn't live as long as Ben, but already Angus had felt the bite of loss of human friends from his childhood.

Tiger would not let them venture any farther into the

house until he'd circled the outside, then walked into every room on the inside. When he finished, he took a seat at the breakfast bar and gave Angus a nod. "Clear. No people, no listening devices."

Angus remembered Tiger saying he could hear the signal a listening device gave off. He and Tamsin exchanged a glance.

Tamsin nodded glumly at him—on the way, they'd agreed Angus would lay out the problem to the others.

Ciaran sat next to Tiger, copying his stance of leaning his elbows back on the breakfast bar. Ciaran would avidly listen to every word, but Angus wouldn't hold back. His son deserved to know the danger.

Angus related the story of his brother and his rebellion, how Gavan had been caught, given a flash trial by Shifter Bureau, and executed, how Angus's mate had been caught and executed with him. He told them how Tamsin had joined the group for a while and then thought better of it when Gavan had showed her his stash of human weapons, collected so he and his band could wreak havoc. Now they had the question of what to do about it.

There was a long silence when he finished.

"So what do you think?" Angus asked them.

Tiger spoke before Ben could. "Destroy it. Weapons reaching Shifter or human hands is a bad idea."

"Agreed. *How* to do that is the problem."

Ben rubbed his chin. "The military gets rid of its surplus by selling things off to other countries—not a viable option. Or they melt things down, explode the ordnance, bury it in a deep hole if it's nuclear." Ben turned a worried gaze to Tamsin. "Please tell me nothing is nuclear."

Tamsin shook her head. "I don't think so, but I'm no expert. I saw guns in racks, grenades, lots of ammunition."

Tiger broke in. "You need special facilities to melt down guns or blow up grenades."

"We couldn't go to the DOD and ask to use a facility for

a little while, could we?" Tamsin asked, then sighed. "Nah, didn't think so."

"Not selling them," Angus said. "Not to people in other countries or to criminals here. Not giving them to Shifters either."

Tamsin held herself tightly, arms folded. "Someone might have found them already—they might not be there anymore. Or Gavan might have moved them or sold them. Or one of his guys did after Gavan was caught."

"If Gavan moved or sold them, that in itself worries me," Angus said. "So first step, find out."

"With Shifter Bureau all over Shreveport watching out for me," Tamsin pointed out.

"That's why you have friends," Ben said. "Friends who are good at stealth. I can look for you."

"Friends who can protect you," Tiger put in. "I will keep you safe."

Tamsin spread her arms. "Aw, you two are so nice. You barely know me—why would you do this?"

"We know Angus," Ben said. "He's cranky, but he's a good guy. And I know about people. Tiger will tell you he can scent the difference between good and evil, and I think he really can."

Tiger's lips twitched, the closest he came to smiling. "There is more to it than that. But I know."

Tamsin steepled her fingers and brought them to her lips, her banter fading. Angus saw thoughts dancing behind her eyes and imagined they were similar to his. They had to decide whether to heave the recon onto Ben's shoulders or risk it themselves. Plus, they had to trust that Ben wouldn't suddenly go wild at the sight of all the weapons and use them himself, such as for avenging the death of his people on the Fae.

"Are you sure you can do it without Shifter Bureau spotting you and following you?" Tamsin asked Ben. "Or anyone else for that matter, like the human police?"

"Hmm," Ben said, and then he vanished.

Tamsin yelped, and Angus jumped. He knew Ben had some magic, but he'd never seen it in action before.

Tiger didn't move, and neither did Ciaran. "He's right there," Ciaran said, pointing to a shadow between the large refrigerator and the hall to the back door.

Angus peered where his son indicated and gradually, Ben's outline became clear, like an object slowly illuminated by dawn light. Ben stepped forward, solid and substantial once more.

"Hard to fool cubs," he said. "They know how to look at things. Can't fool Tiger either."

Tiger only nodded, not boastful.

Tamsin gave Ben an admiring look. "Convinced me. How do you do that? Slip between molecules of air?"

Ben raised his brows. "What kind of books do you read? It's sort of misdirection. Using light and shadow to my advantage. A glam to make watchers look somewhere else. I practice." He huffed on his fingernails and brushed them against his shirt.

"What do you think, Angus?" Tamsin asked. "Have him dodge in and check it out?"

"Your call," Angus said. "Your stash."

"Not *mine*. It belonged to your brother. So *your* call."

Ben let out a laugh. "I don't know if watching you two defer to each other is sweet or hilarious. I should go. If Tamsin is caught, it wouldn't go well for her."

No, it would not. Trusting Ben was the best option. If he tried to do anything duplicitous with the arsenal, Angus would let Shifter Bureau, Dylan, and the human police chase *him*. Angus liked Ben, but he would choose Tamsin's safety, and Ciaran's, over all others. Always.

"Ben goes," Angus said.

Tamsin nodded. "I agree." She let out a breath. "Let me give you the directions."

* * *

Tiger accompanied Angus, Tamsin, and Ciaran back to the carnival, now their self-appointed bodyguard.

Tamsin hugged Ben before he got onto his motorcycle and rode off, her heart heavy. She wasn't sure if she hoped he found the arsenal intact or discovered it had gone. Damn Gavan—what had he been thinking? If Shifter Bureau hadn't caught him when they had . . . Tamsin shuddered. She didn't like to think about what Gavan would have ultimately done with the weapons.

Angus was quiet as they drove back to the field where the carnival was being set up. He returned the truck, then went to help out, after giving Tamsin a long, heartfelt kiss.

Now to wait.

If Ben rode his motorcycle all the way, it would take him at least a day or so to cross through Texas, cutting south and east to Louisiana. Longer if he needed food and rest, though who knew what kind of sustenance a goblin needed? Ben could sure put away the food.

Tamsin tried not to worry about him. Shifter Bureau didn't know about him, Ben had told them. Not much of anyone did. He was good at taking care of himself, he assured them. Had been for a thousand years. The loneliness touching that statement nearly broke Tamsin's heart.

Ben checked in with Tiger later that night—how, Tamsin didn't know, because she never saw Tiger with a phone. Tiger conveyed the message that Ben had made it to Dallas and would sleep and then ride on to Shreveport early in the morning.

After Tiger delivered the message, Tamsin put Ciaran to bed and sat up on the mattress in the back to wait for Angus. She browsed through magazines Celene had lent her, seeing that adorable shoes were in the stores for fall and winter. Maybe Tamsin could use the rest of her poker money to go shopping, now that the carnival was giving her a regular weekly paycheck.

She put any plans aside, along with the magazines, when Angus came in.

He paused to check on Ciaran, who was snoring—in a miniature version of his dad's snores—and started to strip off his clothes.

Tamsin forgot about a lot of things as she watched him. Angus was a big man, tight with muscle, a strong wolf with a broad chest and powerful thighs. Angus put out the light before he slid off his underwear, modest when he wasn't undressing to shift.

Tamsin, in a nightshirt and nothing else, slid over to let him into the bed. Angus settled down, and Tamsin draped herself across him under the covers.

"I need new clothes," she said. "I'm sure Celene doesn't want to share hers with me forever. I saw that Albuquerque has a mall."

Angus rumbled in the darkness. "I thought we were hiding weapons from Shifter Bureau."

"What has that got to do with anything? Ben won't get back to us until tomorrow, and then we'll have to decide what to do. A few hours of shopping in between won't hurt."

Angus rubbed his hand over his face, catching on his beard. "I'll never understand females."

"There's nothing to understand. We are the most logical of beings. We need clothes, we shop. We don't go into denial wearing the same shirt for months until it's a rag held together with a few pieces of thread."

The rumbling deepened. "What are you saying?"

"And we don't automatically assume everything someone says is about us."

"Yes, you do. Women take everything personally."

"*I* don't," Tamsin said with emphasis, then she laughed, skimmed off her nightshirt, and snuggled down with him. "We need to talk."

Angus feigned a shudder. "Why does that fill me with foreboding? What are you going to spring on me now? My brother had *two* arsenals? Or twenty cubs with all these women he mate-claimed?"

"He didn't have any cubs at all. Which is interesting. But no." Tamsin traced a pattern on his bare chest, liking how his wiry hair curled around her fingertip. "What are we going to do afterward? I mean if Shifter Bureau doesn't catch us and kill us. Where will we live? Together? Or . . ."

Angus went silent, and Tamsin's heart thumped. The silence held tension.

"I thought you were happy following the carnival," he said after a moment. "Living the nomadic life."

"I am. For now. But I've been thinking. You have friends in your Shiftertown, good friends, like Reg. Ties. Ciaran has friends there too, and I assume friends at school. Do you truly want to never see them again? Be on the run all the time?"

Angus's faint growl vibrated his chest. "What's this really about, Tamsin?"

Tamsin raised her head, her braid falling across her shoulder. "I'm not sure. I've never wanted to live in a Shiftertown. I don't want to be Collared. I'd die, I think. But then, I want to see my mother. I miss her—I'm crazy with missing her. If I remain a fugitive, I'll never see her again. So it made me think—is that what will happen to *you* if you don't go home? You'll never see the ones you care about again? Is that what you want?" Tears stung her eyes, and she tried to blink them back.

Angus lifted his hand and smoothed a wisp of her hair. "Sweetheart. Why didn't you tell me?"

Tamsin sniffled, swiping at her cheeks. "Which part? I made a lot of statements in that speech."

"About missing your mum. You seem so contented, like it's easy for you to find joy in anything, no matter what."

"I learned to, because if I didn't, I'd sit down and never

get up again. I lost my sister to Shifter hunters. We were close, Angus. I can't explain how close. And then she was gone. My mother was gone too, locked away. I'd made the decision to run when Shifter Bureau came for us. The price has been losing my sister and never seeing my mother. I don't want to risk my mother's relative freedom by trying to contact her—she might be punished with me if I'm caught."

"Goddess, Tamsin, I'm sorry."

"Yeah, me too." Tamsin lay down again, resting her head on his shoulder as he continued to stroke her hair. His large hand was strong, warm in the darkness. "And now I don't want to lose you too. But you're risking everything staying with me."

He kissed her forehead. "You let me worry about that, love."

Tamsin popped her head up. "Sorry, I can't just forget that you and your cub could be arrested for not going home to Shiftertown like good boys. So what happens? Do you throw off your Collar and run away with me? Or do I lock myself into your Shiftertown and pray Shifter Bureau doesn't notice me or execute me? And Tiger let slip that if a Shifter disappears from his Shiftertown, its leader is punished, and other Shifters in that Shiftertown might be too."

Angus's eyes glittered. "Tiger told you that?"

"He was trying to explain to me why he wouldn't be missed from the Austin Shiftertown. He doesn't exist, he said—there's no true record of him. There's a fake one if Shifter Bureau does a head count, but the Morrisseys cover for Tiger if he's off on a mission for them. He explained that if they didn't cover, the Morrisseys might be punished or removed from power, probably both."

"Yeah, I believe it." Angus let out a breath. "When my brother ran off, Spence was called onto the carpet. He was again this year when a Shifter called Brice vanished without a trace, as did a few other Shifters in our and other Shiftertowns. Brice was killed, so at least he's accounted for. Our Guardian sent him to dust. But Spence had to talk fast to keep his position."

"So what will he tell them this time?"

Angus cupped her cheek. "I could always pretend to be dead. Have the Guardian show Shifter Bureau a cloth full of dust."

Tamsin sat up straight. "Fake our own deaths. Oh, that's—"

"*Tamsin.*" Angus slid his hand behind her neck. "I wasn't serious."

"But it's a perfect solution. Then we can—"

Her words were cut off as Angus dragged her down to him for a forceful kiss. "We'll think of something else," he said in a low voice. "Something not so drastic. All right?"

The kiss more than his words made Tamsin want to cease talking. "Sure. We'll think of something."

Tamsin bent to him for another kiss, letting her thoughts scatter as Angus's hands warmed her back. Tamsin slid over him, finding him hard and ready, and she eased herself down on him, letting intense pleasure fill her as he slid inside.

They could talk of the future later. The *now* was plenty good at the moment.

Tiger sought Angus the next morning as he worked to set up the pirate swing ride, perfectly repaired and safe now. Tiger waited until Angus told the guys he'd take a break, and they walked away together. Tiger, as usual, got straight to the point.

"It's there," he said. "Ben found it. He said to tell you that the ball is now in your court."

CHAPTER TWENTY-THREE

Angus asked Dante to watch over Ciaran, and Dante agreed. The only one not happy with the arrangement was Ciaran.

"Dad, I want to go with *you*!"

Ciaran's panic wound around Angus, making him want to say to hell with Gavan's mess and Shifter Bureau and the danger the arsenal posed. He wanted to stay put, hold his cub close, stay next to him forever.

He lifted Ciaran into his arms. As a human boy, he was getting too tall to be picked up, but Angus cared nothing for that. He kissed Ciaran's hair. "I know, son, but you'll be safer here with Dante. What Tamsin and I have to do is dangerous. I can't look after both you and her at the same time. You know what trouble she gets herself into."

Ciaran lifted his head, his stubborn scowl a mirror of Angus's own. "Then Tamsin has to stay with me. Dante and Celene can look after *her* too."

"That's what I want, believe me, but she won't listen."

He and Tamsin had already had a long and loud argument on precisely this topic. Tamsin refused to remain behind. Angus needed protecting, she said, or he'd get himself killed. *She* would evade capture as she had all her life—she was good at it. Angus, on the other hand, was too slow and lumbering, she claimed, and they'd catch him without a problem.

Angus finally gave in only because he knew Tamsin would do something asshole stupid if he tried to leave her behind, like run off in the night to Shreveport alone or follow him. If they went together, at least Angus could keep an eye on her.

Ciaran, on the other hand, needed to stay well away from Shifter Bureau and Shiftertowns. If Angus and Tamsin were caught, Ciaran would be hidden with Dante, well guarded.

Ciaran's mulish look didn't disguise his tears. "What if you don't come back?"

Angus's first impulse was to say, *Of course we'll come back*, but there was a real possibility they might not. He didn't want to lie to Ciaran, who deserved to know, and who was old enough to scent a comforting fib.

"Then Dante and Celene will take care of you," Angus said. "They'll raise you like their own. Dante and I have already talked about it. He's a good guy and will teach you how to be Shifter, but he'll also keep you safe."

Ciaran's breath came fast. "I once thought Uncle Gavan was my dad. I cried a lot, because I was very little, and I didn't like him. I didn't understand why I didn't like my own father. Then I found out *you* were my dad. I was scared of you when you took me away from Uncle Gavan and Mother, because I didn't understand, but *you* acted like a *real* dad. You hugged me and talked to me and cooked me food and told me to clean up my room. I decided I'd never, ever leave you, no matter what." Ciaran fixed Angus with his wolf gray eyes, full of determination. *"No matter what."*

Angus's heart burned, his anger at April and his love for

Ciaran rolling into one fiery ball. "I said the same thing when I brought you home, Ciaran. I want to come back to you, more than anything in the world. I'll fight like shit to get here. But I don't want Shifter Bureau and Haider anywhere near you—I'm leaving you here to keep that dickhead *away* from you. No one will know you are with Dante—Haider and men like him will never find you. I promise."

Ciaran's lower lip came out. "Not the point. I still don't want you to go, Dad."

"I know. I don't want to either. Sometimes we have to do crap we don't want to so more people in the world don't get hurt. I'll have Ben and Tiger with me, and we'll get this done as fast as we can. Just don't give Dante too much trouble, all right? He'll never let me hear the end of it."

Ciaran thought about this and nodded gravely. "I'll try. Can I still do the show?"

"Only if Dante is there to make sure you don't get hurt."

"I won't." Ciaran spoke with the conviction of the very young. "Celene is careful, and what we do looks more dangerous than it is. But I'll be safe," he added quickly.

Angus hugged him, holding him tight. He loved this cub so very much. Part of the reason he was off to clean up Gavan's mess instead of ignoring it and walking away was so that men like Haider and even Dylan wouldn't find the arsenal and endanger all Shifters, including Ciaran. He was also doing it to get Tamsin free of these shitheads forever. After that . . . they'd talk about after that when they were done.

Angus drove them away from the carnival later that day in the pickup he'd borrowed once again. Tamsin sat next to him, her hair in a long braid under a cap that somewhat hid her bright hair. Tiger bulked on her other side, saying little as usual.

Tamsin tried to keep her spirits high. She played the radio and sang, trying to get Tiger to join in. She laughed when Tiger told her, straight-faced, "Tigers don't sing."

"I bet they do," Tamsin said. "How many tigers do you know?"

Tiger considered. "Me. Kendrick. My cub. His cubs."

"I bet your cub's a cutie. Does he sing?"

Tiger shrugged his massive shoulders. "I don't know yet. He gurgles."

"Do you have pictures? You must have pictures."

Tiger produced a wallet with an old-fashioned foldout section with a long string of printed photos. Tamsin exclaimed over each picture in turn.

"He must be the most adorable cub I've ever seen," she concluded when she finished and Tiger folded the photos back into his wallet. "Except for Ciaran, of course."

"Ciaran will be a fine wolf," Tiger said.

Angus felt himself grow absurdly proud. Tiger wasn't known for embellishment—if he said Ciaran would make a fine wolf, he meant it.

Dante had provided a cooler full of food, so they stopped at rest areas to eat and use the bathrooms, keeping to themselves. Tiger had a hat over his eccentric hair, and Angus wore a jacket to hide his Collar.

Angus drove through the night, with Tamsin sleeping slumped against him. Tiger remained awake as well, his eyes glittering in the lights from the road.

In the morning, they crossed the Texas border into Louisiana. At least now Angus couldn't be arrested simply for being out of his Shiftertown's state. For breaking curfew, leaving Louisiana in the first place, helping Tamsin escape, not turning her in, disobeying Shifter Bureau . . . all *that* they'd probably kill him for.

The Red River, which formed the border between Texas and Oklahoma, took a huge bend through Arkansas and then ran right through Shreveport's metropolitan area. Resorts lined the river, and riverboat casinos were permanently stationed next to high-rise hotels.

Tamsin pointed the way across the river, through Bossier City, and out into green countryside filled with tall trees and grassy lots that sometimes contained trailer houses.

They passed a sign for an air force base and one pointing south to another military facility.

"Goddess, is that where Gavan found the weapons?" Angus asked in disgust. "Would he be stupidass enough to steal from the military?"

"I don't know," Tamsin answered, her tone glum. "Probably."

He growled. "Just flipping perfect."

"This way, I think," Tamsin said, pointing down a side road that quickly turned to dirt. "I see motorcycle tracks. Ben's, I'd guess."

Angus hoped so. He didn't want to surprise a motorcycle gang in the middle of doing whatever motorcycle gangs did. He didn't fear fighting them, but they'd have a tale to tell and Angus couldn't afford to let them.

"There's Ben." Tamsin pointed to a dark-haired man leaning on his motorcycle parked in the dark shadow of a tree.

Angus pulled the pickup as close as he could to the motorcycle without risking miring the truck in the mud.

"Well, here we are," Ben said. "You doing all right, Tamsin?"

"As well as any girl can riding for hours and hours with smelly male Shifters." Tamsin let out a laugh. "Is it still there? Are you sure?"

She asked the last question in a small voice, as though hoping Ben would say, *Nah, I was just kidding*, and tell them he'd made them drive all the way to Shreveport as a joke.

No such luck. Ben gestured for them to follow him and led the way down a slick path through some trees.

Angus wasn't certain what he expected. An old bunker or a bomb shelter maybe, built underground and lined with cement, the only entrance a small door set in the earth. Or maybe an anonymous squat gray building with bars on the windows, or no windows at all.

What Ben took them to was a dilapidated mobile home that looked like the next high wind would knock it over. The grimy and rusting white mobile home reposed alone in the middle of a damp, overgrown field, resting on a wooden foundation whose once-blue paint had mostly peeled off.

Wooden steps that had led to the front door now lay in a rotting pile against the foundation. Ben reached over it and opened the door.

"Was it locked?" Angus asked.

"Yep. But the lock was easily broken."

"Shit."

There was no way an arsenal could be kept secure in that trailer. Had Gavan picked the place? Or had whoever sold him the weapons already had the stash here? Either way, it was a dumb-ass place to keep it.

Ben swung himself up into the trailer with ease. "Careful coming in here. Lots of holes and rotted boards."

Angus went next, not wanting Tamsin to enter until he made sure it was safe. Or at least safe-ish. He'd prefer to tell her to stay out altogether, but he knew better than to think she'd listen to him.

He found himself in a dim, musty room that ran the length of the trailer, small windows letting in what light filtered through the trees. If the place had ever had interior walls, they'd been taken out. The trailer floor was covered with thin carpet coming up in patches, but was otherwise empty.

Tiger lifted Tamsin in, then climbed up himself. Tiger stationed himself just inside the door so he could look out without being seen. The spot also gave him a view through the back windows to the field behind the trailer.

"This is it?" Angus asked Tamsin in puzzlement.

Tamsin shivered, hugging her arms to her chest. "Yes."

"I don't see an arsenal."

"It's down here." Ben pulled up a pad of carpet to reveal a rusted ring in a slab of floor. Ben settled work gloves on his hands before he pulled the flaking ring and heaved up the slab.

Angus cautiously leaned down to look inside. Ben flicked on a flashlight and shone it through the hole.

A sort of cellar had been dug under the trailer, a shallow one, or else the trailer had been positioned over it after the cellar had been complete. The underground space was longer and wider than the trailer, and indeed lined with cement. Angus gazed down at racks and racks of guns and rifles of all kinds—he didn't know what they all were. A few bore patches of rust, telling him the cellar wasn't air- or watertight.

That gave him an idea. "We could flood it," Angus said. "Pour water down here and drown the stuff."

"Might neutralize the explosives and ammunition," Ben said. "*Might*. Depending on what kind they are and if they're packed in waterproof containers. But anyone could dry off and repair an assault rifle. Same can be said of driving it to the river and dumping it in. Anyone could find it, clean off the stuff, use it or sell it."

Angus straightened up, anger he'd thought he'd come to terms with a long time ago blazing forth. "Goddess damn my brother. I know he's in the Summerland, but I hope all the Shifters there are kicking his sorry ass."

They closed up the arsenal and prepared to leave. Ben had bought an iron strap, some long bolts, and tools at a hardware store, and he and Angus bolted the strap over the cellar slab so the trapdoor couldn't be lifted without tools and a lot of strength. Ben also secured the front door with a shiny new padlock.

Angus was quiet as they moved back along the path to the pickup truck, more quiet than usual, which, Tamsin reflected, was saying something. Even when Angus didn't talk much, he'd growl, rumble under his breath, or simply glower.

At the moment, Angus strode in silence, his face still. Tamsin wondered whether the rage that kept him so quiet was directed at his brother or at her.

"You all right?" she asked in a low voice.

"Hmm?" Angus reached down and took her hand, but he did so absently. "Just thinking."

"About how you want to run like hell from me and never look back?"

Angus's grip tightened, and now came the scowl that made his eyes glitter. "I'm not letting you out of my sight. You're my *mate*. We stay together."

While Tamsin warmed at that statement, she persisted, "What are you thinking about, then?"

"Ways to get rid of the stash. I have a couple of ideas. But we should talk later. I'll need Ben's help."

Tamsin burned with curiosity, but Angus said nothing more. He helped her into the pickup, Tiger took his place on her other side, and Angus drove them back toward Shreveport, Ben leading them on his motorcycle.

"Where did the agents get killed?" Angus asked Tamsin as they rolled along the highway.

Tamsin shuddered, not wanting to think about it. She swallowed bile and said, "In the park at the lake. Dion was trying to get me to show him the arsenal, but the Bureau must have heard he was in town, or were following him already. They sent two agents . . ." Tamsin trailed off, the memories she'd pushed aside now filling her mind—the horrible snarling as Dion went into his half-beast Feline and attacked. Blood, screaming, the stench . . .

Angus's touch brought her back from the darkness. Tiger, on her other side, put his hand on her arm, sensing her distress, but Angus's touch reached her heart.

Tamsin took a long breath, shaking off the memory.

"We'll avoid the park at the lake," Angus said. "Ben already booked us into a motel room, and we'll lie low there."

The room wasn't in a fancy high-rise resort, but a small chain motel farther down the river. At this point, Tamsin didn't care where they stayed as long as it had a decent bathroom and a bed, and no Shifter Bureau agents.

But maybe one day she and Angus could be truly free to come here on a real vacation and stroll along the river hand in hand. They'd take in a show and a fine dinner, walk in the moonlight as a human couple would. No one would mind that they were Shifter, and they could go where they wanted, do what they wished. Ciaran would never have to take a Collar, and neither would any cub she and Angus had together.

The thought of having a cub with Angus filled her with sudden elation.

All the more reason to get this over and done with. If they destroyed the arsenal, Shifter Bureau would have no more reason to chase Tamsin around—well, apart from the fact that she had no Collar and hadn't been registered and had avoided being forced into a Shiftertown. She'd prove somehow that she hadn't killed the agents, and they wouldn't be able to threaten her or Angus or Ciaran any longer.

Then she'd figure out her life from there.

No matter what happened, she wanted Angus to be a part of that life. Whether they turned revolutionary or moved into Angus's Shiftertown and took up woodworking with Reg, she wanted him by her side, and Ciaran too. A family. And this family would stay together.

Tamsin flopped onto the one bed in the tiny motel room Ben had given Angus the key to. "I could eat something," she said.

"Pretty good pizza place right across the street," Ben offered. "Deep-dish, loaded with meat and cheese."

Angus turned from shutting the door, and Tiger took up a watchful stance by the window.

"Will you two stop talking about food for three seconds?" Angus said impatiently. "It's like being on one of those road trip shows for a food channel."

"I love those," Tamsin said with enthusiasm, and Ben nodded.

"I like the diners one," he said.

"Can we focus?" Angus frowned at them, and deepened his frown when Ben and Tamsin grinned and high-fived each other.

He should know by now that Tamsin babbled nonsense to break the tension. But Angus looked like he'd explode if she teased him any further.

"Focusing now, Captain." Tamsin saluted him, then made a motion of turning a key in a lock over her mouth and throwing the key away.

"Thank you," Angus said in exasperation. "Tiger, I've heard of a guy from the Las Vegas Shiftertown. Name of Reid—not a Shifter but what Dylan calls a dark Fae. Apparently, he can do things to iron, like make it melt, change its shape—something like that. I wasn't clear on the details."

"Stuart Reid," Ben answered before Tiger could. "He's a *dokk alfar*. Much, much more personable than the high Fae, trust me. Reid is what's called an iron master—apparently, he can make iron do his will. The catch is he can only command iron inside Faerie. The talent doesn't manifest in the human world for some reason—he doesn't know why. What he *can* do in the human world is teleport." Ben took on a hopeful expression. "Maybe he could teleport the weapons, or pieces of the weapons, to places all over the country. Scatter their parts so far and wide that no one would be able to use them."

"How long would that take him?"

"Who knows? He can only teleport to places he's seen or been to, and I don't know how much he can do before it spends him. Or whether he can teleport explosives without them going off and killing him, or if he can teleport anything iron or steel at all. If the weapons were inside Faerie, of course, he could reduce them to slag in no time."

Angus shook his head. "I'm not taking an arsenal of human weapons into Faerie for Fae shits to get their hands on. *If* we could even find a way to get it there."

"Would it matter?" Tamsin asked. "The weapons are full of iron. The Fae can't touch them."

"But Fae have recruited Shifters," Angus reminded her. "Stupid Shifters who want to be Battle Beasts again. And I'm willing to bet the Fae have other kinds of lackeys who *can* touch iron. I understand the dark Fae can use it just fine. How well could we trust *them*? What's to say they aren't murdering assholes as well, but Reid happens to be a nice guy?"

"*Dokk alfar* are daisies in the sunshine compared to the *hoch alfar*." Ben spat the last words, as though the syllables choked him. "But you have a point—we can't trust that not one dark Fae would see the benefit of having a pile of automatic weapons land on their doorstep and prevent Reid from destroying them."

"We'll keep Reid on standby," Angus said. "Thinking about Reid gave me another idea. When I was inside Faerie with Jaycee, we met a Fae who was pretty powerful. Lady Aisling—some kind of superpowered Fae. She did things that scared the shit out of me, but she might be able to destroy these things. She said she came into the human world often and that iron didn't bother her as much as it bothers the rest of the high Fae. I don't know if her power would work here, but it might be worth a shot to ask her." He stopped as he noticed Ben staring at him. The man's dark eyes were wide, his face ashen. "What's wrong with you?" Angus growled.

"The woman you call Lady Aisling is one of the Tuil Erdannan." Ben spoke the words carefully, as though fearing dire consequences if he mispronounced them. "Ancient beings, amazingly strong ones, who don't give a shit about the problems of humans, Shifters, high Fae, dark Fae, goblins, or any other living, breathing creature. I'm pretty sure giving *her* access to a stash of weapons is the worst idea of all."

"I met her," Angus said without worry. "I was in her house. She didn't strike me as the type to be excited by human tools of destruction. When Jaycee told her that Fae were recruiting Shifters to fight for them again, it annoyed her but didn't alarm her. She helped us mainly because she liked Jaycee. Maybe if Jaycee asks, she'll do it for *her.*"

"Or crook her little finger and wipe us all off the map," Ben said, the fear in his voice clear. "You don't mess with the Tuil Erdannan, Angus."

Tamsin sat up. "She sounds intriguing. Can I meet her?"

"Not joking, Tamsin," Ben said. "The Tuil Erdannan are seriously badass, and you don't want to mess with them. Even asking one the time of day can get you killed if he or she is feeling peevish."

"Definitely want to meet her then," Tamsin said. "If she liked Jaycee, maybe we should ask Jaycee's opinion."

"Agreed," Angus said. "Ben, can you contact Jaycee? I don't want to risk using my phone."

Ben looked from Angus to Tamsin and shook his head, as though washing his hands of this decision. "Sure, I can ask. I'm going to keep warning you that this is the most dangerous route to take, and maybe you'll listen after a while. Though I won't be able to say *I told you so* if I'm right, because we'll all be a melted pile of goo. What do you think, Tiger? You're usually a good judge of character . . . Tiger? What's up?"

Tiger had gone rigid, his gaze fixed on the parking lot. Without answering Ben, he slipped out the door and vaulted over the balcony, straight down to the lot below.

CHAPTER TWENTY-FOUR

Angus was out the door, but before he reached the stairs, Tiger came back up them with a struggling, hissing Feline. The man was in his human form, but his pupils were slitted with rage, his hands sprouting claws.

Tiger dragged him inside the room, threw the Feline to the floor, and put his foot on him. The Feline squirmed, but it was clear he would not throw off Tiger anytime soon.

Tamsin had bounced off the bed as soon as Tiger came through the door. "Dion!"

Angus snarled, but he'd had the feeling that was who Tiger had captured. "The Shifter who killed the two Bureau agents?"

Dion hissed again, sounding like a leaky tire. *Felines.* "You should be thanking me," he snapped, his voice guttural. "They were dirtbags, hunting down Shifters."

Tamsin came to stand over him, her face flushed, her hands shaking. "They were *people*. With families. We're not murderers. Not only that, but you risked bringing the wrath of Shifter Bureau down on all Shifters. Fortunately, they're only after one suspect for the killings. *Me*."

"So?" Dion's claws receded, and his eyes became human. They were green, his hair lanky and brown. "You took off. You were out of it—what the hell are you doing back here? I was riding by and swore I caught your scent." He took a loud sniff. "It's distinctive. Who are these assholes?"

Angus stepped between the Shifter on the floor and Tamsin. "*This* asshole is her mate."

The Feline opened his mouth to snarl, and then worry crept into his eyes and he shut it again. He'd know that under Shifter law Angus could kill him for putting Tamsin under threat. Killing Dion would break human law, of course, but no humans stood in this room.

Dion switched his gaze to Ben. "What is *that*? Stinks of Fae."

Ben heaved an aggrieved sigh. "I get so tired of this shit." He tapped his chest. "*Not* Fae. If you want to know what kind of being I am and what I can do, here you go."

He made a tossing motion with his hand. Instantly Dion was pinned to the floor, as though a thousand invisible tethers held him down. He struggled for a moment, eyes wide with fear, and then he passed out. His head lolled on the floor, though the rest of his body remained rigid.

Tiger nudged Dion with his foot. "Did you do that?" he asked Ben.

"Knock him out? No. He fainted. Good, because I was already tired of listening to his voice. What do you want to do with him, Tamsin?"

Tamsin gazed down at Dion in worry. "I don't know. We could tie him up and take him to Shifter Bureau, maybe leave a note pinned to him that he killed the Bureau agents, but he might get chatty about us. We could kill him, but then we'd be no better than he is."

"We could give him to Dylan," Tiger suggested. "He knows how to deal with out-of-control Shifters."

Tamsin's face lit, her moroseness vanishing. "Oh, that sounds interesting."

"Meanwhile," Angus broke in, "Ben, can you make sure he stays here and doesn't make noise? While you contact Jaycee?"

"Sure thing."

"Good," Tamsin said, straightening up. "Then we can go try that pizza."

Angus shook his head. "Not going anywhere if Shifter Bureau is still investigating what this guy did and is looking for you."

"We have to eat *something.* I'm starving, and there's no room service."

"Tamsin . . ."

She laughed. "Someday, I'm going to teach you to live for the moment. But I see your point. Ben, can you—?"

"Talk to Jaycee, contain the bad guy, bring home the pizza? Yes. Ben can do it all. Even if he doesn't get the girl." He made *poor-me* eyes at Tamsin.

Tamsin sent him a smile. "One day, you'll get the girl too. I'll put money on it."

"Huh. She'll have to be pretty old. And fearless. Sassy. And cute—I gotta wish for cute."

"Sure you do." Tamsin enclosed him in a brief hug. "I'll take extra pepperoni."

Ben returned the hug enthusiastically but backed off under Angus's glare and glanced at Dion. "He shouldn't be able to move under that spell, even when I'm not here. But keep an eye on him, Tiger."

Tiger gave him a grave nod. Tamsin turned back to look at Dion and wrinkled her nose. "I'm not sure I want to sleep here with him on the floor."

Ben let out another long sigh. "Take my room." He tossed Tamsin the key. "I don't mind terrorizing him a little. Tiger can stay and help me. My room's next door."

Tamsin caught the key, took up her backpack, kissed Ben on the cheek, and walked out.

Angus had to admit the pizza was good. Tamsin ate it with vast enjoyment, washing it down with an oversized soft drink. Foxes could put the food away as much as goblins could, Angus decided.

Ben had contacted Jaycee. She couldn't leave for an unscheduled trip to Shreveport, she said, without Kendrick and other trackers knowing about it. Ben had asked her for strict secrecy—they couldn't risk Dylan getting wind of where they were. Dimitri would know—he and Jaycee never kept anything from each other—but Jaycee promised to get the talisman Lady Aisling had given her to Ben without anyone finding out. She hadn't been specific about how.

Dimitri had asked about his truck. Ben had replied evasively as Angus instructed him, leaving Dimitri growling on the other end.

"I'll get it back to him in one piece," Angus promised. "Not sure what color it will be, but it will be in one piece."

That night, Angus lay down with Tamsin on the lumpy mattress and kissed her lips, which were a little sweet from the soda. "Remember what you said about living for the moment?"

Tamsin stretched against him, pulling him closer. "I remember," she murmured, her eyes closing as he deepened the kiss.

Angus slid inside her, every hurt from his past fleeing as he sank into her. He loved everything about this woman—her taste, her scent, the soft noises she made as he pleasured her. *My mate. My life. I will protect you forever.*

Tamsin smiled up at him, then lost the smile as the two of them dissolved into desire. Angus silenced her cries with kisses, letting out a groan as he released at the same time she did.

"See?" Tamsin whispered as they drowsed together in the darkness. "Spontaneity isn't such a bad thing."

Tamsin woke in the gray light of dawn to a heavy knocking on the door. The sound jerked her out of marvelous dreams where she and Angus made hot love on a cushion of air, surrounded by whipped cream, to find herself on a lumpy mattress in a dingy motel room, traffic roaring by on the highway.

Her fears rushed back at her as Angus got to his feet and cautiously peered out the door's peephole. He inhaled at the same time, taking in the scent of the intruder before he opened the door a foot, darted out his hand, and hauled a man into the room.

Tamsin sat up, pulling the covers to her chin. Zander Moncrieff wore the long black coat Tamsin remembered over jeans and a T-shirt, his beaded white-blond braids swinging. He carried paper bags that smelled of bready things, and Tamsin's stomach growled.

Zander took in the naked Angus and then Tamsin in the bed. "Oops. Am I interrupting something?"

"Nice to see you again, Zander," Tamsin said. "Would you like to sit down? What are you doing here at five thirty in the morning?"

"Bringing Ben a present from Jaycee." Zander glanced at Angus again, who stood tall next to him and didn't move. "Ben told me this was *his* room number."

"We switched," Angus rumbled. "He must have forgotten."

Or not, Tamsin thought. Ben might have thought it funny to send Zander to their mate-frenzied room at dawn. She and Angus had practiced their spontaneity most of the night and hadn't been quiet about it.

"Well, anyway." Zander turned to go, then looked Angus up and down. "You might want to put on clothes before you join us. Don't scare the natives."

He opened and closed the door so quickly, Tamsin barely felt the draft. She heard Zander move to the next door and begin banging on it.

Tamsin was anxious to learn what Zander had to say, but she took a shower first, a quick one, knowing Angus's scent would be all over her. She didn't mind so much, but the teasing would be unbearable. Shifters saw nothing wrong with sex, and lots of it, and could discuss it at length and in detail, but she didn't want to embarrass Angus.

Angus had already dressed and gone by the time she emerged. Tamsin threw on clean clothes and went next door, shaking water from her hair.

Zander had brought breakfast in the bags—pastries, donuts, and bagels. They feasted while Dion remained tethered. Dion was afraid, the scent of his fear cloying, but he'd returned to growling and cursing.

"Should we feed him?" Angus asked.

"Nah," Ben said. "Don't want him to choke. We'll fix him up later. Ready to go?"

"You're going to leave me here?" Dion asked, incredulous.

Ben turned to him, and Dion blenched as soon as those very black eyes were on him. "Yep. I'll deal with you when we get back."

Dion snorted a laugh. "When the maids come in, they'll find me. Or I'll yell, and someone will rescue me."

"Sure you will." Ben approached him, something in his hand, and Dion sucked in a terrified breath. "But, one, no one will hear. Two, you really want them to call the cops? You're wanted for murder, my friend. Keep quiet, and we won't give you to Shifter Bureau. Here's the remote." Ben laid it by his side. "Enjoy yourself."

Tiger took a mug that rested next to the coffee maker in the corner, filled it with water from the sink, and stuck in an extra bendy straw from last night's feast. He set the mug where Dion could turn his head to drink and then nodded for Zander to lead the way out.

Ben closed the door once they were outside then gestured to it and muttered a few words Tamsin didn't understand.

"What did you just do?" she whispered to him as they walked to the stairs.

Ben looked modest. "Nothing too difficult. A glam to keep people from noticing the door or hearing what's inside. I'll have to make my own bed when I come back, but oh well."

Ben must have cast the *don't-notice-me* glam on himself before they drove out, because Tamsin kept losing sight of him on the road, even when she'd been looking right at him the moment before. Tiger rode in the truck with Angus and Tamsin, while Zander brought up the rear on his motorcycle.

Angus drove sedately as usual, winding down the highway toward the location of the trailer and the stash.

As they turned down the lane that led to the clearing with the trailer, Tamsin heard Ben shout and gun his bike. Zander, on his motorcycle, swerved around Angus and raced to see what was wrong.

Angus rattled to a halt near the tree where they'd parked the day before. He and Tiger boiled out of the truck, running down the path after Ben and Zander.

Tamsin scrambled out and followed. She saw what had alarmed Ben when she reached the grassy field that opened out around the trailer.

The door Ben had padlocked was wide-open. About half a dozen men—humans—were climbing into and out of the trailer, all of them carrying the weapons from the cache.

They weren't Shifter Bureau—they were ordinary guys in jeans and T-shirts. When they saw Ben and the three Shifter males racing toward them, they froze, shouted, and then turned the weapons on them.

CHAPTER TWENTY-FIVE

Angus halted at the sight of the guns turned toward them, as did Zander, though Angus reasoned that they likely weren't loaded. The ammo had been stored separately, and these guys had been carrying the weapons out like they were firewood.

But who knew if they'd loaded a few as a precaution?

Tiger had no such worries. With enviable speed, he shifted to his tiger form, his clothes shredding behind him, and sprang in silent fury at the men.

One tried to shoot, proving his pistol at least was loaded. The bullet went through Tiger's hide where his foreleg joined his chest. Blood spattered, but Tiger didn't slow one stride.

The man who'd fired gaped in fear, and Tiger bore him down.

The other men were yelling, calling to others to get out here. Angus tore off his shirt and kicked out of his boots, loosening his jeans as he started to shift. It took him longer than it had Tiger, but at last he shucked his pants and underwear and sprang to Tiger's aid.

Angus's Collar went off, burning his flesh, but he didn't stop. They had to knock these guys out, contain them before they got hold of more weapons or went running off to report a Shifter attack.

A man went down under Angus's paws. Angus held back his wolf instinct to savage, settling for trampling the man on his way to the next one.

He saw a streak of red-orange, a small one, and he cursed. At the same time, a man who'd nearly reached a ring of pickups yelped and jumped high. The red streak zoomed away from him and went to attack the kneecaps of the next man.

Angus chose another and leapt for him. This man brought a rifle to bear, but Angus knocked it out of his hands before he could fire. Angus kicked the gun aside, sinking his teeth into a blue-jeaned leg as the man tried to run away.

Out of the corner of his eye, Angus saw Zander quietly disrobing, no frantic ripping out of his clothes. He didn't tarry but didn't hurry, to the confusion of two men who'd stopped in amazement to watch him.

Zander dropped his shirt, the last thing he'd taken off, gazed at the two men with his black-dark eyes, and started to smile. "How you doing, boys?" And he became a polar bear.

Zander's roar rattled the trees, and he rose high, bulking bigger even than Tiger. The men staring at him must have had no ammunition, or else they forgot what their weapons were for, because they threw down the rifles and bolted, Zander charging after them.

The ground shook under Zander's stride, and then Tiger's. The red furry thing that zigged and zagged and couldn't be caught wreaked havoc. Men were screaming and dancing, trying to hit it, but the fox was never in one place more than a millisecond. Angus imagined Tamsin laughing maniacally as she dashed about.

Angus couldn't see Ben, but he might still be using his glam. The man could take care of himself, so Angus continued knocking over the thieves and stamping on them until they stayed down.

He heard the barking scream of a fox and swung to see Tamsin hanging on to a man's arm while he swung her through the air. She bit down, and he yelled, blood spurting.

The man gave an extra hard yank, and Tamsin came loose, or else she let go, and landed on her feet. The man tried to kick her, but she was gone, racing to the next goon.

A pickup truck started. *Damn.* Men sprinted toward it, diving in as it pulled away. Some who were down crawled to the trees, running when they gained their feet. Angus heard motorcycles roaring to life.

The last man dashed desperately from Angus, though Tiger swerved to cut him off. A pickup careened between Tiger and the man, and one of the man's friends reached down and pulled him on board.

Tiger gave chase, but even he had to give up as the pickup slid around the wet earth, hit the road, and tore out, droplets of mud flying in its wake.

Tiger growled, sitting down on his haunches as though waiting to see if they'd return. Finally he huffed, stood up, and walked slowly to the trailer, his feet leaving giant prints in the mud. He shifted to human as he walked, and as soon as he was upright, began picking up the scattered weapons.

Zander's polar bear charged back from the woods. He took a few seconds to shift, then growled, "Fuck. Didn't get any of them. They knew these woods. Guessing they're locals, stumbling on a lucky find."

Angus shifted, breathing hard as he climbed to his human feet. "If they're local boys, probably Ben and then us coming in and out of here tipped them off. Even if they didn't want the weapons to use themselves, they could sell them for a hefty price. Did we get all the guns back?"

Zander shrugged. "How many were there?"

"I don't know," Angus had to say. "We didn't take an inventory. Tamsin might know . . . Where the hell is she? Tamsin!"

Angus cupped his hands around his mouth as he shouted for her, his heart banging in sudden fear. Had one of those guys grabbed her? Was she racing off Goddess knew where? Or had they injured her, and she was in the woods, her life slipping away?

No, no. She wasn't gone, and she wasn't dead. Angus would know. The mate bond told him she was alive, well, and nearby.

The mate bond . . .

When Tamsin, still a fox, trotted easily back into the clearing, Angus's knees went weak. He wanted to make his way to her, lift her in his arms, kiss her funny fox face, hold her close. He wanted her to shift back to human while he held her, and kiss her lips. Then he'd tell his friends to go the hell away, and take her in the tall grass.

The fact that the local lads might be back, or report that Shifters guarding a stash of weapons had attacked them, didn't interest him. Angus wanted to be with Tamsin—the rest of the world didn't matter.

The mate bond wrapped around his heart, an invisible tether between him and Tamsin that had seeded and grown in the last weeks.

The mate bond didn't always manifest. Angus hadn't formed it with April. Though a Shifter male might make a mate-claim and he and the female have a sun and moon ceremony, they might never experience the mystical bond that all Shifters sought. It was believed that the mate bond was a gift from the Goddess, and Shifters prayed for it.

As Angus stood frozen in the realization that he and Tamsin were mate bonded, Tamsin, who must have wiped the blood from her fur, sauntered past Zander. Zander put his hands on his hips and grinned down at her.

"Aren't you cute?" Zander said. "Aw, you sweet little thing. All right, all right, don't bite me."

Tamsin sat down on her haunches looking smug, lifting her red and white muzzle. She eyed Zander for a moment, then continued to Angus and twined her body around his legs, hugging him with her tail.

The mate bond throbbed, squeezing Angus's heart until he couldn't breathe.

Ben appeared out of a shadow, something glittering in his hand.

"What do we do?" he asked Angus. "Cut and run? Or try for Lady Aisling?"

Angus realized they were all looking at him, Tiger included, who folded his arms and waited for his orders. Tamsin remained a fox, the shimmering bond between them as soft as her fur.

Angus tried to find air to speak. "See if we can find Lady Aisling," he said, his voice grating and hoarse. "If we leave, those guys might return. They can make enough money from these weapons that they'd risk coming back for them."

"Then the police can catch *them* and arrest them for the stash," Zander pointed out. "We'll be out of it."

"A stash with Shifter fingerprints and DNA all over it," Angus said. "Including ours. I doubt my brother was smart enough to wear gloves when handling them. All Shifters were fingerprinted when they were put into Shiftertowns, and about fifteen years ago, Shifter Bureau came by and helped themselves to our DNA. We have to destroy the weapons."

"And if we can't?" Zander asked.

"I don't know." Angus shrugged tightly. "We have to succeed."

Tiger gave them a nod. "Angus is right. We stay and destroy them."

Ben hefted the stone. "All right. Here goes nothing."

He closed his hand around the stone, chanted a few words Angus didn't understand, and then the name *Aisling*.

A breeze blew through the humid air in the clearing, but it was natural, a few clouds rolling overhead.

Angus caught no scent of Fae magic, no sulfur smell of a gate opening between the human world and the Fae's. When he'd journeyed to Faerie—an experience he wanted to forget—the doorway between worlds had emitted a sharp, acrid odor.

"Nothing is right," Zander commented after about ten minutes. He'd restored his clothes, except for his coat.

Ben's chanting died away, and he cleared his throat. He opened his hand and scowled in frustration at the stone on his palm.

"Maybe we have to be in the house for it to work," Zander suggested. The door to Faerie that Angus and Jaycee had used had opened from the haunted house.

"Jaycee said Lady Aisling told her she could summon her anytime, anywhere," Ben answered.

"*Jaycee* can," Zander said. "I'll bet Jaycee has to use the stone."

Ben shook his head. "The Tuil Erdannan are powerful enough to do whatever they want. They don't have to obey the summons of a talisman. They choose. I bet she hears me just fine, but has no interest in answering."

Zander turned to Angus. "Options? Besides having Tiger tear the weapons apart. I hate to risk him accidentally blowing himself up. Carly would never let us hear the end of it."

Angus found his jeans and underwear and pulled them on. "Can we build a big enough fire to burn the trailer down and everything under it? It will create a hell of an explosion, but that will destroy the weapons forever. We disappear and hope the local men don't describe us well."

"Shifter Bureau will just round up any Shifters until they find the right ones," Zander said. "Or make some of them scapegoats—your Shiftertown leader maybe, or all your friends. They'll figure out *you* had something to do with it, since they're chasing you and Tamsin."

And Ciaran, Angus thought but did not say. Who was safe with Dante for now, but would Dante be able to keep Ciaran safe forever? Worry so vast it was physical pain washed through him. Fucking Shifter Bureau.

Tamsin, still in her fox form, now scampered off into the trees. She came back a few minutes later, stuffing her feet in her sneakers before jamming her baseball cap over her mussed hair.

"Can I try?"

"Sure, why not?" Ben scowled. He tossed her the talisman, which Tamsin caught with agility. "She can ignore you as easily as she can me."

Tamsin returned to Angus's side as she examined the talisman. It was a large, uncut amethyst, polished, like the kind sold in New Age stores or souvenir shops. Gold wire twisted around the deep purple stone, glittering even under the clouds that now obscured the sun.

Angus sniffed at it, but he couldn't discern any scent but Shifter. He supposed Jaycee had possessed it long enough to erase any scent but hers.

"What do I do?" Tamsin asked Ben. "I don't speak Fae."

Ben shrugged. "According to Jaycee, just say her name. Lady Aisling. I added polite words, but it looks like they had no effect. Never do, on beings like them."

Tamsin cocked her head. "What do you mean, *beings like them*? I thought you said they were some kind of super-Fae. Not as evil as the high Fae."

"I never said the Tuil Erdannan weren't evil." Ben's onyx eyes sparkled with anger. "When my people were being slaughtered, they did nothing. When the survivors were exiled, they did nothing. My people died off to the last man—me—and they did nothing. Yeah, you could say I have issues with them."

Tamsin sent him a sympathetic look. "I'm sorry, Ben. Maybe they didn't know what was happening. We can always ask her."

"Good luck," Ben muttered. He turned away and marched to the edge of the trees.

Zander watched him go but didn't call him back. Tiger said nothing at all, only folded his arms and waited for what would happen next.

Tamsin tapped the talisman a few times and brought it close to her mouth. "Hello, is this thing on?" *Tap, tap.* "Lady Aisling, this is Tamsin Calloway. You don't know me, but I'm mated to Angus, who's a friend of Jaycee's. I really like her. She's a lady who knows how to get things done. You met Angus, the growly black wolf. And Tiger and Zander. They're here too. We have a little bit of a problem we hoped you could help us with. You might not be able to do anything, as it's a problem very much of the human world, but we would welcome your advice."

She lowered the talisman, keeping her eyes on it, and waited.

Nothing happened. The breeze picked up, and a few drops of rain began falling from the thickening clouds.

Tiger abruptly went rigid, alert, his head snapping around to peer down the trail. "Someone is coming."

Angus heard nothing, but he'd grown to respect Tiger's abilities. "Zander, get the truck ready. Ben!" he yelled into the trees. "Get back here. Make sure Tamsin gets to safety."

Tamsin didn't move. "We'd *really* appreciate any help," she said to the stone. "If that's Shifter Bureau on their way, or the human cops, we might all get slaughtered. Ben maybe not—he's a goblin, and can cast a glam to sneak off without being seen. Shifters can't. If Angus, Zander, and Tiger get killed, I bet Jaycee will be really upset. So will I.

I can *probably* get away, if I change to my fox, but I don't want to leave my mate."

Tamsin glanced at Angus, her eyes the same color as the gold wire around the amethyst. "That's what taking a mate does to us Shifters," she went on to the stone. "We'll die for them, die *with* them, as long as we can stay together. Angus doesn't know it yet, but I'm pretty sure we have the mate bond thing going on, which doesn't always happen, you know. But it's happened to me, and I'll do anything, including stand here and talk to a rock in the hope that it will help my mate survive, to keep him safe. Because in the end, that's what's we have, isn't it? What we do for other people, to make sure they're alive and well, and in the best case, happy too. So if you don't come, I'm going to grab on to Angus and try to get him away from the cops that I can hear now, fend them off in any way I have to, and make sure he gets out of here and back to his cub. It's the best I can do, but it's what I *will* do. The sirens are getting closer now, so I'm going to have to go. Thanks for listening, Lady Aisling. Tell Jaycee I said hi."

Tiger came running back to them as cars and SUVs poured in on them, sirens blaring. Black SUVs were among the cop cars—Shifter Bureau.

Zander had the pickup started. Ben headed for Tamsin. Angus intended to push her at Ben and tell him to get her the hell out. She could go back to Dante and the carnival and hide there.

Zander was un-Collared—he had to get the hell out of here too. Angus was a registered Shifter. Could be that if Angus got word to Dylan after he was arrested, Dylan would insist on due process, and possibly, just possibly, Angus would at least get a trial. Goddess knew what they'd do to Tiger, so Tiger should go with Zander.

Just as Angus put his hands on Tamsin to send her toward Ben, and he raised his voice to tell Tiger and Zander to run for it, everything went silent.

He blinked and realized the sirens had cut off, as had the sound of the engines. Tamsin jerked her head up and stared at the raindrops, her mouth dropping open, but Ben remained frozen in place, his foot raised to take a step.

Angus glanced at what held Tamsin's attention, and started. The raindrops were hovering in place, glittering like diamonds, but not falling. They hovered like a beaded curtain, perfect spheres reflecting the light.

He looked around. The cars and SUVs had halted, as though caught in a snapshot. Birdsong was gone, as was the constant drone of insects.

Tiger had stopped and lowered his arms. He wasn't frozen—he too gazed about in wonder.

Zander in the truck was motionless—Angus couldn't tell from this distance whether he was affected by whatever this was or not.

Only he, Tamsin, and Tiger seemed to be able to move. Angus stepped closer to Tamsin and she to him, the two of them seeking comfort in each other.

The door to the trailer opened, and a woman stood in its opening. She was dressed in khaki pants tucked loosely into boots and wore a white cotton shirt with a khaki windbreaker over it. A broad-brimmed hat half hid hair of flame red that she'd braided and pinned up in loops.

She was Lady Aisling, and she reeked of power just as she had when Angus had first seen her inside Faerie. He'd tried to protect Jaycee from her at the same time he'd realized she could wipe them both out whenever she wanted to.

"Hello, Angus," Lady Aisling said as she leapt lightly down from the trailer's door and strolled toward them. "What is it you want, dear?" she asked Tamsin. "I'm very busy today. We're setting out the bare root roses."

CHAPTER TWENTY-SIX

Tamsin clenched the talisman until it dug into her palm. She didn't reach for Angus, because they needed to be ready to shift, to fight, in an instant. But how could they fight a being who could make the rain stop?

Lady Aisling gazed at Tiger with interest. "You again, eh? I didn't know what to make of you when you intruded upon my home, and I still don't. And what is *this*?" She shifted her gaze to Ben. "A goblin, you called him?"

"Yes," Tamsin croaked through her dry throat. "That's what he said. Or gnome."

Lady Aisling studied him. "I believe he's one of the *Ghallareknoiksnlealous*. But they don't look like *this*." She waved her hand in front of Ben's face.

"He says you didn't help save his people," Tamsin said in a rush. She caught Angus's warning glare, but she couldn't stop. Her anger rose on Ben's behalf. "He says you let them be killed off, and did nothing."

Lady Aisling blinked in surprise. "I didn't know. In

time, I mean. There are so many wars between the various races in Faerie that one can't keep up. I am sorry for him, if the *hoch alfar* destroyed his people, truly sorry. The *hoch alfar* so like to destroy things."

"You could destroy *them*," Tamsin said.

Lady Aisling shook her head. "No, I couldn't. Erasing entire races is forbidden to the Tuil Erdannan. What sort of monster would do that? That would mean killing off even the little children in their cradles who know nothing. I'm glad it's forbidden. The Tuil Erdannan need to keep their egos in check. Annoying and threatening the *hoch alfar*—now that, we can do. But you did not bring me to this damp and smelly place to irritate the *hoch alfar*. If I come to the human world, I prefer large, international cities with many restaurants, but ah well. Can't be helped. You mentioned something about a problem?"

"My problem," Tamsin said. "My mate and friends were drawn into it because of me. They shouldn't die for choosing to help me."

"Very commendable." Lady Aisling's gaze flicked to the motionless SUVs and police cars. "It seems many humans would like to prevent you from doing whatever it is you wish to do. Which is . . . ?"

Angus broke in. "Destroy a cache of human weapons before they get into the wrong hands. Human or Shifter."

"I see." Lady Aisling's very red brows went up. "Whose are the *right* hands?"

"In this case, no one's," Angus answered.

"You've decided this, have you? Weapons are tricky things. They can be used to defend as well as attack. But the distinction is often beyond the reason of the people who wield them. I am pleased I have no need of them. I suppose you would like this taken care of before they reach you?" Lady Aisling glanced at the cars.

"Can they reach us?" Tamsin asked. "They're frozen."

"No, no. Just moving very slowly. Or rather, they are

moving normally, from their perspective. I wanted time to speak to you, so I decided to remove us from the regular motion of the world, just you and Angus. But I did not seem to be able to exclude this one." She pointed at Tiger.

Angus answered. "He's . . . unique."

"So is she." Lady Aisling moved to Tamsin, who clutched the talisman as though it would keep her safe. The scent of lemon clung to Lady Aisling, along with a bite of mint. "A fox Shifter," Lady Aisling said. "Those are rare, my dear, very rare." She lifted a lock of Tamsin's hair, which was nearly as red as hers.

"Like tigers," Tamsin babbled. "I hear they're rare."

"Rare because they were made exclusively for Fae princes and almost died off when they were Battle Beasts. Foxes now. They weren't made by the *hoch alfar* at all. They were made by the Tuil Erdannan."

Tamsin's lips parted in shock. Angus stared at first Tamsin, then Lady Aisling, as though trying to see the resemblance between them. Only Tiger watched, unmoved.

"Not by me personally," Lady Aisling said with a little laugh. "By my friends long, long, long ago. I thought fox Shifters had died out, but of course, foxes are very good at hiding. They were never enslaved by the Fae—never enslaved by anyone. My friends created fox Shifters, patted themselves on their collective backs, and then forgot about them. I'm not surprised the foxes slipped into the human world, and I'm not surprised you have evaded the humans—well, until now." She turned a warm smile on Tamsin. "Sacrificing yourself for your mate. A moving speech, my dear. But I came because I sensed you were different. Call me curious. My gardener says it will get me into trouble one day, and he is usually right, drat the man."

Tamsin gulped, a flood of emotions beating on her for attention. Astonishment, certainly. She'd thought all Shifters had originally been creations of the Fae playing with genetic engineering and magic. Shifters were their own viable species now, but they'd begun, more or less, in a Fae laboratory. Elation—the Fae were horrible, from what she'd heard, and *not* being descended from their creations was a huge relief. Trepidation—were the Tuil Erdannan any better? People so powerful they created species for fun and then forgot them and moved on to their next hobby?

She sucked in air. "I'm going to have a talk with you about my ancestors," Tamsin said, forcing the words out. "A long talk. But right now—can you help us with the weapons? Or not?"

"What? Oh, of course. I'm surprised you haven't figured out how, but no matter."

Lady Aisling turned from Tamsin, pausing at Ben so near. She flicked her fingers, and he stumbled forward, nearly running into her.

"Shit."

"Good afternoon to you too," Lady Aisling said. "Will you show me the way to these weapons? Let me guess. They're in there."

She waved her hand at the trailer. Beyond it, Zander got out of the truck and sprinted to them. Lady Aisling must have released him too.

Zander slowed as he reached them. "Hello again," he said to Lady Aisling.

"Hmph." Lady Aisling looked him up and down. "The young man who sprawled so insolently on my stairs. You are lucky I found you amusing. Well, help me up there. I don't have all day."

Zander blinked, then swung around and headed for the trailer's open door.

Ben gaped after her. "Shit," he whispered.

Lady Aisling paused a stride and looked back at him. "Do goblins, as you call yourselves, know no other words? Perhaps your friends will take pity on you and teach you."

She turned away in a sweep of her jacket, following Zander.

Ben stared after her, his dark eyes huge. "You did it," he said to Tamsin. "Wow. She has a presence, doesn't she?" He sounded admiring, no longer outraged.

Ben started after her. Tamsin, swallowing hard, began to follow, but Angus pulled her back.

"You all right?" he asked.

His solid presence and his touch cut through her shock, curling warmth through her body. "Sure. I think." Tamsin stared down at the talisman in her sweating hand, then slid it into her pocket. "It's not every day you're told your ancestors were made by people who can annihilate whole races."

Angus nodded. "I caught that. She said it's against their rules to, which means they *could* if they chose to break those rules."

"Yes. Comforting."

Angus put his arm all the way around her. "Are you really all right?"

"No." Tamsin gave him a shaky laugh. "But I meant what I said."

Angus didn't bother to ask what she was talking about. He leaned down and kissed her neck, his hot breath tickling her skin. The look in his eyes when he raised his head told her everything. The mate bond they'd formed was real, and Angus felt it too.

Tamsin took Angus's hand and walked with him to the trailer.

Inside, Zander was lifting the door that led to the weapons cache—the local men had broken Ben's iron strap with a sledgehammer. The rifles and pistols were no longer in neat lines, having been jumbled up as the men stealing them had flung them down and fled. Tiger came in with an armload, which he'd been gathering from where the men had dropped them outside.

Lady Aisling dusted off her gloved hands, though she'd touched nothing. "Smelly."

Tamsin scented must from the shut-up half cellar, the

tang of human sweat from the men raiding the place, rust, and oil. Lady Aisling slid a very large linen handkerchief from her jacket pocket and pressed it to her nose and mouth.

"I'm not used to being around so much iron at one time," she said apologetically. "We don't have the anathema to it that the *hoch alfar* do, but it is strange."

"So how do we dispose of these?" Angus rumbled, waving a hand at the weapons Tiger and Ben were sorting through.

"Can you melt them with magic?" Tamsin asked, staying close to Angus. "Beam them into outer space?"

Lady Aisling gave her a perplexed look. "What odd ideas you have, child. I suppose it comes from living among humans for so long. No, it's quite simple. We will break down all parts to the components that make them up. You might not understand the words, but I mean destroy them on the molecular level. Break the bonds and disintegrate the metals into their atomic components."

All four of the Shifters, Tiger included, and Ben, stared at her.

Lady Aisling sighed. "I knew you wouldn't understand. You see—"

"We understand," Angus cut in. "Can that be done?"

"Of course," Lady Aisling said as though he'd asked a too-simple question. "Atoms are mostly empty space. There is a huge distance between the nucleus of an atom and its electrons. The fact that anything stays together at all is rather amazing. If we tear down the weapons into their elemental components of, say, iron, copper, aluminum, and whatever else is in them, then they will fall to bits and be nothing but unusable dust."

"Show-off," Zander muttered and then chortled. "This I gotta see."

"Won't things blow up?" Tamsin asked. "When atoms are split, cities are destroyed."

"Really?" Lady Aisling looked surprised. "Not if we are careful."

"You keep saying *we*," Tamsin said. "But we don't have the ability to disintegrate metal. Well, at least not without special facilities and a lot of heat."

Lady Aisling looked straight at Tamsin, all amusement gone. "*You* do, my dear. But perhaps you never knew this. You were made by the Tuil Erdannan, which means you are not constrained by the limitations of the *hoch alfar*. You are a Shifter, yes, and much like them, but you are a different variety. Like *him*." She pointed at Tiger, who set the last rifle on top of the pile.

Tiger finally spoke. "I was bred by humans. They were trying to make a super Shifter."

"Well, they succeeded," Lady Aisling said. "I wonder if they tapped into Tuil Erdannan magic? Something to think about. And worry about a bit, yes indeed. Anyway, shall we begin? My roses aren't going to plant themselves."

"Shouldn't we stand back?" Ben asked.

"No reason." Lady Aisling put her hands on her hips. "It just takes a bit of concentration. Which means . . ."

The noise outside began with a rush. Rain drummed on the roof, and sirens split the air. The cars and SUVs roared forward, sliding in the mud, surrounding the trailer.

"Even I can only do so many things at once," Lady Aisling said apologetically. "Ben, dear, will you hold my hat for me?"

She swept it from her head and held it out to Ben, who took it with a sort of reverence.

Tamsin stepped back, the carpet feeling tacky under her booted feet. Angus remained in place, partly shielding her from whatever was about to happen.

Lady Aisling's hair was flame red, a more intense red than Tamsin's, and must be very long, because the looped braids wrapped several times about her head and then hung to her shoulders. Delicate pointed ears pricked from among the braids. Tamsin resisted reaching up and touching her own ears. They were ever so slightly pointed at the tip, but she'd always thought that came from being a fox.

Lady Aisling's eyes were a brilliant green, unlike most Fae's, which were dark, like Ben's. The color was brighter than any jewel and glittered in the drab room.

Outside the vehicles halted, doors opening. A man spoke through a bullhorn. "Very slowly, come outside, hands on your heads, and kneel on the ground."

"How rude," Lady Aisling said. "I would get very dirty."

"Now," the man said. "Or we will open fire."

Tamsin twitched, anticipating bullets entering her back. Angus stepped behind her as though to shield her from the humans outside.

Tamsin ducked past him to the door before he could stop her and lifted her forefinger to the mass of police outside the trailer. "Can you all wait just *one* minute?" she called. "We'll be out in a sec."

"Tamsin," Angus said in exasperation.

Whether Tamsin had startled the cops or they weren't in position yet, the bullets didn't fly, and the man with the bullhorn was momentarily mute.

"Tamsin, would you like to assist me?" Lady Aisling asked.

"How?" Tamsin turned to her in bewilderment. She didn't know anything about breaking molecular bonds in gunmetal.

"I will teach you. Take my hand."

Tamsin caught Ben's expression, a warning. Lady Aisling didn't notice, only held her hand out, somewhat impatiently, to Tamsin.

Tamsin slid her fingers around it.

"Now," Lady Aisling said.

And Tamsin could *see.* Everything. What it was made

up of, bone and muscle, metal and wallboard, iron and steel. The lattice structure of every single thing imprinted itself on her mind, showing her the world as a series of geometric shapes, from cubes to tetrahedrons to spheres, like the rain. Even the raindrops outside the door coalesced into crystal lattices.

Lady Aisling herself was a frame filled with pure power. The red-haired woman in gardening clothes was not *her*, Tamsin suddenly understood, but the image she projected.

Everyone in the room appeared like that. Ben's human form was transposed over something huge and dark, bigger than Tiger or Zander, its essence stuffed down into Ben's shorter frame. It was ugly, monstrous, but at the same time, Ben's compassion and sense of fun emanated from it.

Zander shared his human space with a giant polar bear, bear's and human's dark eyes glistening as they focused on her.

This must be how Shifters could shift, Tamsin realized with newfound clarity. They were two-natured, both forms taking up the same space. Her own body was transposed with that of a red furred fox with slender dark legs. Shifters simply became more of one than the other when they chose, she abruptly understood. Anything in the way of that space, like clothes, got torn apart.

Tiger was the oddest, as there wasn't much difference between his human and tiger forms, which were occupying almost the exact the same space. No wonder he shifted so easily—his two natures molded and flowed into each other without impediment.

And Angus . . .

He was a black wolf through and through, his human shape and wolf very close in stature. Dark fur rippled as he moved, his gray eyes narrowing identically in both forms, which made Tamsin want to laugh.

Angus also contained a flame deep in his chest that burned blue white. It matched the glow that shone from within Tamsin herself, and then she saw the silver threads that stretched between them.

"I didn't realize." Tamsin touched the strands, her voice dropping to a whisper. "The mate bond is a real, physical thing. Not just a metaphor for Shifters who fall in love."

Tiger nodded, gazing straight at the shimmering silver threads as though he saw them too. So did Ben. Zander, who obviously couldn't, frowned.

Tamsin put her hand on Angus's chest, right over the glow. It wasn't hot, but soothing somehow. "Mate of my heart," she said, a tremble in the words.

Angus covered her hand with his and then leaned to her and kissed her lips. "Mate of my heart," he said in a gentle rumble. "We're about to be arrested."

Tamsin grinned at him, kissed him one more time, and turned back to Lady Aisling. "Let's do this."

Lady Aisling gave her an *it's-about-time* look, raised Tamsin's hand in hers, and gazed down at the weapons.

She didn't say a word, didn't chant, didn't sing. A jolt went through Tamsin as Lady Aisling simply willed the stiff cubic forms and polyhedrons of the bonded elements in the weapons to revert to their natural state.

Whatever heating, cooling, pouring, or molding had been done to make the guns and the ammunition now came undone. The weapons radiated heat, metal protesting being broken apart, the objects creaking and groaning as they struggled to stay together.

Then they weren't weapons anymore—guns, rifles, the strange avocado shape of the grenades—but parts, shapes, pieces held together with pins, rivets, or the melting of metals. They all shook apart, crumbling, dissolving.

The many carbon-bonded substances that made up the deadly explosives came apart the most reluctantly, but break down they did, their long chains of bonds clinking like real chains as they became carbon, nitrogen, oxygen, and hydrogen. The gases floated away to be absorbed into the air while the rest fell into a carbonate mush.

In a matter of seconds, Gavan's treasured hoard of weapons were nothing but a formless slag covered with dust. The slag itself began to break down, mixing with the dust until a layer of uniform gray about a foot thick coated the space under the trailer.

A puff of this dust wafted up on the breeze through cracks in the floor, and floated away.

Zander sneezed. "Huh," he said, peering into the hole. "Anyone have a vacuum?"

Lady Aisling released Tamsin's hand. The true outlines of everything around Tamsin blurred and returned to what she usually saw. But she couldn't shake the feeling that if she willed herself hard enough, she'd be able to again see what Lady Aisling had shown her.

"That is a gift I will give you, my dear," Lady Aisling said. "The ability to see, and to understand. *You* have it," she said to Ben. "Somewhat."

Tamsin thought she understood what Lady Aisling meant. Ben could meld his true form into anything, including a mimicry of his surroundings. "That is how you make yourself *un*seen," Tamsin said to him. "Wonder if I could do that."

"You already do," Lady Aisling said. "You might think you have escaped detection because you are clever, but it is mostly to do with the abilities the Tuil Erdannan bestowed on your kind. Use them wisely, my dear."

Tamsin shook her head. "It didn't help me when I was running through the woods trying to get away from Angus. *He* caught me without a problem."

Lady Aisling patted her cheek. "Because he's your mate, dear. Now, off you go, and explain things to your human guardsmen. I will give you another gift, Tamsin, because I like you. You have the power, like Ben, to not be noticed and to be quickly forgotten. I sense one man out there is determined to capture or kill you, and I would not like that. You need to practice to fully use your abilities, so I will give you a boost. Now, I really must be going. My gardener is not made of patience, and he is correct—we have a very small planting window. Good-bye, Shifters." She glanced at Ben, a frown puckering her brows as she took her hat from him. "I have a daughter about your age. Perhaps . . ." She shook her head. "No, never mind."

Lady Aisling turned her back on them, walked to the corner of the trailer where the gloom on this rainy afternoon was deepest, and vanished.

"Perhaps," Ben repeated. "Perhaps *what*?"

"Sounds like she's trying to fix you up on a blind date," Zander said in his booming voice. "Don't go for it. Never works out."

"Hey, bear-man, I know how you met *your* mate, so you don't qualify to comment," Ben said. "Shall we, people?"

Angus stepped in front of Tamsin and gave her his fierce glare. "You stay behind me, no matter what happens. Understand? *Behind me.* If it comes to a fight, you let Ben take you out of here."

Tamsin nuzzled his shoulder. "I like it when you're all growly and my alpha mate. I have a feeling we won't have a problem getting away though."

The police had their pistols trained on the trailer, but they had not commenced firing as threatened. Ben walked out first, not because Angus let him, but because he simply slipped by.

"Evening, officers," he said in his laid-back, friends-with-everyone voice. "What can we do for you?"

CHAPTER TWENTY-SEVEN

Angus felt Tamsin up against his back; for once she was using common sense and not darting directly into danger. Her breath warmed his skin, heating the blood beneath.

She'd laid her hand over his heart, right where the mate bond throbbed, and smiled up at him. *Not just a metaphor for Shifters who fall in love.*

In love. She'd fallen in love with him.

His stupefaction at the statement hadn't quite gone away. Watching hard metal become dust hadn't astonished him as much as the fact that Tamsin Calloway loved him.

Angus loved *her.* He loved her smiles, her sassy mouth, her fearlessness. Loved how she protected Ciaran and laughed with him, how she'd look up at Angus and include him in the laughter. Her silly singing, her red hair that flowed over his body in the night, her touch that lit fires all through him.

Angus loved her, the love growing inside him like the

blossoming of Lady Aisling's roses, beauty coming suddenly from nothing.

"You folks all right?" a police officer was asking Ben outside. His voice was no longer threatening but concerned, in a professional way. "Got a call about intruders in this trailer."

Zander jumped down from the doorway, Tiger following. "Yep," Zander said as he landed. "Some local boys thought they'd take over and party. We chased them off, but someone must have called you."

Which was exactly what had happened, Angus thought. Now to see if the cops believed it.

The policemen lowered weapons, taking their cue from their leader. But behind them were Shifter Bureau agents—Zander and Tiger weren't wearing Collars, and Bureau agents were trained to spot Collarless Shifters. Angus held his breath, and Tamsin tensed beside him.

Haider led the three agents as they strode forward. "See any Shifters around here?" Haider asked Zander.

He didn't seem to note that Zander *was* Shifter, though Angus wasn't sure how he could miss the signs. Zander was huge, solidly muscled, with intense dark eyes, and did not bother to dress in a low-key way. His white-blond hair, braids, and black duster coat would make him stand out even if he were human.

"Nope," Zander answered Haider without unease. "This isn't even our trailer. Belongs to a friend. We heard of trouble and came to check it out."

"If you see any Shifters, give us a call," Haider said, his voice still reasonable. "We're Shifter Bureau. Number's on our website."

"Sure thing," Zander said.

"Seriously?" Tamsin whispered. "This is the same guy who forced you to hunt me? Who threatened to dissect me?" She let out a breath. "Wow, Lady Aisling is *good*."

"Is that what she meant about giving you a boost?" Angus whispered back.

"I don't know." Tamsin leaned against him. "Maybe Lady Aisling is letting us elude notice in Haider's brain, like Ben eludes notice by using shadows. That is power. Let's go out and see what happens."

Angus gripped her shoulder to try to hold her back, even though he knew by now Tamsin couldn't be stopped if she didn't want to be. She slipped easily from his grasp, stepped through the door, and dropped to the muddy grass outside, landing with grace, the pattering rain glistening in her hair.

Angus sprang down after her, putting himself in front of her again. She stuck close to him as they walked carefully around the cops and Haider.

Haider didn't notice Angus and Tamsin at all. He'd holstered his gun and stood with arms folded, listening to Ben and Zander explain to the human police how they'd come upon the men who'd broken into the trailer.

A handful of cops moved away to carefully check out the scene. Two climbed inside the trailer while a few others walked around it. The two inside called back when they found the storage area, but reported there was nothing but grainy dirt inside. They emerged again, and the lead cop speculated that a local gang had possibly been looking for a cache of meth to steal.

Throughout these undertakings, none of the police or the Bureau agents noticed Tamsin or Angus.

Tamsin broke from Angus to walk straight to Haider and look directly at him. The man didn't turn his head or so much as glance at her. He didn't appear to see Angus either.

Tamsin turned away, a dazed look on her face. She took Angus's hand and together they walked slowly around the police and Shifter Bureau agents and to the pickup.

Haider continued to watch Zander and the head cop.

None of the humans paid attention to Angus or Tamsin in any way—the two Shifters didn't exist for them.

Angus and Tamsin walked hand in hand to the pickup and got in, and Angus quietly closed the door. In a moment, they were joined by Tiger.

"We should go now," Tiger said.

Angus started the truck as quietly as he could, no gunning the engine. He turned and drove slowly past all the cars, down the lane toward the road.

His heart beat swiftly and his hands sweated on the steering wheel, but no one stopped them, no one challenged them. Even Ben and Zander didn't appear to notice them go. Only Tiger, it seemed, had seen them.

Once on the highway heading back to town, Tamsin blew out her breath and leaned against Angus.

"I never want to do that again," she said. "I thought Haider would look at us any second, stop us, shoot us." She raised her eyes to the ceiling. "Thank you, Lady Aisling."

"It was not Lady Aisling," Tiger said. "It was you."

Tamsin jerked upright. "What?"

"I saw," Tiger went on. "Lady Aisling began it, but you, Tamsin, took the magic and widened it, strengthened it. I can see . . . what others can't." He briefly touched his eyelids.

"How was *I* doing that?" she demanded. Her tension came through the mate bond, and Angus longed to gather her to him, to hold her, soothe her. "I'm a Shifter," Tamsin declared. "I don't know how to work magic." Her voice rose to a frantic note.

Angus broke in. "But you're not a Shifter like I am, or even like Tiger is. If your ancestors were bred by the Tuil Erdannan, created differently, then your abilities will be different. Think about it—your mother was rounded up and you weren't. Your sister, whose genetic makeup went to the Feline side of the family, was caught by hunters and you were not. You thought it was because you were fast, and good at hiding, but what if you instinctively put up this barrier—a glam, as Ben calls it?"

Tamsin paled. "You mean I used magic to escape, when my sister couldn't? When my mother couldn't?"

Angus gentled his voice. "You didn't know you were doing it."

Tamsin put her face in her hands and was silent.

Again, Angus wanted to hold her, shut out the world until her anguish went away. The best he could do while speeding down the road at sixty miles an hour was put his arm around her shoulder and draw her close. "It wasn't your fault, love."

"No," Tiger agreed. "The abilities we are given, whatever they are, were not chosen by us. We have to learn them, understand them, even when they hurt us."

Tiger wasn't a man given to lengthy speeches—these were the most sentences Angus had ever heard him string together—but Tiger was right. All Shifters had to learn what to do with what had been bred into them.

The only reason Haider's men had managed to snap photos of Tamsin was because she hadn't known they were taking them. She'd been a long way off, unaware of the photographer's scrutiny. Angus was willing to bet that if she had known they were there, they'd never have caught her on camera. She'd slipped away from Gavan's group and evaded being rounded up with them, knowing instinctively when to go. She'd speculated Gavan had blabbed to Haider about her—if Gavan had kept his mouth shut, Haider would probably have never realized Tamsin existed.

Angus had spotted her right off without much trouble when Haider had sent him on her trail. *Because he's your mate, dear,* Lady Aisling had said to Tamsin. Angus didn't believe in the your-one-true-mate-is-out-there crap, but perhaps his wolf had known, even then, that Tamsin was meant to be his.

He'd help her get through this. It's what mates did—

comforted, soothed, supported, loved. Angus would put things in motion once they reached the hotel. No more wasting time running from Shifters and Shifter Bureau.

Lady Aisling had given them a gift indeed.

Tamsin's anguish lessened slightly on the remainder of the ride to the motel, which she put down to Angus's touch. But she continued to mourn.

If she had known about her abilities, if she'd been aware she could do something similar to what Ben could, she might have helped her mother, saved her sister.

Also if Tamsin had realized she could move about unseen, she'd have tried to see her mother much more often. She'd given up sneaking into her mother's Shiftertown or convincing her mom to meet her near it, fearing her mother would be punished if Tamsin were caught. It had been hard for Tamsin to make herself stay away.

When they reached the motel, Tiger strode into Ben's room, easily finding the door Ben had glammed, leaving Angus and Tamsin alone.

Tamsin wanted to bury herself in Angus and pour out her troubles, but once he had her safely inside the room, damned if he didn't duck back down to the truck to talk on his cell phone. She supposed he figured it was safe now that Haider seemed to have forgotten about Tamsin.

She showered and dressed in clean clothes, her heart heavy. By the time she finished, she heard Zander and Ben return, and she went out to meet them. She found them in Ben's room with Angus, the three Shifters and Ben gazing down at Dion, who glared back at them.

"So what do we do with him?" Ben asked Zander and Tiger.

"You let me go," Dion snarled. "They were only fucking Shifter Bureau agents."

Zander stepped hard on Dion's leg, and Dion howled.

"Oops, must have slipped," Zander said, but he didn't move his foot. "I think with an attitude like that, you need a little therapy. I know just the guy you can talk to. Name of Dylan Morrissey."

Dion's eyes widened. "Morrissey? He's hand in glove with Shifter Bureau. Everyone knows it."

"Everyone is wrong," Zander said. "I'll take him off your hands, Angus. He might need a healer when Dylan is done explaining things. Or maybe a Guardian."

Dion began to shake.

"Coming with you," Ben told Zander. "Have to, if you want the binding spell to continue."

"What are you going to do?" Tamsin asked Ben, her curiosity working its way through her moroseness. "Have him bound to the back of your motorcycle?"

Ben shrugged. "Should work. Take care of yourself, Tamsin." He enfolded her in a hug. "Come to the house anytime. The door will always be open for you."

"Will open itself for you," Zander corrected. "Creepy house. I like it."

"What about you, Tiger?" Ben asked. "Come with us?"

Tiger shook his head. "I will see that Angus and Tamsin are safe and then return to my mate and cub."

"Yeah, I understand why you want to get home," Ben said. "Give my best to Carly."

Tiger sent Ben a brief nod, but Tamsin saw the warmth in Tiger's eyes when he spoke of his mate and cub. The mate bond was strong in him as well. Tamsin could no longer see hers—not the silken threads she'd observed when Lady Aisling had let her *see*—but the feeling had not ebbed. She was bound to Angus, and he to her, just as Tiger was bound to his mate.

The Shifters managed to get Dion up and out the door, down the stairs, and onto Ben's bike. Dion sat rigidly behind Ben, and Zander dropped a helmet over Dion's head, slapping it in place.

Zander then embraced Tamsin in a flurry of coat, braids, and hard warmth. "Give him hell, Tamsin," he said and kissed her cheek. "And call anytime. I'm living in Montana with Rae now, but we always enjoy a road trip."

Zander pulled Angus into a Shifter hug as well, winking at him before he turned away. "Don't have too much fun, Angus. I know you can really let yourself go if you want to. Later, my friends."

He turned away, straddled his motorcycle, started it, and rode smoothly out of the lot, Ben following with Dion.

Tamsin was in the truck again not long later. Neither she nor Angus much wanted to stay another night in the motel, so they quietly agreed to go. Tiger joined them in silence, and they headed back west toward Albuquerque.

Angus watched Tamsin grow less downcast as the trip wound on. They headed back through Dallas and north to Wichita Falls, then west again to pick up the I-40 in Amarillo, retracing the path they'd taken with the carnival. Tamsin started playing with the radio the morning after their overnight in Dallas, singing along and trying to teach Tiger the songs.

Angus knew Tamsin was still bewildered and uncertain, the revelation about her origins coming as a shock.

He tried to tell her, as they lay in bed together, that it didn't matter. She was still Tamsin, and they were mated. The fact that she might have Tuil Erdannan magic in her and powers like Ben's didn't bother him at all. Angus would be there as she learned all about them.

He wasn't certain if it was his pep talk that helped her feel better or their long night of deep and silent passion and profound sleep, but as the road unrolled beneath them, Tamsin became more like herself, chattering about nothing, trying to make Tiger play road games with her—

Whoever sees a VW first gets to punch the other. She stopped that game because Tiger kept winning.

"There it is!" Tamsin sang out as the road dipped down into Albuquerque. It was twilight, and the lights of Dante's midway flashed into the darkness. "Let's party!"

The first thing Angus saw when he slid out of the truck, glad the long journey was behind him, was Ciaran racing toward him like a shot. Dante was just behind the cub, waving in welcome.

Angus swept up Ciaran, holding him close. Screw Shifter Bureau. He was never, ever leaving his cub behind again.

Ciaran clung to Angus for a long moment, then he launched himself at Tamsin. "I missed you, Tamsin! I mean, Mom!"

Tamsin caught him up and spun around with him. "I missed you too, sweetie." She hugged him close. "I love you, Ciaran."

Ciaran latched his arms around her. "Love you too, Mom."

Angus watched them, his heart full. So were his eyes for some reason. He surreptitiously wiped away tears and tried to focus on what Dante was saying.

"He was a good lad," Dante told Angus with a grin. "Well, more or less. For a Shifter cub. Celene and I have got some pizza, plenty for everyone. Tiger, you coming?"

Tiger had hung back from the greetings and now he shook his head. "I will return home now. Carly and Seth are waiting."

"You need a ride?" Dante asked. "I can see if one of my guys . . ."

"I find my own way," Tiger said. "Good-bye, Angus and Tamsin. Ciaran."

Ciaran squirmed down from Tamsin and raced for Tiger. "Thank you, Tiger, for taking care of my parents. I'm sure they needed it."

Tiger lifted Ciaran for a tight hug, then set him carefully down and bent to speak to him in confidence. "Look after them," he instructed. "I can't always be around to do it."

"Gotcha." Ciaran nodded at him, then Tiger gave Tamsin one last, long look, turned, and faded into the darkness.

"Will he be all right?" Dante asked, peering after him.

"Tiger?" Angus searched the shadows for the big man, but Tiger was already gone. "He's an expert at taking care of himself. If his mate and cub are at the end of the road, he'll get there all the more quickly."

"Hmm." Dante gave the path Tiger had taken another look and then sent a similar assessment over Angus. "Come on. Pizza's waiting."

Angus couldn't take Tamsin off to bed right away, as so many wanted to greet them, and neither of them wanted to leave Ciaran. They had their pizza, then Ciaran did his show with Celene, Angus and Tamsin watching from the audience and cheering him on.

They'd found a home here.

Celene, with keen perception, had Ciaran stay overnight with her family one more day. In the darkness after the close of the carnival, Angus slid himself over Tamsin in their large bed and made swift love to her. She kissed him as she came apart, her body moving with his, the mate bond warm between them.

After they quieted, Angus propped himself up beside her, skimming his fingertips over her soft breasts. "What do we do?" he asked quietly. "Keep following the carnival? Or head back home? To my home, I mean, in Shiftertown."

Tamsin blinked up at him, her eyes full of sleepy contentment. "Is that even possible? I'm not Collared."

"And you never have to be. I talked a lot to Dylan before we left Shreveport. I called him to tell him that the weapons cache was gone, so he could leave you the hell alone about it. Not only did I get him to promise to make a fake Collar for you, but he and Sean can manipulate records so it looks as though you were always in my Shiftertown and never had anything to do with Gavan. If Haider is still fuzzy about you, he'll leave you alone. Dylan is making sure of it."

"Dylan would do that?" Tamsin asked in surprise. "He's not pissed off at us for destroying the arsenal?"

Angus shook his head. "He never wanted the arsenal. He wanted to know where it was, yes, but he wanted to destroy it too. So he told me. He was interested in you not only because you knew where the stash was, but because you were different. He's met another fox, and wants to learn about fox Shifters—without the torture and dissection Shifter Bureau had in mind."

Tamsin huffed. "You mean I dove out the window of that motel in Texas, jumped a barbed-wire fence, and ran through a muddy, plowed-up field for no reason?"

"Not necessarily. Dylan's tricky. But I made him understand that if you help him, it will be on your own terms. And you're protected now by me, as your mate."

Tamsin slid her hand along his bare arm to his shoulder. "I like that."

"So it's up to you, love. Do we continue the life of the carnival? Or do you move into Shiftertown with me? I know it's not much of a choice. Maybe one day I'll be able to offer you more, if Shifters ever get free." Angus touched her lips before she could speak. "There's another choice, you know. Go your own way. Live as you like. As you did before we met."

"*That's* off the table," Tamsin said immediately. "I stay with you, Angus. You know we have the mate bond. Being without you is no longer an option." Her big smile shone forth. "Besides, I'll need your help. Wherever we decide to live, you'll have to help our cub, if she's a fox, understand what being a fox Shifter means and what she might be able to do. And if she's a wolf, she'll need your guidance. And Ciaran's."

Angus gave her a nod. "If cubs come along, yes. Why do you say *she*? The first might be a male."

"She's not. And I mean *when*, not *if*."

Angus stared at her as the meaning of her words penetrated his brain. As he froze, his heart ceasing to beat, Tamsin laughed.

"Tiger told me last night, when we stopped in Dallas. He knows I've started a cub. And he knows it's a she. I told him there was no way he knows I'm preggers when even I don't, but he insisted. He says he can tell these things far in advance of anyone else. I believe him. Angus?" Tamsin lost her smile and touched his face. "You all right?"

Love, hope, fear, excitement, joy swelled up hard in Angus's body and wedged in his throat. Any words got tangled in his brain, and he could only stare down at his mate, his eyes burning.

Then he threw his head back and let out a howling roar, the triumph of a wolf who has found his heart's desire. Tamsin laughed at him and enfolded him in her arms.

In a few minutes, Angus heard small, swift steps, and the door of their trailer banged open, Ciaran appearing on the doorstep in his pajamas.

"Dad," Ciaran shouted. "What's wrong? What the hell?"

Angus was too joyous to admonish him for running from Dante's care. His voice filled the RV. "You're going to have a baby sister, son!"

"Really?" Ciaran sounded dubious, then his tone changed to excitement. "Really? Cool!" He jumped high and punched the air, then started dancing around the trailer.

The RV rocked, and Tamsin continued to laugh. The moon shone brightly through the curtains, the only light now that the carnival had died down, the Goddess joining their celebration.

Angus pulled the sheets high over them and tugged Tamsin into his arms, kissing the mate of his heart while his son cavorted and cheered in celebration of new life.

EPILOGUE

Tamsin chose Shiftertown.

She amazed herself, but she decided she did it for Ciaran's sake. And Angus's. All right, and maybe for hers as well.

Tamsin had thought she'd fall down into depression and be unable to move as soon as she set foot in a Shiftertown, especially with a false Collar around her throat, but to her relief, nothing so dire happened.

The New Orleans Shiftertown—which was about fifty miles west of the city—was an area of brick houses and lush green grass on flat land under a wide sky. Some houses had trees towering over them, planted long ago. No fences ran around the town. This Shiftertown was separated from the rest of humanity by a road on one side, a winding bayou on the other.

The Shifters in Angus's Shiftertown, instead of gazing at Tamsin in suspicion, as she'd expected them to, welcomed her with enthusiasm.

"About time Angus got a life," Reg, the tall Feline, said. He gave Tamsin a hard hug when Angus brought her to the outdoor gathering where she met the entirety of this Shifter-town, and kissed her cheek. "He picked someone cute to do it with too. I kind of figured when I saw you two together it was real."

Reg didn't seem bothered about having to get himself to Lake Charles to retrieve the SUV they'd left there. He was happy he'd been able to evade Shifter Bureau and help them out, he said.

The Shiftertown leader, Spence, welcomed Tamsin as well. Spence was a Lupine in Angus's clan, his eyes a bit darker than Angus's and his hair starting, like Dylan's, to go gray.

"Thank you for bringing Angus home," Spence said to Tamsin when they were formally introduced. "I can already tell you're good for him. He's been through too much tragedy."

"Being rejected by his Shifter leader didn't help," Tamsin said pointedly. "But you probably knew that."

It was none of her business what Angus's Shifter leader had decided in the past, but she hadn't missed the bleak look in Angus's eyes whenever he'd talked about losing his place as second. His position had been taken from him by his brother's actions and through no fault of his own.

Spence acknowledged her hit with a nod. "I'm sorry about that," he said. "They backed me into a corner and gave me no choice. But now that so much time has passed, and Angus has proved he had nothing to do with Gavan's group . . ." He trailed off and shrugged. "Who knows what might happen?"

They had to leave it at that.

Angus had taken her straight to the gathering upon their arrival in Shiftertown. Tamsin understood—she had to be accepted into the community by the Shifters, as a new-comer in their territory. No matter how easily Dylan and

Sean tucked her into the database, no matter what Shifter Bureau thought, the real test was whether the Shifters would welcome a stranger into their midst.

When she'd been greeted without hesitation by Spence—and he'd embraced her—and even more enthusiastically by Reg, the other Shifters grew more interested in her. Tamsin met many people that afternoon, received many hugs, and panicked a little about having to remember all their names. But she'd be living here a while. There would be time.

Her excitement grew as Angus walked them from the gathering in the tree-studded field to Angus's house. His home.

Dimitri's semitruck, restored to gleaming black now that the magnetized carnival curlicues had been removed, rested in the street in front of the house. Dimitri, when Angus had called him to announce he was ready to give it back, had said he'd fetch it when he came for their sun and moon ceremony.

Angus's house was small, one-story, and square, with large leafy trees shading it from the bright sunshine. Angus unlocked and opened the front door to reveal a simple interior—living room with a kitchen beyond in the front of the house, a hall to bedrooms on the left.

Tamsin stood in the middle of the living room and took in the comfortable, worn furniture, a plain kitchen with table and chairs, and oval rugs on the floors. Ciaran had left toys on a table next to the couch, and one of Angus's jackets lay over the arm of a chair.

Tears sprang to her eyes. Though Shifters didn't own their houses in Shiftertowns, the touches of Ciaran and Angus branded this a home, something Tamsin hadn't had in more than twenty years.

"Not much to it," Angus was saying. "I don't have a lot of stuff. You can fix it up however you want."

Tamsin put her hands to her cheeks. "It's perfect."

Angus looked perplexed, but she wasn't talking about

the decor. This was Angus's home, and now hers, where they'd live, love, and share their lives.

"Come and see my room!" Ciaran shouted. He grabbed Tamsin's hand and pulled her down the hall before she could protest. Not that she wanted to resist. He took her to a bedroom that was neat for a kid's. Bookcases held books and numerous toys, mostly trucks and soldiers.

Tamsin listened while Ciaran showed her everything important to him—a favorite book, a toy semitruck like Dimitri's, cards he was learning to do tricks with.

The bedroom across the hall, which she entered when Ciaran became absorbed in his book, was Angus's. And now hers.

Tamsin hung up her few clothes in the side of the closet that Angus quickly cleared for her, and smiled when he blushed about moving his underwear from one drawer to another. His bed wasn't wide, and was covered with a plain bedspread. He only had one picture on the wall, a recent school photo of Ciaran.

The room was barren, but at the same time, so like Angus that she went to him and enfolded him in a tight hug.

Making love under the moonlight in Angus's bed made Tamsin cry again.

"Shh," Angus whispered, kissing her face. "What is it, love?"

"I can be happy here." Tamsin lay against him, listening to the quiet of the night, the soft snores of Ciaran across the hall. "I never thought I'd find a place like this."

"You bring happiness with you." Angus smoothed her hair with a strong hand. "The house has been brighter all day, with you in it."

Angus, the man of few words, always knew the right ones for Tamsin.

She kissed him as Angus slid himself over her and inside her once more. Tamsin didn't mind the small bed, because she and Angus fit together perfectly in it.

* * *

The full moon was due to rise three nights later, and in the bright sunlight of that afternoon, the New Orleans Shiftertown Shifters gathered for a sun and moon ceremony, the official mating of Angus Murray and Tamsin Calloway.

Angus watched Tamsin dance after Spence recognized and blessed the mating under the light of the Father God, the sun. Tamsin was quickly making friends with the other Shifter women, and their cubs liked her too.

Dante had arrived, answering Tamsin's invitation, with Celene and Brina. Dante had worn his feathered hat for the occasion, and its feathers tickled Angus's cheek when Dante pulled him into a full embrace after the mating was declared.

"Lucky bastard," Dante declared, thumping Angus on the back. "But remember, anytime you want to shuck this life for the carny, you call me."

Dante had found himself a fake Collar, courtesy of Tiger, who'd arrived with it. Dante kept fiddling with it, but as there were no humans here to notice, Angus didn't admonish him.

Brina and Ciaran had a loud reunion, and Brina was soon playing with Ciaran and his friends.

Dimitri and Jaycee arrived, both mercilessly teasing Angus and Tamsin, but it was clear they were happy for them.

Tamsin grinned under their banter. She danced with them as music blared from speakers strung through backyards, her body gyrating in the skirt and midriff top she'd chosen for the ceremony.

Zander and Rae were there as well, Zander showing off and dancing like a wild thing, as usual. Rae, when she greeted Tamsin and Angus after the sun mating, revealed that she was also carrying a cub, as Zander had speculated. She and Tamsin spent a long time comparing notes.

Dylan had come with Tiger, who'd brought his mate and baby cub, but Dylan assured Angus he wouldn't pin Tamsin down to question her, at least not today.

"There will be time," Dylan said after sipping from a bottle of beer Angus handed him. "Will she be joining us?"

Dylan had invited Tamsin to participate in the army he was building to fight the Fae when the time came. Tamsin had promised to think about it.

"She probably will," Angus said. "But I think she'll have our cub first."

He warmed every time he thought of it. What would it be to hold their daughter, born from the true mate of his heart?

Dylan only nodded and left it at that.

The special surprise Angus planned arrived just before the moon ceremony was about to take place. Shifters had been partying and drinking all day, and by the time Tamsin and Angus stepped together into the moonlit clearing, excitement was high.

Half the Shifters assumed animal form, and some in human form had thrown off excess clothing to make shifting easy. Mating frenzy was in the wind, and Shifters were already pairing off in the shadows.

A sun and moon ceremony woke the ferocity in Shifters, the need to be with their mates, or to chase mates if they didn't have one yet. The younger Shifters just off their Transitions were growling and impatient, the mating frenzy strongest in them.

Spence sought Angus before he began the ceremony. "Tamsin is right," he said. "I really could use another second. Reg can't do it all. It's been long enough since Gavan—the Shifter Bureau shits can let up and allow you to help me again. I've already spoken to them."

Angus blinked in amazement, but he saw the triumphant look Tamsin shot Spence.

He weighed the idea of tracking for Spence again, which

meant staying in Shiftertown most of the time, though he'd be sent out on dangerous jobs when needed. He put that against his job at the club—which his boss there had told him he still had if he wanted it. Night after night of boring work, making sure drunk humans and Shifters didn't hurt one another. But neither would he have to track danger, nor deal with Shifter Bureau, nor be sent out to protect Shiftertown from any threat.

"I'll think about it," Angus said. He knew he'd pick being a tracker again, doing what he was made for, but he could let Spence sweat a little.

Spence shrugged, pretending it didn't matter, and returned to his spot to begin the moon, or Goddess, ceremony, the more important of the two. "My friends," he began.

He didn't finish, because the surprise for Tamsin arrived just then. A woman walked around Angus's house and down the stretch of yards to the open field. She was a Shifter, tall and straight, her short hair, which was pale in the moonlight, sticking out here and there like the tufts of a bobcat.

Tamsin's body went rigid, her hand falling from Angus's. Angus reached out to steady her, but Tamsin tore from him and ran to the woman, the circlet of flowers in her hair falling unheeded to the grass.

"Mom!" she shouted, and then the two were in each other's arms, crying and hugging, holding on tight.

Angus watched without going to them, letting Tamsin greet her mother in an outpouring of love.

After a time, Tamsin led the woman to the clearing, the two arm in arm. Tamsin had retrieved her circlet of flowers and held it loosely as she and her mother stepped into the beam of moonlight. Tamsin's mother had blue eyes rather than golden, but the shape of them was Tamsin's, as was her look of sharp assessment.

"Angus, this is my mother, Sheila Calloway. But you knew that. You brought her here."

Angus gave her a nod. "I did. With Dylan's help."

Tamsin bent a glare on him. "And you didn't tell me!"

"I wanted it to be a surprise." Angus shrugged. "A mating ceremony present."

"You . . ." Tamsin smacked the circlet of flowers to his gut. "You shithead. You wonderful, wonderful shithead."

She threw herself at Angus, who caught her up against him. The mate bond warmed him through, as did her kiss. Moonlight surrounded them, the Mother Goddess blessing their union.

The white light danced and sparkled in Tamsin's eyes as Angus lowered her to her feet. He helped adjust the circlet of flowers on her bright hair, and in the next moment Spence shouted, "Under the light of the moon, the Mother Goddess—I proclaim you mates!"

The Shifters exploded into insanity, cheering, dancing, howling, roaring. Tamsin went very quiet, touching Angus's cheek before she kissed his lips.

"I love you, mate of my heart," she whispered.

"I love you, Tamsin," Angus said, everything he was in his words.

"Thank you for catching me." Tamsin sent him a sly look, and then she tore the circlet from her hair and tossed it high, laughing.

The musical sound of her laughter rippled into the night, merged with the mate bond, and wrapped around his heart.

Turn the page to read an excerpt from
Jennifer Ashley's new Kat Holloway mystery

SCANDAL ABOVE STAIRS

Coming soon from Berkley

MAY 1881

The clatter of crockery on the flagstone floor broke my heart. I knew without turning that it was my platter of whole roast pig, the crowning glory of the vast meal I'd spent days creating for the supper party above stairs in this grand Mayfair house.

A less capable cook would have buried her face in her apron and sunk down into wailing, or perhaps run out through the scullery and shrieking into the night. I had a better head on my shoulders than that, even if I was not quite thirty years old, and so I stayed upright and calm, though stoic might be the more appropriate adjective.

"Leave it," I snapped at the footmen who were scampering after the clove-studded onions rolling about the floor. "I'll send up the fowl, and they'll have mutton to follow. Elsie, cease your shrieking and scrub those parsnips for me. A dice of them will have to do, but I must be quick."

The scullery maid, who'd screamed and then leveled obscenities at the footmen after being splashed with the juices in which the pig had been roasting, closed her mouth, snatched up the bowl of parsnips, and scurried back to the sink.

I ought to be mortified to serve a joint of mutton with sautéed parsnips at Lady Cynthia's aunt's supper party in their elegant abode in Mount Street. But I was too worn down from the work that had gone into this night, too exasperated by the incompetence of the staff to worry at the moment. If I got the sack—well, I needed a rest.

But first to finish this meal. There was no use crying over spilled . . . pork.

My task was made more difficult by the fact that my kitchen assistant, Mary, whom I'd painstakingly trained all spring, had left a few days before—to get married, if you please.

I'd tried to tell the silly girl that looking after a husband was far more difficult than being in service ever would be. Husbands didn't pay wages, for one thing, and you never got any days out. Asking for extra pin money or an hour to oneself could send a husband into a towering rage and earn a wife a trip to the doctor, both to have her bruises seen to and so the doctor could assess whether there was something wrong with the woman's mind. A true wife was a sacrificing angel who asked nothing for herself.

I had taken time to explain this to Mary, but nothing had penetrated the haze of love into which she'd lapsed. Her young man seemed personable enough, at least upon first assessment. Some married couples rubbed along quite well, I'd heard, which definitely had not been the case for me.

I hadn't exactly given Mary my blessing, but I hadn't hindered her from going either. Lady Cynthia, at my behest, gave Mary a parting gift of a few guineas—or at least, Cynthia borrowed the sum from her uncle to give, as she hasn't a penny to her name.

However generous I'd been to Mary, her going left me shorthanded. The agency had not yet sent a satisfactory replacement, and the other maids in the house had too many chores of their own to be of much use to me. We had no housekeeper, as the woman previously in that position, Mrs. Bowen, had retired in March after a bereavement. None of the potential housekeepers Lady Cynthia's aunt had interviewed had taken the post, so many now that I feared the agencies would stop sending them altogether.

Therefore, the butler, Mr. Davis, and I struggled to do the housekeeping duties as well as our own. So of course Mary chose this very time to run away and leave us.

But I could not worry about that at present. At *this* moment, I had to save the feast.

I at last convinced the footmen to cease trying to put the roast-blackened pig back onto the platter, and to run up to the dining room to receive the two capons laden with carrots and greens I lifted into the dumbwaiter. The downstairs maid cranked the lift upward while I got on with chopping the parsnips Elsie had scrubbed and thrusting them into already boiling water. A quarter of an hour in and they'd be soft enough to brown with onions and carrots and adorn the mutton. A sauce of mint and lemon would accompany the meat, and the meal would finish with various sweet treats.

Those at least I'd made well in advance, and they already waited upstairs on a sideboard—a raspberry tart with chocolate film on its crust, a lemon and blueberry custard, ices in bright fruit flavors, a platter of fine cheeses, a chocolate gâteau piled with cream, and a syllabub. Syllabub was a rather old-fashioned dish, but as it was full of sherry and brandy, I could not wonder that ladies and gentlemen of London still enjoyed it.

I was halfway through preparing the mutton, perspiration dripping down my neck and soaking my collar, when Mr. Davis appeared in the kitchen doorway.

Mr. Davis had been butler to Lady Cynthia's brother-in-law, Lord Rankin, for years, and could be haughty as you please above stairs. Below stairs, he dropped his toffee-nosed accent, sat about in his shirtsleeves, and gossiped like an old biddy. This evening he was in his full butler's kit, his eyes wide with consternation, the hairpiece he wore to cover his thinning hair on top askew.

"Mrs. Holloway." His horrified gaze took in the skinless pig on the floor in a spreading puddle of spiced sauce, and two maids at the table chopping vegetables as though their lives depended upon it. One was the downstairs maid who'd helped send up the capons, the other the upstairs maid, Sara. I'd laid my hands on *her* and dragged her in to help when she'd been unwise enough to come down to the kitchen in search of something to eat.

"What the devil has happened?" Mr. Davis demanded. "I announced the pièce de résistance to Mr. and Mrs. Bywater and Lady Cynthia and all their guests—which include His Grace of Guildford and the Bishop of Dorset, I might add—and I uncover two chickens. The same as their Saturday lunch at home."

I did not bother to look up after one hasty and irritated glance at him. "It is perfectly obvious what happened. Your footmen are clumsy fools. And I'll thank you *not* to compare my *blanquette de poulet à l'estragon* to a Saturday lunch. They will find them tender and declare the fowl the best they've had in years. Now, unless you wish to don an apron and peel carrots, you may leave my kitchen." When he only stood in the middle of the floor, his mouth open, I took up the paring knife that lay next to me. "At once, Mr. Davis."

I'd only intended to hand him the knife and tell him to get on with the carrots if he continued to stare at me, but Mr. Davis eyed the blade, took a hasty step back, and then scuttled away, nearly tripping over the mountain of pig in his haste.

* * *

How we finished the meal, I have little recollection. Somehow, the two maids and I had the vegetables peeled, chopped, sautéed, and seasoned, the mutton sauced and presented quite prettily, and everything hauled upstairs via the dumbwaiter.

Sara, who had at first resented mightily that I'd recruited her for kitchen duty, beamed as the last of the food went up, and impulsively hugged the downstairs maid. Sara looked as though she wished to embrace *me*, but I stepped out of her reach before she could give in to the impulse.

"I'll never doubt you again, Mrs. Holloway," Sara said. "You worked a miracle. Like a general, you are."

I abandoned the kitchen, letting the footmen clean up the remains of the roasted pig—which I knew they'd devour or rush it home to their families as soon as I was out of sight. If I wasn't in the room to see it go, I couldn't stop them, could I?

I'd eaten little tonight, but I crossed the passage to sink down at the table in the servants' hall, thoroughly tired of food. I slumped in my chair a moment until my shaking ceased, and then I drew my notebook from my apron pocket and began to jot my thoughts on the meal.

I did this most nights, especially after I'd prepared a large repast. The notes were for my own guidance or perhaps would be used to train my assistant, if I ever found another one.

Sara brought me a cup of tea, for which I thanked her warmly. She looked upon me with admiration—at last, after my three months of employment in this house in Mount Street, she had found respect for me.

I wrote in relative peace for a time—jotting down what had turned out well in the meal, and what needed more polish. I did my best to ignore the noises across the hall—I heard more broken dishes and made a note to ask for funds to replace them.

Mr. Davis found me there an hour later. I'd long ceased to write, my pen idle on the paper, my thoughts far from the meal and the noises around me.

Earlier this week, on my half day out, I'd gone to a lane near St. Paul's Churchyard to spend the time with my daughter. She'd grown an inch since I'd taken this post, becoming more of a young lady every time I saw her. One day, I vowed, I'd take what I'd saved of my wages, and Grace and I would live in a house together, looking after each other.

My daughter and I always made a special outing when I visited, and that day we'd gone to look at exhibits in the British Museum. Quite a few antiquities had been flowing back to London these days from archaeological digs in Egypt, Greece, Rome, and the Near East, and ladies and gentlemen flocked to see them—mummies, sarcophagi, and little dolls that had accompanied the ancient Egyptians into their tombs; as well as more cheerful things like vases, jewelry, jars, and combs from the civilizations of Greece and Rome, and tablets of writing only scholars could read.

While we'd stood waiting to enter the building, I'd sworn I'd seen the face of a man I knew. His name was Daniel McAdam, a gentlemen I'd come to look upon as a friend—a very close friend.

Of late, though, I'd revised that opinion. I'd seen much of Daniel in the early spring, and then nothing at all in the last two months. Not a sign of him, not a glimpse of him, not a dickey bird, as I would have said in my youth. As I'd lectured Mary about marriage, in the back of my mind was a promise that I'd not make a fool of myself over a man ever again. I vowed I'd put Daniel straight out of my head.

However, when I'd glimpsed a gentleman in a plain suit coming out of another door in the museum, his dark hair barely tamed under a black bowler hat, every ounce of my resolve fled. I'd found myself stepping out of the queue, craning to see him, turning away to follow him when he walked off toward Bedford Square, blast it.

Only Grace's puzzled query—"Where are you going, Mum?"—had brought me to my senses.

Mr. Davis cleared his throat, and I jumped, opening my eyes. I seemed to have dozed off.

"Lady Cynthia wishes to see you," Mr. Davis announced, looking too smug about that. "You're in for it now, Mrs. H."

I gave him a prim stare. "I am quite busy, Mr. Davis. I must prepare for tomorrow."

A cook's work is never done. While the rest of the household sits back and pats their full stomachs, I am in my kitchen starting dough for tomorrow's bread, making lists of what I'd need for the next day's meals, preparing any ingredients I could, and making sure the scullery maid had finished the washing up.

Mr. Davis had shed his coat, and damp patches adorned his shirtsleeves beneath his arms. His brows climbed. "You expect me to go upstairs and tell her ladyship you're too busy to speak to her?"

"She will understand." I liked Lady Cynthia, for all her eccentricities, but at the moment, I did not wish to have a conversation with anyone at all.

Mr. Davis eyed me closely, but I turned a page of my notebook and pointedly took up my pen.

As I bent over my notes, he heaved a great sigh, and then his footsteps receded. He stepped into his pantry—probably to fetch his coat—then I heard him start up the stairs. He was gone, and blissful quiet descended.

The peace was shattered not many minutes later by heels clicking sharply on the slate floor and an impatient rustle of taffeta. A breeze burst over me as a lady stormed into the servants' hall and leaned her fists on the tabletop in a very unladylike manner.

She had a fine-boned face and very fair hair, lovely if

one enjoys the pale-skinned, aristocratic version of beauty. Her high-necked and long-sleeved gown was deep gray with black soutache trim—she wore mourning for her sister, recently deceased.

I jumped to my feet. She straightened as I did so, a frown slanting her brows, her light blue eyes filled with agitation.

"It is important, Mrs. H.," Lady Cynthia said. "I need your help. Clementina's going out of her head with worry."

I had no idea who Clementina was—I assumed one of Lady Cynthia's vast acquaintance.

"I beg your pardon, my lady. What has happened?"

"She was here tonight, very upset." Cynthia waved impatiently at the chairs. "Oh, do let us sit down. Davis, bring me tea to steady my nerves, there's a good chap."

Davis, who'd followed Lady Cynthia down, stuck his nose in the air at being ordered about like a footman and said a haughty, "Yes, my lady." He glided out to shout into the kitchen for someone to make a pot of tea for her ladyship and be quick about it.

I had not seen much of Lady Cynthia since Lord Rankin had retreated to his country estate to console himself. He'd allowed Lady Cynthia to remain living in his London house, which revealed a kindness in him that surprised me. Lady Cynthia had no money of her own, as I've mentioned, and not much choice of where to go. Her parents, the Earl and Countess of Clifford, lived in impoverished isolation in Hertfordshire, and I knew Cynthia had no desire to return to them.

An unmarried lady could not live alone without scandal, however, so Cynthia's aunt and uncle—the respectable Mr. Neville Bywater, younger brother to Cynthia's mother, and his wife, Isobel—had moved into Lord Rankin's house to look after her. Her aunt was content to put her feet up and enjoy the luxurious house in Mount Street while her husband went off to work in the City. The Bywaters were not poor, but they were careful, willing to save money by taking Lord Rankin's free room and board.

"Clemmie's married to a baronet," Cynthia said as soon as she and I sat down. "He is appallingly rich and has priceless artwork hanging on his walls. That is, he *did*—that artwork has started to go missing, whole pictures gone. Sir Evan Bloody Godfrey is blaming Clemmie."

I blinked. "Why should he? It seems a bizarre assumption to make."

"Because Clemmie is always up to her ears in debt. She plays cards—badly—and wagers too much, and she likes the occasional flutter on the horses. As a result, creditors visit her husband. Before this, he'd pay up like a lamb, but a few months ago, he suddenly announced that enough was enough. He forbade Clemmie to wager ever again, but of course, Clemmie couldn't help herself."

"Her husband believes she sold the paintings to pay the debts," I finished as Sara scurried in with tea on a tray and set it carefully on the table. She curtsied, waited for any further instruction from Cynthia, then faded away when Cynthia dismissed her.

I reached for the teapot and poured out a steaming cup of fragrant tea for Lady Cynthia, then topped up my empty teacup. The scent of oolong, my favorite, came to me.

"Exactly, Mrs. H. But Clemmie swears it isn't true. She says she has no idea how she'd sell the paintings even if she did take them, and I believe her. Clemmie is an innocent soul." Cynthia sighed, running her finger around the rim of her teacup. "She says there's been no sign of a break-in or burglary. The paintings are simply there in the evening, gone the next morning."

Interesting. The problem piqued my exhausted brain. However, I did not allow myself to speculate too deeply. Simple explanations are usually the wisest ones—a person can complicate a straightforward situation with unnecessary dramatics and end up in a complete mess.

"Perhaps an enterprising butler is having the paintings cleaned," I suggested. "I understand old paintings can acquire quite a bit of grime, especially in London."

Cynthia waved her long-fingered hand. "I thought of that, but Clemmie swears she's questioned the staff and none have touched them. They rather dote on her, so I'm sure they would tell if they knew anything."

"Hm." Either one of the servants was lying quite fervently, or someone had managed to creep into the baronet's house in the middle of the night and silently rob it. I tried to picture a man walking in, taking a painting from the wall, and walking out again with it under his arm, frame and all, but I could not. London houses had servants roaming them all hours of the day and night, and he'd be spotted.

"You are intrigued," Cynthia said in triumph. "I see the sparkle in your eyes."

"I admit, it is odd," I answered with caution. Lady Cynthia was apt to throw herself into things rather recklessly. "Though I am certain there will be a clear explanation."

"Clemmie will be happy with *any* explanation. The silly cow is devastated her husband doesn't believe her, terrified he'll cut her off without a shilling. She wants to find the culprit and present him to the baronet on a platter."

"If she finds the culprit, she should summon the police," I said severely. "Does she mean to catch the burglar herself, tie him up, and wait for her husband to come home?"

"Ha. Sir Evan is a high-handed, dried-up stick, but I don't want him putting it about that Clemmie is stealing from him. The only reason he doesn't have her up before a magistrate is that he'd die of shame." Lady Cynthia clattered down her teacup and leaned to me. "Say you'll help, Mrs. H. I'd bribe you with extra wages, but Rankin holds the purse strings and my aunt and uncle are parsimonious." She brightened. "But Clemmie can reward you. Her husband might embrace you and give you a heady remuneration if you found his precious paintings. He is oozing with wealth.

Has a roomful of art and antiquities from all over the world—can't think why this burglar is not touching *that*."

Even more interesting.

I was comfortable with my salary, as Lord Rankin paid what was fair for a cook of my abilities and experience. The thought of extra was always welcome, of course—something to put by for my daughter—but that was not why I nodded in agreement. The puzzle did make me curious. Besides, looking for missing paintings seemed far less dangerous than hunting murderers or chasing Fenians.

Sometimes I can be a foolishly confident woman.

Cynthia fixed our date to meet with Clementina the day after tomorrow. Not *tomorrow*, I said firmly, as it was Thursday, my day out. No one, not even a wealthy baron with missing paintings—not the Queen herself—would sway me from taking my day.

Cynthia looked annoyed she'd have to wait, but she knew I was immovable. We'd go Friday after breakfast, we agreed, then she left me. She was going out, Cynthia said as she went, sending me a dark look.

I smothered a sigh. She meant she would be donning gentleman's attire and meeting her lady friends who enjoyed dressing thus. They'd lark about and try to gain admission to seedy clubs where gentlemen slummed. I worried when Cynthia did this, certain one night her uncle would have to retrieve her from some filthy jail, her complete ruin ensured.

I knew Cynthia would not be dissuaded—I had tried to reason with her before. The look she gave me also meant I should see that the scullery door was kept unbolted for her. She had a key to the house's doors, but we drew a bar across the back and front ones after midnight if no one was out, which meant she'd be unable to get in without rousing the house and revealing her truancy to her aunt and uncle. They were amiable people but uncomfortable with Cynthia's wild streak.

Cynthia's mother and father—especially her father—had been wild in their day as well. Still were, from all accounts, though Cynthia's mother had become a near recluse after Cynthia's brother had shot himself years ago.

Mr. Bywater, Cynthia's uncle, seemed to have inherited everything staid in the family. He believed Cynthia should find a husband who would settle her down—his idea was that having a child or two would calm her even more. Mr. Bywater enjoyed inviting eligible young gentlemen to the house, hoping Cynthia would fall madly in love with one of them and accept his inevitable proposal.

Hence the supper party tonight, and Cynthia's rebellion of the moment.

I promised to aid in her deception, and we parted ways.

Cynthia returned safely in the wee hours and crept off to bed. Or so Sara assured me in the morning. I fixed a full breakfast for the household, then put aside enough food for a luncheon for the staff and family. I would be back in time to make supper.

As I prepared the repast I'd leave behind, Mr. Davis, as usual, found time to sit in his shirtsleeves at my table and read bits out of his newspaper to me.

Today it was the French foray into the lands of the Bey of Tunis. Apparently, Tunisian tribesmen there had been crossing into Algeria, a French colony, and pillaging as they saw fit, and the French were retaliating. Mr. Davis read along through the details of the French attack when he paused and looked up.

"Oh, by the bye, I saw that chap who worked here a few months ago—what was his name? Daniel—that was it. Daniel McAdam. In a pawnbrokers on the Strand, of all places." He shook his head. "Dear, dear, how the mighty have fallen."

Ready to find
your next great read?

Let us help.

Visit prh.com/nextread

Penguin
Random
House